PRAISE FOR THE
SUE MARG

Best Supporting Role

"Delightfully funny, deliciously naughty, and compulsively readable."
—Susie Essman, actress, *Curb Your Enthusiasm*,
and author of *What Would Susie Say?*

"This is an absolutely wonderful and engaging book. I fell in love with the characters and laughed my way through the entire novel."
—Chicklit Club

"Funny." —Fresh Fiction

"[This] is a book filled with hopes, dreams, loss, renewal, and ultimately the satisfaction that comes with finding a place to call home, which doesn't always mean a house. Highly recommended."
—Open Book Society

"[This is] a perfect beach read." —Kritters Ramblings

"*Best Supporting Role* is the first book by Sue Margolis that I have read, but it won't be the last! . . . Sarah Green is endearing and easy to relate to. . . . The book was an interesting reflection on risks. Margolis examines risk-taking from several different perspectives. . . . This book will make a great vacation read! It's quick and light yet satisfying at the same time." —The Book Chick

"A wonderful and enjoyable read." —*RT Book Reviews*

A Catered Affair

"Wickedly funny. . . . I laughed until I hurt while reading *A Catered Affair*. It's a delightful romp with a theme lots of women can empathize with, but it's got a lovely message too." —Popcorn Reads

continued . . .

Losing Me

Sue Margolis

NEW AMERICAN LIBRARY

New American Library
Published by the Penguin Group
Penguin Group (USA) LLC, 375 Hudson Street,
New York, New York 10014

USA / Canada / UK / Ireland / Australia / New Zealand / India / South Africa /
China
penguin.com
A Penguin Random House Company

First published by New American Library,
a division of Penguin Group (USA) LLC

First Printing, July 2015

LIBRARY OF CONGRESS CATALOGING-IN-PUBLICATION DATA:
Margolis, Sue.
Losing me / Sue Margolis.
p. cm.
ISBN 978-0-451-47184-0 (softcover)
1. Older women—Fiction. 2. Life-change events—Fiction.
3. Self-realization in women—Fiction. 4. Domestic fiction.
I. Title.
PR6063.A635L67 2015
823'.914—dc23   2015004655

Printed in the United States of America
1   3   5   7   9   10   8   6   4   2

Set in Haarlemmer MT Std

Mrs. Lipschitz falls on hard times. She goes to the synagogue and prays: "Lord, my husband lost his job. We're six months behind with the rent. The triplets are about to start college. Please, just let me win the lottery."

God doesn't reply. Mrs. Lipschitz doesn't win the lottery. Three more weeks, she asks God the same thing. No response.

The fourth week, she begs: "God, why are you ignoring me? We're going bankrupt. I'm on my knees. Please, please let me win the lottery."

Finally, she hears a big voice. "Mrs. Lipschitz, it's God. Do me a favor. Meet me halfway. Buy a lottery ticket."

—traditional Jewish joke

Losing Me

Prologue

"Barbara, before you go, could I have a word?"

"Actually, now's not great. Could it possibly wait until lunchtime?" After everything that had happened that morning, Barbara was feeling the strain. Plus she was due to teach a class in a few minutes. What she needed was a quick breather to clear her head. What she suspected she was about to get—since these days Sandra banged on about little else—was another sermon on the unacceptable levels of swearing in year four. In Barbara's view, it had improved—sort of—and she'd told Sandra so. "At least now when kids call me a cunt, they say, 'You're a cunt, *miss*.'" Sandra flinched. Then she went all head teachery and looked at Barbara over her spectacles. "Barbara, we're talking about ten-year-olds. This is no laughing matter."

She wasn't really laughing. Swearing was an issue. But Jubilee was a school in an impoverished neighborhood. Everybody swore. Kids only copied what they heard. Barbara—along with most of the staff—believed there were more important problems to be tackled, like the four- and five-year-olds starting school not toilet trained.

"I'd rather do it now," Sandra was saying. "If you don't mind."

"Sounds ominous."

"Maybe you should sit down." Sandra gestured to the chair on the other side of her desk.

"OK, now you're making me nervous." Barbara remained standing. She wasn't the leg-buckling type.

"I thought I should tell you before you received the official letter."

"Official letter? I don't understand. Have I don't something wrong? Am I about to get a telling off?"

"No, it's nothing like that. The thing is, earlier this morning I got an e-mail from the Education Department. I want you to know that I've been fighting this for months."

"Fighting what?"

"I do wish you'd sit down."

"I don't want to sit down. Sandra, what's going on?"

"At the beginning of last term, the Education Department wrote to me. I was informed that because of budget cuts, I needed to lose a teacher."

It took her a moment to work out what Sandra was saying. "What?... And you're saying that teacher is me? You're sacking me?"

"Of course not. You're being made redundant."

"Oh, and you think semantics sweetens the pill? You think that being told I'm of no use—surplus to requirements—is an improvement on 'you're sacked'?"

"Barbara, I know you're angry, but please don't take it out on me. This isn't my fault. I sang your praises to the department, told them what a huge asset you are to the school. But a post had to go, and they insisted it should be the person closest to retirement. They thought it seemed fairer that way."

"Retirement? I wasn't remotely thinking about retirement. I've got years left. You know as well as I do that this job is everything to me. It's my life. It's who I am."

"I'm so sorry, Barbara. But there was nothing I could do. In the end, my hands were tied."

Chapter 1

As she sipped her coffee in the early-morning calm, there were no augurs or omens to suggest that before lunchtime, her life would be in the toilet. Her breakfast egg was boiling on the stove. Through the kitchen window the sky was streaked optimistic orange. The elderly heating boiler was roaring away. In a moment the pipes would start their reassuring ticking and knocking. She relished this time to herself—before the day kicked off, before everybody began demanding bits of her. She would have relished it even more if it hadn't been for Mark Zuckerberg.

Barbara had issues with Mark Zuckerberg. Granted, she was fifty-eight, going on fifty-nine, and walking in the valley of the shadow of her seventh decade. But did the boy mogul with practically his whole life ahead of him have to ram the point home quite so often? This morning—as usual—Barbara's Facebook sidebar contained another "fifty-nine next birthday?" ad for a "cheap, no-fuss" funeral plan. Underneath was an invitation to take part in a medical trial aimed at detecting early-onset Alzheimer's. Then there were the plus-size clothing outlets pushing New Year's discounts. Zuckerberg knew she was a size fourteen because he had elves—thousands of invisible Web stalkers—who were forever peering over her shoulder as she shopped. She imagined them sniggering and nudging one another each time she clicked on a pair of big knickers or an XL "leisure pant."

But the advertisement that really got to her was the one for a Norwegian river cruise. In Barbara's book, a cruise ship was God's waiting room. A touring hotel that practically did the sightseeing for you. Effortless—like Velcro, Crocs, or elasticized waistbands—cruises were catnip to people her age. Of course, some of Barbara's friends took cruises not so much to take it easy, but to show off. When couples of a certain age treated themselves to around-the-world cruises, it was a chance for them to bask on the sun loungers of their success. Good luck to them. But it disturbed her that so many people her age had stopped striving and seemed to be happy to talk of their successes in the past tense.

Cruises, no matter why they were taken, were the first sign of the dying of the light and to be fought at all costs. (Elasticized waistbands, on the other hand, had, since the arrival of her ample postmenopausal belly, become her secret pleasure.)

Barbara topped up her *Queen of Fucking Everything* coffee mug that her best friend, Jean, had given her for Christmas and checked the time on the kitchen clock. Just past six. She always got up early on school days. After thirty-odd years as a teacher, she still panicked about being late and even more so on the first day of a new term, which it was today. Her anxiety stemmed from her miserable childhood.

She spooled down the page of status updates. Her sister-in-law, Pam, had posted another selection of kitten pictures. She and her husband, Si, had recently moved to the Costa del Sol—somewhere near Málaga. For months she had posted nothing but beach snaps: "Me on the beach," "Si on the beach," "Me and Si on the beach."

If they weren't lazing on the sand, they were to be seen basking by the pool knocking back sangria. "This is the life," Pam would proclaim with a line of exclamation marks. For the first few weeks she got twenty or thirty "likes" every time she posted a picture. But the thumbs-ups and "lucky old you" comments gradually waned as people got fed up with hearing about Pam and Si's sun-and-sangria life. Pam appeared to take the hint—which was unusual for her. From then on the beach and poolside photographs stopped and she went back to her pre-Spain habit of posting syrupy animal snaps.

Today there were kittens poking their doe-eyed faces out of saucepans and toilet bowls. There were kittens cuddling puppies, kittens lapping from dinky bone-china teacups. Farther down, she had added one of her bumper-sticker affirmations. The fancy lettering wafted out of a sun-dappled bluebell wood: *Life isn't measured by the breaths you take but by the moments that take your breath away.* "So true," Pam's old school friend Heather Babcock had commented, adding a line of hearts and smiley faces.

Barbara couldn't understand why, the moment they hit fifty, so many previously cool, fun women turned into syrupy sentimentalists. Take Heather Babcock for example. In 1983, at Pam's hen night at a pub in Camden Town, Heather had stood on a tabletop and sung a "feminist" song she'd penned. The chorus went: *Oh . . . don't go jogging in a white tracksuit when you've got a heavy flow.* Even the blokes had joined in.

Now Heather, Pam and their ilk were cooing over infant animals on Facebook and buying tapestry cushions and bookmarks embroidered "To my dearest hubby." Their living room shelves were rammed with snow globes, faux Fabergé eggs and porcelain babies dressed as angels. It seemed to Barbara that as soon as women ran out of estrogen and could no longer reproduce, they became driven by a new biological imperative—to fill their houses with kitsch crap. Old Mrs. Brownstein from down the road called them her *tchotchkes*. Barbara had once made the mistake of agreeing to a cup of tea with Mrs. B. What had followed was an hour-long guided tour of all her china ballerinas and harlequins. It upset the old lady no end to think of her children disposing of them after she'd gone.

If she was honest, Barbara had felt twinges of the condition herself. These had resulted in her dispatching more than one birthday e-card depicting penguins cutting a rug to the "Minute Waltz." And although she had watched *Breaking Bad* and appreciated its genius, another of her secret pleasures, along with the elasticized waistbands, was an evening in with reruns of *Roseanne* or *The Golden Girls*.

Pam, on the other hand, combined her syrupyitis with a fervent desire to bring back hanging. What was more, she had no qualms about expressing this on Facebook. Her posts on the subject—invariably accompanied by a picture of a giant noose—appeared every time a black person was convicted of killing a white one. Barbara had thought about unfriending Pam—but in the end she decided against it. Pam would find out. There would be an argument, which would result in a family rift. Best to leave well alone.

Out of politeness, Barbara "liked" both the kittens and the affirmation. Pam almost never returned the compliment. She steadfastly refused to "like" or comment on Barbara's links to newspaper articles on child hunger or first-world poverty. Maybe she thought the way to deal with it was to hang the poor—or give them a kitten.

She dunked Marmite soldiers into her boiled egg. The yolk wasn't as runny as she liked it, but it was her own fault. She'd got so wound up about Facebook that she'd left it on the stove for too long.

She wondered if it was possible to e-mail Mark Zuckerberg—not to complain about Pam et al., but about his ageist advertisements. She knew she'd never get around to it, but she hoped others might. He should be taken to task—left in no doubt that people of a certain age didn't care to be reminded of their mortality over their morning boiled egg. They were perfectly capable of doing that for themselves, thank you very much. Maybe he was like the Apple chap. People had been able to e-mail him and apparently he even replied to a few. What was his name? Always wore black polo-necks. The one who died. For crying out loud, he'd been one of the most famous people on the planet. But his name escaped her. These days Barbara had a real problem remembering names—and not just people's names. It was the same with objects.

Last week it had been "colander." She'd been simmering chicken joints and vegetables on the stove to make stock and needed to drain off the liquid. She'd taken the saucepan to the sink and asked her husband, Frank, if he would go to the cupboard and fetch her "the whatsit . . . you know . . . the strainy thing."

"That would be the colander," Frank had said, getting up from behind his newspaper. He duly located it, handed it to his wife and went back to his newspaper. Meanwhile, Barbara poured the golden chicken stock into the colander. Then, for what must have been a full five seconds she stared into the sink, convinced that some kind of magic was about to reverse the calamity. But it didn't. The last drops of stock flowed into the plughole. All she had left was a colander full of overcooked meat, bones and veg. Frank thought it was hilarious, but Barbara was close to tears. "I never forget to put a bowl under the colander. Never."

"Well, this time you did."

"Yes, because I'm going bloody senile."

"Oh, stop it. We're all going bloody senile. The other day I found myself on the landing and I couldn't remember if I'd just come upstairs or was heading down."

After the chicken stock debacle, they'd gotten changed for Jean's party. It was her sixtieth birthday, and she'd got caterers in to do posh bangers and mustard mash, along with a trio of puddings. Frank put on his navy Paul Smith suit that they'd bought at an outlet mall last year. Barbara could never get over the effects good tailoring could have on the chunky male figure. He'd teamed the suit with a white button-down collared shirt, open at the neck, and trendy black suede brogues. When he sat down there was a glimpse of bright pink sock.

"You know," he said, looking at himself in the full-length mirror, "for a paunchy middle-aged git, I still scrub up OK."

She had to admit that he did. When he was at home he shuffled around the house in the baggy old jeans and jumpers with elbow holes that she threw out when he wasn't looking, but when he went out he liked to look a bit sharp.

"So, what about me? How do I look?" She was wearing a knee-length black tunic with a dramatic asymmetrical hem, over leggings and high-heeled boots.

"Great. But you always do. Have I seen that top thing before?"

"Only about a dozen times."

"Really? Well, I like it. Suits you."

As soon as they arrived at Jean's, Frank disappeared to the loo. His prostate didn't care for the cold weather.

Barbara helped herself to a glass of seasonal mulled wine and went in search of the birthday girl. She spotted Jean's sister, Val, on the other side of the packed room. They shouted "hi" and exchanged waves but couldn't get close enough for a proper hello. From what Barbara could tell, the only other family members in attendance were Jean and Ken's boys, Oliver and Adam—along with Adam's fiancée, Emma. Mostly the gathering was made up of the usual crowd—Ken's colleagues from the gastroenterology department at King George's.

Years ago, when Barbara and Frank were first introduced to them, they were skinny junior doctors in flares and mullets who told drunken stories about digital rectal exams and—famously—the guy who came into the ER insisting that his penis was dead. Now they were tubby senior consultants with ear hair and unruly eyebrows.

"I don't get it," Frank had said on the way over. "Ken's still a good laugh. But his mates seem to have become so bloody dull as they've got older. Not one of them has got any real conversation. If they're not talking shop, they bore on about wine and all the posh restaurants they've been to. Then they get on to hitting things with sticks." Frank referred to any sport that wasn't football as "hitting things with sticks." It was partly a class thing. He loved the grassrootsness of football. Everything else was for posh boys or just plain pointless—although he did make a notable exception for cricket. He thought golf was especially preposterous and had no qualms about offending golfers he met.

"Ah, Jeff, I hear you play golf. So, do you own your own bag of bats?"

Eventually Barbara spied Jean, who was wearing a pair of big sparkly antlers, handing out nibbles on the other side of the room. "Suburban snacks, anybody?"

Try as she might to reach her, Barbara kept getting waylaid by doctors' wives—whose names she couldn't bring to mind—eager for a natter and a catch-up.

"Barbara! Long time no see. Come over here and say hello to my new knee."

But before she could reach the knee and its owner, another familiar face she couldn't put a name to was smiling a greeting.

"Barbara, how are you? Frank still working?"

"Actually, we both are."

"Good Lord. You're real suckers for punishment. Graham took retirement a couple of years ago. Couldn't wait. It's bliss. I cannot tell you. He's busy working on his autobiography, which he's planning to bring out as an e-book later in the year. I walk the dogs, potter in the garden. My asters did awfully well last year. Oh, and I've just started this brilliant antique-collecting course."

Barbara couldn't imagine a life being reduced to asters and antiques. She knew she was being snotty and contemptuous, not characteristics that she admired in herself, but she couldn't see the point of carrying on if you didn't have a proper, people-are-depending-on-you reason to get up in the morning. On the other hand, she was envious. These people could afford to give up work. She and Frank couldn't, even if they wanted to.

Barbara finally caught up with Jean at the bar. This was actually Jean's dining room table covered in a white cloth and bottles of supermarket fizz.

"Hey, birthday girl," Barbara said, giving her friend a hug. "You're looking gorgeous . . . and I'm lovin' the antlers."

"Ken thought I should wear a tiara, but since it's still Christmas, I thought these were more seasonal."

"Quite right. So have you had a good day?"

"Fabulous—and thanks again for the pressie. You really shouldn't have. Issey Miyake perfume *and* body lotion. You must have spent a fortune. That said, it is my fave."

Barbara had been worried about sending a parcel full of glass in the post, but she'd wanted to make sure it arrived that morning. Jean was a big kid when it came to her birthday. Every year she opened

her presents in bed with Ken while they ate warm buttered crois-
sants and drank champagne with floating strawberries.

"Oh, who cares about money?" Barbara said. "You're only sixty
once." Since her credit cards were maxed out, she'd put the Issey
Miyake on the charge card she'd used to pay for all the family Christmas presents. She dreaded to think how much she'd spent. Since
Boxing Day, she'd been fretting about the bill landing on the mat.

"So," Barbara said, "what did Ken get you for your birthday?"

"A fancy-schmancy spa day, and he's whisking me off to the
South of France for a week in July."

"Wow. Lucky old you. Your old man's still nuts about you. You
know that, don't you?"

Jean laughed. "I do . . . and you're right. I am a very lucky girl."

Just then Ken appeared, glass in hand.

"So what do you think of the wife? Isn't she gorgeous? I keep
telling her she doesn't look a day over thirty-five."

"Idiot," Jean said, bashing him on the arm.

"Right, I suppose I should go and mingle," he said. "Barbara,
where's that husband of yours? Talking to him makes such a change
from all these boring old farts. You know they're all retiring, don't
you? Bloody idiots. Mark my words, they'll be dead in ten years. It's
what boredom and lack of purpose do to you."

"Ken fully intends to keel over at ninety, shoving a tube up some
poor sod's rectum—don't you, Ken?"

"Too bloody right. . . . OK, I'm off to find Frank."

As he turned, he started to sway. Barbara and Jean exchanged
glances.

"Ken, just look at you. You know you can't hold your booze like
you used to. Now do as I say and switch to water."

"You know I really love it when you're bossy." He squeezed Jean's
waist.

"Believe me, if you don't do as you're told, there's plenty more where that came from."

"I can't wait." He winked at his wife and left.

"I do envy you two," Barbara said to Jean. "So loved up after all these years."

It wasn't long before everybody was merry on mulled wine and Tesco Finest bubbly and Jean was organizing party games. After "Gargle That Tune," there was "Murder in the Dark" and "Pin the Lips on Mick Jagger." This was followed by dancing. Funny, Barbara thought as she dragged a protesting Frank into the melee—how the middle-aged women could still get their groove on, whereas most of the men—Frank included—could manage only the kind of jerky-limbed abandon that would have had their children and grandchildren squirming and covering their eyes . . . before sharing the video on Facebook.

At midnight, Barbara, Jean and Jean's sister, Val, who by now were all pretty worse for wear, found themselves sitting on the sofa, getting maudlin.

"So Ken thinks we should buy a futon," Jean said, adjusting her antlers, which kept slipping down over her eyes. "He reckons it'll be good for our backs, but I've told him there is no way that my death-bed is going to be a bloody futon."

"Too right," Val said as she flicked cigarette ash into her empty champagne glass. "You tell him. Oh, and talking of deathbeds, Steve and I have found *the* most incredible burial plots."

Jean looked at her sister. "Bloody hell, Val. You're not even fifty-five."

"I know, but it was a once-in-a-lifetime offer. The plots are in this glorious little glade. It's like this dinky fairy glen. . . ."

"But when the time comes," Barbara said, "won't you and Steve be too dead to notice?"

"That's not the point. . . ."

"I wanna be stuffed," Jean declared. "And have the boys and Ken bring me out every Christmas. They can sit me at the top of the table and stick these antlers on my head."

"I'd like to die having an orgasm," Val said.

Jean laughed. "Good for you, hon. I'll drink to that."

"OK, I think we should stop all this talk about death," Barbara said. "It's depressing. I don't know about you two, but I've still got plenty of living left to do. Everybody says sixty is the new forty."

"Then that would make thirty the new ten," Jean said.

"Not necessarily."

"Yes, necessarily," Val came back. "It's simple arithmetic."

"I don't care," Jean said. "It's legacy that counts. You need to leave a legacy. You know . . . like Einstein. Or Cher."

"We really ought to do it," Frank said to Barbara as they got into bed. "It's been ages. I'm worrying that we're getting out of the habit. And I really fancied you tonight."

"Ditto. You looked incredibly handsome."

"On the other hand, it's one in the morning and it's such a bloody rigmarole. It means I've got to get up and take a tablet. Then we have to wait for it to work."

"I could put the kettle on."

"Oh, very erotic . . . sitting in bed drinking a mug of Yorkshire Gold while I wait to get a hard-on."

If she was honest, she wasn't that bothered about sex these days. There had been a time when she liked Frank to tie her up. When had that waned? Around the time her hot flashes and vaginal dryness had waxed. HRT patches had helped improve her libido a bit, but it wasn't what it was, and like Frank said, these days it was such a rigmarole.

"Let's just have a cuddle?" she said.

Barbara snuggled into him. After a couple of minutes, Frank said his nostrils itched. He got out of bed to find his nose hair trimmer.

Back in the kitchen, Barbara fancied another slice of toast, but she was watching her carbs. Post-menopause fat cells—particularly the ones around her middle—seemed to swell up if they got even the faintest sniff of a scone or hot buttered crumpet. She'd just put the loaf back in the bread bin when her cell rang. She padded over to the kitchen table and picked it up. When she saw the number, she let out a groan. Even for her mother, this was early.

"Hi, Mum. How are you?"

Rose would have been up since five, had her up-and-down wash, eaten her muesli and banana, and now she was bored and looking for some action.

"I'm fine. I was just calling because I've forgotten what time you said you'd be over today."

"I told you last night. I'll be there straight after school. If the weather's not too bad, maybe we could go for a walk in the park. It'll do you good."

"Lovely. I'll make sure I'm in."

Barbara found it both sad and amusing that her mother, who these days left her flat only to go shopping or to the hairdresser, always spoke as if her social calendar were packed with engagements. Right now she would be staring out of her living room window, waiting for it to get light and for the postman to arrive. Frank said she was becoming agoraphobic like Stan—Barbara's late father. Barbara didn't agree. Rose went out every day to shop and run errands. When necessary, she even took the bus. Barbara put her mother's behavior down to nothing more than inertia. In the last few years so many of her friends had died. On the one hand, Rose was lonely. On the other, she couldn't see the point of going out and making new friends who would only die on her.

"But you need to do something to keep yourself occupied," Barbara had said repeatedly. "What about joining a seniors club?"

Rose could think of nothing worse. "What, and spend my days being patronized by idiots who assume that as soon as a person turns seventy, their brain seizes up and all they're interested in is playing bingo and doing the 'Hokey Pokey'? No. I'm better off on my own."

So she spent her days standing at the window or sitting in front of the TV.

Barbara still wanted more toast. Instead of reaching for the bread, she forced herself in the direction of the fruit bowl and helped herself to a handful of blueberries. Above her the floorboards creaked. Frank was up. She would take him a cup of coffee.

She found him in his study, staring into his laptop. When he made no effort to relieve her of the mug, she made some space among his mess of papers and put it down.

"You're welcome," she said.

"Oh, right, cheers," he said, eyes still fixed on his screen. Then: "Oh, for fuck's sake. I don't believe it."

"What?"

"The exec producer at Channel Four is saying they want an entire re-fucking-edit of the Bolivia film. That's going to take forever."

"Frank, calm down. It's not like this is the first time this has happened. So you'll negotiate more time, and it'll work out like it always does. But getting het up isn't going to help. Come on . . . drink some coffee."

"I don't think I can manage it." He grimaced and let out a long belch. "Bloody stomach acid. And I can't find my pills."

Frank made TV documentaries—the kind that came with a warning: "The images you are about to see may cause distress." Did they ever. Audiences wept watching them. Frank got acid reflux making them.

Informing the world about torture, human trafficking, war crimes—essentially any kind of human rights abuse—was Frank's passion, if "passion" was the right word. Maybe "calling" was more apt. His work frequently involved him putting himself in danger. To make his award-winning film *Inside North Korea*, he'd got himself into Pyongyang on an official tourist trip. But each day he'd managed to give the tour guides the slip for a few hours and hook up with a group of activists who took him to wretched, impoverished neighborhoods full of starving families and street children. Barbara was Frank's most ardent advocate and admirer—his enthusiasm and energy were the things that had drawn her to him all those years ago—but that didn't stop her worrying herself sick that one day he would get captured by bad people on one of his escapades and be left to rot in some third-world jail. Or worse.

"They're on the shelf in front of you," Barbara said, regarding the pills. She stretched across, grabbed the box and handed it to him. "So you in for dinner?"

"Nah. Too much on. I'm going to be working late on this reedit."

The story of her life.

Years ago—when their eldest, Jess, was a baby and Barbara was fat and lactating—it occurred to her that Frank wasn't spending all those nights working late and that he was cheating on her. Once, around midnight, she'd shown up at his tiny office in Soho—Jess asleep in her buggy. All she found was her husband cursing into a TV screen as he alternately downed mouthfuls of meat samosa and

Cobra. He was really hurt and angry that she'd felt the need to check up on him, but more than that, he was furious with her for dragging Jess from her cot. She was forced to agree that removing her sleeping infant from her bed and schlepping her to town on a freezing winter's night, purely to indulge her own paranoia, wasn't entirely sane.

"You have to start trusting me," he'd said afterwards, when they were in bed. "I have absolutely no interest whatsoever in other women. It's you and our little family that I want, but at the same time, my work means a huge amount to me. I never made a secret of it. You knew what you were getting into when you married me." He was right. She had gone into the marriage with her eyes wide open. In the end she just accepted her lot as a married single mum and got on with it.

Jess and Ben, who had no idea what it was like to have a dad who worked nine to five and had never known anything different, didn't seem to mind. In fact, their dad being away so much had definite advantages. When he returned, he always came laden with gifts. Ben still remembered being three or four and Frank arriving home from a trip to Tokyo and presenting them with a giant McDonald's restaurant kit complete with paper hats and plastic burgers and pickles.

"So if you're not in for dinner, what will you do?" Barbara said.

"I dunno. I'll probably get a curry."

"You eat too many curries. They're full of fat, which is bad for your reflux. . . ."

Not to mention his weight. He must have put on forty pounds in the last couple of years. But she rarely raised the subject with him, and when she did, she was always tentative. Reason being: she knew from her own experience how hard it was to shed pounds in middle age. If she ate like a bird for a month she could drop a pound or two, but that was as good as it got. When she complained about her weight, Frank accused her of boring on. He said she was fine how she was and so what if she'd gained a few pounds. It happened at their age. She found it hard to nag him when he was so accepting of her.

Nevertheless, she wished Frank would make some effort. Yes, he looked great in a suit, but that only disguised the problem. She was in no doubt that it was the stress of his job that made him eat too much. He self-medicated with food.

The kids didn't hold back though. Jess would pat her father's paunch and say things like: "So, Dad, you opting for a natural birth or an epidural?"

"OK, I'll get sushi," Frank said to Barbara now. "So long as you give me a break."

"I'm sorry, but I worry about you, that's all. Maybe after you finish the edit, you should get a checkup."

"I'll do it when I've got time."

That would be a no, then.

"Oh, by the way," Frank said, popping one of his proton pump inhibitors out of the foil. "I got the go-ahead from BBC Two for the Mexico film." This was going to be about human rights abuses in the Mexican mental-health system. "Not sure how long I'll be away. Could be a while."

Barbara was so used to these announcements—so used to him leaving her for weeks or months at a time—that they barely registered. But lately—over the past year or so—she'd started to feel sad and resentful when he told her he was going away. "So, when are you off?"

He downed the pill with some coffee. "Dunno. It's all up in the air right now, what with this reedit. Plus we've still got to agree to the budget. But I'm hoping to get away in a couple of weeks."

"But you've only just got back." He'd spent the last month making a film about the use of child labor in Bolivian silver mines. While he was there, his car had been followed and he'd received death threats from mine owners.

"Bar, the day has hardly started and so far you've done nothing but give me a hard time. You've never nagged me about going away. Please don't start now. What would you have me do?"

She resented him accusing her of nagging. He was right. Over the years she'd been positively stoic about him being away so much. It was only now that they were getting older that she thought they deserved some time together.

"Come on," she said, trying to sound loving rather than combative. "You know I loathe the idea of retirement as much as you do and I'd never ask you to stop working. This job is your life, and for your sake I hope you carry on doing it until you're ninety, but couldn't you cut back just a bit? And maybe you could think about covering stories that don't put your life in danger." She looked at his belly, the way it strained against his T-shirt and hung over his boxers. "I don't want to lose you."

"I'm always careful. You're not going to lose me. And you know as well as I do that I can't cut back on work. We need the money."

He was right again. They did need the money. Contrary to popular opinion, TV documentary makers—even award-winning ones like Frank who were always in demand—didn't make a great deal of money. Over the years they'd remortgaged the house twice to help pay for the kids' education. Among their friends, they were the only couple that didn't own their house outright. They were also the only ones who hadn't come into a substantial inheritance. When Frank's parents died a few years back, there had been no property to pass on because they'd rented their flat. Their only hope was Rose. But if the time came when she needed to go into a care home, her place would have to be sold. Private care cost a fortune, so all the equity would be swallowed up in fees. That would leave them with nothing. They'd be forced to sell their home to finance their old age and be left eking out their days paying rent on some rabbit hutch of a rented flat.

"I know we need the money," Barbara said, "but I hate seeing you under so much stress. If third-world thugs don't kill you, then stress will."

"I appreciate the sentiment, but whether you like it or not, I plan to carry on working and earn enough money to pay for our old age. In other words, I fully intend to have my cake and eat it. So, unless you have another solution . . ."

"That's not fair. Don't make this my problem. It's our problem. We need to work it out together."

"Look, I can't have this conversation now. I've got a stack of e-mails to reply to. Then I need to get in the shower."

It seemed to her that he always found some excuse or other not to have *this* conversation.

"Oh, by the way," he said. "My sister's been posting more pictures of kittens on Facebook."

"I know. I saw. And some affirmation about life being less about breaths you take and more about the moments that take your breath away."

"I don't get it," Frank said. "Pam's always liked to show off and flaunt her money, but she's never been a flake."

"That's what menopause does to you," Barbara said. "Lack of estrogen makes women crave all things saccharine and schmaltzy."

"Really?"

"Well, that's my theory, for what it's worth. I'm not sure it would stand up to rigorous scientific analysis. . . . With me it's *The Golden Girls*."

"Huh . . . I hadn't noticed."

Of course he hadn't. He was never here.

"I don't know how you can watch that rubbish," he said.

"Yeah, well, I'd rather have my brain go a bit syrupy than succumb to the male meno-Porsche."

"Male meno-Porsche? Me? What are you on about? You and I share a crappy old Saab."

"Yeah, but that's only because you can't afford a Porsche. If you had money, you'd be so in there. . . ."

"Actually, I wouldn't get a Porsche. I'd get a Harley." He started making vrooming noises. "Come on . . . be honest. How much would it turn you on to see my paunch encased in skintight black leather?"

"You have no idea," she said, grinning.

Since Frank would probably be at his desk for another few minutes, Barbara decided to grab the first shower. On her way to the bathroom, she stopped to listen at Ben's door for signs of him stirring. Some hopes. The TV was on quietly, which meant he'd probably been up most of the night and had dozed off in front of it. She opened the door a crack. Her son was asleep on his back, arms splayed, mouth slightly open. His laptop, along with the stinky remains of a plate of bacon, eggs, beans and ketchup, was on his nightstand. Dirty socks, pants and towels were scattered over the floor. She could only guess what time he'd fallen asleep. Ben—eighteen months out of uni—was trying to make it as a music journalist. He wrote at night, claiming that he worked better in the quiet. "Stop worrying," he'd say, whenever his mother registered concern about his unhealthy sleeping pattern. "I was the same at university. My whole life was spent pulling all-nighters."

What Barbara knew for certain was that her son would remain

unconscious for most of the day—probably emerging from his adolescent pit about the time she got home from work. She closed the door as quietly as she could.

The point was, of course, that Ben wasn't an adolescent. He was twenty-three. But in many ways he was still her baby. A couple of years after having Jess, they'd tried to get pregnant again, but each month had ended in disappointment. There was no obvious physical reason. Just bad luck, the doctors said. Then, almost a decade later, when they'd given up hope, along came Ben: their little miracle.

"This can't go on," Frank had said last night when Ben was out. "Us bankrolling him while he sleeps all day. We're too bloody soft on him. Have you any idea how much his December phone bill was—the one that I just paid? Two hundred quid. And that's on top of the ton of money you spent on Christmas presents and Jean's birthday."

"It was bloody Christmas, for crying out loud. And Jean was sixty. What was I supposed to do?"

"Spend less."

"OK, next year you can be in charge of all the present buying. . . . Look, I know Ben's costing us a fortune, but it's hard for kids these days. They come out of university with decent degrees only to discover that nobody wants to employ them. This is the worst job market in decades. Lots of his friends are in the same boat. According to the Office for National Statistics, one in three men aged twenty to thirty-four still lives with his parents. I read it in the *Guardian*."

"Sod the Office for bloody Statistics and sod the *Guardian*. It's indulgent *Guardian*-reading parents like us who've mollycoddled our kids since they were born who are responsible for all this. We've infantilized them, turned them into these delicate flowers who are too scared to go out into the world and get their hands dirty. Ben needs to find a job. Any job. That's all there is to it."

Barbara reminded him that Ben volunteered twice a week at the food bank, distributing groceries. "He's a good kid. His heart's in the right place. He takes after you."

In the seventies, Frank had spent some time volunteering at a soup kitchen.

"I also had a paid job."

"Yes, but right now there are no jobs."

"There are if you're prepared to get your hands dirty."

Then Frank went on about how, during his gap year—when the economic situation was so bad that the population was working only a three-day week—he'd found work as a porter in a hospital mortuary. "In my day kids had initiative."

"And you enjoyed that job, did you?"

"It was OK, and anyway, it wasn't about enjoyment. Coming face-to-face with death toughened me up—made a man of me."

"Really? Because according to your mum, you lasted less than a day. She said a leg on one of the corpses shot up and you ran out, screaming like a girl."

"Rubbish. I didn't scream like a girl. I screamed like a man."

Barbara turned on the shower and got undressed. She couldn't help feeling sorry for Ben, but Frank had a point. They were being too soft on him. From the moment Ben moved back in they should have laid down some rules. Rule one: if he wanted to make it as a music journalist he needed to meet the world halfway and start typing stuff out.

Granted, he was doing a bit, writing blogs for online music magazines, but it wasn't enough. And mostly he wrote for free. A few magazines paid, but rarely more than fifty quid.

She'd read some of his stuff. Most of the time she hadn't the foggiest what he was going on about. He tended to write about obscure bands with "fearless sonic curiosity" or whose latest "tensely coiled" offering had "an alchemical knack of deriving inspiration from limitation."

Ben's knowledge didn't surprise her. He'd been immersed in music since he was a teenager. He'd taught himself to play guitar at age fourteen, and in his first year at university he formed a punk band called Grandma and the Junkies. They were pretty good by all accounts. By the time the boys left university, they were gigging all over the country—mostly in crappy clubs in godforsaken towns, but that was the way it worked. You slogged away for years, and if you were any good, you might get a break. But after a year or so they realized that none of them had the stomach for the long haul. What's more, the lack of any A&R interest—despite them posting endless videos on YouTube—prompted a reality check. Grandma and the Junkies were good, but they weren't great. They were just another standard uni band.

They broke up. It was the first time in his life that Ben had failed at something, and for a while he was pretty miserable. It didn't help that despite the recession, the other boys landed on their feet and found jobs.

Ben wasn't saying anything, but Barbara suspected that even now, months later, he was still reeling from his failure. He'd been denied his dream. She imagined how angry he felt. He was clearly sleeping to hide from his emotions. Despite his bits of writing, she suspected that deep down his passion for music had faded. His heart wasn't in it. Barbara had tried talking to him about how he was feeling.

"I know you're miserable, but you did your best to make a go of the band. And people in the music industry are always going on about how success is so often down to luck more than talent. Plus you admitted that none of you really had the commitment to keep going."

"We didn't have the commitment.... But you've got this all wrong. I'm over what happened to the band. Honest."

But she wasn't buying it.

Sad as she felt for him, it didn't alter the fact that Ben needed to earn some money. It wasn't simply that they couldn't afford to keep financing him. It wasn't good for him to be in his twenties and so dependent on his parents. She dreaded to think what effect it was having on his self-esteem. He needed to get a part-time job with a paper hat and start paying something towards his upkeep. She resolved that she and Frank would sit down and have a serious talk with him. And sooner rather than later.

After her shower, Barbara dried her hair, checked her chin in the mirror for whiskers and replaced her HRT patch. She'd tried coming off the hormones, but within a few days the hot flashes returned and she turned into Crazy Psycho Woman. Frank said it was like living with Mrs. Satan with PMS. Her doctor said she would probably need to be on HRT for life.

Getting dressed was easy—thanks to her stomach bulge. Barbara's tight tops and jeans were long gone. She slipped on a navy tunic and a pair of matching palazzo pants. These days her wardrobe was full of dark palazzos, leggings and long A-line tunics that skimmed her upper body and vaguely hinted at a waist. According to the magazines, tunics, long scarves and heels lengthened the torso and drew the eye away from a thickened midsection. Today she accessorized her uniform with chunky earrings, a couple of thick bangles and the obligatory long, jazzy scarf.

Her mother, Rose, is getting ready to go out. She and Stan—Barbara's dad—have been invited to something called a "function." This is a sort of party. Her parents go to lots of functions. As usual, Mrs. T is coming to babysit. Mrs. T is old and seems to like Barbara. She's teaching her how to knit.

Barbara goes upstairs to watch her mother dress. Rose's wardrobe is full of beautiful clothes. Barbara likes the evening gowns best. She sits on the big bed studying how her mother applies her eye shadow, the way she dots her face with Pan Stik and then with swift, skillful strokes, smudges it over her face so that it's perfectly even. She watches her adjust her breasts in her low-cut, floaty chiffon dress covered in twinkly beads. "You look like a princess," Barbara tells her mother. She stands up on the bed, reaches over and throws her arms around Rose's shoulders. She gives her a big kiss on the cheek.

"What's that for?" It's her mother's usual response when her daughter attempts to show her affection. Barbara is confused. Is it wrong to kiss your mum for no reason?

"Barbara, please let go. You're spoiling my makeup."

Barbara missed clothes shopping. Even in her forties she'd still been slim and able to find the odd thing in Topshop that she could get away with. That seemed light-years away now.

Jean was one of the lucky ones who hadn't put on weight in her fifties. "Look at you in your tight jeans. You still look amazing."

"No, I don't. I look like Andy Warhol." She was referring to her flyaway bleached-blond hair.

Being overweight in middle age did have one compensation, for which Barbara couldn't help being grateful. Fat was a natural filler, and even if she did say so herself, her face was holding up rather well. That said, it hadn't stopped her being pissed off about her thirty-nine-inch waist. A few weeks ago, Pam had posted on Facebook that when she felt old and unattractive, she thought about the young women she'd known who had died. Thinking about those beautiful women who didn't make it always makes me feel grateful for what I've got—even if these days Father Time and Mr. Gravity are taking their toll. For me it's a privilege just to be alive.

Sanctimonious cow.

Barbara closed the front door behind her. Steve Jobs! That was the name of the Apple bloke. She felt a bit less senile now that she'd remembered.

Chapter 2

On a good day it was no more than a ten-minute drive to Jubilee Primary. The school was over the road from Orchard Farm. It went without saying that this was neither an orchard nor a farm, but a public-housing estate. It was also one of the worst in London. Orchard Farm: a mean joke of a name, Barbara thought. The *Daily Mail* referred to the place as the "Hammer Housing Estate of Horror." As soon as they turned five, all the Orchard Farm kids started at Jubilee.

There was a reason apart from her punctuality neurosis that Barbara liked to get in early. Each morning, the school provided breakfast for the pupils, and she thought that it was important to be there. It was a chance for her to sit down and chat with the most underprivileged, vulnerable youngsters and check how they were doing. She knew these kids well, as they tended to be the ones who left their classes for a few hours each week to come to her cubbyhole of an office for extra tutoring. Barbara was one of the school's remedial teachers, although the staff were careful never to use the word in front of pupils. But even the little ones had her sussed. "Oy, miss, is it true that people only come to your classes 'cos they is retards?" Her charges were often bullied and taunted in the playground. "Tyler is special nee-eeds. . . . Tyler is special nee-eeds." Despite frequent lectures from the principal in school assembly, the harassment didn't stop.

In Barbara's opinion, many of the children who came to her were perfectly able. It was their emotional problems, which resulted in them acting out or throwing violent temper tantrums, that affected their ability to learn. She'd spent years trying to get the local education authority to fund a permanent on-site counselor, but there was never any money. Class teachers tended to be at their wits' end with these children. How did you even begin to teach a class of thirty when some kid with attention deficit disorder was throwing books and chairs about? Barbara provided the teachers with a break.

Since university, all Barbara had ever wanted to do was try to make a difference—to help kids like the ones at Jubilee—kids whose lives were threadbare and godforsaken. And she'd always known she would be good at it because in some ways she could identify with neglected kids. Granted, she'd never been cold or gone hungry. She hadn't grown up with useless, drug-addled parents, but she knew how it felt to be neglected emotionally. She'd also read enough pop psychology books to realize that by trying to rescue other children, she was trying to rescue the abandoned child in her. That was one of the reasons that her work was so addictive and why she couldn't contemplate parting with it.

Over the years, several head teachers at schools where she'd worked had suggested—always with a nod and a wink—that she apply for this or that senior post or headship, but she'd always refused. She was a teacher, not a manager.

A few hundred yards down the road, Barbara pulled over and ducked into Bean and Gone to pick up a double-shot latte. The hit from her early-morning mug of coffee was starting to wear off.

Barbara and Frank had moved to the East End soon after they got married—because it was cheap. Back in the midseventies, the first wave of gentrification was just beginning to hit. They'd bought their tiny flat for less than ten grand, when the only place approaching a coffee shop was Jim's, the greasy spoon on Mare Street. It was always full workmen and blokes in flat caps reading the *Racing Post* while they downed bacon, eggs and beans—and maybe a slice of Jim's fried bread. Jim didn't serve poncy, frothy coffee. That was for poofters. It was either thick orange builder's tea or instant coffee. By the eighties they had moved around the corner, into the Victorian terraced house where they still lived. Today there were two independent coffee shops, a whole-food deli, a Reiki healer and an organic butcher within two hundred yards of Barbara's front door.

Bean and Gone used to be an ironmonger's. The owner had been a bloke called Derrick. In the warm weather, his old mum used to sit outside on a kitchen chair, resting her bulk on one of those three-pronged metal walking sticks. The entire neighborhood called her Grandma. Presumably Derrick knew her actual name, but nobody thought to ask. You couldn't pass the shop without being collared by Grandma. Barbara had one memorable encounter: "Aw right, darlin'? 'Ere, jew know everybody can see your arse in that skirt?"

A workman on some scaffolding had heard her and yelled: "No, Grandma—you sing it and I'll hum along."

Grandma burst into a bronchial cackle. "Still you've got the legs for it. Good luck to yer, darlin'."

Barbara missed the old characters. She wondered what Grandma would have made of all the hipster newcomers. "Oy, mate . . . yeah, you in the woolly hat. You do realize it's bleedin' August, don't you?"

That said, Barbara loved the energy, the cosmopolitan-ness, the twenty-four-seven, artisan macaroonness of the new East End. What she loathed were the dirt, the bag people, the smell of exhaust, the sirens, the gangs, the knife crime. As she returned to her car with her latte, a dispatch rider with a wobbly exhaust roared off, leaving a toxic cloud of black in his wake. There were times when she found herself craving a life in the country. She yearned for fields, woods to wander in, babbling brooks, birdsong that wasn't drowned out by traffic noise, a rolling hill or two. But the desire didn't last long. She couldn't imagine living in one of those twee hang-'em-and-flog-'em Tory stronghold villages where you never saw a black or brown face from one fox-hunt ball to the next. The countryside was also where people her age went to retire—to play bowls on the village green, to exchange gossip about the latest parish council meeting or church bazaar . . . to embrace the dying of the light. Barbara leaned forward and turned on the CD player . . . *Like a bat outta hell I'll be gone when the morning comes* . . . As she pulled away, she turned up the volume and sang along while beating out a rhythm on the steering wheel.

A few minutes later, as she pulled up at a red light, she was still singing and thinking that she must tell the kids she wanted them to play Meat Loaf at her funeral. She was paying almost no attention to the Porsche in front of her and would have carried on paying it no attention had the driver not rolled down his window and dropped a paper cup onto the road. She waited for a couple of moments to see if it had been accidental. Surely the driver was about to open his door and get out to retrieve the cup. But he didn't.

Aware that the light could change any second, Barbara was out of her car. She was always saying that one of the best things about being a stout middle-aged woman was that you looked harmless. Barbara had learned that she could confront people in public about their rudeness or blatant disregard for civic duty and mostly they didn't pull a knife.

She tapped on the driver's window. Inside, the thirtysomething chap in a Mr. Toad check jacket and flat cap looked taken aback. The window slid down.

"Er, excuse me, sir . . ." She always began by being superpolite in these situations. Not that she'd been that polite to the antiabortion protesters she'd come across last week, camped outside the offices of British Pregnancy Advisory Service. She'd shouted and hectored them about how banning abortion would force women to return to the days when they bled to death on the kitchen tables of backstreet abortionists. Today, faced only with a litter lout, she was feeling far less combative.

"Sorry to trouble you, but I think that somehow this cup found its way out of your car and onto the road." By now she had picked it up and was dangling it in front of the driver.

"Oh, right. Gosh. Most awfully sorry. My mistake." He took the cup.

If she'd been younger, he would have continued to behave like the asshole he was and ignored her or told her to fuck off. But she probably reminded him of his nanny. Posh, well-brought-up assholes didn't dare tell Nanny to fuck off.

"No worries." Barbara smiled. "You have a nice day."

The light had changed, but she hadn't quite made it back to her car. She expected the traffic to be honking like crazy, but the woman behind her was beaming and giving her a thumbs-up. "You're a braver woman than me," she called out through her window. "I wouldn't have dared to challenge him. You never know what they'll do."

One of the many things that pissed Barbara off about the world was people seeing wrongdoing and refusing to get involved or speak up. Why was everybody so feeble? She blamed the *Daily Mail*. If you believed their hype and scaremongering, half the population was armed with knives.

As she pulled away, she checked the time on the dashboard clock.

Her mother is standing in front of the hall mirror, spending what seems like hours doing her hair and makeup. The wrought iron and frosted-glass telephone table is littered with lipsticks, pots of eye shadow and rouge—a giant can of Aqua Net extra hold. Barbara is standing beside her in her green gymslip and crested blazer, checking the minute hand on her Timex watch. Barbara enjoys watching Rose get ready to go out, but not when school starts in less than fifteen minutes.

"Mummy, hurry up. I'm going to be late again. . . . Mummy, please. You always make me late. . . ."

"Will you stop nagging?" In as ladylike a fashion as she can muster, Rose spits onto the solid block of mascara and scrubs at it with her brush. "So what if you're a few minutes late?"

"I'll get kept in at playtime." Barbara is close to tears.

They arrive at the school gates to find the bell has gone and the playground empty. Once again, Barbara is made to stay in at break and do hard division sums.

When Rose collects her from school, Barbara grizzles and whines about the sums and how she missed playing with her friends. "It was horrible. I was all on my own. Please can we get to school earlier?"

"Oh, stop making such a fuss," her mother says, handing her a packet of cheese and onion potato chips. "At least you didn't have to carry three bags of shopping home in the teeming rain. Missing playtime is hardly the end of the world. You'll play with your friends tomorrow."

Whenever Barbara moans to her mother—which isn't often—Rose makes her feel as if she's being selfish and naughty.

———————

Barbara had just parked her car in her usual spot around the corner from the school when her cell rang. Jess.

"Mum, I know it's short notice, but I was wondering if you could pick the kids up from school and look after them for a few hours. I wouldn't ask, but I'm desperate. We're doing this outside catering job, and I'm in the middle of making two hundred vegan canapés. The babysitter's got this stomach thing that's been doing the rounds, and I'm not sure I'll be finished by school pickup time."

Jess and her husband, Matt, had just opened their own organic deli-cum-grocery-cum-eatery a mile or so down the road from Barbara and Frank. Since it was early days, the only help they could afford were a couple of part-time assistants-slash-waitresses. Jess, who always said her culinary talent came about as a reaction to her mother's lack of interest in cooking, prepared all the ready meals and did the baking. Matt worked behind the counter, took care of the ordering and did the books.

"Sweetheart, you sound really stressed. You sure you OK? You know, I do worry that you and Matt have taken on too much. I mean, what with the kids . . ."

"Mum, don't do this now . . . please. I'm too busy. I just need to know if you can get Atticus and Cleo."

"Of course. No probs, but they'll have to come to Nana's with me."

"Fine. Get her to show them her photographs from the *olden days*. They love that."

Jubilee School was a dirty, yellow brick, churchlike edifice surrounded by asphalt and tall railings. It still had its original stone plaque in the shape of a shield over the main entrance: JUBILEE MIXED INFANTS AND JUNIORS. 1887. It also had the original two

entrances—one for boys and one for girls, which had been pre-
served purely for historical interest.

Barbara opened the school gate and made her way across the
playground. A group of year-six lads—white, Asian, black, Eastern
European—were kicking a ball around and yelling at one another in
half a dozen languages. Some of their mates were leaning against
the wall trying to look cool as they played games on their phones.
Phones weren't allowed in school, but the oldest kids in particular—
not to mention their parents—weren't about to be told. Whenever a
phone was confiscated, an irate mother or father—who had never
shown up to a single parents' evening—came marching into school
insisting that they knew their rights and accusing the school of
abuse. In the end Sandra had decided it was a battle she couldn't win.
She relented and let the top years bring in their phones. "What I
don't understand," she had said to Barbara the other day when they
were chatting in the staff room, "is why families who are struggling
always make such bad choices. I mean, if you or I were hard up, we'd
buy food, gas and electricity—not big-screen TVs and smartphones
for our kids. And they wonder why they're always in debt."

Sandra—Mrs. Nichols to the kids—had worked at Jubilee for
five years. Before that she'd spent two decades teaching at a small
private school just outside Oxford. By the time she'd left, she was
deputy head. She was married to a wine merchant named Charles.
There were no children. Whether that was down to bad luck or lack
of desire, Barbara had never been able to establish. Since Sandra
never raised the subject, she suspected it was bad luck.

Barbara—along with most of the staff—had always considered
her an odd fit for a school like Jubilee.

"I needed a challenge," she'd said when Barbara had asked her
why she'd given up such a comfortable, stress-free job. "In the end,

comfortable becomes tedious, and superbright, privileged children can be so dull. They're like automatons, a lot of them. The boys know they will go into the law or banking. The girls end up in PR or working in art galleries. As a teacher, you start to think, what's the point? What do I have to offer?"

What Sandra liked to think what she offered Jubilee kids was discipline. She insisted on teachers setting homework three nights a week—although little got done. Children had to wear the regulation blue sweatshirt with the school logo. Sandra believed that taking pride in one's school led to greater self-esteem. It didn't. Stewart, the deputy head, summed up what the rest of the staff already knew: "All it does is make it easier for the police to identify the little buggers."

Sandra's other innovation was playtime detentions. Miscreants would be made to sit alone and write apologies to their victims. Most were short—on words as well as remorse: *Soree I stabbed you in the neck with my pensel. I will give you a kwid after school.*

Their contrition, such as it was, lasted until the next time they thought it might be fun to stick somebody with a pencil or demand money with menaces.

Stewart, the young deputy head, did his best to explain that kids often behaved badly to get attention. "They spend their lives being ignored by their parents. In the end they get so angry and frustrated that they lash out—at somebody or something."

"But surely there are parenting classes they can go to. . . ."

"These people don't need parenting classes. Most of them are suffering from depression."

Now Barbara waded in. "Stewart's right. It's the reason they turn to booze and drugs. That's why they treat themselves to fancy phones and big TVs. It's all about escapism."

"I don't think all these people are genuinely depressed," Sandra said. "If you ask me, it's laziness. Nobody on that estate seems to have any ambition or drive. They're all so passive and happy for the government to take control of their lives."

Barbara often imagined Sandra in a previous life, ministering to the poor in a big hat as she handed out thin soup and admonishments.

The two women had been having this debate—which never amounted to more than good-natured sparring—since Sandra took over at the school. Sandra would accuse Barbara of being a namby-pamby liberal. In her view, pandering to the underprivileged did them no favors. It simply disempowered them. Barbara would accuse her of spouting Tory claptrap. How could forcing people to live on these wretched housing estates possibly be described as pandering?

Then the end-of-play bell would go and they would abandon their discussion, agreeing only to disagree.

Barbara fell in behind a group of younger girls making their way inside for breakfast. They were yakking at the tops of their voices. Barbara couldn't help smiling. How old were they? Eight? Nine? And already they were engaged in proper conversational back-and-forth. Boys were so much slower that way.

She was about to climb the stairs to the staff room when a small voice piped up behind her. "Hi, Mrs. Stirling. Did you have a good Christmas? Miss, if there was a booga competition, I'd definitely win it, 'cos I can eat a hundred in an hour." Jordan Duffy—year two—waved his index finger at Barbara.

"Wow, Jordan. That's great. Thank you so much for sharing."

He raced off towards the dining hall.

"Hey, Jordan! No running!"

Grim as the school looked from the outside, the interior couldn't have been more different. Visitors stepped into an ocean of primary colors and kids' artwork. Ten years ago, after local worthies had spent decades lobbying the government, the Education Department had finally caved in and agreed to renovate the building. This happened to be around the time that the *Daily Mail* first referred to the neighborhood as the Hammer Housing Estate of Horror. The initial article turned into a campaign that ran for months—attacking residents, referring to them as scroungers and criminals.

It was moot whether the government relented for altruistic reasons or purely to get the right-wing press off its back. Whatever the truth, they shelled out the best part of two million pounds to give Jubilee a face-lift. There was new wiring, plumbing and heating. There was even carpeting in some of the communal areas. The brown-and-green wall tiles had been painted white. All the old classroom desks and chairs had been replaced with bright, modern furniture. The lunchroom now had a large kitchen extension, from which decent, healthy meals were produced every day. Each class had a couple of computers and Internet access. When the building work was finished, the school was officially "relaunched." The Labour government considered it an event worthy of the prime minister's presence. The staff got dressed up. The kids got excited—not so much about being in the presence of Tony Blair, but because the school was going to be full of TV cameras. "Miss, miss . . . does that mean I'll be on the telly, miss? Does it?" The PM made a speech about the renovation of Jubilee school being another major example of Labour's commitment to education and inner-city regeneration. He hailed education as the key to success. Every child, no matter what their background, should feel they had a right to succeed. The staff all exchanged glances at this. Barbara couldn't help thinking that the hapless kids on the social services at-risk register might have laughed if they'd understood what was being said.

In the staff room, everybody was exchanging cheery "Happy New Year's," along with tales of Christmas triumphs and disasters.

Christine, a year-one teaching assistant, had broken her wrist skiing and was in plaster up to her elbow. A few people were poring over the newspaper and moaning about education budget cuts. "Well, if you ask me," Christine said, "job-wise this has to be the safest school in London. Why would the government plow all that money into the refurb only to cut our jobs? Makes no sense."

"But that was the last government, and it was ten years ago," Stewart said, stirring his coffee. "In case you've forgotten, this is austerity Britain."

This morning about a dozen kids had turned up for breakfast in the lunchroom. "Not a great turnout," one of the serving ladies said to Barbara. "You know, it's the ones who don't make it that worry me." She was right. The kids who really needed feeding tended to arrive late for school, or simply didn't show up.

Barbara helped herself to a banana. She was wondering if she had time for another cup of coffee before school started when she noticed Troy from year three. He was stuffing beans on toast down him like there was no tomorrow. She wondered when he'd last had a decent meal.

Troy was one of her remedial kids. With his dark chocolate eyes and thicket of golden hair, he looked almost beatific. But Troy was prone to angry outbursts. His mum, Tiffany, did her best for him and his baby sister, Lacie, but she was on her own, living on benefits and clearly weighed down by life on the poverty line.

Tiffany had come in recently, at Barbara's request, to discuss Troy's temper tantrums. She'd brought Lacie, who was in her buggy feeding herself cold weak tea from a bottle. Occasionally, Tiffany handed her bits of jam doughnut. Tiffany was pretty, but she did her best to disguise it. Her scraped-back hair, heavy black eyeliner and matching eyebrows made her look positively fierce.

"It ain't Troy's fault that he keeps losing it," Tiffany insisted.

"Night after night he sees me crying because there's no money. He wants to help and he can't because he's eight. And he gets angry 'cos I can't buy him stuff the other kids have. And in case you hadn't worked it out, that's also why he's backward. He's brain's too full of other stuff to concentrate on his work."

"You're right about Troy. You don't have to convince me. And I know you struggle financially. I do understand."

"The fuck you do. People like you know nothing. You're all piss and paninis. There are days when I have to decide do I put money in the meter for the electric or do I put food on the table? If I thought I wouldn't get caught, I'd start thieving. And I'm not going to one of them food banks, neither. I'm not a bloody beggar."

"But don't you have any family who can help out?" Barbara was aware that she sounded like some lady bountiful social worker from the fifties.

"They're either dead or locked up. Next question."

Tiffany thought she was hard, but her fingernails bitten to the quick and the scars on her lower arms from cutting herself were testament to something very different.

Tiffany was messed up the way that so many poor, vulnerable women were messed up. Self-harm was only one of her problems. Barbara knew—via on- and off-the-record conversations that Sandra had had with social services—that Tiffany was drawn to violent men and had been since she was a teenager. Nearly all her boyfriends—including the fathers of her children—had treated her like a punch bag. She'd ended up in hospital with broken ribs more than once. The police did their best to persuade her to press charges, but she always refused.

"Tiffany, is everything all right at home? Are you keeping yourself safe?"

She swore she wasn't seeing anybody right now.

"Tell me something—has Troy ever seen you being hurt by these men?"

"Never. On my life. I swear to God."

This was the story she always told the police and social services. They bought it because they couldn't prove otherwise. And Troy certainly wasn't telling. In the end it was decided that the children could remain in her care, but they would be put on the at-risk register.

"Because if Troy has ever seen you being attacked," Barbara went on, "he would be very angry and frightened, and it would explain his behavior."

"I'm telling you, he's upset because there's no money and he worries about me. Why can't that be enough? Why do you people always have to keep digging and prying?"

"I'm sorry if you think I'm prying, but I'm just trying to help."

"We don't need your help. We don't need anybody's help. We're fine as we are."

"Let me ask you a question. The last time you ended up in hospital with broken ribs, what did you tell Troy?"

"That I had an accident."

"And you think he believed you?"

"Of course he believed me. He's a kid. Why wouldn't he believe me? Who do you think you are, interrogating me? You think you're so perfect, so bloody high and mighty. Well, you know fuck all."

With that Tiffany snatched hold of the buggy and steered it out of the room.

Barbara swallowed the last of her banana and made her way over to Troy. "Hi, Troy. Good Christmas?"

A shrug. Then he looked down at his plate. Troy had never been big on eye contact. It was one of the things that worried her about him. "Wayne got us a big-screen TV. But it was for everybody."

Barbara lowered herself onto one of the child-size dining chairs. "So you missed out on getting something just for you. That's a shame. On the other hand, TVs cost a lot of money."

"S'pose."

"So who's Wayne?" she said. "Is he a new friend of your mum's?"

Troy concentrated on shoveling beans and toast into his mouth. "Yeah. He stays in our house. He lets me play *Grand Theft Auto*."

Of course he did. "Right. So what else did you get up to on Christmas Day?"

"Not much. I just wish that Santa had brought me what I wanted."

"What was that?"

"A chimney and a Christmas tree like you see on TV."

Barbara could feel herself welling up. It was as much as she could do to stop herself scooping up the poor little chap and taking him home.

"Well, at least you got one nice present."

"I suppose." As he reached for his carton of milk, the sleeve of his school sweatshirt rode up to reveal two circular angry sores.

Cigarette burns. She would put money on it.

"Ooh, they look nasty," Barbara said, making sure to keep her voice level. She didn't want to freak him out. If Tiffany's new boyfriend was responsible, then Troy would only get more of the same if he found out the kid had been telling tales to his teacher. "Tell you what. After you've eaten, why don't we go the medical room and put something on them."

They stopped off at Sandra's office en route. "Mrs. Nichols," Barbara said. "Would you mind coming with me?"

"What?" Sandra mouthed.

Barbara jerked her head in the direction of the medical room. They sat Troy down, and Barbara rolled up his sleeves. His arms were dotted with burns. Both women winced. Barbara dabbed the two fresh sores with antiseptic—the others appeared to be scabbing over—and said she'd check on them again tomorrow.

When Troy had gone, Barbara said they ought to call social services. "This is bound to be the work of Tiffany's new boyfriend. Lacie could be in danger, too. Those kids are meant to be on the at-risk register. Who the hell's looking after them?"

"Right," Sandra said. "Why don't you get on to it?"

"Me?"

"Oh, come on. You know how scary and intimidating you are. You're so much better at dealing with social services than me. You know how I loathe confrontation."

Sandra was a puzzle. When it came to debating politics in the staff room, she was happy to take on all comers. But if she needed to confront social services or her bosses at the Education Department, she preferred to delegate. Usually she asked Stewart. Sometimes she leaned on Barbara. It was pretty obvious to both of them why she did it: Sandra knew she wasn't a great fit at Jubilee. The last thing she wanted was to rock the boat with anybody in authority, so she got other people to rock it for her. Barbara had wanted to raise the issue with Sandra, but Stewart begged her not to. He wasn't a boat rocker either.

She said that she would make the call during first break. There wasn't time now because the bell was about to go and she had four kids from Troy's year—Troy included—coming to her for a lesson.

Armani was the first to arrive. She was a cute, smiley child with cornrows and bows and startling blue eyes. Today she had glitter all over her hands. "Goodness, where did all that come from?" Barbara said, taking Armani's hand in hers.

"I was doing sticking before I came to school," she said, joining Barbara at the round table.

Here was one child, at least, who spent time at home engaged in creative activity.

Troy was next to show, along with Baillie and Kane. Troy offered Barbara a tepid smile. He even made eye contact with her. Whenever he did that, it gave Barbara hope. It made her feel that one day she might truly reach him. Baillie and Kane sat down and immediately began to fiddle with the paper and pencils on the table.

"Kane, please don't stick pencils up your nose. It's not funny. Do you see me laughing?"

"Miss is right," Armani said to him. "If you fell over with the pencil up your nose, it could stab you in the brain. And all this brain gunge would come out of your eyes and your ears and your nose."

Kane pulled a face. "Gross. Is she right, miss?"

"Well, she's probably exaggerating a bit, but that doesn't make it safe." Barbara paused and turned her attention to the whole group. "Right, so why don't we get started? I thought that today it might be fun to do some measuring."

Barbara was aware that, as usual, Baillie was attempting to pull out her eyelashes. Barbara needed to distract her. She reached into her bag.

"Baillie, do you know what this is?" Barbara was holding up a large thermometer.

"It's a ther-momenter."

"Almost. It's actually pronounced ther-mometer. Baillie, sweetheart, can you try to look at me when you give an answer?"

Like Troy, Baillie struggled to make eye contact. She looked steadfastly down at the table.

Barbara tried again. "OK, so, can you tell me what a thermometer measures?"

"Heat," Armani piped up. "And it's really, really hot in Jamaica, where my gran comes from. I'm going there one day. On a plane. Have you ever been to Jamaica, miss?"

"I haven't. Come on, Armani. How's about you try concentrating for a few minutes."

The child put her finger to her lips and giggled. "OK, miss. Sorry, miss."

Kane was the quietest of the four. Barbara was aware of how easy it was to ignore him. "So, Kane, have you ever had your temperature taken? Sometimes when you get sick, you get hot. Perhaps Mum has put a strip across your forehead to check how hot you are?"

He was holding a couple of pencils like drumsticks and beating out a rhythm on the table. Barbara made him stop and repeated her question. His face was a picture of blank regarding the forehead thermometer

"They took my temp-ri-ture when I was in the hospital," Troy said. "They put this thing in my ear."

"Yes, that's how nurses take your temperature. So, when were you in the hospital?"

"Christmas. I hurt my leg."

"And how did you do that?" Barbara said, immediately realizing how stupid it was to think that he'd tell the truth with other children there.

"Playing."

"I see." There was no point pushing him. She would see what social services knew about his hospital visit. "OK, so the thermometer I've got here tells us how hot it is in this room. I'd like you all to look at it and see if you can work out how to read the temperature."

"You look at the red line," Armani said, stretching across the table and tapping the glass. "And match it to the number. It's sixty-eight degrees in here." There was no question in Barbara's mind that this child was perfectly able, if not highly intelligent. The only reason she was being sent to Barbara three times a week was because she never stopped yakking and her class teacher had had enough. She was simply bored and in need of individual attention and stimulation. Like that was ever going to happen.

"Well done, Armani." Barbara put the thermometer in the center of the table. "Now, can everybody else see that?"

Without any warning, Troy snatched the thermometer off the table and threw it on the floor. It lay there in tiny pieces, amid spreading beads of mercury. Before she had a chance to react, Troy was ripping up his exercise book. His face was contorted and red. Tears were falling down his face. Barbara got up and wrenched the book from his hands. "Hey, come on, hon. Calm down. It's OK." The next moment, he was hitting and punching her. "I hate you. I hate you." He was small and light, but he was coming at her with all his strength. Eventually, she got him in a bear hug. He fought, wriggled and squirmed. "Shhh, sweetie. It's OK. You're OK. I've got you." After a minute or so the fight went out of him and he sat sobbing quietly.

Barbara sent the other children back to their class. "Armani, on your way, could you go to Mrs. Nichols' office and ask her to come here?"

A couple of minutes later, Sandra appeared. "Now what?"

Barbara was sitting rubbing Troy's back. "Major tantrum. He totally lost it."

Sandra pulled up a chair. "Troy, Mrs. Stirling and I are worried about you. Has somebody been hurting you?"

Troy stared at the floor.

"It's safe to tell us. I promise. If you let us know what's been going on, we can help you."

Still nothing.

Finally Barbara and Sandra went into the corridor so that they could speak out of Troy's earshot.

"There's nothing we can do," Sandra said. "This isn't the first time he's become violent. He's a danger to the other kids. We have to send him home."

"We can't. Who knows what we're sending him back to? What if the boyfriend's home and he turns on Troy?"

"We have no choice. I have other children to think about. We're teachers, not social workers. We'll hang on to him for the rest of the day. Meanwhile, you need to make that call to social services. Use my office."

Barbara spent ten minutes on hold. Eventually she was put through to a woman in Child Protection called Jan, who was meant to be Troy's caseworker. Only she wasn't.

"It was actually one of my colleagues who visited the family. But she left back in September."

"OK, so after she'd gone, who took over?"

"I'm not sure. Bear with me. . . . OK, I'm just downloading the family's file. . . . Right, well, it would appear that nobody from the department has visited since their caseworker left."

"You are kidding me. We are talking about an eight-year-old child and his baby sister—both of whom are on the at-risk register—and you're telling me that nobody has visited since September. Are you people complete idiots?"

"Mrs. Stirling, please don't take that tone with me."

"What tone do you expect me to take? His mother has clearly hooked up with another maniac, and now her son has cigarette burns all over his arms and apparently he ended up in casualty over Christmas. I have no idea if the baby's OK."

"All right. I'll get somebody over there."

"When?"

"As soon as I can."

"What does that mean?"

"It means I will do my best to send somebody today."

"Well, so far your best hasn't been good enough."

When she came off the phone, Barbara couldn't help thinking she hadn't been anything like scary enough.

"Any luck?" Sandra said, coming back into the office with a thick file of papers. She dropped the file onto a spare chair and sat down at her desk.

"They're sending a social worker to see Tiffany."

"When?"

"Possibly today, but who knows. Bloody social workers. They're just so complacent. There's no sense of urgency."

"What do you expect? They're overworked and understaffed. It's not that they don't care. They just get jaded."

Barbara sighed, "I know. I do get it, but there's a child in real danger here. God forbid something happens to him. Do you think I should go round to the house? Check that everything's OK?"

"No. You can't step on social services' toes. We've informed them. Now we have to let them do their job."

"That would be fine, if we could be sure they were going to do it." Barbara stood up. "Right . . . I need to get going. I've got another class in a few minutes."

It was then that Sandra asked if she could have a word. She took off her specs, laid them on the desk and began fiddling with one of the arms. When she started to speak, she hedged and fudged and made oblique references to official letters. Finally she got to the point. Barbara no longer had a job. She was surplus to requirements. Then Sandra got to the bit about how she'd been fighting this for months, how she'd gone to bat for Barbara, how hard she'd fought in her corner and how, in the end, her hands had been tied.

Barbara's initial shock and anger turned to bewilderment.

"But I don't understand." She lowered herself back into the chair. "I thought I was good at what I did."

"You are. You're brilliant. I know we don't always see eye to eye, but that doesn't alter the fact that you're one of my best teachers."

"Then how could you let them get rid of me?"

"Barbara, you have to believe me when I say there was nothing I could do. It was a fait accompli. If it's any comfort, they're offering you a pretty good severance deal, and of course, you'll be allowed to work until the end of term."

"Well, yippee."

"I can't tell you how much I wish this wasn't happening."

"Yeah. Me, too." By now tears were falling down Barbara's cheeks. "I can't believe it. I feel like I'm going to wake up in a moment."

Sandra handed her a tissue. "I'm so sorry, Barbara. I don't know what to say."

"It's not your fault. You have a job to do." Barbara dabbed under her eyes. "Could you just do me one favor and tell the rest of the staff for me? I'm not sure I can face doing it."

"Of course I will. Now, then, why don't I make us a cup of tea?"

"I don't have time. I've got a class to get to."

"Forget the class. I'll find somebody to cover for you."

"Thanks, but if you don't mind, I'd rather go."

"OK . . . but if there's anything else I can do . . ."

Barbara nodded.

"You're strong," Sandra said, putting her specs back on. "You'll pick yourself up, find a new direction. I know you will."

Barbara blew her nose and left.

Chapter 3

Barbara made her way back to her room and sat at the table staring at the wall. Bastards. After all her years of hard work, how could they do this to her? Discard her like an old dishrag. Some bean counter who knew nothing about the lives these kids led and probably cared even less had put a stop to her doing the job she loved—had put a stop to her trying to make a difference. Bastards. And had Sandra really gone into bat for her, or had she simply done as she was told? Barbara suspected she'd probably written a formal letter registering her "disappointment and regret" at the council's decision, but little more. And that comment she'd made about Barbara being strong. That said it all. *You don't have to worry about Barbara. She always copes. She'll bounce back.*

Barbara wiped her eyes and glanced at her watch. Still a couple of minutes before the next group arrived for a lesson. She took her phone out of her bag and hit Frank's number. Voice mail. She sent a text. Need to speak to you. Call me during lunch.

She finished her last class of the morning a few minutes early. That gave her time to run up to the staff room and collect her coat without being seen. By now Sandra would have started spreading the word. Barbara couldn't face all the teary hugs and condolences. Instead she would skip lunch and take a walk. She needed to get some air.

She ended up in the middle of the Orchard Farm Estate—breathing in the poverty and the piss, avoiding the dog shit and litter. She headed for the children's playground, which seemed bright enough, if a bit battered, and sat down on one of the red metal benches. Somebody had carved "Stacey is a slag" across the back of the seat.

It was getting colder now, and it had started to drizzle. Barbara wound her scarf around her neck and surveyed the concrete low-rise blocks, their walkways clogged with abandoned supermarket trolleys, the walls festooned with old satellite dishes. Around her, bits of tissue and foil stained with crack drifted in the breeze like autumn leaves. A couple of teenage lads loped by, their jeans slung so low that they reminded Barbara of toddlers with overfull diapers. A few yards away a couple of surly-looking teenage mothers with hooped earrings pushed their toddlers on the swings.

The boys in jeans headed to the cage-windowed mini-market, where they sold single cigarettes for ten pence each. It was the only shop left on the estate. The rest were long gone, boarded up, covered in graffiti. The social center had closed down, too. It had been opened with such fanfare—a scaled-down version of the Jubilee relaunch. The social center was going to stop the kids getting up to no good in the stairwells and get them playing football, taking drama, dance and music classes. But the funding dried up. Youth workers were let go. Volunteers kept the place running for a while, but with no money for equipment, teachers or sports coaches, they couldn't deliver. So they gave up.

Barbara was certain there was some erudite literary term for when physical surroundings reflected the watcher's mood. She'd been taught it at university. But of course she couldn't bring it to mind. Three years she'd studied English Lit. She must have used it dozens of times in essays. She was still trying to remember what it was when Frank called.

"Hey, I got your message. Sorry I didn't get back to you straight-away, but I've been in meetings all morning and I had my phone switched off."

"I've been made redundant."

"What? You're kidding."

"I wish I were. They've given me a term's notice."

"But you're one of their best teachers. Why would they get rid of you?"

"Cuts. A job had to go. I was the closest to retirement, so they chose me."

"Bloody hell. . . . How are we going to manage without your salary? You're going to have to find another job."

"Frank, you're not listening. You know as well as I do that they're making cuts all over the place. There are no jobs. And even if there were, who's going to take me on at nearly sixty?"

"You'll have to find something else—outside teaching."

"I don't want to find anything else. This job has been my life for nearly forty years. I love it. I love the kids."

"Barbara, you're going to have to forget all the emotional stuff. We need the money. You'll just have to take what you can get."

"My career has just come to an end, and that's all you've got to say? That I need to forget the 'emotional stuff'? How do you think you'd feel if nobody wanted your films anymore? You'd feel like your heart had been ripped out."

"It's not the same."

"Why isn't it the same? Because you make important, socially relevant TV documentaries and win awards and I just have this little teaching job?"

"That's not what I meant."

"Yes, it is."

"Look, you're upset. . . ."

"Of course I'm *upset*. I'm devastated."

"And you have every right to be. I'm sorry if I sounded unsympathetic, but it's a shock for me, too. I just panicked—that's all. Let's have a proper talk when I get home."

"OK. Try not to be late."

"I'll do my best. And don't worry. I love you."

"Love you, too."

She had half an hour before the start of afternoon school. She found herself walking over to the group of teenage mums. "Excuse me. Do any of you happen to know where Tiffany Butler lives?"

One of the girls pointed. "Over there. Ground floor. One with the blue door."

Barbara thanked her. Despite Sandra's warning not to tread on social services' toes, she found herself walking the couple of hundred yards to the building. Small chunks had been chiseled out of the paint-blistered door. It looked to Barbara as if the locks had been changed. She tried the bell. Dead. She tapped on the door. There were footsteps, the sound of a baby crying.

Tiffany opened the door—Lacie in her arms—wearing a white toweling dressing gown covered in tiny pink hearts. Her trademark eyebrows hadn't been painted in. Ditto the black eyeliner. Her hair hung loose and unwashed. Without her armor, she looked childlike and vulnerable. She also looked done in.

Tiffany took one look at Barbara and rolled her eyes like a surly adolescent. "What do you want?" she said, bouncing Lacie in an effort to soothe her. "I told you I don't need your help. Why can't you stop interfering and just piss off and leave me alone?"

"Tiffany, Troy's got cigarette burns on his arms."

"It was an accident." Her voice was full of defiance. There was some fight left in her after all. She turned away and began blowing raspberries on Lacie's cheek. The child started laughing.

"I don't think it was an accident. Please can I come in? Maybe we could have a chat?"

"Look, it's all sorted. Wayne's gone, OK?"

"That's good, but maybe we could talk anyway. Please?"

"Whatever." She stood to one side and let Barbara into the flat. They walked down the narrow hallway—regulation lino tiles, walls painted tangerine in a failed effort to brighten the place up.

"Tiffany, it's freezing in here."

"Wayne fucked off with all my cash. I haven't got money for the electric meter. Me and Lacie have been staying in bed to keep warm."

The new flat-screen TV looked out of place in the bedraggled living room. There was a tatty leatherette sofa, a couple of sad mismatched armchairs, a few tenth-hand baby toys scattered over the floor. There were no pictures, no photographs, no tchotchkes. Barbara lowered herself into one of the armchairs. Tiffany sat on the sofa, Lacie on her lap. The baby immediately started to grizzle. Barbara reached into her pocket and took out a miniature pack of chocolate digestives that she kept for low-blood-sugar emergencies. "Do you think she'd like one of these?"

"Lacie never says no to a biscuit, do you?"

"Here you are, sweetheart. Try this."

Lacie grabbed the biscuit and began munching. In a few seconds her mouth was covered in chocolate. Barbara wondered when she'd last eaten.

"What's really been going on?" Barbara said gently.

"You really want to know?... OK ..." Her voice was raised now in what was probably a combination of fear, exhaustion and fury.

Tiffany lowered her dressing gown to reveal livid purple bruises over her shoulders and arms. "It's the same all over my back. He knew not to touch my face. Bastard didn't want anybody seeing what he'd done."

Barbara grimaced. "Have you seen a doctor?"

"It's nothing much. I've had worse than this."

"Christ, Tiffany. It's not nothing."

"I'm fine. Don't start getting busy."

"And just to be clear—Wayne did this?"

She nodded. "Troy was so brave. He kept kicking and punching and trying to stop him. Wayne would turn on him and stick him with his cigarette."

"What about Lacie?"

"He never laid a hand on her.... When I said I was calling the police, he threatened to kill me. Said he'd cut my throat."

Barbara sat stunned. Tiffany took her silence as an attack.

"You think I'm weak, don't you? You think I'm a terrible mother."

"That's ridiculous. Of course I don't."

And she meant it. She had no idea how she'd cope as a young, practically destitute single mother.

Tears were falling down Tiffany's face now. "Let me tell you something. I love my kids. They're my life. I'd do anything to protect them. And I've done my best...."

"OK, what if we called the police right now?"

"Are you having a laugh?"

"What do you mean?"

"People like you actually think the police are going to give a fuck. You think I can waltz into the police station, tell them what's been happening and they'll put Wayne right at the top of their to-do list."

"They'll do something."

"No, they won't. They never do. That's why so many women end up dead. And you know what? Even if they found him and locked him up, he'd send somebody to get me. I'd never be safe. It's better like this."

"Then at least let me call social services and ask them to find you a place in a women's refuge."

"No point."

"Why?"

"He's gone. Wayne's a bricklayer. He got a call about a job up north."

"But what if he comes back?"

"He won't. He lives up north. He was only down here for a few weeks working. But the bastard went off with my spare keys, so I borrowed some money and had the locks changed, just in case."

Barbara tried to convince her that she still wasn't safe and urged her again to call the police or think about going to a refuge, but Tiffany was adamant that she was doing the right thing.

"How did Troy hurt his leg?" Barbara said.

Tiffany said that Wayne had got angry with him and pushed him down some steps at the park.

"It's fine though. The hospital said his leg was just bruised."

"But what if Wayne comes back?"

"He won't," Tiffany said. "He's hundreds of miles away. He's probably found another woman to batter by now. It's how these blokes operate."

Barbara wasn't sure whether to be relieved or petrified for some other unsuspecting girl. She reached into her bag and took out her purse. "I want you to have this," she said, taking out three twenty-pound notes. "Go and buy some food and put some money in the meter."

"I'm not taking your money. I've told you, I'm not a beggar."

"I know you're not. And even if you were, it wouldn't matter to me. I want you to have it."

"No way. And anyway, teachers can't go round handing out money to kids' parents. It'll be against some regulation or other."

"I have no doubt that it is, but since I've just been sacked, I don't really give a crap. What are they going to do? Sack me twice?" She slipped the money under an overfilled ashtray. "Take it. I won't hear another word."

Lacie reached into the ashtray full of cigarette butts and grabbed a handful.

"They've sacked you?" Tiffany said, struggling to prize open her daughter's hand. "Why? Troy says you're the best teacher in the whole school. He thinks you're great."

Barbara explained.

"I'm sorry you're going," Tiffany said. "Troy's really going to miss you." By now she was sweeping cigarette butts and bits of tobacco off Lacie's hand and into the ashtray.

"And I'll miss him." Barbara looked at her watch. "Look, I have to get back. But will you do me a favor?"

"What?"

"Promise you'll call me if you're in trouble or you need anything. Day or night, it doesn't matter." She picked a coloring book up off the floor and wrote her number on the inside of the cover. "Tear this off. Please don't lose it."

"I won't."

Barbara got up to go.

"Mrs. Stirling . . . thanks for the money and everything. I was really horrible to you and you've been so kind. I'm sorry."

"Forget it. Just get the heating back on and go out and buy some food."

Tiffany managed a smile. "I'll go out now and get some change for the meter."

"Make sure you do. And promise you'll call if you need me."

"I promise. And, Mrs. Stirling . . . Thanks again."

Barbara got through the rest of the school day on automatic pilot, just about managing to hold back the tears. It didn't help that having skipped lunch, her blood sugar was low. She was choked up and angry for Tiffany as much as for herself. She hoped to God that social services were going to up their game and keep a proper eye on her and the children.

School ended at three. Her instinct was to make a quick exit. She still couldn't face all the pity waiting for her in the staff room. But she'd wimped out at lunchtime. She needed to show her face and get it over with.

People hugged her and said it was a disgrace that she'd been sacked. A few of the women cried. Everybody was angry. It wasn't that she was ungrateful for their sympathy. She could feel their warmth, and she knew it was genuine. On the other hand, part of her suspected that her colleagues felt the way people often did at funerals—sad, but hugely relieved the angel of death has passed them by.

It wasn't until she was walking to her car that she remembered she was picking up Atticus and Cleo and taking them to her mother's. There was no getting out of it. Jess was relying on her. And seeing her grandchildren would cheer her up.

She popped into the sweetshop on the corner and bought chocolate bars, crisps and juice boxes. All the things her grandchildren weren't allowed. But feeling the way she did, she wasn't about to spend forty minutes driving to her mother's place with two kids in the back while suffering from low blood sugar. Today she would feed them crap and she would feel not a smidgen of guilt.

Atticus and Cleo didn't finish at St. Mungo's for another half hour, and since it was only a couple of miles down the road and the traffic tended to be pretty light, she rarely had a problem getting there on time.

Barbara could never get over how different St. Mungo's was from Jubilee. Like most inner-city schools, it still had its fair share of impoverished, needy children, but mainly the pupils at St. Mungo's came from middle-class professional homes. As Barbara cruised the side streets looking for a parking space, she was aware how dilapidated her ancient Saab looked among the shiny SUVs.

In the playground, the mothers in their fur gilets and UGGs exchanged "Happy New Year's" and air kisses. Somebody was talking in a loud voice about the family's Christmas trip to Tuvalu— wherever that was.

Another group of women was discussing a child called Casper. "So anyway, apparently he goes round the playground rubbing his penis against other children."

"He must be gay."

"Oh, stop it. The kid's five. And anyway, he does it to both sexes."

"Well, if he's not gay, he needs to see a shrink."

It was all Barbara could do to stop wading in. Of course the poor child didn't need a shrink. He needed his mother to sit him down and explain calmly and gently that rubbing his penis against other children was unacceptable, but in the privacy of his own room he could fiddle with himself all he liked.

That was another thing that pissed Barbara off about the world— especially the respectable middle-class bit of it. Even now, in a society where you couldn't get away from sex, parents still didn't discuss the subject with their children. Barbara had a theory. She had a lot of theories. Being nearly sixty did that to you. She was convinced that parents were the best people to tell their children about sex. She believed that keeping this conversation in the family created intimacy between parents and their offspring. Once kids knew that sex wasn't a taboo subject and that they could feel relaxed and safe talking about it at home, they wouldn't feel scared to bring their worries and problems to their parents as they got older.

As it happened, she'd shared her theory with Frank a few nights ago, while they were lying in bed, reading.

"I know I did the right thing being open with the kids about sex and masturbation when they were growing up. Neither of them has got the remotest hang-up about sex."

"Too true," Frank said from behind his Kindle. "I mean, didn't we laugh when our four-year-old daughter announced to the milkman that she had a clitoris?"

"Stop it. That was cute."

"But not nearly as cute as when Ben told his teacher that masturbation is normal, the whole world does it and that it's a great way of discovering what you enjoy. That was really cute."

"Well, at least he didn't go around rubbing his penis up against all and sundry. So what are you saying?"

"I'm saying that being open about sex is all well and good, but you also need to help them set boundaries. Kids need to know when to shut up about that stuff. But clearly Ben took all your advice about masturbation to heart."

"Meaning?"

"It would appear that at twenty-three he's still trying to work out what he enjoys, which is why he spends all day jerking off in his room instead of getting a job."

"He doesn't jerk off—at least not all day. He's too busy sleeping."

Barbara was still eavesdropping on the posh mummies' conversation about poor Casper and his penis when she felt a tap on her shoulder.

"Hi, Mrs. S." It was Martha. Today she had replaced her usual peasant scarf with cold-weather headgear, a knitted Peruvian hat with earflaps. She'd teamed it with an ethnic, Indian cotton baby carrier and an expertly swaddled infant. "I didn't think it was your day for picking up the kids."

Barbara explained about Jess being rushed off her feet at the deli. "Oh, poor thing. But she knows I would have had them."

"She probably thought you had enough on your hands."

Martha was Jess's closest mummy friend. Her two eldest, Linus and Juniper, were the same ages as Atticus and Cleo. The baby, a girl, if Barbara remembered rightly, had to be nearing six weeks.

"And look at this little cutie," Barbara cooed, stroking the baby's cheek. "The last time I saw you, you hadn't decided on a name."

"Minnie."

"Oh, how lovely," Barbara said, remembering her smelly aunty Minnie with the white lips that she got from sucking too many indigestion tablets. "And she's doing OK?"

"Actually, she's got a bit of a runny nose and a temperature, but I haven't taken her to the doctor. He'll only give her antibiotics. I'd rather she got my immunity through breast milk."

Barbara refrained from sharing another of her theories—namely that antibiotics, overused as they might be, were still capable of fighting childhood diseases and saving lives. To her knowledge, there were no peer-reviewed studies that suggested breast milk did the same. Theories like that didn't go down well with hummusy mothers like Martha and Jess—the ones who knew all the best placenta recipes, used menstrual cups and loved nothing more than a good chicken pox party.

The hummusy mummies were the other major contingent at St. Mungo's. As a result of her conversations with Jess and Martha, along with the occasional playground chat with a rich mummy or two, Barbara had managed to establish the following: The hummusy mummies despised the rich mummies for destroying the planet with their gas-guzzlers, for wearing cosmetics that had been tested on animals, clogging landfill sites with disposable nappies and hiring tutors for their four-year-olds. The rich mummies despised the hummusy mummies because they dressed as if they were on their way to Woodstock circa 1969, went around with Kegel balls in their vaginas and refused to feed their children ice cream, favoring breast-milk parfait instead. What was more, they drove these same children—helmetless—on London roads in homemade wooden carts attached to their bikes. On the bike issue, Barbara was absolutely with the rich mummies. She thought that anybody who put their children in one of those go-kart contraptions—particularly without a helmet—should be hauled up in front of a judge.

"So the big ones aren't jealous of their baby sister?" Barbara asked Martha.

"Oh, we've had a few tantrums, but the chicken coop's arriving later on today. I'm hoping that feeding the chickens and collecting eggs will give them something else to focus on."

Just then they were joined by Martha's friend Bryony. Barbara remembered her from one of the children's birthday parties. Bryony seemed positively elated. "Great news. I managed to score some raw milk at the weekend, so if either of you would like a couple of pints, pop round."

Barbara had a theory about unpasteurized milk, too.

The children came charging out of school in their scarlet sweat-shirts, dragging their coats and scarves along the ground.

The moment Atticus and Cleo caught sight of their grandmother, they sprinted towards her. Barbara held out her arms for hugs and kisses.

"Mum never told us you were coming," Atticus said, automatically handing her his coat, reading folder and lunch box. Cleo did the same. The identical transaction was happening all over the playground. Folders and lunch boxes, not to mention football kits, class hamsters, giant papier-mâché artworks, violins and trumpets were exchanged for snacks. Mothers left the playground looking like well-groomed Sherpas.

"I thought I'd give you a surprise," Barbara said. "How do you fancy going to see Nana Rose? I suggested to her that we go for a walk, but maybe you'd prefer to watch a movie. Later on she could show you more of her old photographs."

"Movie," they declared in unison.

"OK, and as a special treat we can order pizza."

"Cool."

While Martha and Bryony handed out kale chips to their off-spring, Barbara held out chocolate bars and crisps. Atticus had no qualms grabbing his. He was eight and well up for some skullduggery. It was little Cleo who held back. "But, Grandma, we're not allowed."

"You know what?" Barbara said. "You are today. Because this is a special day."

"What sort of a special day?" asked Atticus.

"Oh, I don't know . . . but it has to be special for somebody somewhere."

Cleo thought for a moment or two, after which she decided to go along with Barbara's proposition. Grinning, she accepted her treats. Their friends looked on, their never-been-sullied-by-soap faces pictures of envy. Barbara was in no doubt that Martha and Bryony would tell on her. That meant she would have to own up first and spend ten minutes being chastised and lectured to by her holier-than-thou daughter.

"Gran'ma," Atticus said as the three of them headed towards the car. "Linus and Juniper have got a tortoise. And they've called it Usain Bolt. Isn't that a great name for a tortoise?"

Barbara laughed. "It's an excellent name."

"Why is it?" Cleo said.

"Because," Atticus said, "Usain Bolt is this really fast runner, and tortoises move very, very slowly."

"I don't understand."

"Duuhhh . . . stupid . . . it's funny."

"OK, I get it."

But Barbara knew she didn't.

She helped the children into the back of the car, and in Cleo's case—because she was only five—onto her booster seat.

"Ha-ha, Cleo is a baby," Atticus taunted. "She still needs a booster seat."

"Atticus, don't be so unkind. May I remind you that you needed a booster seat until recently? Now say sorry."

Atticus mumbled an apology. Cleo poked her tongue out at him.

"Right, who's for OJ?" Barbara said, handing them both a carton of juice.

While the children sucked on their straws and finished their crisps, there was silence.

Barbara didn't attempt to engage them in conversation. She craved a few moments' peace. She wanted some time to replay the day and feel sorry for herself. She needed to curse—albeit in silence. But she was tired. She couldn't focus. Her mind flitted from thought to thought. One moment she was back in Sandra's office, getting the sack, the next she was in Tiffany's front room. Then she was back in bed with Frank, sharing her thoughts on child sex education. She could see him looking up from his Kindle. "Barbara, have you any idea how much you toot your own horn? You know it's your worst fault, don't you? I mean, what makes you such an expert on teaching kids about sex?"

"I don't think I'm an expert. That said, I've raised two kids of my own, and I've spent the last forty years teaching some of the most difficult children you could ever hope to meet. Aren't I entitled to a child-rearing theory or two? And it's not like I ever toot in public."

"No, you just confront people in public."

"Self-empowerment is another thing that comes with age."

"You can be empowered without being confrontational."

"I can't. I'm a battle-ax. What can I say? And anyway, in my opinion, the world would be a much better place if we confronted casual, day-to-day wrongdoing instead of constantly turning our backs."

"You've missed your vocation. You should have gone into politics, not education."

"You always say that, but you know I've never been interested in party politics. And anyway, I'm not smart enough."

"Now you *are* talking rubbish."

"Well, it's how I feel. I know I keep coming up with all these theories about the world, but you know as well as I do that one of the reasons I do it is to prove to myself that I'm not stupid."

"Excuse me while I fetch my violin."

"You can be so mean sometimes. Do you know that?"

Barbara went back to her book—unlike Frank, she hadn't made the transition from paper—but she couldn't concentrate.

"So, Grandma," Atticus was saying now. "What apps did you have when you were a kid?"

"Come again?" Barbara said, stirring from her reverie.

He repeated the question.

Barbara burst out laughing and almost missed a right turn. "Oh, darling, we didn't have apps. They hadn't been invented when I was little."

Barbara is nine and her teacher Mrs. Emmet is reading out the end-of-term exam results to the forty-one children in Barbara's class. Like most years, she's come in fortieth. She sits at her desk overwhelmed by the familiar feelings of shame and humiliation, trying so hard not to cry that her throat aches.

Later on that day, she and her mother are back at school for parents' evening. "We realize that Barbara will never be a high achiever," Rose says to Mrs. Emmet. "At the moment she wants to be a hairdresser, but between you and me, I don't think her diction is good enough."

Mrs. Emmet looks at Rose, clearly at a loss for how to respond. Barbara is too young to realize that her mother is talking claptrap. She feels worthless and, quite literally, good for nothing.

For the best part of this year, Barbara has been in pain when she walks. She's complained regularly to her mother about the throbbing "black thing" on the edge of her foot, an inch or so from her little toe. Tonight when she's in the bath she checks it out again and discovers it has spawned a cluster of black specks.

"Mummy, please come and look at my foot. It's got really horrible."

"I'm cooking. Bring it down here."

Barbara dries herself off and goes downstairs to present her foot.

"It's nothing," Rose announces. "It's just a mark. Why do you always have to make such a fuss?"

Barbara tells her that the thing has become so painful lately that she's limping.

"Don't be ridiculous."

Barbara goes away and makes a protective pad with some cotton wool and a Band-Aid. The next day Mrs. Emmet asks Barbara why she's limping. She explains. Mrs. Emmet sends her to see Mrs. Pierce, the principal's secretary who doubles as the unofficial school nurse. Mrs. Pierce tells Barbara that she has a very nasty verruca and calls Rose. Of course Rose takes it out on Barbara.

"That woman really embarrassed me. Why did you have to show her your foot?"

Rose makes a doctor's appointment for Barbara. "You poor thing," he says. "That looks really painful." He turns to Rose. "Mum, why on earth didn't you bring her in earlier?" The verruca needed to be frozen with liquid nitrogen. The treatment was painful and Barbara will need to return for treatment once a week for several weeks.

To her credit, Rose looks shamefaced and apologizes to the doctor. On the way home she even buys Barbara an ice cream.

Growing up, Barbara was always aware that the only person Rose really cared about was Stan. She did everything she could think of to lift his mood. She cooked him fancy dinners, baked him cakes, chose books she thought he would like from the library. She even arranged for a counselor to visit him at home. The lady counselor told him write down his wartime memories and when he was done, he should burn them. He told her to her face that she was an idiot and refused to see her again. Barbara knew this because she heard him shouting. In later years she realized that her mother had fallen in love with a handsome, vigorous young soldier. Then he was gone. Rose had spent her entire marriage trying to get him back.

Stan only ever picked at Rose's food. If he was in the mood, he might flick through one of the library books she had so carefully chosen. Then he would go back to watching TV. He loved sitcoms and game shows. Barbara worked out that they made him feel safe.

Although Stan was incapable of taking an interest in Barbara's life, he did show her affection—something that Rose never resented. In fact, she encouraged it. "Go and give Daddy a cuddle. It'll cheer him up." Father and daughter would snuggle on the sofa in front of *My Favorite Martian*. Seeing Barbara laugh made him laugh—and that appeared to give Rose hope. When it was Barbara's bedtime, Stan would look at his daughter with his watery, melancholy eyes. "How much do you love me?" When she was little she would tell him: "A million, billion, zillion pounds." When she got older, it was: "Come on, Dad, knock it off. You're being boring—you know I love you loads."

Barbara was a grown woman before it dawned on her that Stan never once said how much he loved *her* and that their cuddles were all about his little girl making *him* feel better. He never thought about what he, as a parent, might give her.

Mrs. Emmet didn't write Barbara off. She knew about Stan's psychological problems—most likely through playground gossip. Rose would never have said anything to the school for fear of the authorities poking their noses into her business.

Whether Mrs. Emmet was spurred into action by Rose's hairdresser remark, Barbara never found out, but the following term she took Barbara under her wing. There was extra tutoring during lunch breaks. She gave Barbara pep talks, insisted that she wasn't stupid. Barbara's problem, she said, was her inability to concentrate because she was anxious and miserable. Mrs. Emmet set her a challenge—to leave her worries at home. She even made her stand in the playground, name each of her concerns in turn and wave them goodbye. Cognitive behavioral therapy—before it was even a thing. She mentioned to Rose that Mrs. Emmet was giving her extra tutoring. Rose said that was very kind of her, but not to worry if her grades didn't improve. After all, she was a girl. She didn't need a proper career, because one day she would meet a nice boy and get married.

Barbara had the sense not to mention Mrs. Emmet's self-styled behavioral therapy. She knew that Rose would be furious if she found out that her daughter was discussing their family situation.

With practice, Barbara learned to put her worries away for a few hours and concentrate. When her mind wandered, Mrs. Emmet noticed and brought her back into the moment. As her grades improved, she began to believe that Mrs. Emmet was right and she wasn't stupid.

Mrs. Emmet died in the early nineties. Barbara found out by chance as she skimmed the death notices in the *Times*—something she almost never did. She had always meant to write to her and thank her for all her kindness and care and to tell her that if it hadn't been for her, she would never have become a teacher. But she'd never got round to it.

With every exam Barbara passed, her confidence grew. Rose couldn't understand why her daughter was so determined to carry on studying beyond high school. Barbara told her that all her girl-friends were applying to university. What was more, their parents were behind them. But Rose couldn't see the point. And what was all this studying going to cost?

But Rose gave in and Barbara went to university, got a respectable degree in English and went on to study for her teaching certificate. There were still times though—even after she'd married and had Jess—when she still felt pretty wormlike. When Jess was a few months old, that changed.

The baby developed a high fever. Then a rash appeared. Barbara bundled her into the car and rushed to the ER. A junior doctor examined Jess and assured Barbara that the symptoms weren't serious. He told her to go home and keep up the Tylenol. But what about the rash? It was nothing, he said. An allergic reaction maybe. "Look, you're a first-time mum. You're bound to be a bit neurotic. . . ." That was it. Something clicked inside her. Barbara wasn't about to be dismissed as a stupid, irrational mother by some wet-behind-the ears schoolboy with a stethoscope. She stood her ground and refused to leave until she'd seen somebody senior. Eventually, a nice lady doctor came along and agreed to do some blood tests. They were all negative. Jess did not have meningitis. But fighting for her child, being her advocate, spurred Barbara on. She had found her voice, and she was damned well going to use it. Before she knew it, she was asserting herself more in school staff meetings and standing up to the occasional senior member of staff who tried to bully her. Three decades later, she was holding up traffic to confront litter louts and tooting her horn to Frank. But after a bad day at work—if she felt she hadn't gotten her point across in a meeting with social services and therefore failed to advocate for one of her pupils—Barbara could still reach inside herself and find the little girl in Mrs. Emmet's class who had come fortieth.

Jean had views on Barbara's horn tooting. She believed it was born of frustration.

"I can't help thinking about how over the years you turned down all those offers of promotion. You always said it was because you were a teacher, not a manager. But has it occurred to you that deep down you thought you weren't good enough?"

"I've never really believed I was good enough," Barbara said. "You know that."

"I understand, but feeling like that has done you no favors. It's left you frustrated. Look at you. You tackle people in the street, you take on social services, but you've never been the one in charge. What you need is a chance to throw your weight about a bit, impose yourself."

Jean's theory hit a nerve. It was true. Her lack of confidence had been a factor when she'd decided not to go for a promotion, and these days her lack of professional clout had left her feeling frustrated. But she was fifty-eight. At her age, what possible hope did she have of scoring a job where she could throw her weight around and impose herself? In the end, she decided there was no point dwelling on her mistakes—particularly as she couldn't put them right. Nevertheless, from time to time, that conversation with Jean still troubled her.

The traffic was heavy heading out of town. It took more than an hour to get to Rose's flat. Once Cleo and Atticus had finished their snacks and juice, the questions kicked off. Cleo wanted to know if before they got caught, fish fingers could swim. Atticus wondered if in the olden days everything was in black-and-white.

"So, Grandma," Atticus said. "What's your favorite food?"

"I don't know. Curry probably."

"Mine's ramen."

Of course it was.

"The children need to take their shoes off," Rose said by way of greeting. "I don't want mud all over the carpet."

"And hello to you, too," Barbara said, giving her mother a peck on the cheek. It was only as she stepped back that she saw the exhaustion on her face. Tiny and birdlike as she was, Rose never got tired. It was one of the side effects of her thyroid medication. "Mum, you OK? Is something the matter?"

"Rotten day."

"Makes two of us." But her mother didn't hear. Atticus and Cleo were already clamoring for her attention.

"Nana, Nana, can we watch *Mary Poppins*?"

"Don't I get a kiss hello?"

They obliged, but without much enthusiasm. In recent years Rose had managed to acquire a bristly upper lip. The children hated the way it scratched when they kissed her. They had made their objection clear to both Barbara and their mother. Jess kept nagging Barbara to buy Nana Rose some depilatory cream, but Barbara didn't want to offend her.

"So, Nana," Atticus said, rubbing his cheek, "now can we watch the film?"

Rose didn't own a DVD player. All she had was an ancient VHS video player and a selection of old Disney films. Their favorite was *Mary Poppins*.

"No. Not today. I'm fed up with all the noise."

"Awwww."

"What noise?" Barbara said. Her mother's small apartment block was in a suburban cul-de-sac. Dogs were banned, loud parties discouraged. So apart from the occasional sound of building work—which was permitted only on weekdays and strictly between the hours of nine and four—the place was silent.

"This damned music. It hasn't stopped all day. It's been going since nine o'clock this morning and still no letup. It shouldn't be allowed."

"What music? I can't hear anything."

Barbara shooed the children into the living room and carried on listening.

"'Chattanooga Choo Choo.' Can't you hear it? There it goes. . . . *Pardon me, boy. Is that the Chattanooga Choo Choo . . . ?*"

Barbara strained to hear. "Mum, honestly. There's nothing."

"Don't be so ridiculous. Are you deaf? It's blaring out."

Barbara's faculties might be declining in late middle age, but so far she hadn't been beset by deafness. There was nothing blaring out. "Look, why don't we let the kids watch *Mary Poppins*? You and I can sit quietly in the kitchen, and I'll make us a cup of tea."

Rose nodded. "OK, you two," she said, poking her head around the living room door. "You can put your film on."

"Yaaay."

"But please keep the volume down. Nana's got a bad headache."

Rose lowered herself onto a kitchen chair and began rubbing her forehead. Barbara offered to fetch some ibuprofen from the bathroom cabinet.

"No. A cup of hot tea will work just as well."

"But I don't understand what's going on," Barbara said, filling the kettle. "Is it possible you're imagining the music?"

Not her smartest move, suggesting to an eighty-three-year-old that she was losing her marbles.

"Of course I'm not imagining it. I'm not senile, you know. Somebody's got a record player on. I've been up- and downstairs knocking on doors, but nobody's prepared to own up. It isn't right."

"And you can hear it right now?"

"Yes."

After she'd made tea, Barbara went around the flat, trying to locate the noise. She even opened the windows. There was no big band. The music had to be in her mother's head. Of course, there was no way Rose would agree to see a doctor—not if he was going to start questioning her state of mind. Barbara decided she would have to go behind her mother's back and call him herself.

A few minutes later the kids came running into the kitchen asking for something to drink. Rose said there was apple juice in the fridge.

"Barbara, please don't let them take it into the living room. They'll get it on the sofa."

Rose had always been house proud. Barbara believed it was an

extension of her vanity. She could still remember her mother cleaning the spout of the dishwasher liquid bottle with a toothbrush.

"Your hair looks nice, Mum," Barbara said after Atticus and
Cleo had disappeared into the living room. "You just had it done?"

"Yesterday." She patted her blond cotton-candy helmet. "And I
bought this little cardi. What do you think?"

She got up and gave Barbara a twirl. The scarlet cashmere cardigan was dotted with black seed pearls. She was wearing it over tai-
lored black trousers. Even now—mustache aside—her mother hadn't
lost her flair.

"Twenty pounds on sale. It was the only one left."

"Good for you."

When Rose's parents died in the early sixties, she'd inherited a lot
of money—enough to keep the family afloat and bankroll her
clothes spending. Rose had never needed to work. These days there
wasn't much left, but with her state pension, she got by.

"Your dad always loved me in red," Rose said. "I once had this
crimson evening dress. He said that when I wore it, I lit up the room."

"You still miss him, don't you?"

"Not a day goes by when I don't think of him. This year it will be
thirty-seven years since he passed away."

Rose always referred to Stan as having "passed away." It was as if
he hadn't died, but instead had dissolved like a sugar lump in tea.

Stan had been sitting in his chair watching *Name That Tune*
when he started complaining of chest pains and shortness of breath.
Rose had called an ambulance. Weeks later the coroner said that had
he made it to hospital, they could probably have saved him. But
because of his agoraphobia, Stan had refused to get into the ambulance. Instead the ambulance drivers—it was long before the days of
paramedics—laid him on the sofa and called the GP. He arrived an
hour later. By that time Stan was gone.

"I should have tried harder to get him into that ambulance," Rose said.

"You did all you could. Everybody said so at the time. In the end it was his choice."

"And he chose to leave me."

"Come on, Mum. You have to stop torturing yourself. He adored you. He was petrified of leaving the house, that's all."

Rose sipped her tea. "I know, but it's still hard. He should have lived. He could still have been around today if he'd only . . ."

Her mother was tearing up. Barbara reached across the kitchen table and took her hand. For a few moments neither of them spoke.

"Still, what can you do?" Rose said eventually. She pulled her hand away from her daughter's. "Life goes on. You just have to keep going." She let out a long breath. Her expression brightened. "You know, you could wear one of these short cardis if you lost that weight round your middle."

"Mum, please don't give me a hard time. I know you've had a bad day, but mine hasn't been that good either."

"Why? What happened?"

"I lost my job. I've been made redundant."

"Heavens. That's not good," her mother said. Then she waved a hand in front of her. "But you're young. You'll find another one soon enough."

"What are you talking about? I'm nearly sixty."

"You want to try being my age? Stop fretting. Something will turn up. You've always been such a worrier."

"No, I haven't."

"Look how you used to fuss about getting to school on time."

"Only because you used to make me late every day."

"Oh, I'm sure I didn't. Why would I have done that?"

Barbara decided not to go there. Not today. "And for your

information, there are no jobs. The government is making cuts right across the public sector."

"Well, at least you don't wake up every morning wondering if it will be your last. That old woman from downstairs died last week. You know, the one with the square head. Looked like a toaster."

Barbara laughed at the image. "Stop it. You are not about to keel over. You just had a checkup. The doctor said you've got years left in you."

"What does he know?"

By now it was nearly six. Barbara decided to order pizza. "Make sure there are no green peppers on mine," Rose said. "They repeat on me. I'll be up half the night."

By the time the pizza arrived, Rose was saying that the big-band music was fading. She started to cheer up, and for once she agreed that they could eat on the sofa so that the children could watch the end of *Mary Poppins*. She even sang along to "Feed the Birds." Barbara was in no doubt that her mother was so starved of company that this little gathering felt like a party. When the film was over, she started chatting to Atticus and Cleo about what they were doing at school.

"Do you know when my mummy was at school," Rose said, "there weren't computers? There wasn't even much paper. They wrote with chalk on a sort of mini blackboard called a slate."

Barbara told them to think of it as an old-fashioned iPad, which seemed to confuse them even more.

"And in the war," Rose went on, "when the air-raid siren went and we knew the bombs were coming, we had to rush down to the shelter at the bottom of the garden. If it was in the night, we had to get dressed as fast as we could and run. But my sister, Freda, could never find her knickers, so she always came without any."

Atticus and Cleo had heard this story dozens of times, but it still made them laugh.

"Nana Rose, can we get the photograph albums out and look at the pictures of the olden days?"

"Sorry. That's going to have to wait for another time," Barbara said. "I need to get you home."

Rose gave the children bristly kisses. Then, as usual, she handed each of them a two-pound coin. "Buy yourselves a treat."

"Wow. Thanks, Nana."

Rose even gave Jess and Ben money when they came to visit—although since they'd gotten older, she'd upped it to a tenner.

"How's the music now?" Barbara asked her mother as they were leaving.

"Would you believe it's started up again? First thing in the morning I'm going to speak to the chairman of the management committee."

When they reached the deli, Jess was swabbing the marble countertop. The shop had originally been a dairy and still had most of its Victorian features: the blue-and-white wall tiles, the mosaic floor, the marble and mahogany counters. It smelled of what the children called posh "pooh cheese" and olives.

Jess came out from behind the counter. She looked flushed and worn-out.

"Hi, guys. Did you have a good time at Nana's?"

"Great," Atticus said. "Nana gave us two pounds each."

Jess gave her mother a kiss hello. "Sorry if I smell of garlic. I've been chewing it all day. I think I might be coming down with a cold."

"You're working too hard," Barbara said. "You're exhausted." She looked at her daughter. She'd barely changed since she was five: those cute, chocolate button eyes, the wavy chestnut hair. But today her eyes were heavy and glassy. Her long hair was falling out of its claw clip.

"We watched *Mary Poppins*," Cleo said. "And Grandma let us have chocolate and crisps."

Jess put her hands on her hips. "Mum . . ."

"Actually, it gets worse. I also let them have undiluted fruit juice and pizza."

"But why would you do that?"

"I'm sorry, but it was a special occasion."

"What sort of special occasion?"

"I lost my job today."

"What? . . . Shit."

"Mum said shit! Mum said shit!"

"OK, kids—your dad's waiting upstairs to give you a bath. And then afterwards he'll help you practice your juggling. Why don't you go and find him?"

The children raced over to the stairs. "Dad! We're back!"

The shop had come with a small-to-the-point-of-cramped three-bedroom flat. Despite the lack of space, Jess always said that living above the shop was their saving grace. If she and Matt had needed to commute back and forth to work, she wasn't sure either of them could have coped. This way, when it was quiet, she could shove some laundry into the washer or—on very rare occasions—put her feet up for ten minutes.

Barbara followed Jess to one of the long wooden tables (reclaimed railway sleepers bolted together).

They each took a stool (reclaimed industrial metal).

The deli was called the Green Door on account of (a) it having a green door, and (b) all its produce was organic and ethically sourced.

"So what happened?" Jess said. "Why did they fire you?"

"Cuts. Sandra had to lose a post."

"But I thought she loved you."

Barbara shrugged. "It wasn't her fault. She was forced to pick the person closest to retirement. And that was me."

"So what will you do?"

"I'll work out my notice, but beyond that, I have absolutely no idea." She looked at her watch. "It's getting late. I need to get going. Your dad said he'd try to get back at a reasonable time tonight so that we could talk."

"Sure, but come and say hi to Matt first."

As the two women climbed the stairs, they could hear the children splashing about in the bath.

"Hurry up, you two," Jess called out. "Grandma's leaving."

Matt was sitting at his desk, staring into the computer and pulling at the hairs of his ironic muttonchops. Hanging on the wall, directly above his head, was a pair of antlers. Barbara went over and gave her son-in-law a peck on the cheek. "Matt, you do realize that you've got antlers growing out of your head."

He rolled his eyes. "Yes, I know. They need moving. I hung them too low."

"They're nice though. Very stylish."

Not that that the antlers were quite Barbara's thing. Style-wise she had taken a while to warm to Jess and Matt's flat. An edgy interiors magazine would have described it as "an homage to upcycling."

All their friends upcycled. It was the epitome of early-twenty-first-century boho chic. It was also cheap. Once they'd bought the business and paid six months' rent on the premises up front, Jess and Matt had almost no money left. The flat had a decent kitchen and bathroom, but it was dark. Not only did it need brightening up, but it needed tables, chairs and sofas. Until now Jess and Matt and the kids had lived in a furnished apartment. They owned nothing by way of beds, tables and chairs.

The first thing they did was strip the walls and floorboards and paint them white. Then came the upcycling. They started filling the flat with objects they found in Dumpsters or thrift shops. But not before these items had been "converted." It worked like this: Jess would happen upon a couple of battered tennis racquets that she thought would make "amazing" wall mirrors. Or she'd pay pennies for a hard-sided fifties suitcase that she "just knew" would work as a small living room table. Her friend Lola, who was an artist and performance poet, did the converting, but she refused to take cash. Jess and Matt paid by barter. In return for turning a couple of bowler hats into lampshades and an old door into a dining table, Jess and Matt would provide Lola and her family with home-cooked vegan dinners for a month and a few bottles of organic merlot.

Eventually, Barbara had to admit that this quirky little flat with its bent-wrench coat hooks and walls of pictureless picture frames had real charm. If the deli failed, they could go into business as interior designers.

Then one day Jess and Matt came over to Frank and Barbara's full of excitement. Matt had found "the most fantastic sofa" sticking out of a Dumpster down the road. "It's a bit shabby and stained, but with a bit of work . . ."

Barbara was horrified. There was no way she was going to have her grandchildren sitting on some stinky, flea-infested sofa with horsehair sticking out.

"Tell you what," Barbara said. "Dad and I haven't got you a house-warming present yet. How's about we buy you a couple of Ikea sofas?"

"A couple?" Frank said, the color draining from his face.

"But, Mum, you can't afford it."

"'Course we can. Can't we, Frank?"

"Well . . ."

"Right, that's settled."

"OK, if you're sure."

After Jess and Matt had left, Barbara and Frank had had a huge fight. "What the hell do you think you're doing, offering to buy the kids two sofas? Where do you think we're going to find the money?"

"Take it from the pot we've set aside to pay the next tax bill."

"Excellent idea, and how do you propose we pay the bloody tax bill?"

"We'll find a way. Anyway, I'd rather be in hock to the tax people than have our grandchildren catch tetanus."

"What? People get tetanus from dog bites and rusty nails, not old sofas."

"Well, they could catch something. The thing's probably infested with bugs and weevils."

In the end, Frank threw up his hands in defeat.

Matt was still staring into the computer screen. "Jess, I thought you said you'd ordered *late*-harvest olive oil."

"I did."

"Nope. You ordered *early*-harvest."

"Sorry. Does it matter?"

"Of course it matters. Our customers are the sort of people who know the difference. You need to start concentrating. You're just so bloody vague all the time."

"I'm not vague. I'm just human and overworked like you. I make mistakes."

"Which I have to sort out. Now I'll have to send it all back."

"Ignore him," Jess said to her mother. "He's been in a lousy mood all day. . . . So anyway, I have news. We've made a decision. . . . We're giving up loo paper."

Barbara blinked. "O . . . kay . . . How does that work?"

"You buy this stuff called family cloth."

"Family cloth?"

"Yeah, squares of fabric—some people like Martha cut up their own. And you wash it and reuse it."

"What? You're being ridiculous. Have you any idea how unhygienic that is?"

"It's not. You soak it in green disinfectant before you wash it."

"Oh, for heaven's sake."

"Did you know that loo paper is really harmful to the skin because it contains dangerous chemicals?"

"Really? So how many people do you know with arse cancer? Jess, this is madness."

"Well, it's all the rage in parts of the US."

"Rubbish. Among a few loonies, maybe. Do you honestly think Michelle Obama expects her staff to wash her pooh-covered bum cloth?"

"Well, we're going give it a try. . . . Aren't we, Matt?"

"Give what a try?" He was still staring into the computer.

"Family cloth."

"I guess. Hang on. I need to read this e-mail. . . . Oh, fabulous. The olive oil suppliers say they can't change the order. We're too late. They've sold out of late-harvest oil."

Matt stood up and bashed his head on the antlers, which promptly fell to the floor. "Shit. That hurt." Rubbing his head, he bent down to retrieve them.

Jess threw up her arms. "Now look what you've done." A couple of nails and a load of plaster had fallen off the wall along with the antlers, leaving a large hole in the wall.

"I'm sorry. I'll deal with it, OK? Just don't go on."

Jess looked repentant. "No, I'm sorry. It wasn't your fault. It was an accident." She turned to her mother. "Apologies for the bickering. It's just that we're both really stressed."

"Why? What's happened?"

Matt explained that a few months back they'd catered a couple of big lunch parties—one for a local PR company, the other for an IT firm. The PR company had gone bust. The IT people were ignoring their invoices. Between them they owed Jess and Matt more than five grand.

"It wouldn't be so bad if this was just a one-off," Jess said. "But this stuff just keeps happening. We thought small-scale catering was going to bring in a bit more money, but people just aren't paying their bills."

"I'm so sorry," Barbara said. "That's awful. Do you stand any chance of recouping the money from the PR company?"

"Not a hope in hell. Apparently, they owe thousands in unpaid tax. The Revenue always gets first dibs."

Just then the children came tearing in, dripping and naked.

"Dad, Dad, can we do juggling now?" Atticus said, launching himself at his father.

"I think you both need to go and get dried off first," Jess told them.

They protested. Why couldn't they dry in the air? Their mother shooed them back to the bathroom. There would be no juggling unless they returned dry and wearing their pj's.

The children disappeared.

Barbara looked at her daughter and son-in-law. "OK, tell me honestly. How serious is this problem?"

Jess shrugged. "Most small businesses are struggling right now."

"That's not what I asked."

"We're fine," Matt said. "It's just me panicking, that's all."

"But I worry. . . . OK, here's what I think you should do. You need to rent out this flat and come and live with your dad and me. At the same time you could speak to our accountant. Maybe you're not claiming all the allowances you're entitled to. I bet there are ways you could be saving money."

"Mum, does your advice center ever close?"

Barbara gave them a sheepish look. "Sorry. I worry, that's all."

"I know," Jess said. "And we appreciate it. But this is our problem. One way or another, we will come through it."

"You're right. Of course you will."

"And you've got your own problems to think about just now."

"What problems?" Matt said.

Jess explained.

"That's awful," Matt said. "I'm really sorry. Look, if there's anything we can do."

"That's kind, but short of getting me my job back, I don't think there's anything anybody can do. . . . Right, I need to get home."

The children returned still damp of head but otherwise dry. Both were in their pajamas.

"Grandma's off now," Jess said. "Come and kiss her good-bye and say thank you for all your treats."

"Bye, Grandma," Cleo said. "Thank you for my treats."

Then it was her brother's turn: "Grandma, can it be another special occasion very soon?"

Barbara bent down to hug both her grandchildren. "We'll see," she said.

Ben was sitting with his feet on the kitchen table, channel surfing. Beside him was an empty plate. Judging by the crumbs and caked-on light brown smears, it had recently contained beans and toast. Barbara would say one thing for her son: when it came to feeding him, his preferences were pretty basic.

"Ben, please take your feet off the table. Those things you're wearing are filthy."

Ben looked at his beaten-up Converse and put his feet down. "But they're all I've got. . . . *Storage Wars . . . Storage Wars . . . Murder, She Wrote . . .* Oh, and look, *Storage Wars . . .*" He turned his head away from the screen. "Where have you been? You're never this late back."

"Nana's with Atticus and Cleo. I just dropped them back home."

"So how's my bonkers sister?"

"Don't be unkind. She's not bonkers." Barbara took off her coat and draped it over the back of a chair.

"Really? Well, I have two words to say to you: family cloth. It's reusable toilet paper."

"Yes, I know what it is. She's been telling me all about it."

"Not to mention everybody on Facebook."

"You're kidding."

"I'm not. You're friends with her. Take a look if you don't believe me. . . . You do realize this means that every time one of us visits her, we'll have to go armed with a secret stash of loo roll."

"OK, I admit, it is a bit out there."

"It's more than 'out there.' They're all going to die of cholera. . . . *Storage Wars . . . The Real Housewives of New Jersey . . . Keeping Up with the Kardashians . . . Storage Wars . . .*"

Barbara noticed the sink was full of dirty dishes.

"What's all this?"

Ben said he'd been tidying his room.

"And the reason you haven't put all your penicillin-encrusted plates in the dishwasher is . . . ?"

"It needs unloading. I was going to get round to doing it. Honest."

"No, you weren't. You were leaving it for me."

"I wasn't."

"Have you any idea how fed up I get being treated like the hired help? I shouldn't have to come home to this." She snatched the remote from him and zapped the TV.

"Hey, take it easy."

Barbara pulled out a chair and sat down. "I'm sorry. I know I shouldn't be taking it out on you. But I've had a crap day."

"What happened?"

She rubbed her fingers over her forehead. "I lost my job."

"What? You're kidding. Bloody hell. What are you going to do?"

"I don't know. The thing is that without my salary coming in, your dad and I are really going to be struggling financially."

"Shit. So are you kicking me out?"

"What? Of course not. We'd never kick you out. But you can't go on like this. You need to start earning some money."

"Look, I'm doing my best. OK?"

"Ben, please don't get defensive. It doesn't help." After the day she'd had, the last thing she wanted was a fight. "I mean, surely you can get some bar work."

"You think I haven't tried? I've trekked all over town with my CV. There's nothing."

"I know." She felt as hopeless as he looked. His generation hadn't bargained for this. These were the kids who'd been breast-fed parental approval. Every flower they painted, every poem they wrote, every goal they scored had been celebrated. They grew up believing they were special. For them the future held only possibilities. These children knew that when the time came, all they had to do was go out into the world and claim their due. Then the world changed. Instead of offering opportunities, it hurled lemons.

Barbara decided to change the subject.

"So," she said, "what time did you get in last night? I didn't hear you."

"Dunno . . . threeish. Maybe four."

"Go somewhere nice?"

"New bar in Whitechapel with some mates. And no, I didn't ask Dad for cash. I paid for it with some birthday money I had left."

"So . . ." She hesitated, but as usual, her curiosity got the better of her. "You seeing anybody at the moment?"

"Not really."

"What does 'not really' mean?"

"God, Mum . . ." He did that weary, adolescent eye-roll thing. "It means I'm getting the occasional shag, but there's nobody serious. Is that what you wanted to know?"

She supposed it was. "Look, I know I'm interfering, but I worry about you getting depressed living at home. I like to know that you're getting out and doing stuff."

"Don't worry. I'm doing stuff. And I'm sorry I keep asking for money in order to do it."

She was wary of steering him back to the main agenda, but he seemed to be heading that way without her help.

"So how's the writing going?" she said.

"OK."

She knew it wasn't remotely OK. In the last couple of months he'd submitted a hilarious piece to another Web magazine about what it was like being a graduate living back home with his mum and dad. He'd also sent a couple of on-spec music reviews to the *Guardian*. The Web magazine had used the piece, but as usual, there was no fee. The *Guardian* hadn't even bothered to get back to him.

"Ben, tell me something. Are you absolutely sure you want to be a music journalist?"

"Why do you ask?"

"I dunno. I just get this feeling that you're not as enthusiastic about it as you once were. If you've changed your mind, it doesn't matter. I mean your dad and I think that with your music background, journalism would be great for you. But if you're thinking of going in a different direction, it's not too late."

"I'm fine. Honest. Please stop worrying. . . . And I'm really sorry about your job. It's crap. But you're a great teacher. Something will turn up."

"I'm not holding my breath, but let's hope so."

"And I will start earning some money soon. I promise. I hate being dependent on you and Dad, and now with you losing your job, I feel even worse."

"I don't want you to feel bad. Just so long as you're trying. That's all we ask."

"I am. And please don't think I'm not grateful to you guys. I just need a bit more time to sort myself out. Please, you have to trust me."

"It's not that I don't trust you. I'm just not sure how you're going to do it."

"Just leave it with me. I'm working on it."

"Working on what?"

"It. . . . Please can we let the subject drop now?"

He got up and started to unload the dishwasher. Meanwhile, his mother prayed that "it"—whatever "it" might be—would come to something.

A text pinged from inside her bag. It was from Frank. Exec producer coming this evening to check how edit progressing. Couldn't put him off. Should be back by ten.

In Frank speak, that meant midnight.

After a long soak in the bath, she lay on the sofa, nursing a glass of Scotch. Ben helped himself to some Ben & Jerry's and took it up to his room.

Ten o'clock came and went with no sign of Frank. She thought about calling him, but she wasn't about to beg him to come home.

She switched on the news. More floods in Wales. Evil bankers bankrupting struggling businesses in order to boost their own profits. Good Lord, what if that happened to Jess and Matt?

It occurred to her to call Rose to see if the music had disappeared, but having been up since five, her mother would be asleep by now. Unless, of course, the music was keeping her awake.

Barbara decided to see if Dr. Google had anything to say about Rose's disorder. By now she was starting to think that there could be something seriously wrong with her. The words "brain" and "tumor" had popped into her head more than once this evening. She fetched her laptop from the kitchen and set it up on the coffee table. She typed: "hearing imaginary music." And there it was, an entire page on something called musical ear syndrome. It drove sufferers crazy with frustration but was entirely benign. It tended to affect the elderly, people with tinnitus, or those who lived in quiet surroundings. Rose had never complained of tinnitus, but she was certainly old and her surroundings were quiet, verging on monastic. According to one Web site, the brain compensated for the silence by creating its own sounds. There was no treatment, although encouraging patients to bring real sounds into their world—from the radio or TV—was thought to help. Well, that was a relief. Barbara would still have a chat with her mother's GP, but it seemed like there was no cause for panic.

Now that she was online, she thought she might as well see what was happening on Facebook. At the top of her news feed was Jess's YouTube link about family cloth. Going to try this out. Will keep you posted.

"Please don't," Barbara said under her breath.

Martha and a few more of Jess's hummusy friends had "liked" it.

Jess wasn't normal. What sort of a person shares their family's bottom-wiping habits with the rest of the world? "This is all my fault," Barbara muttered. Frank was right. When the children were growing up, she'd failed to teach them about social boundaries, when to self-censor and shut up about intimate stuff. But whereas Ben appeared to have taught himself to do it, Jess hadn't. This was a rerun of the milkman and the clitoris. And it was too late to do anything about it.

Barbara hadn't posted a status update in ages. She decided to announce that she'd lost her job. She wasn't sure why. She certainly wasn't in need of any more sympathy. Or maybe she was.

Lost my job today due to education cuts. Farewell, Jubilee Primary. Hard work, but I had the best time. Can't begin to describe how much I'm going to miss all my wonderful kids. She hit "enter" and started to cry.

Finally, she took herself to bed. She tried to read but couldn't. She tried to sleep but couldn't.

Her brain refused to switch off. She kept thinking about the future. Without a job, she would fall apart. She needed a plan.

There was only one way forward. She would have to take on some private tutoring. With so many underprivileged, underperforming kids out there, the thought of abandoning them turned her stomach. She felt like a traitor. But the going rate for tutoring was fifty quid an hour. She would get in touch with one of the agencies.

Frank came in bang on midnight. He practically fell onto the bed.

"Please don't shout. I know I said I'd try to be in at a reasonable time, but you have no idea of the day I've had."

"The day you've had?"

"Sorry. . . . I know you had a shit day, too. But these bloody people at the BBC . . . They're trying to fuck me over on the budget for the Mexico film. They're offering almost half what I asked for. Bloody cutbacks. On top of that, they're expecting me to lay out for flights, hotels and car hire and then claim it back. I don't bloody have it."

"Raid the tax pot."

"Again? It isn't bottomless, you know. Soon there'll be nothing left."

"So we'll be late paying and we'll get a fine. I don't see you have any other option."

"Probably not. Bastards. I need a shower."

"Now? But it's after midnight. You'll wake me up when you come to bed."

He said he'd be as quick as he could. Barbara lay in bed waiting for him to finish.

"So how are you feeling?" he said when he finally climbed in beside her.

"Crap, since you ask. On top of everything else, my mother seems to be suffering from something called musical ear syndrome." She explained about Glenn Miller and "Chattanooga Choo Choo."

"Great. That's all we need, your mother going bonkers."

Barbara said it was an ear thing rather than a brain thing. "I need to get her hearing checked out. . . . Oh, and Jess and Matt might be in financial trouble. They've been doing all this outside catering and nobody's paying their bills."

"They'll sort it."

"What do you mean 'they'll sort it'? What if they don't?"

"Barbara, they're intelligent, industrious kids. They'll find a way through this. You can't keep assuming the worst. Stop worrying."

"And how's about—just for once in your life—you started worrying about somebody who isn't you."

"OK, if this is still about me coming home late, I'm sorry. This bloody exec producer seems to have no home to go to and insisted on coming over to see the film tonight. What could I do?"

"All I wanted was for us to sit down with a bottle of wine and have a talk."

"I know, but I'm here now. Come on . . . cut me some slack."

"Frank, I've cut you enough slack over the years to make you an overcoat."

He made his daft, please-forgive-me puppy face. She laid her head on his chest.

"By the way, I had a talk with Ben. He says he's doing his best to earn money and that we need to trust him. He seems to have some kind of plan up his sleeve. He didn't want to discuss it and I didn't push him."

"About bloody time. Perhaps he's starting to get his act together."

"Maybe. It wouldn't surprise me if it had nothing to do with music journalism though."

"What makes you say that?"

"Dunno. I've just got this feeling that since the band broke up, the taste has gone out of his chewing gum. Of course, he denies it."

"I guess all we can do is wait."

He asked her if she'd had any thoughts about where she went from here, job-wise.

"Tutoring, I guess."

"Makes sense. Three kids at what—fifty quid a time? A hundred and fifty quid a day. You're sorted."

"No, Frank, I'm not *sorted*," she said, sitting up. "I might be able to find work, but that doesn't alter the fact that my career is over. Why can't you see that?"

"I do see it, and I'm truly sorry about what's happened, but we have to be practical. Look, we're both knackered. Let's have a proper talk tomorrow."

"'K . . . Oh, I didn't tell you—one of my kids came to school today covered in cigarette burns. He's meant to be on the at-risk register. I don't get it. . . . Why doesn't anybody do their job anymore?"

"Let me guess: the mother's boyfriend. And don't tell me you got straight on to Child Protection and read them the riot act."

"Of course I did. What else would you have me do? A kid's life could be in danger. And I went round to see the mother to see if I could help."

"And could you?"

"Not really. The boyfriend's done a runner." She paused. "Please don't be angry, but he stole her money and she had no heat or food. So I gave her sixty quid."

"Fine. Why didn't you make it a hundred? According to you, there's loads in the tax pot."

Barbara described the cold, desolateness of the flat, the bruises on Tiffany's body. "You'd have done the same—admit it."

Her husband grunted. "Maybe."

"Frank, who's going to do this stuff when I'm not there?"

"What, hand out wads of our cash to the needy?"

"You know what I mean."

"You know what your problem is?"

"I toot my own horn. I know."

"Not just that. You think you're indispensable."

Frank said he really was too tired to talk anymore and turned over. He was snoring in a matter of minutes. Barbara still couldn't sleep. It didn't help that on top of all the other emotions she was feeling, she was still angry with Frank for not making an effort to come home at a reasonable time tonight. It wasn't often that she asked him for anything.

Outside the night had turned wild and stormy—the tail end of some Caribbean hurricane, apparently. She lay there listening to the howling wind, the rain beating at the old sash windows making them rattle.

Pathetic fallacy. It had come to her—the phrase she'd been trying to remember in the playground—the literary term for when physical surroundings echoed a character's mood.

Chapter 4

The bald woman in the photograph was smiling a wan but courageous smile. She held up a placard: *My last chemo. "Like" if you hate cancer.*

So if she didn't click on "like," Barbara thought, did that mean she loved cancer? That she actively supported it? The picture had been posted by some women's group calling themselves "Feminists Against Cancer," which seemed to imply there were some feminists out there who were all for it.

Barbara was sitting at her kitchen table in her dressing gown, getting her usual early-morning caffeine and Facebook fix. She carried on spooling down the page. She reached her own status update from the night before. Nine people had "liked" it. She'd just announced that she'd lost her job and nine people seemed to think it was reason to give her a thumbs-up.

Pam had commented, When the Lord closes a door, somewhere He opens a window—Maria, The Sound of Music. Other people had left messages of condolence and fury at the government cuts, which she appreciated. Jean had commented: Bastards. Shame

on them. They're losing a talented and truly committed teacher. Love
you. xxx

Barbara "liked" all the comments and posted a general thank-
you, saying how much people's support meant to her. She felt guilty
that Jean had heard her news via Facebook. She should have called
her last night. What had she been thinking?

She was about to get off Facebook, but instead she went back to
the picture of the smiling cancer woman. *"Like" if you hate cancer.*
Barbara had no idea if the directive had been designed to instill
guilt, but it had succeeded. If she ignored this woman, Barbara
would spend the rest of the day thinking she was a bad person. She
hit "like" and went upstairs to take a shower.

She was just leaving the house—Frank had left before she was
even awake—when her cell rang. It was Jean.

"Jean, I'm so sorry you had to find out on Facebook. I should have
called you last night."

"Don't you dare apologize. You were probably in no fit state to
talk. Listen, I haven't got long. I'm at work, grabbing a quick break. I
just wanted to check how you're holding up."

"Yeah, I'm OK, I guess."

"How about I pop round when you get back from school? I've got
to dash now. I've got a geriatric primigravida down the corridor
who's fully dilated and screaming blue murder."

"OK, go. See you later."

As soon as she got to school, Barbara headed for the lunchroom.
This morning, probably because it was so bitterly cold, a few more
kids had turned up for breakfast. She helped herself to a bowl of
cornflakes and looked round for Troy. She wondered if Sandra had
gone through with her threat to exclude him. She hadn't. He was
sitting at a table on his own, struggling to get the top off his boiled
egg. Rigid as Sandra could be when it came to school regulations,

she had clearly come to the conclusion that this was the safest place for the child.

"Hey, Troy, mind if I join you?"

He looked up briefly. She took that as an invitation and sat down next to him.

"Why don't you let me show you how to do that?" She demonstrated how to bash the eggshell and take the bits off with the spoon handle. "Or you can use your fingers like this."

She watched him break into the egg white with his spoon and scoop up the yolk. Once again she was overcome with the urge to wrap this sad, vulnerable little scrap in her arms. She wanted to make him feel safe and cared for, but she couldn't. Over the years there she'd taught dozens of children like Troy. She'd wanted to rescue them all. Frank accused her of having a Mother Teresa complex. Barbara agreed that she probably did. At the same time, she thought it was a bit rich coming from a man who thought TV journalism could save the world.

"So how are you feeling this morning?"

"OK," Troy said.

She reached for a butter knife and cut his toast into soldiers and handed him one. "See, that way you can dunk the toast into the yolk. It's really good."

He dunked and ate but refused to make eye contact, let alone engage in conversation.

"Troy, do you know if anybody called round to speak to your mum yesterday?"

"Dunno."

"OK. Not to worry. Tell you what, when you've finished breakfast, how's about we go to the sickroom and put some more antiseptic on your arm."

"It's fine. I mustn't show anybody."

"Who told you that?"

He carried on eating his egg.

Just then Sandra appeared and beckoned Barbara over. "I decided to let him back because he'll be warm and safe here and he'll get two decent meals. But that doesn't mean I'm not worried about the other children."

"OK, tell you what," Barbara said. "Why don't I keep him with me for the day?"

"You sure?"

"Positive."

Barbara asked Sandra if she could use her office to put in another call to social services. "I'm not sure anybody's called round to see Tiffany. I need to find out what's going on."

"Sure. I'll watch Troy."

It turned out that Jan, the woman she'd spoken to yesterday, wasn't due in until after lunch. Barbara was put through to her boss—a woman called Maureen Taylor. Barbara introduced herself and gave a brief summary of her conversation with Jan. "I was expecting a social worker to make an emergency visit, but I'm not sure if anybody's been."

"Sorry. When did you say you called?"

"Yesterday morning."

"And it's Mrs. Stirling from Jubilee Primary?"

"Yes."

"Well, I'm looking at the log, and there's no record of your call or any notes."

"I don't believe this."

"Let me see if there's anything on Jan's desk. Bear with me for a sec. . . . Right . . . No, there doesn't appear to be anything. . . . No . . . wait . . . hang on. . . . There's a Post-it note. Got it. Sorry. It was buried under her papers."

"So she lost it."

"Oh, I'm sure she would have found it."

"When? Next week? Next month? By then we could have a dead child on our hands. Why have you people got no sense of urgency?"

"Look . . . I appreciate your concern, but getting angry isn't very helpful. Of course we have a sense of urgency. But my team is overloaded with cases. They have to prioritize."

"And Jan decided not to prioritize Troy."

"It's not like that."

"Then what is it like? Tell me."

"Mrs. Stirling, you need to calm down. We are doing our best. I assure you that somebody will visit the family."

"But when? I've talked to his mother. Her boyfriend has been physically abusing Troy. His arms are covered in cigarette burns. He seems to have done a runner, but I'm not convinced he won't be back."

"OK, I've made a note. Tell you what. I don't usually do home visits, but this situation worries me. I'll call in on my way home."

Maureen's appreciation that the situation was urgent and that she was prepared to go out of her way to visit Tiffany and the children threw Barbara. She'd been ready for a fight, and now that the wind had been taken out of her sails, she didn't quite know what to say.

"Right . . . well . . . thank you. I really appreciate that."

At twelve thirty, Barbara took Troy back to the lunchroom and sat him down at a table with Baillie and Kane. She needed a few minutes' break to eat something and drink a cup of coffee, so she asked the young, newly qualified teacher on lunch duty to keep a special eye on Troy and to watch out for kids calling the group "retards." Baillie and Kane would probably retaliate with no more than a few "fuck yous." Despite being hyperactive, they were good-natured kids and rarely violent. Troy was the one likely to go nuclear.

Once Troy was settled, Barbara took herself up to the staff room. People were sitting around, eating packed lunches and reading the papers. At Jubilee, staff only ever read the tabloids—the more down-market and outrageous, the better. They provided much-needed light relief.

"Here, listen to this: 'Bigfoot kept lumberjack as love slave.'"

Barbara joined in the laughter and took a bite of the ham and mustard sandwich she'd brought for lunch.

"No . . . wait . . . Get this . . . 'Severed leg hops to hospital.'"

While the room erupted, Barbara sat rubbing her chest. She assumed the pain she was feeling was indigestion. She put down the sandwich. The pain was getting worse. What was more, it didn't feel like that familiar sharp, bubble-of-air sensation. This felt like some-body had put a belt around her chest and was pulling it tighter and tighter. Her heart was racing. Suddenly she was struggling to breathe. She darted to the window and threw it open.

Somebody called out to her to shut the window because she was causing a draft.

"Can't breathe. Chest hurts. Going to faint."

A moment later she was surrounded by alarmed faces. Instruc-tions seemed to be coming from every direction. "OK, keep calm. . . . Come and sit down. . . . Somebody fetch a blanket. . . . Try to breathe. . . ."

"But I can't bloody breathe."

"That's because you're panicking."

Of course she was panicking. This was how her father died. Somebody made her sit down and put her head between her knees. Somebody else called 999.

The ambulance seemed to take forever but in reality probably took only a few minutes. It rolled into the playground, blue light flashing. The paramedics gave Barbara oxygen, checked her blood pressure and bundled her onto a stretcher. Since it was still lunchtime, the kids were in the playground. Despite the best efforts of the teachers on playground duty, they swarmed around the stretcher. "Miss . . . You ill, miss? Is it your appendix, miss? . . . Miss . . . did you get stabbed? . . . You going to die, miss?"

Sandra offered to come with her to King George's. "No. Stay with Troy. My friend Jean works at the hospital. I'll get somebody to page her. If you could possibly call Frank?"

"No worries."

Twenty minutes later Barbara was lying on a bed in the ER. She was wired up to an ECG monitor and wearing a hospital gown that gaped at the back. Not that this concerned her. She was too busy thinking that she was about to die. A chirpy young nurse had taken some blood and left her with a blood pressure cuff around her arm. This automatically tightened every few minutes and gave a readout. By now the pain in her chest had eased and she didn't need the oxygen mask, although the nurse insisted she keep it on. Barbara was anxious to make contact with Jean. "I was just wondering," she said, pulling off her oxygen mask, "if there was any chance you could call the labor ward and leave a message for a friend of mine to say I'm in casualty. She's a midwife. Her name's Jean Bishop. She's probably really busy. Tell her not to panic."

The nurse said she would do her best, so long as Barbara kept her oxygen mask on. Barbara duly replaced it, but as soon as the nurse disappeared, she took it off again. She tried calling Frank, but as usual, he wasn't picking up. She left a message. "Frank, I'm in casualty at King George's. I think I might have had a heart attack. Please can you come?"

Fifteen minutes later, the ECG complete, the nurse tore off the ticker tape.

"How's it looking?" Barbara said.

"Sorry. Above my pay grade, I'm afraid. I'm not allowed to say anything. One of the doctors needs to take a look at it."

"Do you know how long that might take?"

"Could be a while. The ER's heaving right now."

The nurse disappeared with the readout. Meanwhile her blood pressure and heart rate were still being monitored. She tried closing her eyes but couldn't. Even though the pain wasn't so severe, her heart was still pounding. She had to stay awake and vigilant in order to stop herself dying. Every so often the cuff would tighten around her arm. She studied the pointy peaks and troughs of her heartbeat on the monitor. Any minute now she would flatline. Her father had clearly passed his crap genes on to her. Once her heart stopped, an alarm would go off and doctors would come running with electronic paddles and shots of adrenaline and attempt to bring her back. Meanwhile, she would be setting off on her journey down the tunnel of death that she'd read so much about in all those tabloid articles on near-death experiences. Her spirit would float down the tunnel, towards the bright light. She would be met on the other side by all her dead relatives. Knowing her luck, though, her dad wouldn't show up on account of his agoraphobia, which naturally had continued into the afterlife. The only person to make the effort would be her smelly aunty Minnie (who, amazingly, would still be smelly).

Barbara was still in the midst of her death reverie when a junior doctor stopped by to check her vital signs. He hadn't checked her ECG readout—a more senior doctor would be doing that—but her blood pressure and pulse seemed fine. There didn't appear to be any immediate cause for concern. What was that supposed to mean?

Either there was cause for concern or there wasn't. Christ. And why hadn't Frank called?

"Right, Mrs. Stirling, what we're going to do next is get a chest X-ray, just to check your heart and lungs look normal."

Barbara shuffled forward until her skin was pressed against the X-ray plate. She found herself apologizing for the size of her breasts. "They won't get in the way, will they?" The kindly woman radiographer assured her they wouldn't. She gently shifted Barbara into the exact position before disappearing behind the screen.

"OK, my love—deep breath now and hold it . . . hold it. . . ."

She couldn't begin to express the extent to which she didn't want to die. Her eyes started to fill up. "And just one more for luck." She wanted to see her kids successful and thriving. She wanted to dance at her grandchildren's weddings. Her life couldn't end here. There was stuff she still needed to do. So much she wanted to achieve.

Once she was back in her cubicle in the ER, she tried calling Frank again. Still nothing.

Then Jean appeared in her blue midwife scrubs, her face full of concern. "I just got your message. They said you came in by ambulance. What on earth happened?"

"I had this terrible chest pain and I couldn't breathe. It may have been a heart attack. Jean, I'm really frightened. I think I'm going to die."

That made Jean laugh. "Oh, for heaven's sake. Look at you. Of course you're not going to die." She peered at the monitor. "Your BP and heart rate are fine."

"That's what the doctor said. But are you sure?"

"Positive. Sweetheart, please try to calm down. Whatever's wrong, you're certainly not at death's door."

"Not that you'd tell me if I were."

"Of course I would. You know me. By now I'd be asking if you wanted to be burned, buried or stuffed."

"Hang on—didn't we have this conversation at your birthday party?"

"Yeah. I think I decided I wanted to be stuffed and brought out at Christmas."

Jean majored in jovial calm. She absorbed other people's panic like human Bounty. When friends described her as solid and capable, she always complained. "It makes me sound like one of those burly women gym teachers." But capable she was. Not to mention sensible and wise. Her sister, Val, called her an old soul. Jean hated that, too, because it suggested some forlorn phantom haunting the Tower of London. Unless she had reason, Jean was anything but forlorn. In fact, it was her humor that first brought Barbara and Jean together.

It was 1980 or thereabouts. Barbara had picked up a flyer in the local library publicizing a new women's group. She decided to go along to the first meeting and check it out. The flyer had suggested that group members could look forward to lively debates on subjects like equal pay and the division of domestic labor. The last thing Barbara had expected was a turgid lecture by a feminist academic with an overabundance of armpit hair on whether $E=mc^2$ was a "sexed" equation. From what Barbara could gather, it privileged the speed of light over other vitally necessary speeds.

The young woman sitting next to Barbara had clearly noticed her yawning. "Why doesn't somebody tell her to shut up and shave?" she whispered.

Barbara burst out laughing and was told to shush.

"I'm Jean, by the way."

"Barbara. I don't know about you, but I need to get out of here."

Giggling like a pair of naughty schoolgirls, they hotfooted it to the pub.

"Tell you what," Jean was saying now. "Why don't I go and find a doctor? I think you need to know what's going on."

Before she had a chance, a hand pushed back the cubicle curtain and a doctor appeared. Dr. Sykes was a specialist who'd been sent down from cardiology to take a look at Barbara's ECG results. At a guess, she was about Barbara's age. Gray hair. Sensible flats. Eminently trustworthy. "Well, the good news is everything's perfectly normal. Your X-rays are fine. There's nothing on your ECG or in your blood tests to suggest a heart attack."

"Really?"

"Really."

"So I'm not going to die."

Dr. Sykes smiled. "I'd say you've probably got a year or two left."

"What did I tell you?" Jean said.

"Then what happened? It certainly felt like a heart attack. I had pains in my chest. I was gasping for breath."

"I'm pretty certain you had a panic attack."

"But I never panic. I mean, I get worked up about stuff and things are pretty stressful at the moment, but I never panic."

Dr. Sykes asked what kind of stress she'd been experiencing.

Barbara went through the list. She'd just been sacked. Then there was Troy and the social workers. Oh, and Ben living at home earning no money, Jess and Matt struggling to make a go of their business.

"Is that all? Well, if you ask me, you've got one heck of a lot going on. I think this is your body telling you everything's gotten to be too much."

She said Barbara was free to go, but suggested she see her family doctor to discuss antianxiety medication. She also told her that she needed to take things easy.

"Take things easy?" Barbara said to Jean after Dr. Sykes had gone. "She's having a laugh. Oh, and I forgot to mention to her that my mother thinks Glenn Miller and his orchestra have moved into her building."

"Come again."

"I Googled it. Apparently, it's a thing. It's called musical ear syndrome."

"I've heard of that," Jean said. "There was a chap in the old-age home where Ken's dad lived. He had it. Thought the cast of *Hello, Dolly!* was camped on the lawn."

"Sounds about right."

"But listen, the doctor's right. You do have to start taking it easy."

Just then Ken appeared. Shirtsleeves. Stethoscope around his neck.

"Hi. Jean texted me. What happened? You OK?"

"Oh, Ken, you're such a sweetheart to come and check on me, but I'm fine. It's all been one huge fuss about nothing."

"It's not nothing," Jean said.

Barbara gave him the bullet points.

"You poor old sausage. Sounds to me like you could do with getting away for a week or two. Couldn't Frank get some time off?"

"I doubt it. He's off to Mexico in a couple of weeks."

Just then Barbara's mobile rang. Speak of the devil.

"Bar, what's been going on? Are you OK? What have the doctors said?"

"It wasn't a heart attack. The heart specialist is pretty certain it was a panic attack. It's stress, apparently. But I honestly thought I was having a heart attack. I had these terrible chest pains. I couldn't breathe. I was sure I was going to die. Frank, I've been so scared."

"Christ, I bet you were. And they're absolutely sure it was just a panic attack?"

"Yes. They want me to go on antianxiety meds."

"Makes sense."

"Look, you wouldn't come and pick me up, would you? I'm still feeling pretty shaky. I could really do with a cup of tea and a hug."

"I'm sure you could. You've had a nasty scare. The thing is, I'm really up against it here." She could hear the panic in his voice. Then came the silence while he tried to decide what to do. "OK, don't worry. I'll get the tube over to the hospital. I'll be with you in half an hour or so. Then we'll take a cab home."

"Thanks, hon. I really appreciate it."

She said her thank-yous and good-byes to Jean and Ken.

"Promise you'll call if you need me," Jean said, hugging her. "Day or night. It doesn't matter."

"I promise."

"You're going to be fine. Try to get some rest. Love you."

"Love you, too."

Barbara got dressed and made her way to the reception area to wait for Frank. While she waited, she called Sandra.

"So in the end it was just a panic attack."

"Thank the Lord for that. No, that came out wrong. What I mean is, I'm relieved it's nothing life-threatening. We've all been so worried about you."

"I have to say I feel like a bit of a fraud."

"What? Don't be daft. Of course you're not a fraud. I dropped a huge bombshell on you yesterday. I'm not surprised you had a reaction. But like I said, I did my level best to fight in your corner with the Education Department. They simply refused to listen."

"I know. Look, forget about it. What's done is done."

"So I'm assuming you've been told to take it easy for a while."

"Yes, but how can I? I have to earn a living. I need to start job hunting. Not that I'm going to have much luck at my age."

"You mustn't think about any of that for a few days. Take some sick leave. Go for walks. I find a good long walk in the fresh air bucks me up no end."

Barbara said she'd think about taking some time off. "So, how's Troy?"

"He's absolutely fine. He's here in my office. We've been doing some coloring. Now, go home, put your feet up and stop worrying."

Barbara said she would do her best.

It was more than an hour before Frank appeared.

"Sorry to take so long. Bloody Central line's out again. In the end I got a cab. Then the traffic was a nightmare. Anyway, I asked the driver to wait. Taxi's outside."

In the cab he kissed her and put his arm around her. "How you feeling now?"

"Still a bit shaky. Honestly, I thought I was dying back there. All I could think about were the things I still want to do and achieve."

"What? Like skydiving?"

"No, not like skydiving," She managed a smile. "Like making something of the next few years. I want to go out with a bang, not a whimper."

"You will. But for now you have to take it easy. Understood?"

"I suppose." She sank into him, felt his warm breath on her cheek.

As the taxi turned in to their street, Frank told the driver he'd be needing a ride back into town.

"What? You're going back to work?" Barbara said.

"I've got to. I'm up to my eyes with this edit. Tell you what; I'll make sure I'm back by seven and I'll bring in a curry. How does that sound?"

"But what if I have another panic attack in the meantime?"

"Ben's around. If you feel wobbly, just get him to call the doctor."

"You sure you can't stay?"

"I'm sorry. I really have to get back."

"OK." Only it wasn't OK. It was anything but.

"Don't worry. You'll be fine. I'll be back at seven with food."

The taxi pulled away. Barbara rummaged in her bag for her house keys. She stepped inside and closed the door. Usually after a long day she found comfort in the silence. But right now she couldn't. The silence, the emptiness made her anxious. She felt as if she'd been cast adrift in a vast ocean with no life raft. She needed somebody to cling on to, to make her feel safe. She knew that Ben was upstairs, but if she had another panic attack, he wouldn't know what to do. He would most likely get frightened and make things worse. Her heart was starting to race. She took her phone out of her pocket and hit Jean's number.

"Hey, sweetie. You OK?"

"Not really. Frank had to go back to work, and I'm not sure I want to be on my own."

"Don't worry. My shift finishes in half an hour. I'll come straight over."

"You sure?"

"Of course I am. Just sit tight. I'm on my way."

Gradually Barbara's parents stop going to parties. Rose says, "Daddy isn't well." But he's not in bed or in the hospital or anything. Instead her father sits in the chair all the time. He always wears the same gray cardigan and his eyes look sad. When she goes to give him a kiss, his face feels all bristly. Rose keeps nagging him about his hair. She says if he doesn't get it cut, she'll have do it. "And get out of that jumper and let me wash it—before the thing walks off you."

Barbara pesters her mother for an explanation. Rose says that the war affected his nerves. Now it's getting worse, and he finds it difficult to leave the house. She's cross with him because he refuses to take the pills the doctor's prescribed. He's told her they make him feel drowsy and nauseous. Rose thinks he should persevere.

Barbara decides that if she'd been in the war, all the bombs and shooting would have affected her nerves, too. She feels sorry for her daddy.

One day she overhears her mother talking about Stan on the phone. "The army doles out this paltry pension and then abandons him. I'm the one left to cope every night when he wakes up screaming. If only he'd talk about it, but he can't. God knows those poor people suffered in Belsen. It's beyond imagining, but the soldiers who went in and liberated them have their own nightmares." Barbara isn't quite sure what any of this means, but she knows that Rose is sad, too. She must try harder to make her happy. She must stop whining and complaining and being selfish.

Jean put the kettle on and opened a packet of chocolate gingers. She brought the tea and biscuits into the living room, where Barbara was sitting on the sofa, wrapped in a duvet. The heating was on, but she couldn't get warm. "Why am I shivering?"

"You're still in shock," Jean said, putting the tray down on the coffee table. She passed Barbara a mug of tea. "Take a biscuit, too. You could probably do with the sugar."

Barbara helped herself to a chocolate ginger and demolished it in two bites.

"It was ever so kind of Ken to come and check on me. I mean, it was kind of you, too, but he's not my closest friend the way you are." She sipped her tea. "Funny how Ken dropped everything, but Frank hardly ever puts himself out for me. While I was in labor with Jess, he spent most of the time sitting next to me reading the papers. Afterwards he said it was because he was terrified. I, of course, wasn't remotely scared."

"I've known you forever, and this is the first time you have ever complained about Frank. You've always been so stoic."

"I had no choice."

"Don't get me wrong," Jean said. "Frank's a good man. He spends his life trying to expose the suffering in the world, but at the same time, he can be so self-centered."

"So you don't think I was wrong for wanting him to stay with me after we got back from the hospital?"

"Of course you weren't. Imagine if the tables had been reversed. You wouldn't have abandoned him."

"You know it's only recently," Barbara said, "that I've started to work out why I rarely make a fuss when Frank treats me badly. Growing up with parents who neglected me emotionally left me with a profound sense that I didn't deserve to be loved. I still struggle with it." She said that the likelihood was she would always have fallen for a workaholic, self-absorbed man like Frank. If he was what she deserved, what right did she have to complain?

"And yet you don't question whether you deserve to be loved by your kids."

"I know. I can't explain why. Maybe it's because they've loved me from when they were tiny and I've just taken it for granted. I've never taken Frank's love for granted."

"Why not?"

"I worry about being too needy. Frank loathes needy people. He's such a contradiction. When it comes to global suffering, he's brimming over with compassion. When it comes to me, he shows very little emotional support. . . ." She trailed off. "Sorry—now I'm just feeling sorry for myself."

"No, you're not. You're being honest. Frank isn't an easy man to live with."

"He just seems incapable of understanding how relationships work—that caring is a two-way street. I know it's late in the day, but I'm starting to wonder if he's ever so slightly autistic."

"He could definitely be on the spectrum," Jean said.

Barbara smiled. "You think everybody's on the spectrum."

"No. Only men."

"Ken's not. You've always said that you two get on like a couple of girls."

"OK, I admit that Ken is the exception."

Just then a text pinged on Barbara's phone. She reached over to the coffee table. "It's Ben. . . . Little sod. Get this: 'Mum, is that you downstairs? If it is you and not a burglar, could you possibly bring me up a cup of tea with two sugars and one of those chocolate ginger biscuits?'" She texted back: No can do. I'm the burglar.

Two minutes later, Ben appeared.

"Hey, Mum. Guess I'll have to go without tea, then. But don't you worry about me."

"I'm not. Now say hello to Jean."

"Hi, Aunty Jean."

He went over and gave Jean a kiss on the cheek. She wasn't his real aunt, of course, but when they were little, Ben and Jess had decided that she was and "Aunty Jean" had stuck. By the same token, Adam and Oliver called Barbara "Aunty Bar."

Jean asked him how the writing was going. He said OK. Jean knew enough about Ben's situation to have the good sense not to push it and demand details. Instead she remarked on his hair. "With that mop of yours, you're looking more like Bob Dylan every time I see you." She turned to Barbara. "And of course Bob Dylan was the image of Frank when he was young. Or should that be the other way round?"

Ben said it was funny that Aunty Jean should bring up the subject of his hair, because it could actually do with a cut.

"Don't even go there," Barbara said. "The bank's empty." It seemed that the kid who felt so guilty about living off his parents was still capable of reverting to being a teenager when it suited him. She looked at her watch and then at her son. "It's only four o'clock. What's the matter? Couldn't you sleep?"

"Very funny. . . . Look, Mum, instead of a haircut, could I possibly have fifty quid for some new Converse? These are falling apart."

"I just told you, there's no money."

"Please? I'll pay you back."

"How are you going to do that?"

"I'll look after you and Dad when you're old and incontinent. Of course, by that I mean I will get carers in. I'm not going to actually wipe your bums."

"Well, that's good to know—on both counts," Barbara said, shaking her head in mock despair. "So you want fifty quid? For plimsolls."

"It's not my fault. That's how much they cost." Only now did he notice that his mother was wrapped in a duvet. "Mum, you OK? If you're coming down with something, don't come near me. I've got this gig tomorrow night."

"And you'll be wanting money for that, too, I presume."

"Come on. You love me really."

"You think?"

"So are you ill?"

"Not exactly."

Barbara told him the tale.

"You'll be fine," Ben said. "My mate Chris used to have these terrible panic attacks. He'd totally freak out if we were at a gig and it was rammed. He's on meds now, and he's completely OK. . . . So can I take your credit card? I promise I won't take more than I need."

"I suppose so. And put your big coat on. It's freezing."

After he'd gone, Barbara turned to Jean. "He's so like his father. I could be having a nervous breakdown here and all he's interested in is himself."

"Maybe it's not as simple as that. Kids get scared when their parents get ill—even adult kids. I remember reading about it when I was doing my nursing training. And it's true. Deep down they think you might be about to die and abandon them. Ben's just too macho to show it."

"Perhaps. I just worry that sometimes he behaves like such a spoiled brat. One minute he's telling me how much he hates living off me and his dad. The next he's coming round me for cash, just like a kid."

"Ken and I had all this with our two. Don't forget Oliver and Adam both went through what Ben's going through. The kid's unemployed. His band crashed and died. He's got no money. So he reverts to being a teenager. I know it's hard, but what are you going to do? Kick him out?"

"Some parents would."

"I know, but I'm not sure tough love is the answer. People don't understand that these kids can't see a future for themselves. They're frightened. But eventually my two sorted themselves out. Ben will, too. You just need to sit tight and not panic."

"I wish you'd tell Frank that. He won't listen to me." Barbara arranged the duvet, which had slipped off her shoulders. "I know I moan, but if I'm honest, I'll miss Ben when he finally moves out."

Jean said she'd cried for a month when her last layabout left. "It's not the laundry, the picking up after them that you miss. It's the having them around—cracking jokes, squirting cream into their mouths straight from the can. Then, before you know it, they get engaged and married and there are in-laws to contend with."

Barbara said they didn't see much of Matt's folks because they'd retired to Devon. "To be honest, we don't really know them. Apart from the wedding, we've met only a couple of times, but they seem like really lovely people and Atticus and Cleo adore them."

"Bully for you. We had Felicity over for dinner last night." Felicity was the mother of their future daughter-in-law. It was the first time Jean and Ken had met her, and it hadn't gone well.

"We adore Emma, but her mother is a real piece of work. Terrible snob. We both tried to give her a bit of leeway because she just lost her husband, but I ended up wanting to throttle her." She explained how the conversation had got round to the royal family and Felicity had kept going on about how Kate was so nouveau and not remotely good enough for William and how the Middleton girls had always been known as the "Wisteria Sisters"—highly decorative, terribly fragrant and with a ferocious ability to climb.

"Then she starts on immigrants and people living on benefits. And what does Ken do?"

"Buggers off to the pub?"

"Not quite. He pretends he's got to call the hospital to check on a patient and retreats into his study for half an hour. I was furious with him. But he said it was either that or he would have shown her the front door. Afterwards poor Emma couldn't stop apologizing for her mother. Adam and I were trying to calm her down. Meanwhile Ken sat himself down in front of the football."

"Well, it's good to hear everything's got off to such a good start," Barbara said.

They both started to laugh, and Barbara realized she was feeling warmer.

"Where does the time go?" Jean said, shaking her head. "You raise a family, and then suddenly it's just you and the old man staring at each other across the dinner table, wondering what to talk about."

"Stop it," Barbara said. "You and Ken have a brilliant relationship. You've never had that problem."

"OK, maybe not that exact problem, but there's no such thing as a perfect marriage, you know. Ken and I have our ups and downs."

"Of course you do. Doesn't everybody?"

Jean looked down at the mug of tea she was nursing. "We hardly ever have sex," she blurted out. Then she pursed her lips as if she regretted her revelation. It seemed pretty clear that Jean had been bottling up this information for a while.

"Come on," Barbara soothed. "You've been married since ever. Sex gets boring. Plus we're all getting older."

"It's nothing to do with age. Right from the start, sex has been an issue. Ken has never been what you'd call a sexual being. When he's in the mood—which is rarely—he can perform perfectly well. But the truth is, he's not really interested. Over the years, he's seen specialists, had his testosterone levels checked. He's had umpteen sessions with shrinks. And before you ask—no, he's not gay. Nor is he repressing memories of sexual abuse—which is what we thought at first. He simply has a very low sex drive. It happens."

"So was he like this before you got married?"

"Pretty much, but I put it down to our mutual lack of experience. I thought that, given time, we'd be able to sort it out."

"Oh, sweetheart. I'm so sorry. But why have you never said anything?"

"I couldn't bear to. I felt that once I'd said it out loud, it would become real. While I was keeping it to myself, I could pretend it wasn't happening—or at least that it wasn't so bad. And like you, I felt there was no point complaining. There was nothing to be done. I just accepted it. And it wasn't like we were having no sex at all. That's what kept me going."

"Even so. You must have felt so rejected by him."

"I did. But on the other hand, Ken is so loving and affectionate. He's always telling me how much he adores me. He pays me no end of compliments. He fusses over me. I've always felt loved, and I know he wants to be with me."

"Funny. When I saw the pair of you flirting at your birthday party, I was convinced you were still swinging from the chandeliers."

"Nothing could be further from the truth. I think we do it for show."

"Have you ever thought about having an affair?"

"Many times. But the danger of an affair is that you end up falling in love and walking away from your marriage. I could never put our marriage at risk. I love Ken and I want to be with him. We're best friends. We have a good life."

"With virtually no sex."

"I manage." A thin smile crossed her face. "The Rabbit is a wonderful invention." Jean was trying to make light of it all, but Barbara wasn't laughing. "The thing is," Jean went on, "when I hit menopause I thought my libido would start to flag and Ken and I would be on the same page desire-wise. But it didn't. So I finally came up with a solution."

"Don't tell me you've found yourself a gigolo."

Jean took a mouthful of tea. "I did. His name's Jenson."

"Brilliant," Barbara said, laughing. "Jean and Jenson. So, come on. What was your actual solution?"

"That's it."

"What is?"

"Jenson."

"My God—you're serious? You're having sex with a male prostitute?"

"You make it sound so sordid. Jenson's a gigolo."

Which didn't sound remotely sordid.

"Of course, Jenson's not his real name. All the guys at the agency have made-up gigolo names."

"I'm speechless. I mean, what if Ken found out? What if you caught some disease?"

"Bar—this is me you're talking to. Do you honestly think I'm going to have unprotected sex? And Ken isn't going to find out. I meet Jenson at this place he rents—purely for entertaining purposes—and I pay him cash from the money I inherited when my mum died. And before you ask, yes, I keep it in my own private bank account. And if the worst did happen, I think that, once he got over the shock, Ken would understand."

"You really think that?"

"Yes, I do. He's under no illusions. He knows how much I have struggled over the years."

"So you don't feel guilty?"

"Actually, I don't. I've spent a long time thinking about doing this. Then, after my sixtieth birthday, it hit me that we only have one shot at life. I don't know how many years I've got left on this earth, but I don't intend to spend them living like a nun. I went online, found an agency and called them."

"So how old is this Jenson?"

"I don't know—thirty-five maybe. And he's gorgeous. Tall, dark. Magnificent body. At first I wouldn't let him see me naked. But he convinced me he's absolutely fine with my saggy bits. He actually kisses my stretch marks. Can you believe that? And when he goes down on me, it's otherworldly. I feel like I'm having an out-of-body experience. He flicks my clitoris with his tongue and . . ."

"Oh God."

"It drives me crazy. And then he flips me over and takes me from behind. Next week I'm going to let him tie me up. Bar, I'm having so much fun, you wouldn't believe." She stopped herself. The delight drained from her face. "I'm sorry. I'm being thoughtless. I'm meant to be looking after you. I shouldn't be sitting here telling you what a great time I'm having."

"Yes, you should. Hearing all this is taking my mind off things. Honestly. You carry on."

"You sure?"

"Positive.... But I won't pretend I'm not shocked."

"Why? Because I'm a midwife married to a surgeon and I'm meant to be a pillar of the community?"

"It's not that. It's more about you as a person. I mean, your entire house is painted magnolia. You have an automatic bird feeder in your garden. You own a Hostess Trolley."

"And bloody useful it is, too.... So, you're saying I'm boring and suburban."

"No. I'm saying you're conventional."

"Well, it turns out I'm not as conventional as you thought."

"You're right. I appear to have misjudged you.... But tell me—because I'm concerned—what do you know about this guy?"

"Not a lot. That's part of the deal. It's to protect clients from forming attachments and putting their marriages or relationships at risk. All he's told me is that he's a struggling jazz musician. He plays the saxophone."

Barbara decided this was code for layabout. But she wasn't about to upset Jean by saying it.

"So how much does he charge?"

"Not as much as you'd think. His older women tend to see him for a couple of hours in the afternoons, so we get a special senior rate."

"Your gigolo cuts you an early-bird deal? Now I've heard everything."

"I guess older women aren't quite as demanding as the younger ones. I'm exhausted after an hour or so. The others want him for longer."

"And you trust him? I mean, you don't think he could turn nasty?"

"Good Lord, no. Jenson is one of the most gentle people I've ever met. . . . The way he strokes my face, caresses my inner thighs, teases me . . . Bar, have you ever had a full-body orgasm?"

"What, you mean, like, in my elbows?"

"Elbows, knees, fingers—everywhere."

"Nope. Pretty sure I haven't."

Jean bit into another biscuit. "I've disgusted you with all this, haven't I?"

"No. Like I say, I'm taken aback and concerned for your safety, but I'm not disgusted. I totally understand why you're doing it. I just wish there were some other way to resolve all this."

"Believe me. There isn't."

Barbara nodded.

"I'm glad I told you," Jean said.

"I'm glad you told me, too."

Jean went to make more tea, leaving Barbara to ponder full-body orgasms.

As promised, Frank arrived home bang on seven with curry. He put the foil containers in the oven to keep warm and poured them both a Scotch. They sat on the sofa with their drinks.

"How you doing?" he said, putting his arm across her shoulders.

"Not too bad. Jean's been here. I asked her to come over because I didn't want to be on my own. She only left a few minutes ago."

"That's kind of her. . . . You know, I got such a fright this afternoon. I was scared shitless."

"That makes two of us. You know, I would have really appreciated you staying with me after we got home."

"I'm sorry, but you've no idea the pressure I'm under at the moment."

"But I needed you. Just for once would it have hurt you to drop everything?"

"Bar, you had a panic attack, that's all. Frightening, I grant you. But please don't start turning it into something it isn't. Apart from anything else, it won't help you get better."

Barbara didn't get a chance to turn on him, to tell him how much it hurt her to hear him belittling what had happened. Instead the key went in the door and Ben appeared, wearing a pair of new green Converse.

"So how much did those cost me?" his father said by way of greeting.

"Fifty quid. And Mum paid."

"Fifty quid? For a bit of canvas and rubber?"

"Dad, please don't give me a hard time. What do you want from me? I'm not living off you because I enjoy it. I'm trying to get myself sorted. I just need a bit more time."

"Time for what? You lie in bloody bed all day."

"I work at night. My brain seems to function better. I was the same at uni. It's how I am."

"So what is it you're working on all night?"

"A thing."

"What sort of thing? Is it to do with your writing?"

"It's a thing. That's all."

"And that's all you're going to tell me?"

"For now. Yes."

Frank threw up his hands and looked at his wife. "You hear that? I'm supporting him so that he can work on *a thing*. Do you mind telling me what's going to become of him? If he's not careful, he's going to end up sweeping the bloody roads."

"Cheers, Dad. I appreciate that."

"Well, it's true."

"No, it's not. When have I ever let you down? I worked hard at school. I got a decent degree. I've never been in trouble. I volunteer. Why can't you have a bit of faith in me?" By now Ben's face was crimson with fury. "I'm not listening to any more of this. I'm going back out."

Barbara grabbed his arm. "Please don't."

Ben yanked his arm from his mother's grasp. "I'm doing my best. I practically live off beans on toast. My underpants are full of holes. I'm not having him speak to me like that."

"What do you expect me to say?" Frank came back. "You need to pull your finger out."

"So you think I'm lazy."

"Do you think you're lazy?"

"You have no idea! No fucking idea!" Ben headed towards the door.

"Ben, stop! OK, that's enough. Both of you." Barbara could feel her body trembling. She took a breath. "Reluctant as I am to make this about me, can I remind the pair of you that I ended up in the hospital today, and if you don't start behaving, I will probably be back there before the night is out. Just sort this thing out. Now."

She flounced out and took herself into the kitchen. Frank was right behind her.

"I'm sorry," he said. "I got so angry that I forgot about what happened today. I shouldn't have lost my temper." He hugged her. Barbara's arms remained at her sides. He took the hint and pulled back. "I was too hard on him. It's just that I panic, that's all. What sort of a future is he going to have?"

"You think I'm not worried? But how is losing your temper going to help?"

"I don't know. It's what I do."

"It's what you do? That's your answer? Frank, you know as well as I do that losing your temper achieves nothing. All it does is add to everybody else's stress. Mine included. I've got enough on my plate right now. I need you to be a husband and a dad, not another child."

"I know. You're right. I'll apologize to Ben." He took a couple of Cobras from the fridge and went back into the living room.

By the time Barbara returned with plates of lamb rogan josh and mushroom rice, Ben and his dad were sitting side by side on the sofa watching football.

"Does this mean we're not going to eat at the table like civilized people?" Barbara said.

"But it's Manchester United versus Arsenal live," Ben said. "Can't we eat off our laps?"

"But you can still see the TV from the table."

"It's not the same."

"Come on, Bar. Don't be mean."

"Yeah, Mum."

Barbara gave in. She was too tired to argue, and on the upside, they were mates again. She ate with them—plate on her lap in front of the TV—but she found football tedious. In the end she went upstairs and called Jess to tell her about her panic attack.

"Mum, that's awful. It's all this bloody stress you're under from losing your job. Why didn't you call me? You know I'd have come over."

"I know you would, darling, but you're busy and Jean happened to be around."

"So how are you feeling now?"

Barbara said the same as she'd said to Frank, that she was still a bit wobbly.

"Mum, listen to me. Please don't let them put you on pharmaceuticals. All antidepressants and antianxiety meds are addictive, and nobody knows what their long-term effects are."

Barbara was to go to the health-food shop and buy Rescue Remedy and valerian. Apparently valerian was "nature's tranquilizer." "Oh, and eat a lettuce sandwich at night. Lettuce leaves contain valerian, too." Catnip, kava kava and chamomile were also good for anxiety. She would make a list and e-mail it to Barbara. "I'll call you tomorrow. Love you."

"Love you, too, hon."

The following morning Barbara called her GP's office and managed to get an appointment for midday.

Dr. Johal agreed with Dr. Sykes the heart specialist. Barbara was suffering from stress, and future panic attacks couldn't be ruled out. He recommended antianxiety pills. He also suggested that she take a few weeks off work. Barbara said that the idea of being at home all day doing nothing terrified her. Work—even if it was only until the end of term—would be the best therapy. And she was worried about taking pills—not because of Jess's scaremongering—but because she thought they were a sign of weakness, a sign that she was giving in.

Dr. Johal smiled that tolerant smile of his. He had known Barbara for years, and far from feeling threatened, he seemed to enjoy the way she questioned his advice. She would come armed with a diagnosis from Dr. Google—invariably correct, as she frequently reminded him. Her trigger finger, a slight but bothersome ailment she'd developed last year, being a case in point. This had required precisely the minor procedure that Barbara slash Dr. G had advocated.

"Barbara, why did you come and see me if you already knew how you were planning to deal with this problem?"

"I want your opinion."

"No. What you want is my approval to do nothing. Well, I'm not prepared to give it. I think you need medication and rest. And perhaps even some therapy."

"OK, I hear you, but as I've only had one panic attack, I'd like to hold off and see what happens."

"Fine, but I want to see you in two weeks to check how you're doing. Agreed?"

"Agreed."

She got back to her car and called Sandra to say she'd be back in school on Monday. Sandra said she thought she was crazy, but it was up to her and they would certainly be glad to have her back. She also said that she'd heard nothing from social services and had no idea if anybody had visited Troy's family. Barbara said she would give Maureen a call straightaway.

It turned out that Maureen had kept her promise. She had been to see Tiffany and the children. "Like you said, Tiffany's covered in bruises, and the marks on Troy's arms are definitely cigarette burns. But neither he nor his mum are prepared to speak to the police. And Tiffany swears she's got no idea where Wayne is—other than he's gone back up north."

"But if you went to the police, it's possible he might be known to them and they could find him."

"But without Tiffany and Troy's testimony, they'd have no proof. I'm really sorry. There's no way she's going to be persuaded. Meanwhile, the children will remain on the at-risk register, and I promise we'll keep a really close eye on them."

"Thank you. It's just that I'm going to be leaving Jubilee at the end of this term, and I'd like to know that somebody's looking out for him."

"Don't worry. From now on, there will be."

Barbara thought she might go for a swim. She needed the exercise, and being in water always relaxed her. She was about to head off home to pick up her swimsuit when her phone rang.

"Mrs. Stirling?"

"Yes."

"Sergeant Lisa Banks here from Brentvale Police. I'm with your mother at her flat."

Barbara's heart started to race. She dreaded what she was going to hear next. "Is she OK? What's happened?"

"She's absolutely fine physically, but I am slightly concerned about her mental state. She's gone to make a cup of tea, so since she gave me your number, I thought I'd give you a quick call."

It seemed that Rose had gone to her local police station to complain about the loud music being played in her building. The kindly sergeant Lisa had walked her home to check it out.

"I can't hear a thing, but your mother insists somebody's playing something called 'A String of Pearls' at full volume."

"Oh God. Not again. I'm so sorry. You've been dragged out on a wild-goose chase, I'm afraid."

"This has happened before?"

Barbara explained that the music wasn't real and that her mother appeared to be suffering from musical ear syndrome. "She's not going gaga. It's actually a problem with her ears. I'll come over right away."

Sergeant Lisa insisted on staying until Barbara arrived.

Barbara turned the ignition and pulled away. She'd driven no more than a few hundred yards when the chest pain started. Then she couldn't breathe. She gave a sharp twist of the wheel and pulled over. The driver in the car behind hooted loudly and accelerated past her. She opened the window. The rush of bitter cold air seemed to help her breathing. She kept telling herself to stay calm, to take slow breaths. "This is just a panic attack. You are not dying." After about fifteen minutes, she felt the pain ease. Her breathing returned to normal. She was still feeling sick and panicky though. She was in no fit state to drive to her mother's. What she needed to do was hotfoot it back to Dr. Johal, apologize for being such a know-it-all and get some meds. Meanwhile, she picked up her phone and pressed the "home" button. "Siri—call Ben." (Her son was always telling her how much time Siri saved and that she should use it more.)

"I'm sorry I don't see Jen in your contacts."

"No, not Jen . . . Siri . . . Call . . . BEN!"

"I'm sorry, I don't see Hen in your contacts."

"You stupid imbecile!"

"Calling Aunty Celia."

"No . . . I don't want Aunty Celia."

By that stage Siri appeared to get offended and cut her off. She went to her contacts list and hit the number for her son's cell. Ben wasn't answering. Of course he wasn't. He was asleep. She tried five more times. On the sixth, he picked up.

"Shit, Mum, this'd better be important. I'd just dribbled around Iniesta and was about to score the winning goal in the World Cup against Spain."

"I don't care. Listen, I'm on my way to see Dr. Johal. Nana Rose is at home with a policewoman and I need you to go over there and sit with her."

"Why? What's she done? Oh God, she hasn't been arrested for shoplifting, has she? My friend Jake, his old gran gets arrested in shops all the time. Last time she got caught walking out of her local deli carrying an entire kosher salami."

"No, she hasn't been arrested." Barbara explained about her musical ear syndrome. "At least that's what I think it is."

"No shit. That's really cool."

"Ben, it isn't remotely cool. If it carries on, it's going to drive her insane. I need to call her doctor and get her ears checked."

"So I have to go right now?"

"Yes, please."

"But I need a shower."

"Forget about a shower. You've still got my credit card from yesterday. Just call a cab and go. I'll be with you as soon as I can."

Five minutes later, Barbara was back at the doctor's surgery, pleading with the receptionist to let her have two more minutes with Dr. Johal. The woman was adamant that there were no appointments left. Barbara would have to come back tomorrow. "But all I need is a prescription. Please can I see him?" She laid it on about just having had a panic attack in her car. "I could have caused a serious accident. I really do need some medication."

The receptionist finally took pity on her and said she would try to squeeze her in.

Barbara thought that Dr. Johal would give her an I-told-you-so lecture, but he didn't. Instead he wrote out a prescription for an SSRI.

"Now, then," he said, "SSRI stands for . . ."

"Selective Serotonin Reuptake Inhibitor."

"Stupid of me to think you wouldn't know that. And do you know what they do?"

"They make your brain produce more serotonin, which makes you feel less depressed and anxious."

"Exactly. In fact, the one I'm going to prescribe you is specifically designed to combat anxiety."

He said they would take a few weeks to kick in, so in the meanwhile she should absolutely stop working.

"In fact, since you only have this term left, I'm going to insist you don't go back."

"But I have to. There are children who depend on me."

"Nobody's indispensable. You have to stop working. It's time you put your welfare before the welfare of others."

He would see her in a month.

Barbara collected her tablets from the pharmacy over the road and took herself home. The first thing she did was call Frank. It was a reflex. She knew she was unlikely to get much by way of sympathy, but something made her keep on trying. For once he picked up on the first ring. "I had another panic attack," she said. She told him about the call from the policewoman and how Dr. Johal had signed her off work.

"I think he's right. You should start taking it easy. And we need to get this thing with your mother sorted before her problems make you worse."

"I know that. But I have to work. I'll shrivel and die if I can't."

"No, you won't." He said he had to go. "Talk later."

Barbara made herself poached eggs on toast and a mug of tea. After she'd eaten, she went to lie down on the sofa. So that was it. Her career was actually over. She'd only just called Sandra to say she would be back on Monday. Now she would have to tell her that she was never coming back.

Without her job to define her, who was she? A woman of no substance. A shadow that would briefly grow longer before fading into eternal night. She could hear Frank telling her to stop being so bloody melodramatic. But she couldn't help it. What was to become of her? She wasn't ready to turn into another invisible middle-aged woman who, when she wasn't doting on her grandchildren, collected schmaltzy knickknacks and wandered around garden centers.

She supposed that most people who got the sack—whatever their age—felt a similar loss of identity. But the young could still live in hope. At almost sixty, she had little chance of kick-starting her career. She was washed up and irrelevant. Redundant.

Despite being on the cusp of her seventh decade, Barbara wanted her mum. She wanted to climb onto her lap and tell her about the panic attacks. She wanted Rose to hold her in her arms and rock her, tell her she was there, that it would be all right. But Rose had rarely offered Barbara comfort in the past when she needed it. She was hardly going to change now. If Barbara went to her, she would be given cold comfort. "What have you got to panic about?" Rose would say. "You want to try waking up every morning facing the prospect that this could be the day you drop dead? Now, that's a proper reason to panic."

Eventually, Barbara dozed off. When she woke it was getting dark. She looked at her watch. It was four o'clock. She'd been asleep for two hours. She never slept in the day, let alone for two hours.

She called Ben. He was going to be furious with her for not being at Rose's yet.

"Hey, Mum, you all right? Nana and I are watching the snooker."

Since when had her mother taken an interest in snooker?

When she arrived an hour later, Ben and his grandmother were drinking tea and eating Kit Kats. They were still glued to the snooker.

"It's getting so exciting," Rose said to Barbara. "The one in the green waistcoat just made a break of a hundred and thirty in the opening frame."

Barbara looked a question at Ben.

"I've been teaching her," he said. "She really seems to be enjoying it."

"Now I need to go and have a pee," Rose said. "Damn. I don't want to leave the game."

Ben reminded her that all she had to do was press the "live pause" button on her remote.

"I know, but I don't like using it."

"Why?"

"Because it's not fair on all the other people."

Ben started laughing. "What? No. . . . The other people carry on watching."

"But how can they if I've just paused the program?"

"You haven't paused it for everybody. It only affects your TV."

"No! Really? Well, that is clever. The things they think of."

Barbara asked Ben to make them all another cup of tea. Rose disappeared to the loo, happy now to put the TV on live pause.

"So, Mum," Barbara said when she returned, "about this music you're still hearing . . ."

"Ben says I'm not to worry and that I'm definitely not going gaga. It's just a problem with my ears. Is he right?"

"I think so. I've looked it up on the Internet, but we still have to get your hearing checked out."

Barbara said she would make an appointment and go with her.

"I'm perfectly capable of going on my own," Rose said. It wasn't that she minded being looked after; she didn't. In fact, she relished it because it gave her a chance to criticize the quality of the tending—particularly where Barbara was concerned. What she hated was being patronized and treated like a child.

But Barbara insisted on coming.

"Thanks for stepping into the breach today," Barbara said to Ben as she drove them home. "I really appreciate it. Did you apologize to the policewoman and thank her for all her trouble?"

"I did."

"Good boy."

"Actually, Nana and I had fun. She got out all the old family albums. . . . So did you get your meds?"

Barbara said that she did. She also explained that she'd been signed off work. She didn't mention the second panic attack because she didn't want to worry him. Nor did she say anything about how distraught she was feeling about having to say good-bye to all her kids.

"Come on, Mum. Cheer up. Dad said you're going to try your hand at tutoring. You'll be brilliant at it. And the meds will sort you out in no time."

"You reckon?"

"Absolutely. . . . So what's for dinner?"

She was unloading the dishwasher—a prebedtime ritual because it saved time in the morning—when she heard Frank's key in the door.

He kissed her and asked how she was doing.

"Not great, to be honest." She loaded a stack of dinner plates into one of the kitchen cupboards. "Frank."

"What?"

"Please don't go to Mexico. I'm not well, and I don't want to be on my own." She hadn't planned on asking him to abandon his trip. It just came out.

"What? But I have to go. It's all arranged."

"Couldn't you unarrange it—just this once? I really need you around just now, and it would do us good . . . give us time to reconnect. Forget about the money—we'll work it out somehow."

"I can't forget about the money. I have to keep earning. I'm sorry you're going through a rough patch, but maybe we can spend a couple of weeks together when I get back."

"But I'm scared. What if I'm cracking up?"

"Bar, calm down. You've had a couple of panic attacks, that's all.

It means you need to slow down for a while, but it doesn't mean you're cracking up. And you're strong. You'll come through this. I promise. Plus you've got Jean and Ken. Ben's around. God knows he's not exactly busy. And Jess is only down the road."

She put down the clean Le Creuset casserole dish she was holding. "You're simply incapable, aren't you?"

"Incapable of what?"

"Of showing me the remotest concern or sympathy."

"That's ridiculous. I was scared shitless when I thought you'd had a heart attack. What more do you want?"

"I want *you*."

"You've got me. I'm here."

"No, it's the Mexicans and the rest of your third-world victims who've got you. They will always have you. I never will."

"Oh, stop being such a drama queen."

"A drama queen? Is that how you see me?"

"Yes. You're blowing everything out of proportion. I do my best. If that's not good enough, then I don't know what else I can do."

"As usual, I have to put up or shut up."

He didn't say anything.

She picked up the Le Creuset again and went to put it away. Inside she was raging. She was furious with Frank for calling her a drama queen, for neglecting her all these years. Mostly she was furious with herself for putting up with it. But at the same time, her internal debate continued. Was she too greedy for love? How much did she deserve?

"So when do you go?" she said.

"A week from Sunday."

"And when will you be back?"

"I dunno. A couple of months. Could be more. Look, I know it feels like I'm neglecting you. . . ."

"It doesn't just feel like it. You *are* neglecting me."

"And I'm sorry. I admit that this job couldn't have come up at a worse time. But I'll keep checking in. We'll phone and Skype. You have got me. Honestly. Come on. . . . You'll be fine."

"And if I'm not fine?"

She allowed him to draw her towards him and put his arms around her.

"You will be," he said, stroking her hair. "I know you will."

Chapter 5

Sunday, midday, and the hipsters were up and about and piling into the Green Door—the young men in artfully arranged woolly hats and big headphones, the Etsy entrepreneur girls in their pastel lace-up brogues and big horn-rimmed specs. Barbara was waiting tables. Jess and Matt had done their best to persuade her to stay at home and take it easy, but helping out at the Green Door on a Saturday or Sunday was part of Barbara's routine. She looked forward to it. On top of that, Jess and Matt needed her. They took turns taking weekends off to spend time with the kids. Today it was Jess's turn. Right now she was upstairs helping Atticus and Cleo make a farewell cake for Frank. He was leaving for Mexico the following morning, and Jess had organized a family dinner. Barbara supposed that she should have been the one organizing Frank's send-off, but she was too angry with him.

Barbara had been on her medication a couple of weeks—not that it had kicked in yet—and she worried about getting more panic attacks. On the upside—such as it was—Sandra had assured her that having been signed off work for health reasons, she would receive her salary until the end of term. Everybody told her to think of the next few weeks as a paid holiday. She did her best, but the feelings of emptiness and hopelessness continued. Then there were the times when she felt as if her entire being—body and soul—were about to disappear, fuse with the ceiling or the sky. Jean said that sounded like a different form of panic attack. She told her that when it happened she should pinch herself or tug at her hair. "Apparently, the pain brings you back—helps you to reconnect with the world." It seemed to work—as did playing "Bat Out of Hell" at full volume.

When she went back to school to say good-bye, Sandra said she hoped Barbara was starting to "buck up" and reiterated her advice about long walks. Barbara said she was swimming most days. "Jolly good. That's the ticket."

She still doubted that Sandra had put much effort into trying to save her from the sack. She was still cross with her, but not as cross as she had been. Sandra might be a bit weak, but she was well-meaning. She did her best. And even if she had tried to fight Barbara's dismissal, she wouldn't have won. Barbara knew how these things worked. The department always knew they had the upper hand and would have refused to budge. Sandra wasn't lying when she said the whole thing was a fait accompli.

"I do feel like I'm deserting the kids," Barbara said at one point. "It feels so mean to be going off to tutor privileged children for private-school entrance exams. I know smart middle-class kids have problems, but they will never need me the way the Jubilee kids do. And I need to be needed. I can't help it. That's who I am."

"And I have every faith that once you're over this wobble, you'll find your niche again. What you must do is stop worrying."

A "wobble." That's how she saw it.

On the grounds that Barbara hadn't chosen to leave and it was breaking her heart to go, she asked Sandra not to organize a leaving do for her. Sandra agreed. She did, however, organize a gift. The staff clubbed together to get her a two-hundred-pound Conran Shop voucher. Barbara couldn't have asked for a better present. The nearest she'd come to owning something from Conran was pressing her nose against the shop window and salivating over a Philippe Starck chair or a piece of Danish glass.

Before she left she made Sandra promise that she would keep a special eye on Troy. "You have my word," Sandra said.

Barbara gave Sandra a hug good-bye, but despite feeling more warmly disposed towards her, it wasn't as heartfelt as it might have been.

Afterwards she took a final wander around the school. When she got to her room, she found herself patting the walls. Afterwards, she went up to the staff room to say her farewells. Since it was lunchtime, nearly everybody was there. People hadn't seen her since she'd been stretchered off the premises. They all wanted to know how she was doing. After she'd explained that she'd been ordered to rest, there were more hugs, tears and promises to keep in touch. She'd known some of these people for two decades. Leaving wasn't just breaking her heart. It was killing her.

She had no idea how she was going to cope with saying good-bye to "her" kids. She headed downstairs and into the playground. They, too, hadn't seen her since she'd been carted off in the ambulance. As soon as they caught sight of her, a small crowd came running towards her.

"Miss, miss . . . are you better now, miss? Are you coming back to school? We've really missed you, miss."

Barbara explained that although she was feeling much better, she wouldn't be coming back to school.

"Ohhh!"

"But why? Is it because really you're dying, miss, and you don't want to tell us?"

She assured them that she absolutely wasn't dying. "I'm leaving because I've been sick and I need some rest."

A couple of bottom lips trembled. Armani threw her arms around Barbara's waist. "You're my favoritest teacher ever, miss. Please don't go."

"Tell you what—I'll write you all letters to let you know how I'm getting on and you can send me all your news. How's that?"

That seemed to cheer them up.

Barbara noticed that, as usual, Baillie and Kane were hanging back, not saying anything. She went and gave each of them a hug and told them how much she was going to miss them. For once they both managed a smile.

She couldn't see Troy. Maybe it was for the best. If anything was tearing her apart, it was deserting him. Then he appeared, running out of the main door. He looked forlorn.

"My mum said you were leaving. So, are you going right now this very minute?"

"I am. I'm so sorry, Troy. I'm really going to miss you. But I promise I will keep in touch."

"No, you won't. You're lying. You'll forget about us."

"Troy, I couldn't possibly forget about any of you."

"Yes, you will."

"No," she said emphatically, her eyes filling up. "I won't."

By now the others had wandered off. She crouched in front of him and took his hands in hers. "I want you to promise me something. If anybody hurts you or tries to hurt you again, you will tell your class teacher or Mrs. Nichols. Please, please promise me."

Troy looked at the ground.

"No, that won't do. Sweetheart, I know your mum doesn't want anybody to find out about what happened, but you're just a little boy. If anybody hurts you, it's important to speak up. Do you understand?"

He shrugged. That was the best she was going to get.

"I'll be thinking about you."

He ran off. No hugs. No tears. Just his back turned against her.

Barbara walked across the playground and out of the school. There was the familiar clang of the gate as she closed it behind her.

As she ran around, trying to remember who wanted the soy no-foam latte, who wanted the half caff at a hundred and twenty degrees, who wanted "one of your amazing gluten-free cardamom thingies," Barbara was able to stop ruminating about Frank abandoning her and the loss of her job. Rose was always saying how being busy "takes you out of yourself." Not that these days her mother knew much about being busy. But she was right. Being rushed off her feet helped Barbara forget her problems. Plus she found the hipsters amusing.

"You know those nights when you're finding it hard to sleep? Has it occurred to you, like, maybe you're awake in somebody else's dream?"

"Do you think it's OK to dump a guy because he has a rubbish mustache?"

"Where are we gonna eat tonight? Who's up for global fusion ?"

"So is your dress vintage or preloved?"

"I loved her latest piece. The woman totally boogies in the VDU of her existence."

Those who weren't hanging out with friends were sitting behind their MacBooks, punching up their movie scripts or latest Web design. Occasionally they paused to take photographs of their food with their iPhones.

A gang of women had colonized a table by the window. They were spreading raw Himalayan honey on their scones and discussing their dyke visibility.

"Excuse me," a waifish girl called out to Barbara. "Do you have a vegan menu?"

"Actually, we don't, but we do have an excellent red lentil bake today, which is vegan."

"I'm allergic to red lentils. Maybe I'll have the chicken salad. Is the chicken organic?"

Barbara duly recited her script, opting to mention that chicken wasn't strictly vegan. But, yes, the chicken was a hundred percent organic and had been raised with enough space to express its distinctive behaviors. It had been fed on goat's milk, alfalfa and cottonseed meal.

As she was taking Waifish Girl's order, Barbara noticed Brian and Eric sitting at a table by the door. They were American actors who had temporarily relocated from New York to London after Eric landed a part in *Ripper Street*. The men were also dads to Travis. Travis was black, cute as a button and spoke mainly French.

Barbara made her way over to their table.

"Hey, *bonjour*, Travis—*comment ça va?*"

"*Bien, merci. Et toi?*"

"*Tres bien, aussi.*"

In her best Franglais, Barbara asked Travis what he would like to eat.

"Quinoa and black-bean wrap," he replied, opting for English. Of course. What else would an eight-year-old ask for? What's more, he pronounced it "kee-nwar," the way you're meant to.

The first time Barbara heard the family speaking French, she asked the dads if Travis was from Haiti. She assumed that Brian and Eric had adopted him after the earthquake.

"Oh, no," Eric said. "He's from the Bronx."

Apparently, a child raised to speak French was the latest must-have accessory in Brooklyn.

Yet again it occurred to Barbara how bemused elderly East Enders must be by this latest wave of trendification. It was one thing ordinary middle-class people like Barbara and Frank moving in, renovating old properties and sending house prices rocketing—a consequence that elderly residents appreciated but younger ones who were trying to get on the property ladder most definitely did not. But what did they make of the hipster-and-hummus brigade with their artisan soap shops, froufrou boulangeries and mandolin festivals? She supposed they'd seen it all before. Not so many years ago Barbara's generation had gone around in antiestablishment Afros and afghans. These days young people demonstrated their independent expression and countercultural politics by riding fixie bikes and playing their music on vinyl.

By one o'clock people were queuing for tables and Matt and the other weekend helpers seemed to be doing a brisk trade at the counter. Even though they were owed money, Barbara couldn't understand how the Green Door wasn't turning a decent profit. Jess said it was the location. The deli was hidden down a side street. This didn't matter at the weekends because all the locals knew where to find them, but during the week there wasn't much passing trade. They'd made a terrible mistake, and she would give anything to turn back the clock.

By the end of the day, Barbara was exhausted—but in a good way. Her body was tired, but her mind, having been forced to lie fallow for a few hours, felt relaxed. While Matt and the others swabbed tables and counters, she mopped the floor. When everything was done, the helpers left and Barbara and Matt headed upstairs.

Frank was already there. He was sitting on the sofa, his arm round Jess. They were drinking wine and going through a giant box of family photos. The box had lived with Jess and Matt for a couple of years—ever since Jess had volunteered to transfer the pictures into albums. She still hadn't got around to it. At the same time, everybody agreed that whenever they were overcome with the urge to see pictures of Frank in flares and a droopy mustache, it was probably more fun to tip them onto the floor and rummage.

"Umm, something smells good," Barbara said.

"Lasagna." Jess had made two for the deli plus one more that she'd kept back for tonight. She offered her mother a glass of wine.

"No, don't get up," Barbara said. "You're covered in photographs. I'll get it."

Barbara headed to the kitchen.

"No, Grandma. You mustn't come in!" It was Atticus. "You have to keep out. It's a surprise."

"But I only want to get a glass of wine."

"You can't," Cleo said.

Matt called out to Cleo, telling her not to be so rude. Then he went into the kitchen to fetch Barbara a drink.

"They're icing a secret bon voyage cake for Dad," Jess said in a stage whisper.

"At least somebody loves me," Frank said to Barbara.

Barbara rolled her eyes but let the remark go. Matt handed her a glass of wine and said he needed to get back to the kitchen to supervise icing operations.

"Oh, look at you in this picture," Frank said to Jess. "You were about to start school and Mum had taken you to get your hair cut. I loved you with that fringe. You looked so cute. Why don't you wear your hair in a fringe anymore?"

"That would be because it makes me look like a cute five-year-old."

"That's what I like about it."

"I wish you weren't going away for so long," Jess said.

"Can't be helped. It isn't easy going to a country like Mexico and trying to infiltrate its health system."

"When you say 'infiltrate'—you're not going to be doing all that hidden-camera stuff, are you?"

"Probably."

"I really worry about you. What if you get arrested?"

"I'm not going to get arrested."

"You don't know that."

"On the upside," Frank said, "prison would be a great dieting opportunity. At least I'd lose some of this." He patted his belly.

"Idiot," Jess said, smiling.

Frank put down his glass and gave her a cuddle. "Come on, it won't be so bad. We can Skype."

"No, we can't. Not when you're in the back of beyond."

Frank and Jess had always been close. Barbara supposed it was the father-daughter thing. Daughters and dads forged special bonds. Not that it was saying much, but Barbara supposed she had been fairly close to her own father. That said, there were times when Barbara couldn't help feeling jealous of Jess's relationship with Frank. It didn't take hold very often, but it was happening now, as she watched the two of them snuggling on the sofa. It had happened a few weeks ago. Frank had been getting ready to go to some posh dinner and Jess and the kids were visiting. Instead of asking Barbara what tie he should wear, he'd asked Jess. She hated herself for feeling the way she did. Barbara adored her daughter and knew full well that Jess wasn't trying to "steal" Frank or usurp Barbara's position in the family. This was all about her feeling neglected by Frank. She was directing her anger at Jess. It was wrong, and she knew she should curb her feelings.

The sound of the downstairs doorbell interrupted her thoughts.

Matt went to answer it. Ben and Nana Rose had arrived at the same time. They trooped up the stairs, Nana panting and grumbling about how steep and narrow they were.

She came into the living room, hand clamped to her chest. "Next time when I come," she said, "you're going to have to hoist me up by crane."

Jess got up and took Rose's coat. Rose handed her a plastic carrier. This contained a Marks & Spencer chocolate fudge cake plus Snickers bars and M&M's for Atticus and Cleo. Rose never arrived empty-handed. On the other hand, she always seemed to forget that her granddaughter baked for a living and that the children weren't allowed sweets.

"I am absolutely gagging for a cup of tea," Rose said.

"Sit down, Nana," Jess said. "And I'll put the kettle on."

Once again Matt said he would do the honors.

"What a lovely boy," Rose said, lowering herself onto the sofa next to Frank. "But none of that hawthorn and tree-bark stuff you gave me last time. Plain will be fine."

Matt said that he was sure they had some somewhere.

"So, Frank, Barbara tells me you're off on another one of your jaunts."

"Yep, you know me, Rose. A life full of jaunts."

His sarcasm failed to register with his mother-in-law. "I don't know why you don't make a documentary about that Hoff chap."

"Hoff?"

"She means the Hoff—David Hasselhoff," Ben said.

Frank frowned, none the wiser.

"What a life that man's had. The women, the drink, the daughters who've stood by him. People love all that."

"I'll bear it in mind," Frank said.

By now Jess was kneeling on the floor putting photographs back in the box. "Hey, Ben," she said. "Come and see this picture of you with no clothes on, peeing on a flower bed. It's so cute. You were only sixteen."

"Oh, the wit! . . . But at least I grew up knowing how to use loo paper. How's your foray into medieval toilet practices working out? Caught any good diseases yet? Shouldn't be long before the first boils appear in your armpits."

"Very funny. And FYI—the plague was carried by rat fleas."

Ben produced a roll of toilet paper from his shoulder bag. "And FYI to you . . . I intend to make my own arrangements arse-wiping-wise."

"I have loo roll," Jess said. "I'm not forcing guests to use family cloth."

"What's family cloth?" Rose piped up.

Ben was more than happy to oblige with an explanation. "It's toilet paper made of cloth that you wash and reuse."

"Oh my God," Frank said, pulling a face. "Please tell me you're not serious."

Rose was still trying to take in what Ben had said. "What? You mean you wipe your backside and then you wash the cloth?"

"Why is everybody so against this?" Jess said.

"Er . . . let me think," Ben said. "That would be because it's about the most unhygienic thing imaginable."

"No, it isn't. You soak everything in disinfectant before you wash it."

"And you end up with buckets of shitty disinfectanty rags sitting about the place. Nice."

Jess was getting worked up. "Ben, you're such a jerk. What you don't seem to understand is that millions of trees are cut down to make toilet paper. That makes it really bad for the environment. On top of that, when you flush, the mulch goes into the sewers and the chemicals kill fish and make women grow facial hair."

"And which peer-reviewed study did that last piece of information come from?"

"It's common knowledge."

"It isn't common to me."

"Well, I need to spend a penny," Nana said, lifting herself off the sofa with an *oomph*. "Ben, pass me the loo roll."

Jess actually stamped her foot. "I *have* ordinary loo roll." But Nana had already taken Ben's and toddled off.

"OK, you two," Barbara said. "That's enough bickering." She turned to Ben. "Stop teasing your sister. This is hers and Matt's decision. It's nothing to do with you. Now, butt out."

"Your mother's right," Frank said. "I'm sure Jess has views on you not having a job, but she keeps them to herself."

"No, she bloody doesn't," Ben shot back. "She's always calling me a layabout."

"It's true," Jess said. "You are a layabout."

"See what I have to put up with?"

"Jess, that's mean-spirited. You know how hard it is these days for graduates to find jobs. You had it easy in your day. Now, apologize to your brother."

Jess snorted the way she used to when she was a child and Barbara made her apologize to her brother. "Sor-ree."

By now Rose was back. "I only did a number one, so I only needed a couple of squares," she said to Ben, handing him back the loo roll.

In an attempt to steer the conversation away from the family cloth versus loo roll debate, Barbara asked her mother if she was still hearing Glenn Miller. By now Barbara had taken her to see a hearing specialist who had reassured her that she wasn't going senile and had reiterated Dr. Google's advice. Rose needed to fill the silence in her flat.

"Almost gone. I'm doing what the doctor said. I keep the radio on low all day, and it's made a real difference. Funny what your mind can do. I still can't get over how real it sounded."

Barbara noticed that Ben was about to speak. Fearing he was going to start teasing his sister again, she leaped in a second time.

"Journey OK, Mum?"

"Excellent. Taxi turned up right on time. What a lovely driver. As soon as he saw me coming, he got out and opened the car door for me. They can be such gentlemen, some of these colored chappies."

"Mum, please . . . nobody says 'colored' anymore. It's racist."

"Why? I don't mean anything by it. And he was colored."

"He was no more colored than you are."

"He was black. How's that not colored? Black is a color. White is no color."

"OK," Ben whispered to his mother, "watch and learn. See how skillfully I change the subject."

"So, Nana Rose," he kicked off, "what do you think about all these Eastern European immigrants, then?" He grinned at his mother.

"You little sod," she hissed, bashing Ben on the arm.

"Send them all back, that's what I say. Scroungers, the lot of them."

"What about Arek, who owns the Polish grocery shop down the road from you?" Ben said. "You like him, don't you?"

"Oh, now, he's a lovely man. He used to be a chemical engineer back in Warsaw. He's different, though. He's a superior one."

As if on cue, Matt emerged from the kitchen to say that the lasagna was ready to go and that everybody should sit down at the table.

Atticus came in carrying a bowl of salad. Cleo was behind him, both hands wrapped around the bottle of dressing, which no longer had its stopper. Barbara had to resist the urge to take it from her in case she dropped it. Of course she didn't. Instead she placed it carefully on the table.

As usual, Atticus and Cleo were allowed to dominate the conversation. Barbara didn't entirely approve of Jess and Matt's child-centered approach to family mealtimes. She was a great believer in children being encouraged to participate in adult conversation, but she also thought it was important for them to practice listening. That was how they learned.

"I hate lasagna," Atticus harrumphed.

"Darling, you love lasagna," Jess said. "It's one of your favorites."

Matt suggested making him some eggs.

Nana Rose's eyes widened. "Don't you dare, Matthew. Children must learn to eat what's put in front of them."

"But Atticus can be a robust refuser," Matt said.

"So let him refuse. Send him to bed hungry. He won't do it more than once."

It wasn't often that Barbara agreed with her mother, but right now she couldn't have been more on her side. As the family matriarch, Rose had no qualms about speaking her mind. It was a privilege born of age, and nobody took offense. Barbara had yet to earn that privilege. She still caused offense when she voiced opinions contrary to those held by her children.

Atticus, clearly intimidated by his great-grandmother's stern forthrightness, got busy with his knife and fork.

"There you are," Nana Rose said to Matt. "What did I tell you?"

"So," Atticus said through a mouthful of lasagna, "if a starfish fought a crab, who would win?"

Nana Rose told him that it was rude to speak with his mouth full.

"It's not rude," Atticus replied. "Mum says only 'fuck' is rude."

Jess didn't seem remotely embarrassed. "Actually, that's true," she said to her grandmother. "Matt and I aren't very strict on table manners."

Rose gave a regal snort. "So I see."

"Nana," Cleo said. "How old are you?"

"I'm eighty-three years young," Rose said, beaming now.

"That's not young. It's old. So, when are you going to die?"

Rose hooted. "Oh, darling, I don't know. Not for a while, I hope."

"And will you go to heaven?"

"I very much hope so."

"Are there dinosaurs in heaven?" Cleo said.

"If they were good while they were on earth, they will be," Nana told her.

"Why only if they've been good? What if they've been bad?"

"Then they burn in hell," Atticus said. "It's full of flames and people are in agony forever and ever."

"No, they're not! That's horrible. Stop saying those things." With that Cleo punched her brother.

He burst into tears and ran into the bedroom. His sister called after him:

"Ha-ha! Atticus is a crybaby."

Their mother's threat of no cake persuaded the children to call a truce.

After dinner they persuaded everybody to let them show off their juggling skills. Rose made her disapproval clear. Who in their right mind let children play with balls in the house? Something was bound to get broken. Jess assured her that they would be fine. While the adults sat, Atticus and Cleo stood in the middle of the room, two colored balls apiece. Matt had supposedly been teaching them to throw both balls in the air at the same time and catch them with the opposite hand. Each time Cleo attempted this most basic of juggling moves, she dropped both balls. Atticus was only slightly better. After repeated attempts, they both looked close to tears. The adults responded with applause and shouts of: "Yay . . . Well done. Good effort."

Only Rose looked perplexed. "But they were useless," she whispered to Barbara. "Why on earth would you praise failure?"

"Right. I think it might be cake time," Jess announced.

Atticus and Cleo presented Frank with the carrot cake they'd made. It was covered in splodges and smears of red and green frosting (stevia for sweetness, plus natural colorings). On top of this they'd arranged a selection of Lego people and birthday candles. Matt lit them, and the children insisted everybody sing "Happy Mexico to you" to Frank. Afterwards, he blew out his candles.

"Make a wish, Granddad. Make a wish."

Frank made a face to suggest that he was thinking very hard indeed.

"But you mustn't tell anybody," Cleo insisted.

Frank promised he wouldn't.

Barbara watched him as he cuddled his grandchildren and told them how much he was going to miss them. She could tell he'd been touched by the cake and the singing. "Suddenly I'm feeling really sad about going and leaving you all," Frank said.

She wondered how sad he felt about leaving her.

"So, don't go," Rose said. "Stay and make a documentary about the Hoff. That'll put bums on seats."

That night in bed, Frank put his arms around Barbara's waist and began kissing the back of her neck.

"Frank, if you're after going-away sex, I can't do it."

"But I just took a pill," he said. "And it was what I wished for when I blew out my candles."

"Well, you don't always get what you wish for."

"But I don't want to leave with you still angry with me. I hate going away when there's an atmosphere."

"I'm sorry. But you're asking me to make you feel better, and I can't."

"Fine," he said, turning his back on her. "And I'm sorry, too. I'm sorry I can't be the husband you want. But like I said, I do my best."

At seven the next morning Frank and Barbara were standing in the hall waiting for Frank's taxi. Barbara was in her dressing gown, nursing a mug of coffee.

"I'll call you as soon as I land," Frank said.

"Sure . . . Did you remember your indigestion tabs?"

"In my hand luggage."

"Good."

Silence. They'd been like this since they got up: awkwardly polite or silent—neither of them wanting to start a fight.

Ben broke this particular silence. He came thumping down the stairs, his face creased with sleep, his hair looking like a family of small rodents had overnighted in it. He extended his hand towards Frank. "Cheerio, Father. Give the Hun hell."

"Roger that. Good-bye, old bean." The two men shook hands and exchanged backslaps. Ben had invented this gung ho, wartime comedy routine when he was thirteen or fourteen and starting to find paternal displays of affection embarrassing. Frank had been happy to go along with it. But it upset Barbara that they had chosen to stop kissing and hugging. When she'd raised the subject with Frank, he'd told her to stop interfering. It was their relationship, and they would conduct it how they chose. Barbara had realized she had to respect this and did as she was told.

A car hooted.

"Right, that's me." Frank slung his bag over his shoulder.

"Safe journey," Barbara said.

He gave her a kiss on the cheek. "I do love you, you know," he whispered.

She nodded. It was all she could offer.

He wheeled his two enormous suitcases out to the cab. As he looked back, she managed a halfhearted wave. She closed the door. It was then that the familiar feeling crept over her. She knew she deserved to be loved, but at the same time, she couldn't help feeling that by leaving, Frank was punishing her for being bad. And rightly so.

"Mum," Ben said, following his mother into the kitchen, "is everything OK between you and Dad?"

"Sure. Why wouldn't it be?"

"I dunno. Lately you've seemed a bit off with each other."

The comment surprised her. She thought her son existed in an egocentric fog, barely noticing anything that went on outside his own orbit. Clearly she was wrong.

"It's nothing. Your dad's got himself really wound up about this trip. There's been so much to organize. You know what he's like when he's stressed. He's been irritable and it's been getting me down, that's all."

"You sure? 'Cos I was wondering if you were upset with Dad for going away. I'd get it if you were. I mean, what, with you losing your job and having these panic attacks—you could probably do with him being around."

"Are you worrying about my panic attacks?" she asked, remembering Jean's theory about children burying their fears when parents got sick.

"A bit. I'm not used to you being ill."

"I'm not ill exactly. I'm just finding life a bit of a struggle right now. And I'll be absolutely fine without your dad. I don't want you worrying. You've got enough on your plate."

"Come on, sit down. I'll make you a cup of tea."

"Excuse me? You're offering to make *me* a cup of tea?"

He grinned. "I might even be persuaded to make you a slice of toast."

"Good Lord. I'm honored."

"Yeah, but don't start getting the wrong idea. This is strictly a one-off gesture."

"Oh, absolutely."

"And there is a quid pro quo."

"Of course there is."

"Do you think you could get my black jeans washed and dried by tonight?"

Chapter 6

At the age of fifty-eight, she realized she'd never ride through Paris—or even Hackney—in a sports car with the warm wind in her hair. "The Ballad of Barbara Stirling." That first week after Frank left, she found herself singing her own modified version of the Marianne Faithfull song a lot—even though the words "fifty-eight" didn't remotely scan.

Not that she had any particular desire to ride through Hackney in a sports car, since the wind—warm or otherwise—smelled of exhaust fumes and the likelihood was that as soon as she pulled up at a traffic light, some crazy would lob a half-eaten kebab into the car. What she wanted was a future.

But like Lucy Jordan, the lonely housewife in the song, she cleaned the house for hours. Once or twice she even rearranged the flowers. Unlike Lucy Jordan, though, she made no attempt to hurl herself off the roof. Barbara was miserable, but she was nowhere near suicidal.

Instead she tackled all the domestic jobs she hadn't got round to in years. She washed paintwork, sprayed chemicals on the mold around the bath, cleaned away twenty-odd years of gunk from behind the fridge. A full-time job had left her with neither the energy nor the inclination to do much more than a weekly vacuum and dust. That said, she had always given the kitchen floor and the bathroom a quick going-over every day. Her mother had always drummed it into her that a dirty kitchen floor and skid marks in the loo were the mark of a slattern.

With no job to go to, she could really get stuck in. One day she actually found herself bleaching the inside of the teapot.

Mornings were spent mopping, swabbing and dusting. Afternoons were set aside for more challenging tasks like cleaning the oven or turning out the kitchen cupboards. She was aware that she hadn't cleaned the cupboards in months—possibly as many as eighteen or twenty-four—but it still came as a shock to find spiders dead in their webs suspended in the corners.

At the start of the week she also wrote a letter to her kids at Jubilee telling them how much she was missing them. Sandra forwarded the twenty-odd replies. Armani's happened to be the first in the pile. "Dear miss—missing you, miss." Her letter was full of how when she grew up she wanted to be a Kardashian—or babysit small animals, brackets nonevil. She'd drawn a picture of herself with her new hamster called Mr. H. Nearly all the kids had signed off with a picture, self-portraits mainly. They were garish and ham-fisted and none bore the remotest resemblance to the sender, but each one brought tears to Barbara's eyes.

There was nothing from Troy. He was clearly still angry with her for abandoning him. Barbara sat down and wrote him his own letter, telling him again how sorry she was to have left the school and all her special children. She explained that she'd been sick, that she really hadn't wanted to leave and that she thought about him a lot.

When he still didn't reply, she called Sandra to find out how he was doing. "He's fine. If you ask me, he's just cross with you for going and doing his best to make you feel bad."

"Maybe," Barbara said. It was typical of Sandra to write kids off as manipulative when they were crying for attention.

"Stop worrying about him. He's fine. I got a call from Maureen at social services. Tiffany's doing much better, too. No sign of the boyfriend. Things really seem to have calmed down."

That, at least, was something.

"And how are you?" Sandra said.

"I keep finding myself singing 'The Ballad of Lucy Jordan.'"

Sandra laughed. "Don't we all. But you have to stay positive. This isn't the end. I just know something will turn up."

"But what?"

"I don't know. Sometimes life has a way of surprising us."

"Well, in the last few weeks, it's certainly done that."

At lunchtime she tended to take a stroll to the French coffee shop. She would bag the table in the window and sit with a salami salad baguette and a decaf Americano. Dr. Johal had said that caffeine could aggravate panic attacks. She'd thought about registering with one of the tutoring agencies and taking on a few hours of work, but she decided against it. She couldn't risk scaring a child by having an attack while she was tutoring.

Sometimes as the afternoon rolled round, she realized she couldn't face more housework. Then she would go for a swim at the large municipal pool. The place was always full of shouty school-children who left gum on the changing room benches and muddy footprints all over the floor. Half the pool was reserved for the kids. The other half was divided into lanes for people who wanted to swim lengths. Barbara always chose the "Nice 'n' Easy" lane along with the pregnant women and the whiskery old ladies who for some reason favored billowing shower caps over swimming hats. They chugged up and down, the elderly, the expectant and her— mismatched ducks in a row.

When she swam, she concentrated on her breathing. She listened to the lapping of the water, the bellowing of the school kids' instruc- tor. For half an hour every day, she stopped thinking—a bit like she did when she worked at the Green Door.

Frank was based in Mexico City. He phoned every couple of nights. They'd tried Skyping, but the picture kept freezing or one or both of them would turn into pixels. He called ostensibly to find out how she was doing, but he was always full of his own troubles. People who'd promised him and his crew access to psychiatric hospitals now wanted paying. He was also worried that somebody in the Mexican Department of Health had got wind of what they were doing. "I hope to God I'm just being paranoid. If I'm not and things really are going tits up, then we're fucked."

Barbara said she was sorry he was having problems and she meant it. But she didn't really care—not the way she had in the past. How many nights had she spent lying awake with him, offering con- cern and counsel? And how often had he returned the gesture? Now he'd abandoned her when she needed him most. She wasn't sure if she could forgive him. Did she even love him anymore? She cer- tainly couldn't locate any tender feelings. Whenever she looked for some, all she could find was anger.

She was still having the occasional panic attack. She'd had one the night after Frank left. She woke up at three a.m., heart pounding and fighting for breath. As per Dr. Google's advice, she tried to con- vince herself that she was in no danger and that her fear was irratio- nal. But logical thought had no place in this nightmare. The adrenal glands didn't speak English. The panic continued.

Feeling desperate but not wanting to go charging into Ben's room and frighten him, she reached for the scrap of paper on which she'd written the number for one of the twenty-four-hour panic helplines. She picked up the phone and dialed.

On the first ring, a tepid female voice came on the line in the form of a recorded message. "Helloo," she cooed, not so much a counselor as a new and rather shy neighbor trying to introduce herself over the garden fence. "My name is Paul-een and you are having a panic attack."

You think?

"You will get better."

Barbara could hear the trembling in Pauline's voice. To say she didn't sound exactly sure would be putting it mildly.

"No, I won't, you idiot. Can't you see I'm dying here?"

"What I need you to do is place your hand on your abdomen and breathe with me. Here we go. . . . In one, two, three, four . . . and out two, three, four. Are you starting to feel better?"

"No. I'm hyper-fucking-ventilating and seconds from passing out."

What happened next startled her, but it stopped her from passing out. For some reason—probably because she'd messed up the setting—the radio alarm went off. Suddenly she was listening to a late-night football phone-in. A player had fouled an opponent in some important playoff a few hours before, and everybody was up in arms that the referee had chosen to ignore it. Barbara couldn't have been less interested, but she forced herself to listen and concentrate. As she did, her symptoms eased. She realized that her brain couldn't panic and concentrate on the radio at the same time.

Dr. Johal had warned her that while she was waiting for the medication to start working, the panics would continue. But for how long?

By now she was exhausted. She sank back into the pillows and eventually nodded off. It was past nine when she woke. She was making a cup of tea when Jean called to ask how she was doing. Barbara told her about the latest attack. Jean assured her that the pills would take effect soon, but meanwhile she had to be patient. "Tell you what—my shift finishes at two. I need to go home and get changed. Why don't we meet for a cuppa around four?"

They decided on Le Salon de Thé in Islington. The chap serving insisted on taking them through the entire tea menu—the Assams, the Darjeelings, the China black teas. Then there were the flavored teas: autumn cranberry, blue ginger, chocolate mint.

When they told him that regular English Breakfast would be fine, he seemed genuinely disappointed. They ordered scones and homemade jam just to cheer him up.

"I'm so sorry you're going through all this," Jean said. "You don't deserve it."

"I'm just so scared."

"Of?"

"The panic attacks, the future . . . Without my job, I feel I've lost my sense of self. It feels as if my life is over, that there's nothing left for me."

She told Jean how she sometimes got an image in her head of an old hag with a grizzled claw beckoning her over the hill towards lonely cronehood.

Jean laughed. "Oh, behave. These days, sixty is nothing." She bit into her scone. "Look, I know I keep saying it, but you will get better. Whoever invented SSRIs deserves a bloomin' Nobel Prize. They do work, but it takes a while."

"Well, I wish they'd get a bloody move on."

"Meanwhile," Jean said, "I've got something that'll cheer you up. I think I may have found you a tutoring gig."

Jean had a friend who had a friend who was looking for somebody to tutor her ten-year-old son for his private-school entrance exam.

"But what if I have a panic attack while I'm with him? It would freak him out. No, I've decided I should wait a bit longer before I think about doing any work."

"Barbara, you've just been telling me that you feel your life is over. This isn't the time to walk away. Yes, panic attacks are scary, but you can't live in fear of the fear. Plus they *will* stop. Come on. It's not like you to walk away from a challenge." Jean took a piece of paper out of her pocket. "I've written down this woman's contact details." She slid the paper across the table.

"I know it's not like me, but for once in my life, I'm really frightened." Barbara read the name: Sally Fergusson. There was a phone number and an e-mail address.

"I know you are, hon. But think what Pam would say: 'Face the fear and do it anyway.'"

Barbara snorted.

"But in this case she'd be right. You mustn't let fear take over."

Barbara carried on staring at Sally Fergusson's details. "OK. I'm not happy, but I'll do it." Barbara picked up the piece of paper and put it in her bag. "And thank you. You've been such a good friend while I've been going through all this. I don't know what I would have done without you."

"You don't have to thank me," Jean said, topping up Barbara's cup. "Just get back out there."

It was only now that Barbara noticed what Jean was wearing. "By the way, I'm loving that top."

"I wondered if it was a bit too low-cut. You don't think it looks tarty?"

Barbara assured her it was perfect and that the raspberry shade complemented her blue eyes.

"And I got this little skirt to go with it," Jean said, standing up to show off the raspberry-and-navy tweed pencil skirt. "I thought it had a touch of Chanel about it."

Barbara agreed that it did. "Fabulous."

"You don't think the tweed makes me look fat?"

"Oh, for crying out loud. Turn you sideways and you'd disappear."

"Actually, I think maybe I *have* lost a few pounds." Jean was glowing. As she sat down, she tucked her hair behind her ear. There was something almost coquettish about the way she did it.

"You're off to see Jenson, aren't you?"

"How do you know?"

"The sexy new top? The skirt? The fact that you've lost weight."

"Well, I like to look nice when I go there."

"Jean—are you falling for this guy?"

"Don't be ridiculous. Of course I'm not. We have an arrangement. It's sex. Damn good sex, I admit, but it's nothing more. He goes back to his life. I go back to mine."

"And you never fantasize about being a part of his life?"

"Once in a while maybe. A girl is entitled to the occasional soppy dream. But the truth is that where Jenson is concerned, my feet are firmly fixed on the ground."

"You sure?"

"Positive."

That evening Barbara e-mailed Sally Fergusson. She called the following day sounding pathetically grateful that Barbara had got in touch.

"I'll be honest with you," Sally said. "We've been through quite a few tutors, but Freddie hasn't responded very well to any of them."

"And why do you think that is?" Barbara asked, alarm bells positively clanging.

"They didn't challenge him. It's the same at school. Without the proper stimulation, he refuses to work. His teacher says he's lazy. She says he daydreams all the time instead of getting on with his work. But Freddie is really bright. I know that with the right coaching he'll walk into a decent school."

Barbara asked if she could meet Freddie. They made a date for after school the following Thursday.

On the morning of her appointment with Freddie—domestic chores abandoned for once—Barbara started on her reading. Despite having a literature degree, there were so many classics she'd never got round to reading. This break from work would be the perfect opportunity for her to catch up. A few days ago she'd printed out *Newsweek*'s list of the hundred best books ever written. She'd ordered *The Iliad* and *The Odyssey*, which had arrived first thing. By midday she'd given up on both on the grounds that there were too many "rosy-fingered dawns" and "wine-dark seas."

After an early lunch she went for her induction session at the "nonjudgmental gym." She had joined after Christmas in a fit of post-Christmas-gluttony angst but had found endless excuses not to go. Only recently had it occurred to her that since swimming was having such a calming effect on her mind, the treadmill and stepper might do the same. So she arranged to have her induction. Ten minutes in, she walked out—on the grounds that the nonjudgmental gym was too judgmental. She was surprised she'd lasted as long as she did. She should have realized from the beginning that things weren't going to end well.

"Sorry," Barbara had said to the skinny orange girl in a Juicy Couture tracksuit. "But I'm not having you grasp my spare tire with those calipers. You can see I'm overweight. Can't we just leave it at that?"

Barbara had been expecting a chilled dude with dreadlocks, not Paris Hilton.

Apparently they couldn't leave it at that. Orange Girl, whose name was Chanel, had boxes to tick. The calipers were applied. A sharp intake of breath from Chanel. Barbara had a body mass index of thirty.

"So, Barbara, have you considered cutting out carbs?"

"I watch my carbs, but why would I want to cut out an entire food group?"

"OK, if you're not keen on doing that, people do say vinegar shots are good appetite suppressants."

"Lovely. I'll bear that in mind."

"But personally," Chanel said with a flick of her hair extensions, "I'm into the Facial Analysis Diet. If you don't mind me saying, your face is looking a little red and puffy. That could indicate you have a dairy intolerance."

Barbara leaned forward in her seat. "Chanel, tell me something. Have you been through menopause?"

"You trying to be funny? I'm twenty-two."

"Then let me explain something to you. When your ovaries shrivel and die, as yours surely will one day, your estrogen levels will fall, giving you hot flashes, wrinkles, a dry vagina—oh, and excess fat around your middle. For some women this weight is very hard to lose."

"I'd have it all lipoed."

"I don't doubt that for a second. But as we get older, some of us try to accept ourselves as we are and recognize that we bring more to the party than a size-eight figure."

"What party?"

It was then that Barbara made her excuses and left.

The Fergussons' cream stucco Victorian villa formed part of a grand Islington square that overlooked a pretty communal garden. Ornate railings protected the lawn and flower beds from incursions by undesirables. Each resident would have a key, though. Barbara imagined the summer drinks parties: women in floaty pastels, men in linen suits and Panama hats—all knocking back Sea Breezes.

You couldn't get farther from the Orchard Farm Estate than this. The irony was that most of the people who lived in this part of town thought of themselves as liberals. They voted Labour. They read the right newspapers, held politically correct views. But they preferred to hold them from behind their original Victorian shutters. Not that the area didn't have its underprivileged multiethnic bits. The rich liberals liked this, too. They were virtually rubbing shoulders with the needy. How intrepid was that?

Sally Fergusson opened the front door accompanied by an ochre Labrador who immediately launched itself at Barbara, depositing muddy paw prints on her silk scarf.

"Gosh. I am so sorry. Bertie—naughty boy. Down." Sally grabbed the dog's collar and did her best to pull him off, but he was too busy licking Barbara's face. "You must be Barbara. . . . How do you do? I'm Sally. Bertie! No! . . . He does get rather excited when we have visitors." She gave one final tug on the animal's collar. "That's better. Good boy." She shooed him down the basement stairs.

"No harm done," Barbara said, looking at the marks Bertie had left on her hundred-quid scarf.

Sally was exactly as Barbara had imagined—shoulder-length blond hair, the color accentuated by subtle tones of honey and corn—at more than three hundred quid a pop. She was wearing it in the standard posh-mummy half updo. The top and sides had been pulled back and were held in place with a barrette. It was a look that Barbara didn't much care for. She thought it made women look like little girls. All Sally needed was a school blazer, a violin case and a patch over her lazy eye. Not that she had a lazy eye. Both of Sally Fergusson's gray eyes darted with nervous energy.

Barbara followed Sally and Bertie downstairs into the vast basement kitchen. Barbara took in the built-in deep-fat fryer and indoor barbecue, the fancy Italian coffeemaker that clearly never got used, since there was a jar of instant sitting on the countertop. Unless, of course, that was for the help, which, thinking about it, it probably was.

Sitting on the sofa, staring into his Xbox, his thumbs going like pistons, was a handsome, fair-haired boy, his arms still tanned from the family's winter break. His long legs were tucked underneath him. Barbara was in no doubt that this child was a full head taller than the average ten-year-old at Jubilee. "Stunted urchins," Sandra called them.

"Freddie, this is Barbara. Do you remember me saying that she'd be popping in?"

Freddie looked up. "I don't want another tutor. I've already told you." He went back to his Xbox.

"He's just a bit shy, that's all," Sally said.

Barbara wasn't sure that shyness was his issue.

"Freddie, while Barbara and I have a chat, would you like a snack?"

"What is there?"

His mother ran through a list of options.

"Cheese and onion crisps and a Snickers," he said. There was no "please." Nor did Sally demand one.

She went to fetch her son's snacks. When she returned, she put them on the coffee table next to him. He didn't look up, let alone offer her a thank-you.

Sally made tea, and the two women sat at the island at the other end of the kitchen, out of Freddie's hearing. Sally explained that she and her husband, Jeremy, were both bankers. He was working in Hong Kong for the next month or so. She was off to Washington the next morning for a meeting with representatives from the IMF. That was why she'd been able to finish work early today—to prepare and pack.

"We're always flying from hither to yon," she said with an eye roll. "It's so hard on poor Freddie. I'm sure he feels we neglect him."

"It can't be easy," Barbara said. So that was why Sally didn't discipline her son. She felt guilty about being away so much.

Sally explained that, for the most part, Freddie was looked after by au pairs. "They've all been useless, though. In fact, I had to let another one go this morning. The moment Freddie has a tantrum, they can't handle him. I need somebody with a sense of humor who doesn't make a drama out of everything."

Until Sally found a new, undramatic au pair, Freddie's granddad would be coming down from Gloucestershire to look after him.

Barbara asked Sally why she thought Freddie had tantrums.

"Simple. As I said on the phone, he's not being sufficiently challenged at school. The upshot is, he's become unmotivated. He's either having tantrums or daydreaming and not getting on with his schoolwork. That's why we're frantic with worry that he won't get into a good school."

"I see. And what does his teacher say?"

"She wants him to see a child psychologist."

"And you don't think he needs to?"

"No, I don't." She clearly found the suggestion outrageous, bordering on offensive. "Freddie behaves like he does because he isn't getting what he needs. Of course he's lagging behind. The poor child is bored. That said, Jeremy and I should take our share of responsibility. We were the ones who decided to send him to a state school. We wanted to do the right thing—you know, let him mix with children from different backgrounds and ethnic groups for a few years—but it was clearly the wrong decision. There are thirty-odd kids in a class. Some of them don't speak English, and if you ask me, Freddie is being ignored."

Barbara asked if she could have a chat with him.

"By all means."

She went over to the sofa. "Hey, Freddie, mind if I sit down?"

A shrug. She took this as an invitation to sit.

"So what are you playing?"

"*Lego Movie.*"

His mother, who was hovering nearby, was quick to point out that the game was purely cartoon knockabout violence and had absolutely no blood or gore. "Jeremy and I are pretty fanatical on that score."

"Is it good?" Barbara asked Freddie.

"It's a bit tame." His eyes were glued to the screen. Those thumbs were still going.

"And we're very strict about limiting his screen time to an hour a day."

"So what else do you like doing, apart from playing computer games?"

"Dunno."

"Oh, come on, Freddie. You go to football club twice a week. You love that."

"I don't. I hate it. I'm hopeless at all sports. Everybody laughs at me." He paused. "I like drama though. I played Bono in the school nativity play, and I got to sing in front of everybody."

"Freddie's school takes a peculiarly secular approach to Christmas," Sally said. "I'm not sure I approve, but Freddie was magnificent."

"I bet he was," Barbara said. She turned back to Freddie. "So . . . you don't want another tutor."

"No. I hate tutors. They suck."

"What makes you say that?"

"They make me do fractions and decimals."

"And you don't like that?"

"It's boring. It's what I do all day at school. I don't want to come home and do more."

Barbara said she understood. "Tell you what, if I made a really big effort to make the time we spend together as unboring as possible, would you give me a chance?"

"You can't. It's always boring."

"It doesn't have to be. Why don't you give me a try? Just once."

"Just once?"

"Yep, and if I don't measure up, you can sack me."

Another shrug. "Fine, whatever."

Barbara and Sally agreed—assuming Freddie didn't give her the sack—that he would have two one-hour sessions a week, on Tuesdays and Thursdays.

"Freddie, Barbara's going now. Come and say good-bye."

A grunt from the sofa.

"He's still a bit wary of you," Sally said. "But I'm sure he'll come round.

"Freddie," his mother called out again. "I need you to take a bath now. We're going to Aunty Pru's tonight, and there won't be time when we get back."

"Later."

"I think now would be better."

"I said *later*."

"OK, if you think you won't be too tired."

The two women said their good-byes. Barbara's polite smile disappeared the instant the front door closed behind her.

The kid was a rude, truculent little despot. Not that it was his fault. It didn't take an expert to see that he'd got like this because his parents neglected him and then tried to compensate by spoiling him and refusing to discipline him. His teacher was right. The child did need to see a shrink. Barbara was used to dealing with problem kids—kids who lashed out, spat and called her a cunt and a slag. But they were poor and deprived. This kid was rich and, God forgive her, she held it against him. But at fifty quid an hour she wasn't about to walk away. She could do it, she reasoned, so long as she kept on reminding herself that rich nutty kids were just as deserving as poor ones.

Frank was delighted that Barbara had found some work. "Even a bit of money coming in makes a difference." But as usual the conversation soon got around to him. He was convinced that he and his crew were being tailed by Mexican government heavies.

"Fabulous," Barbara said. "Something else for me to worry about."

"I'm used to it. They're only trying to frighten us. If they try anything, I'll pay them off. These goons can always be bribed. I keep a wad of cash on me for that very purpose."

"I just hope you know what you're doing."

Ben congratulated Barbara in his usual Ben way: "Well done, Mum. Now go and put the kettle on. I could murder a cuppa."

When Barbara called to tell Jess her news, her daughter couldn't have been more pleased, but it wasn't long before she was quizzing her mother about the natural antianxiety remedies she'd recommended.

"So have you tried any of them?"

"Not exactly," Barbara said.

"What does that mean? Please tell me you're not taking pharmaceuticals."

"Actually, I am."

"But, Mum! How could you? These companies are all corrupt. They make money from filling people with poisons."

Vulnerable as she felt, Barbara wasn't about to be browbeaten. "Listen to me . . . The next time you're having a panic attack and you think you're about to die, feel free to trot off and make yourself a lettuce and valerian sandwich or rub your kidneys in a clockwork direction. I have decided that, flawed as the pharmaceutical industry undoubtedly is, I intend to put my trust in chemicals—at least for the time being. And I would really appreciate it if you accepted and respected my decision."

"But what if you become addicted? Or you get terrible side effects?"

"That's my problem, not yours. If any of that happens, I will take full responsibility and deal with it. Now, please stop trying to tell me what to do."

"Well, at least now you know how it feels when you boss us around."

"Fine. Point taken," Barbara said. "I'll try to do better."

"Mum," Jess said. Her voice had become meek and childlike. "Are you OK? 'Cos I'm really worried about you—particularly as Dad's not around. I've had so much on my mind that I haven't thought about it until now, but he really shouldn't have left you when you weren't well. I should have said something to him."

"Of course you shouldn't. That's not your job. Thank you for worrying, though. I do appreciate it. But once the meds start working I'm going to be fine. And your dad had signed a contract. He had to go to Mexico."

She was determined not to involve Jess in her marriage or turn her against her Frank.

"He does love you, you know," Jess said.

"What on earth made you say that?"

"I dunno. It just occurred to me that you might be sitting on your own thinking he doesn't care about you. But he does. He's just so self-absorbed and taken up with saving the world. That's who he is. I love him to bits, but I know he's not easy."

"I suppose I'm used to it."

"You know, I do realize that you raised me and Ben pretty much on your own. And you were amazing. It's only since I've become a mum that I've started to appreciate how hard it must have been for you. I find every day a struggle—and I've got Matt around."

"You're right. It wasn't always easy."

"Well, I want you to know that I get it."

"Thank you, my darling. I appreciate that."

If Jess had been standing in front of her, she would have hugged the life out of her. She felt ashamed that she'd ever felt jealous of her daughter.

Tuesday arrived and Barbara realized that she hadn't had a panic attack for more than a week. She hesitated to say it, but the pharmaceuticals appeared to be doing their work.

She swam in the morning. After lunch she got started on the first volume (there were seven) of *The Life and Opinions of Tristram Shandy, Gentleman*. She had a degree in English literature. She was used to heavyweight tomes, but this, like *The Iliad* and *The Odyssey*, had her nodding off after half a dozen pages. At three she set off for Islington—armed only with a Monopoly set and a copy of *The Fabulous Fart Machine*.

A gray-haired man with a welcoming smile opened the door. He was wearing a floral Cath Kidston apron. Bertie was nowhere to be seen.

"You must be Barbara," he said, extending his hand. "Jack Dolan, Freddie's grandfather—aka, the temporary au pair."

He had clearly noticed her noticing the apron. "Shrove Tuesday," he said. "Freddie and I have been busy making pancakes. You must come and try one. Although I can't promise it will be the finest you've ever tasted."

"I'd love one," Barbara said, following Jack Dolan downstairs. "I'd completely forgotten it was Pancake Day."

She noticed Bertie fast asleep in his bed next to the radiator.

"Granddad, I flipped this one. I actually flipped it. Yaay." Freddie gave a little jig.

Barbara was taken aback. What had happened to the sullen child she'd met the week before?

"Well done," Jack said. "Now tip it onto a plate, and don't forget to turn the gas out. There's lemon and sugar on the table."

"Hi, Freddie," said Barbara. "How are you?"

"Fine." On seeing her, the excitement left his face. "It's Pancake Day. I don't want to do work."

"He'll buck up once he's eaten. He's just got in from school. Low blood sugar."

Freddie sat down at the table and squeezed lemon on his pancake. "I will not buck up."

"Now, then, Barbara, before you get to work with young Fred, let me make you a pancake." He turned to his grandson. "Or maybe you'd like to make it—show Barbara how it's done."

"Don't want to."

"Come on, don't be like that."

But Freddie refused to make Barbara a pancake.

"In which case," his grandfather said, "I will do it."

Barbara was starting to feel a bit awkward. "Honestly. You don't have to."

"Nonsense. My pleasure."

Barbara and Jack ate their excellent pancakes at the table while Freddie made another one for himself. Only then did she realize how much Freddie and his grandfather resembled each other. The same long legs, the same strong, handsome features—although Jack's had softened a good deal with age and his hair was white. He reminded her of that actor. What was his name? Oh, for heaven's sake. The one who played the handsome silver fox in *Mad Men*.

"So, have you had to take time off work to look after Freddie?" Barbara said, by way of making conversation.

Jack said he was pretty much retired. She asked what he'd done before gave up work.

"I was in the building trade."

Barbara was taken aback for the second time in as many minutes. The diffident English charm, the cut-glass accent, the brogues that she would have put money on being handmade, did nothing to suggest that this was a person who used to throw up house extensions for a living.

"Not that I ever got my hands dirty." He'd clearly read her thoughts. "I ran a building company."

Then it hit her.

"Goodness . . . You're Dolan—as in Dolan's who build half the homes in Britain."

"I wouldn't go quite that far," Jack said. "But, yes, we own a healthy market share."

"So you're the company chairman?"

"Was. I took over from my father, who inherited the business from his father. He was an immigrant Irish laborer and he started the company. I still have a seat on the board. But these days my role doesn't extend to much more than showing up to the occasional meeting."

"So you keep your hand in without any of the stress. Sounds perfect."

"It is rather."

John Slattery. That's who he reminded her of.

He asked her how long she'd been tutoring.

"I probably shouldn't be saying this, but Freddie is my first-ever tutee." She found herself telling him about her job at Jubilee and how she'd been made redundant.

"And I'm guessing that with all the cuts, it won't be easy to find a new job."

"Plus my age is against me. Who's going to employ somebody knocking on sixty?"

"Good Lord. You're nearly sixty? I would never have guessed—not for a second."

"Well, thank you very much," Barbara said. "That's the nicest thing anybody has said to me in a long time. Flattery will get you everywhere."

"No, I mean it. I wouldn't put you a day over forty-five."

"Huh. As old as that?" She watched his face turn pink. "It's OK. I'm only pulling your leg," she said. "I appreciate the compliment. Really."

Still looking uncomfortable, Jack turned to see how Freddie was doing. "Is that the spattering of oil I can hear? Remember what I said about not using too much. That's the secret to great pancakes—a hot pan, not much oil." He carried on watching. A moment later Freddie was tossing his pancake.

"Done it again." Another jig.

"I have to admit I'm puzzled," Barbara said to Jack. "This isn't the boy I met last week. Back then he was sullen and irritable, dishing out orders to his mother. OK, I admit he's not particularly pleased to see me, but otherwise he seems completely different. And if you don't mind me saying—so does Bertie."

"All Fred needs is love, attention and a firm hand. It's the same with the dog. I keep telling Sally and Jeremy, but they seem incapable of grasping it." Barbara got the impression he was about to say more, but Freddie reappeared with his pancake. His grandfather ruffled his head. "Well done that, boy."

"Do I have to do schoolwork?"

"Come on. It's only for an hour."

"And I've brought a brilliant book," Barbara said.

"Not more Roald Dahl."

"Uh-uh." She took the paperback out of her bag.

Freddie managed a smile. His grandfather burst out laughing. "Come on, Fred. A book called *The Fabulous Fart Machine* has to be worth a try."

"I thought we could read bits aloud and then talk about it," Barbara said.

"Only if Granddad can join in."

"Sure . . . Jack—what do you say?"

"If I'm invited, I'd be more than happy to oblige."

Despite its scatological title, *The Fabulous Fart Machine*, invented by a mischievous boy who loved nothing more than causing his stiff and prim parents maximum embarrassment at inappropriate times, was fast becoming a children's classic.

When it was Freddie's turn, he read without a single stumble. He paused at all the right places, understanding instinctively how to read for dramatic effect. He gave the characters comedy voices. More than once he had Jack and Barbara laughing out loud. Afterwards he was able to answer all Barbara's comprehension questions, which she'd disguised as general discussion. His grasp of the vocabulary was excellent, too. She was impressed. Sally appeared to be right about her son. Maybe he wasn't getting the stimulation he needed.

"OK, so, who's for a game of Monopoly?" Barbara said. "Grand-dad can play, too."

Freddie seemed positively eager. Barbara suggested that he be banker. "That means you're in charge of all the money."

Since he hadn't played the game before, much less been banker, Barbara was prepared to give Freddie a good deal of leeway arithmetic-wise. But from the get-go it was clear that he was strug-gling. The average six-year-old could add and subtract better than he could. But he enjoyed the game. It helped that Jack and Barbara rigged things so that he could win. When the hour was up, Freddie was forced to admit that he'd enjoyed himself.

"So can I come again?" Barbara said.

" 'K. But it has to be this good every time."

She promised to do her best.

Freddie helped her pack the game away without being asked. "So, Freddie," Barbara said as he arranged the bank notes in order, "can you help me with something? If it's the fourth today, what's the date going to be a week from now?" She took out her diary to make it look like a genuine inquiry instead of a test.

"I dunno."

"You need to start with four and add seven," Jack said.

"Why seven?"

"Come on, Fred. . . . That's how many days there are in the week."

Freddie began counting on his fingers. "Monday, Tuesday, Fri-day, Wednesday, Saturday . . ."

"OK, not to worry," Barbara said. "So, Freddie, remind me—what month are we in?"

"Winter."

"And can you tell me the months of the year?"

He got as far as April and gave up. "I'm bored. I don't want to do this anymore. Can I go?"

"Don't worry, hon. That's fine. Off you go." Then: "Right, I should get going, too. Freddie, what's the time?"

He stared at his wristwatch. "Dunno. Battery's run down."

Barbara was pretty sure it hadn't.

Freddie handed her the pile of the Monopoly banknotes he'd collected and headed upstairs to his room. Jack asked Barbara if she had time for a cuppa.

"That would be great," she said.

"So," Jack said as they sat drinking more tea. "What do you make of young Fred?"

"Well, his reading and comprehension are excellent. He's a bright kid."

"And his arithmetic?"

"It's hard to say. It's not great, but he could have been a bit anxious because I was there and he felt as if he was being tested. Plus I've only had an hour with him."

Jack put down his mug of tea and crossed his arms. "Come on. I can tell you're holding back. What do you actually think?"

"Goodness, you're really putting me on the spot."

"Sorry. It's my worst habit. My late wife was always telling me that I tend to interrogate people rather than simply show an interest."

Barbara smiled. "Look, I can see that you're worried about Freddie, but I would need more time. It's far too early. . . ."

"Do you think he could be dyslexic? I've been doing some research on the quiet and I know that you can read and write perfectly well and still be mildly dyslexic."

"That's true," Barbara said. "I couldn't say for certain, but it's possible. Like I say, his maths skills aren't great, but then again, kids fall behind for all sorts of reasons. The bigger concern is the way he got confused over the months and seasons and the fact that he can't recite the days of the week in order."

"And his watch hadn't stopped. I know for a fact that it was working perfectly."

"I guessed that." She paused. "And there are other clues. He says he's not great at sports. Lack of coordination can be another sign of dyslexia."

"So do you think he stands any hope of getting into a posh school?"

"Not without a vast improvement. But I can see why his parents think he's a high achiever. His language skills, his comprehension and his vocabulary are all excellent. He really is a smart kid. He's lucky. Not all dyslexic kids are smart—if that's what he is."

"Well, for what it's worth, I think he probably is dyslexic. And all the reading I've done seems to confirm it. In some ways it's not Fred who's the problem. It's Sally and Jeremy. They're both high achievers. The idea of their son being anything less is unthinkable. At the same time, they neglect the poor boy. If you ask me, he's sullen and badly behaved because he's desperate for attention."

"It's possible," Barbara said, doing her best to be diplomatic. It wasn't her place to wade in with her opinion—which was that Sally and Jeremy needed to spend more time with their son and stop compensating for their absence by spoiling him rotten and turning him into a monster. "But there's another problem. Freddie knows he's struggling at school. He probably thinks he's thick. That's another reason he gets so frustrated and angry."

"That makes perfect sense. I hadn't thought of that. So what do we do?"

"He needs to be assessed. After that his parents can take advice about where to go from there."

"They'll never agree to it."

"I'm not sure they have much choice."

Jack asked Barbara if she would speak to Sally. "I'm afraid I tend to charge in like a bull in a china shop. She might take it better coming from you."

Barbara agreed to call her.

This time she came away feeling really sorry for Freddie. Poor neglected little mite. Still, at least his granddad paid him attention and was prepared to fight his corner. Kids like Troy had nobody.

Barbara decided she needed cheering up. She got into her car and hit Jess's number. She would ask if she felt like seeing a movie. Jess hardly ever got out. It would do her good.

"I'd love to, but Cleo has got a temperature and she's a bit chesty. I'm about to call the emergency homeopath."

Barbara bit her tongue regarding the homeopath. "OK, darling. Not to worry. Maybe another time. So, is Cleo very sick?"

"She'll be fine. It's just a chest infection. The homeopath has got her on Pulsatilla. Martha said it worked wonders on Linus."

"Well, give her a big hug from me and say Grandma wishes her better."

"Will do."

Barbara turned the car ignition. Why hadn't Jess taken Cleo to a proper doctor? What was wrong with her? Where had all this alternative hippie, hummusy daftness come from? Certainly not from her or Frank.

She switched on the radio. Paul Simon was singing "Mother and Child Reunion." It occurred to her that she hadn't seen her mother in almost a week. Maybe she should pop over. Not that visiting Rose would cheer her up exactly, but at least it got a chore out of the way. She hated the way she'd come to think of visiting her mother as a chore, but that was the reality. She didn't particularly enjoy seeing her. There was no mutual affection, no bond. All that held them together was blood and—for Barbara—a bucketload of unhappy childhood memories.

"Mummy, I bought you this. I got it with some of my birthday money." Barbara, age eight or nine, jigging with excitement, presents her mother the gift she's wrapped in peach Kleenex and secured untidily with bits of Scotch tape.

"What's this?" Rose says, carrying on with her ironing. Barbara wonders why her mother sounds irritated. Barbara is never annoyed when somebody gives her a present.

"Open it and see." Barbara is still jigging.

Rose turns the iron on its end and begins unwinding the tissue paper. She discovers a china poodle with painted eyelashes and a pink bow in its hair. It's attached to a tiny cart full of pink China roses. It cost a whole two shillings—half of the savings in her money box. Barbara thinks it's the cutest thing ever. She waits for her mother to beam and embrace her and say how much she loves it.

"Very nice. Thank you very much. Why don't you go and put it on the shelf."

"I love you, Mummy," Barbara said.

Rose was examining a stain on one of Stan's shirts. "Oh, for heaven's sake. I've half ironed this thing and now I'll have to wash it all over again."

Barbara pressed the downstairs bell. When Rose didn't answer, she tried again. Still nothing. She hit the bell a third time. Surely her mother wasn't out. Not after seven. Then:

"Hello? Who is it?"

"Mum, what took you so long? It's me. I'm downstairs."

Rose buzzed her in. Barbara took the lift to the third floor.

"I've twisted my ankle," Rose said by way of greeting. "I can hardly walk."

"Oh, for goodness' sake. Why on earth didn't you call me?"

Leaving Barbara to shut the front door, Rose began hobbling back into the living room, grasping bits of furniture along the way. Barbara followed.

"I was waiting for you to call me."

"Because somehow I knew telepathically that you'd twisted your ankle," Barbara said, taking off her coat.

"No. You owe me a call."

This was how her mother had always operated. Ever since Barbara could remember, Rose had kept a mental record of all social calls made and received. Friends—back in the days when she had them—who failed to call her as often as she called them were ignored until they made up their shortfall. Nevertheless, Barbara was surprised her mother hadn't called. She wasn't one to hold back when she was suffering.

"What was the point of calling? There's nothing you can do. I just have to wait for the swelling to go down."

It turned out that Rose's ankle had given way a couple of days ago as she stepped down from the bus that brought her home from the shops. Terry, the building caretaker, had seen her topple over and helped her to her flat. "He's been getting my shopping, bless him. He's such a lovely chap. He'd do anything for you."

OK, now she got it. Rose was feeling neglected and was making her point by not phoning.

As Barbara dropped her keys into her handbag, she noticed a packet of sweets. She'd bought them for her mother days ago and had forgotten about them.

"Oh, I got you some more peppermint creams. You said you'd run out." She handed her mother the packet.

"I've gone off peppermint creams," she said, waving them away. "I'm into toffees again."

Barbara put the peppermint creams back in her bag and felt the familiar feeling of rejection.

Rose maneuvered herself onto the sofa and lifted her foot onto the leather footstool. Her *Thorn Birds* video was playing in the background.

"Mum, can't we turn this off while we talk?"

"No. This is the best bit. It's the beach scene where they make up." Her mother reached into the sweet dish and unwrapped a toffee. "You used to love Richard Chamberlain."

Since her mother clearly wasn't going to offer her one, Barbara helped herself to a toffee. Richard Chamberlain, or to be more specific Dr. Kildare, had been Barbara's first pinup. She'd sent off for a signed photograph, and it had hung over her bed for years—until she'd replaced him with David Cassidy. Even though she'd been in in her forties when she'd discovered Chamberlain was gay, she'd still been upset.

Barbara knelt down and felt Rose's ankle. It was puffy and purple, but her mother seemed to have no trouble moving it.

"It's not broken," Rose said. "Terry's wife's a nurse. She came up and looked at it. She said I'd be in more pain if it was broken."

Barbara was inclined to agree.

"So how are you managing in the bath and getting dressed?"

Rose said she'd had a quick up-and-down wash each morning, but she couldn't manage to get in the bath. Barbara asked if she'd like a bath now, while she was here to help her.

"Well, if it's no trouble. I don't want to put you out."

"You aren't putting me out."

When the bath was ready, Barbara helped her mother into the bathroom and sat her down on the loo lid. "You've forgotten my bath salts," Rose said.

Barbara picked up the jar of lavender bath salts and started sprinkling.

"That's too much. Now you've made the water all slimy."

"No, I haven't. The water's fine. Now, come on. Let's get you undressed."

Barbara hadn't seen her mother naked in decades. Not since before she left home.

"Look at me," Rose said. "I'm nothing more than a sagging old prune." The leg with the good ankle was already in the bath. With Barbara holding her arm, she was able to draw the other one across. "And I used to have such beautiful firm breasts. Look at them now—a couple of empty, shriveled paper bags."

"Oh, stop it. You're eighty-three. Of course you've got a few wrinkles and saggy bits. But your figure's great. You still go in at the waist."

"True—which is more than you do."

"Mum, I just paid you a compliment. I'm not asking for one in return, but could you at least stop criticizing me for five minutes?"

"Oh, stop being so sensitive. You need to take a chill pill."

Little did her mother know that she was on twenty milligrams a day.

"I'm not being sensitive. You're being rude. Now behave, or I won't scrub your back."

Rose snorted and grabbed the handrail on the wall. Barbara carried on supporting her other arm. Gingerly, Rose lowered herself into the water.

Barbara reached for the soap and the loofah mitt.

"Ooh, that is bliss," Rose said. "I can't remember the last time somebody scrubbed my back." She paused. "I can still picture bathing you when you were little. Do you remember how we used to make that unicorn horn with your hair?"

"I do. And I used to hate the way you scrubbed my ears."

"But you know why I did that?"

"Yes, because cabbages would grow in the dirt if you didn't."

"That's right."

"Every day when I shower," Barbara said, "I remember you telling me that."

Rose chuckled. "Ooh, I nearly forgot. Talking of prunes, I must ask Terry to get me some. These days they're the only things that keep me regular."

"Mum, you can't keep asking Terry to do your shopping. He's not your personal butler."

"He doesn't mind. And I always get him a bottle of Scotch at Christmas."

"So what? You're using him, and it isn't right. Just tell me what you need and I'll order your shopping online."

"What? No way. I don't want strangers choosing my fruit and veg. They'll give me any old overripe rubbish."

"But you're happy for Terry to do it."

"He knows how fussy I am."

"OK, I'll do it."

"All right . . . if you're sure."

"I'm sure."

"Well . . . I suppose it's not like you've got a lot on at the moment."

Rose sat in her dressing gown and made a shopping list while Barbara made her mother supper: eggs, lightly poached, on Marmite toast—brown not burned.

The evening traffic was so bad that it took Barbara nearly two hours to get home. She located a year-old spinach cannelloni in the deep freeze and shoved it in the oven. While it was cooking, she poured herself a Scotch and took it into the living room. She sat on the sofa and found herself thinking about ear cabbages. Had she and Rose shared a moment back there?

Chapter 7

Pam had posted a new status update. Oh-em-gee . . . Susan Boyle in concert last night at the Apollo. Voice of an angel. Such an inspiration. *fills up.*

"Gawd . . . Aunty Pam's been to see Subo."

"Thank you, Ben," Barbara said. "I *can* read. And FYI, my Facebook newsfeed is private. Would you mind not peering over my shoulder? And how come you're up so early on a Saturday morning?"

"My day at the food bank."

Her son ambled over to the fridge.

"Of course, you know why women your age are into Subo," he said, taking out a carton of milk. "Because she gives them hope. I mean there they are, sad and middle-aged, their lives practically over, and she's telling them not to give up. So why haven't you and Aunty Jean been to one of her gigs? You're totally her demographic." He began pouring milk over a bowl of Honey Shreddies.

She knew he was taking the piss, but it didn't stop her picking up a tea towel lying on the back of a chair and throwing it at him. It fell onto the floor, a foot or two short.

"Arrogant little sod. How dare you suggest my life is practically over?"

He was grinning as he bent down to pick up the tea towel. "It was a joke. Of course your life isn't over."

"Thank you. And Susan Boyle happens to put a smile on people's faces. What's wrong with that?... Oh, and if you're planning on taking cereal up to your room, don't get milk over the duvet. I only changed the cover yesterday."

He picked up the bowl and turned to go.

"Mark my words," Barbara said. "One day you'll be fat and middle-aged with bushy eyebrows and an enlarged prostate. Wait until your kids call you sad and pathetic. Then you'll be laughing on the other side of your face."

Ben turned round and grinned. "Not gonna happen."

"You reckon?... Oh, and FYI, when I die, I want 'Bat Out of Hell' played at my funeral."

"Really? But Subo's got the voice of an angel. Surely you'd prefer her."

"I want 'Bat Out of Hell' and 'Praise, My Soul, the King of Heaven.'"

"Mum, I don't quite know how to break this to you, but 'Praise, My Soul, the King of Heaven' isn't actually a Meat Loaf song."

"Duh."

"God, you're weird."

"Thank you," she said. "I'll take that as a compliment."

Barbara dutifully "liked" Pam's status update and went to take a shower. She'd promised to do an afternoon shift at the deli. Before that she planned to do a supermarket shop for Rose and drop it round. She had her coat on and was hunting for her keys when the phone rang. It was Sally Fergusson. She sounded tense, and there was a certain amount of throat clearing.

"I just wanted to call and say thank you for seeing Freddie, but we won't be needing you anymore."

She knew that Sally had form, sacking tutors, but she hadn't been expecting to get her marching orders quite so soon. "Goodness. Would you mind telling me why? It's just that I thought our session went rather well."

She came straight out with it. "My son is not dyslexic. I'm horrified that you could even suggest such a thing."

Great. So after he promised not to, Sally's dad had gone wading in.

"Sally, has your father been speaking to you?"

"You made sure you got him on your side, didn't you?"

"This has nothing to do with sides. He's worried about Freddie, that's all, and he asked my opinion."

"I'm Freddie's mother. It's me you should be speaking to, not my father."

She was right. Barbara shouldn't have discussed Freddie with a third party—even if it was his grandfather. "I apologize. It was very wrong of me. But you weren't there, and your dad seemed anxious. Not that that's an excuse. Believe me, I was planning to call you to talk about Freddie."

"I don't understand what there is to talk about. It's simple. Freddie is a highly intelligent child who is simply not getting the stimulation he deserves. Why is it that his father and I are the only people who get it?"

"That's not true. I get it. Freddie is a smart boy. Be in no doubt about that."

"Then how can he possibly be dyslexic?"

"Smart kids can be dyslexic."

"And what gives you the right to diagnose him? Are you an expert?"

"No, I'm not, and I have absolutely not diagnosed him. He would need to be properly assessed. All I've done is voice my concerns."

"Oh, I get it. You've got some kind of agenda. Everywhere you go, you see dyslexia. You're like one of those crazy social workers who think everybody's sexually abusing their children."

"That's ridiculous. I am no such thing, and if you carry on speaking to me like this, I'm going to hang up."

Sally didn't say anything. Barbara decided to take her silence as something approaching a climbdown.

"Look," Barbara said, doing her best to stay calm. "I know you're upset and angry. Why don't I come over sometime? It might be easier if we discussed this face-to-face, and afterwards you can decide whether or not to let me carry on tutoring Freddie."

Sally took a moment to consider Barbara's proposal. "Fine. Whatever. But you'll need to come straightaway. Freddie's at a friend's house for a few hours. I don't want to have this conversation with him around."

Barbara didn't take kindly to Sally's summons to come immediately. Plus schlepping to Islington right now would leave her short of time. There was no way she'd be able to fit in Rose's supermarket shop, let alone drop the groceries in. Her mother would not be pleased. On the other hand, this was about Freddie, and she cared about him. "OK . . . Give me an hour."

She put down the phone and went in search of her mother's shopping list. It was lying on the hall table under her keys. She brought it over to her laptop, went onto the Tesco Web site. Just this once her mother would have to make do with a supermarket delivery.

A bit later she called Rose from the car.

"Well, if the apples come bruised, I'm sending them back. And I like my bananas green—so they last longer. I hope you told them that."

"You don't actually get to talk to a person, but I've done my best."

"But why can't you do my shopping?"

Barbara explained that she'd started doing some private tutoring. "There's this kid who's having problems. His mum is really upset about him and wants to have a chat."

"I see. So I suppose I'll just have to wait my turn, then."

Yeah, just like I did all those years, Barbara thought. *Only my turn never came. And it wasn't like I even had brothers or sisters.*

Jack opened the door. "OK, before you say anything ... This is all my fault and I am truly sorry. I know I promised not to say anything to Sally, but in the end I just couldn't hold back."

Barbara's response was polite but no more. She wasn't about to let him off the hook. "These things happen," she said.

"And I overheard what Sally said to you on the phone. She shouldn't have spoken to you like that."

"It's fine. I realized she was upset."

By now they had reached the basement. Bertie was amusing himself with a lamb bone. Sally was in sweats and perfectly pedicured bare feet. She was standing at the kitchen counter pouring coffee into a mug. She looked up when she saw Barbara.

"Thank you for coming. Look ... I was appallingly rude to you on the phone. I'm sorry. I got myself worked up, that's all."

"I'm sorry, too. I should have spoken to you sooner."

"Right, now we've got that sorted," Jack said, "maybe we should all sit down and have a cup of coffee." Jack paused and looked at his daughter. "Unless, of course, you'd rather I wasn't here."

His daughter rolled her eyes. "No, Dad. It's OK. You can stay."

Sally took two more mugs off the shelf. Jack produced a box of shortbread, and the three of them sat down at the kitchen table. Bertie padded over to join them and made himself comfortable at Jack's feet.

"Freddie's dad still away?" Barbara said, reaching over to scratch Bertie under the chin.

Sally nodded. "I'm not sure when he'll be back. . . . So . . . maybe you could explain why you think Freddie's dyslexic."

"Like I said on the phone, I don't know for certain that he is."

"But you suspect he might be?"

"It's possible. The fact is that Freddie is a smart, articulate boy with excellent reading and comprehension skills. . . ."

"You don't have to tell me," Sally said. "I know all this."

"But do you also know that he can't recite the months of the year or the days of the week in order?"

"That's absurd."

"Have you heard him do it?" Barbara helped herself to a finger of shortbread.

"No, but it's ludicrous to think he can't do something so basic."

"I think he might also be struggling to tell the time."

"What? The child is ten. That's crazy."

"Again . . . have you ever checked he can tell the time?"

"I don't know. But at some point, surely I must have. . . ."

"What's more, his mental arithmetic is well below what I'd expect from a child of his age."

Jack looked at his daughter. "Isn't that what his class teacher told you?"

"I've told you," Sally shot back, "the woman's an idiot."

Jack shook his head. "Why is it that everybody who doesn't agree with you is an idiot?"

"Look . . . Freddie is bored. How many more times do I have to say it? He's lost the incentive to learn."

"You could be right," Barbara said. "On the other hand, he may have real problems, which need to be identified and addressed."

"But I don't understand. Jeremy and I never had problems academically. Why would Freddie?"

"I can't answer that," Barbara said, "other than to say he's Freddie. He isn't you or your husband."

As she struggled to take it all in, Sally looked close to tears. "So what do we do?"

"Get him assessed," Barbara said. "Once you know what you're dealing with, you can take it from there."

"What does that mean?" Sally said. "That he's going to end up in some boys' academy for kids with special needs?"

"Oh, for heaven's sake," her father came back at her. "Stop being so dramatic. Of course it doesn't mean that."

"Your dad's right. There are plenty of mainstream private schools with programs suitable for Freddie." She couldn't resist the add-on: "He's one of the lucky ones."

Barbara took out her phone and found the number for the North London Dyslexia Clinic. Sally took it down and said she would make an appointment.

"Promise me you'll let me know how it goes," Barbara said.

"I will. . . . So would you like to carry on tutoring Freddie?"

"Definitely—if you're happy. But let's get the assessment first. Then I'll know how best to help him."

Sally managed a smile and thanked Barbara for coming.

"I know this has all come as a shock," Barbara said. "But Freddie is bright. With the right help, he's going to be fine. I promise you."

"Freddie's all we've got. All our hopes and dreams are invested in him."

"Come on, love," Jack said, patting his daughter's hand. "Freddie's brain might be wired a bit differently from most people, but he's by no means a lost cause. You're just going to have to modify your hopes a bit, that's all. Is that really such a big ask?"

Barbara thought it might well be.

Jack showed her to the door. "Thank you so much for that. You did brilliantly. Far better than I could have done. I'm such an oaf, the way I go blundering in. My wife was always telling me off. I do miss her being there to keep me on the straight and narrow."

"When did she die?"

"Eighteen months ago. Breast cancer."

"I'm sorry."

"Doctors did all they could, but in the end . . ." His voice trailed off. "Then you're left alone to pick up the pieces. It hasn't been easy. . . ."

"I've not been widowed," she said, "but I do know how it feels to be on your own." She told him about Frank's job and how it took him away for weeks and months at a time. "When Frank was away and my son, Ben, was at university, I hated that feeling of coming home from work to an empty house. Frank's in Mexico right now, but at least this time I've got Ben at home to keep me company."

"Ah, returning-graduate syndrome. I've read about this in the papers."

"Actually, to be precise, it's called unemployed-graduate-dependent-on-the-bank-of-Mum-and-Dad-syndrome."

"Point taken," Jack said, laughing. "So, Barbara, one last thing before you go. When do you think we should tackle Sally about how she and Jeremy are failing to meet Freddie's emotional needs?"

"We?"

"Yes. I mean you're so good at this. . . ."

"That's because education is my field. I can't start accusing Sally of being a bad parent."

"But Freddie's being neglected and then they make up for it by spoiling him. Surely you can see that."

"I can, but it's not my place to raise the issue. I'd be crossing a boundary. And anyway, you should meet some of the cruel, dead-beat parents I've come in contact with. In the scheme of things, Sally and Jeremy are great parents. Ask me again when they turn the house into a crack den."

After she'd finished at the deli, Barbara didn't feel like going home. It was the weekend. Ben would be going out and she couldn't face another Saturday night on her own with a microwave spag bol and bad telly.

"Tell you what," she said to Jess. "Why don't you and Matt have a night out? Let me babysit. I'd enjoy spending a few hours with the kids."

At first Jess wouldn't hear of it. Her mother needed to go home, put her feet up and rest. She didn't need to be running around after Atticus and Cleo.

"Actually, that's exactly what I need. You'd be doing me a favor. It's too quiet at home. Come on, what do you say? You and Matt haven't been out in ages."

They promised to be back by half past ten. Barbara called Jean and asked if she fancied coming over after the children were asleep. Jean couldn't have been more grateful for the invitation. Ken was at a medical conference in Stoke-on-Trent, and she was on her own, fuming about the wording of the wedding invitations.

"Of course it's all down to bloody Felicity. Get this: 'Mrs. Felicity Monkton, together with Mr. and Mrs. Kenneth Bishop, invite you' . . . et cetera, et cetera. I mean, since when has my name been Kenneth? And I loathe that phrase 'together with.' It's such appalling, clumsy English."

Barbara agreed that the wording wasn't ideal. "What do Adam and Emma say?"

"Oh, you know. What do they ever say? They're good kids. They just want to keep the peace. They take the view that Felicity's just been widowed—what's the harm in giving her what she wants? But it's not like she's even paying for the wedding. Ken and I are paying. Shouldn't we at least have a say?"

"Of course you should. But if the kids are happy . . ."

"I know. . . . I should pull back. It's not my day; it's theirs. I do try, but it's so damned hard. You were so lucky with Jess and Matt's wedding."

Jean wasn't wrong. Jess and Matt's wedding had been a pretty modest affair. The bride and groom had rolled up at the registry office in an ancient VW camper. Jess wore a vintage flapper dress that had cost a couple hundred quid. After the ceremony, family and close friends gathered for a roast beef lunch at the Cat and Whistle—an old East End boozer turned gastropub. Beer was served in old-fashioned dimpled mugs with handles. Red and purple anemones were arranged in vintage china teapots. For Barbara and Frank, the organization had been minimal, the cost just about doable and the aggravation nonexistent—beyond Jess and Matt constantly fretting about the provenance of the lunch ingredients.

"I'll be over about half past eight," Jean said. "I'll pick up Chinese on the way."

"By the way," Jess said as she and Matt were leaving, "Cleo is still a bit chesty at night. She's been having these terrible coughing fits, but loads of kids have had it and all the mums say it sounds worse than it is. If you're worried, call the homeopath. She'll probably up the dose of Pulsatilla. Her number's on the fridge."

Barbara knew she shouldn't interfere, but the words had left her mouth before she could stop them. "Darling, do you think maybe she should see the doctor? I mean, this cough has been going on for a while."

"I agree," Matt said. "But you try convincing your daughter."

"But what's the doctor going to do?" Jess said. "He'll only give her antibiotics, and I refuse to go down that road." She looked at Matt. "I thought we were agreed on that?"

"Usually, yes. But she's had this cough for so long. I'm not happy. You should have let me take her to the doctor when I wanted to."

"Matt, stop worrying. It's just a standard chest infection. She'll be fine."

Barbara wasn't about to wade in, but she couldn't help thinking that had Ben been there, he wouldn't have held back. He was always having a go at Jess about homeopathy. She hadn't forgotten his most recent attack before Christmas.

"What kind of idiot believes that diluting an active medicinal ingredient until it's nonexistent makes it more potent? It's a massive con. The UK homeopathic market is worth more than two hundred million pounds a year. You can't abide Big Pharma, but you support that."

Jess went on about how it had been proven that water had memory. "When you dilute a chemical in water, it sets up a vibration and you still get the amount you need."

"OK, so if you're collapsed on the floor with a stroke, I'll remember to call the homeopath while Mum feeds you Rescue Remedy."

Jess and Ben hadn't spoken for days after that spat.

"So, Grandma," Cleo said after her parents had gone. "Do you want to see the spider we caught? It's huge."

"That depends. . . ."

"It's OK," Atticus said. "You don't have to be frightened. He's in a jar with the lid on."

"Oh, well, in that case . . ."

Cleo ran to fetch the spider, coughing as she went. Barbara didn't like the rasping sound she was hearing, but her granddaughter seemed lively enough.

Inside a Manuka honey jar was a house spider—disarmingly thick of leg and thorax.

"He's called Cyril," Cleo said.

"Are you sure he wouldn't prefer to be released into the wild?"

Cleo shook her head. "No. He's a house spider."

"But Mum's scared of spiders," Atticus chimed in, "so we can't keep him here. She says we need to rehome him."

"You're going to rehome a spider."

"Yes, but we need to find a family who will feed it lots of crickets and mealworms."

How far the world had come, Barbara thought. Back in the twenties—so family legend had it—her grandmother used to pay Big Vera ten bob to come in every few months to drown the family dog's latest litter. A hundred years later her grandchildren were interviewing prospective carers for a house spider.

While Atticus tucked into the chicken casserole Jess had left for supper, Cleo barely touched hers. Later on Barbara read the children a few pages of *The Twits*. Cleo wanted to be cuddled and snuggled into Barbara. Once or twice she had to stop reading while Cleo had a coughing fit. She gave her water, but it didn't seem to make much difference. Bedtime was eight o'clock, but they begged Barbara to let them watch a bit of *Britain's Got Talent*. Atticus jumped up and down on the sofa, hooting and mocking the acts, thoroughly enjoying himself. Cleo sat on Barbara's lap, clutching her blanky, barely able to stay awake.

"Mum and Dad never let us watch *Britain's Got Talent*," Atticus said as an ad break started. "Mum says it's part of our"—he paused as he searched for the words—"globalized, trans-fat, Pop-Tart culture. What does that mean?"

"You may well ask," Barbara said.

Cleo swallowed the tiny Pulsatilla pills and Barbara kissed her good night. "I'm only in the living room if you need me." She went into Atticus's room. He was next to his bed, practicing his juggling. "Look, Grandma, look." But he hadn't really improved since the last time she'd watched him. "Wow. You're getting there," she said.

"Nah. I'm rubbish. Nana Rose was right. She told me I should retire gracefully."

"Nana told you to give up?"

"Yes. And she's right. Why do parents always tell you you're great at everything when you're not?"

"They're trying to encourage you—that's all."

"Well, it doesn't work. All it means is that you can't trust them."

Barbara picked the juggling balls up off the floor. "I can see that," she said. "But years ago children didn't get much encouragement, and nowadays people try to make up for it."

"So when you were a child, didn't you get any encouragement from your mum and dad?"

"Not really."

"The olden days must have been horrible."

Barbara laughed. "They weren't so bad. We got to eat lemonade powder and chips out of newspaper. Now, come on, you. Into bed."

"Lemonade powder?"

"It came in a bag and it was bright yellow. You dipped your finger into the sour sugar granules and sucked it off. We loved it."

"I bet it rotted your teeth, and food colorings are really bad for you."

"I know. But we enjoyed it. Back then they hadn't invented kale."

Atticus climbed in and pulled the duvet up to his chin.

"Grandma, can you read just a few more pages of *The Twits*? Please. Please. Then I'll go to sleep. I promise." Barbara obliged, and twenty minutes later, much to her surprise, Atticus fell asleep.

Jean arrived with enough Chinese for six people. "I made the mistake of buying food when I was starving," she said. "I'm afraid I made a start on the spring rolls in the car."

They laid out the cartons on the coffee table and sat on the sofa to eat. As usual, Jean couldn't stop admiring the flat. "I am loving the antlers. I'm sure they weren't here when I came last time. . . . And who thinks of turning a bowler hat into a lampshade? It's all so wonderfully boho."

"I know. I've often thought that if the deli goes down the pan, they could turn to interior design."

"Why should it go down the pan? I thought it was doing brilliantly."

She explained about the lack of passing trade and the clients who'd gone bust owing them money.

"It's hit them really hard. They're struggling to make ends meet."

"Come on," Jean soothed. "You can't take Jess and Matt's money worries on board. You've got your own problems."

"I know, but when you're a mum you never stop worrying."

"Tell me about it."

For a few moments, they carried on eating in silence. "So," Jean said eventually, "how are you doing apart from worrying about Jess and Matt?"

"Well, on the plus side, I haven't had any more panic attacks. On the downside, I'm not sure I love my husband anymore."

"You two need to talk about what's going on," Jean said, stabbing a sweet-and-sour pork ball with her fork. "It's the only way forward."

"I've tried talking to him, but he doesn't get it. It's this old thing about him thinking I'm too needy. All he says is that he does his best and if that's not good enough . . ."

"You can walk."

"He hasn't said as much, but it's what he means."

"It's sheer bravado. Frank loves you. He'd be bereft without you."

"I don't doubt it. Who else would run around after him? But at the same time, he didn't really care about leaving me. He knew how much I needed him and he still walked away. I wouldn't have minded if it had been for a week or so, but I've no idea when he's going to be back."

"Not his finest hour, I admit. But if your marriage means anything, the pair of you must keep talking."

"Did you and Ken talk about how you never had sex?"

"A great deal."

"And look where it got you."

"It's different with us. I'm not sure we could ever have resolved our issue. Ken is just wired differently from other men. He can't change. Frank might."

"You think?"

"I admit that at his age, you're not going to turn him into the ideal husband, but don't give up. Eventually you will get through to him."

"I'm not so sure. And to be honest, I don't think I've got the energy to keep trying." Barbara bit into a kung pao prawn.

"I won't be easy. You've been in the wars and Frank's behaved badly. . . ."

"And not for the first time. You know as well as I do that I've had decades of his selfishness."

"You don't have to remind me. It's just that deep down I don't think Frank's a bad man."

"Of course he isn't. But knowing that doesn't help me."

"So that's it—you're going to walk away?"

"I don't know."

They ate in silence for a few moments.

"So how's it going with Jenson?"

"Still pretty amazing. I bought him a gold earring stud . . . you know, just as a token."

"I see," Barbara said, doing her best to sound noncommittal, but suspecting she sounded decidedly committal.

"What does 'I see' mean?"

"You tell me."

"Look, I am not falling in love with him."

"Then why—on top of paying him—are you buying him *tokens*?"

"I like him. Aren't I allowed to like him?"

"I guess so," Barbara said. "But it's more than that, and you know it. You've formed an emotional attachment to him, and you know how dangerous that is."

"It's fine."

"No, it's not."

"It is. I've got the whole thing under control."

"I hope you have, because falling in love with a thirtysomething guy you pay to have sex with you may not be your smartest move."

"I'm not in love with him. Honestly. I like him, that's all. And he makes me happy. Now, can we just drop this? I know you're worried and I appreciate it, but really there's no need."

Barbara shrugged. "OK. If you say so."

They fell into silence for a second time.

"By the way," Barbara said eventually, "Freddie, the boy I'm tutoring—the one you hooked me up with—could be dyslexic."

"Well, at least his parents have got the money to get him the help he needs. The kids you teach aren't so lucky."

"I know. Why is life so bloody unfair?"

"OK, enough miserablist talk. Get this . . . So my cell goes on the way over here. It's Adam with the latest wedding update. . . . Felicity wants doves."

"Doves? Aren't they a bit nineties?"

"A bit? And even then they were tacky. But apparently Felicity thinks releasing doves is spiritual."

"Not very spiritual when they crap all over you."

"That's what Ken said when I called him. He said we have to put our foot down."

"Good luck with that."

They suddenly became aware that Cleo was coughing. Barbara went in to her. She was sitting up in bed. Every so often she would cough so hard that she retched. Barbara gave her some water. The cough eased off for a few moments and then started up again.

"Goodness, you're burning up," Barbara said, feeling her granddaughter's forehead.

Jean tapped on the door. "Mind if I come in?"

"Cleo, you remember Aunty Jean, don't you? She's a nurse."

"I thought she helped get babies out of mummies' tummies."

"Well, that's a type of nurse," Barbara said. "So it might be a good idea to let her take a look at you."

Cleo nodded as she hacked. Jean took her pulse and felt her cheeks.

"Bar—can I have a quick word outside?"

Barbara followed her into the hallway.

"She's terribly hot and her pulse is racing," Jean said. "And I recognize that cough. It's an asthma cough."

"I'm not with you. I though asthmatics wheezed."

"Some do. Some get a bad cough, which often starts as a chest infection. Hasn't Jess taken her to the doctor?"

"Homeopath."

"Oh, for crying out loud."

"Jess doesn't approve of antibiotics. The homeopath's got Cleo on something called Pulsatilla."

"What she needs is drugs. I really don't like the look of her. Did you notice how rapid her breathing is? I think we need to get her to the hospital."

"You think it's that serious?"

"It could get that way. Look . . . you take her. I'll stay here and look after Atticus. Oh, and I'll call Jess. Leave me her number."

Barbara helped Cleo pull a sweater on over her pajamas. Jean shoved her bare feet into trainers. As soon as Cleo stood up, she said she felt dizzy. Cleo was no small weight, but Barbara managed to carry her down the narrow staircase and out to the car.

By now it was past ten, but for a Saturday night it was still early and the ER wasn't too busy. A gang of teenagers—high on who knew what—had brought in their mate who had fallen out of a tree and appeared to have dislocated his shoulder. While the lad sobbed with pain, his mates assumed comedy poses and took larky selfies with him. A few feet away, a human-shaped bundle of filthy coats, jumpers and matted hair was sprawled across three metal seats. It was being asked to leave by a security guard. "I know it's cold out, mate, but you can't come in here to get warm, not stinking like that you can't."

The homeless man wiped his nose with the back of his hand. The skin was gray with muck, the overlong nails curled and ragged. "I haven't eaten since yesterday."

"Well, you'd better get on yer bike, then. There's a homeless shelter down the road."

"It's full."

The security guard looked over at the two middle-aged women on reception. "No room at the inn apparently."

The women looked at each other. "Don't be too hard on him,

Gordon," one of them said. "He'll freeze to death if you throw him out."

"I'm too soft, that's what I am," Gordon grumbled. Then he offered to get the chap a cup of tea and a sandwich, so long as he promised to sit at the back of the waiting room and make no trouble.

"That man looks very poor," Cleo said between coughs. "Doesn't he have somebody to look after him?"

"It doesn't look like it." Barbara rearranged Cleo in her arms, but however she tried to hold her, the child didn't get any lighter.

"That's sad. Do you think he'd like Cyril for company?"

It occurred to Barbara that the man already had several Cyrils—or similar—about his person.

"If he's not very well," Barbara said, "I'm not sure he could cope with looking after a pet."

They headed towards reception. An elderly woman was lying on a trolley next to the lift. "Is she dead?" Cleo asked.

"Of course she isn't. Look, her eyes are open."

"She could still be dead."

"She's not dead. She's breathing. Can't you see her chest going up and down?"

"Nope. Her chest isn't moving. She's definitely dead. Cool. Now I can tell everybody at school I saw a dead person."

Cleo was taken into triage straightaway. A nurse took her temperature. A hundred and three. "And I don't like the sound of that cough." A doctor was brought in. He listened to Cleo's chest.

"How long has she been coughing like this?" His tone was faintly accusatory. Barbara was vague. A few days maybe.

Jean's diagnosis turned out to be right. Cleo's chest infection had triggered asthma. "We'll admit her and put her on a nebulizer overnight."

"What's that?" Cleo said.

The doctor explained that she would have a mask over her face and a machine would pump out a mist of medicine, which would clear her airways and make her cough go away.

"Am I going to die?"

"Absolutely not," the doctor said. "In fact, if the medicine does its job tonight, you might even get to go home tomorrow."

"Good. And if I can't go home, can Cyril come and stay with me in the hospital?"

"Is Cyril a relative?"

"No, he's a spider."

They had to wait in the ER until a bed could be found on one of the wards. Barbara wondered what was keeping Jess and Matt. She called Jess. Her daughter picked up on the first ring.

"Hey, Mum, I was about to call you. Don't worry—we're on our way. Aunty Jean finally got me. She'd been trying for ages, but I couldn't hear my phone in the restaurant. How's Cleo?"

"It's asthma. I don't think it's too bad, but they're keeping her overnight."

"Overnight? OK, tell her we'll be five minutes."

By the time Jess and Matt arrived, Cleo still hadn't been taken up to the ward, but she had been hooked up to the nebulizer. Jess looked frantic, more so when she saw her pale, glassy-eyed daughter breathing through a mask. She shot over to hug her. Matt said nothing. His face was taut. He seemed more angry than anything.

"Sweetie," Jess said, stroking Cleo's hair. "I'm so sorry it's taken us so long to get here. How are you feeling?"

Cleo pulled off her mask. "Fine. Everybody's been really nice. And I saw a dead person."

"She didn't," Barbara whispered.

"I heard that. I did see a dead person. So there."

Matt told Cleo to put her mask back on because she was wasting the medicine.

"I need to talk to the doctor," Jess said. "What is it they're pumping into her? It's steroids, isn't it? I'm not having her filled up with steroids." She turned to Matt. "Maybe I should call the homeopath."

"Are you serious? I can't believe you just said that. Sod the bloody homeopath. Our daughter has asthma. And if she needs steroids, she's bloody having steroids. We should have taken her to the doctor like I said. If she'd had proper treatment for her chest, this wouldn't have happened."

"So it's all my fault. As usual. Why didn't you take her to the doctor?"

"Because you wouldn't let me."

"What? Like I could have stopped you."

"OK, you two," Barbara said. "Do you think you could have this argument outside? You're upsetting Cleo."

"No, they're not. They're always arguing. Me and Atticus are used to it."

"Don't be silly," Jess singsonged. "Of course we're not always arguing."

"Yes, you are."

"She's right," Matt said. "And since Cleo's been ill, it's been about effing homeopathy."

"What's *effing* mean?"

"What I don't get," Matt went on, "is why you allow yourself to be bullied by that ignorant mummy mafia you hang out with. When the kids were teething, you put them in those ridiculous amber bead necklaces. If they had a cold, you'd treat it with breast milk—like it was some magic cure-all. Now Cleo has ended up in hospital. See what you've bloody done."

"Stop it. This isn't just about me. You were in favor of homeopathy, too."

"Well, I've done some reading and I've changed my mind."

"Well, thanks for telling me."

"I have been telling you. I keep on about all the studies that prove what bollocks it is, but you refuse to listen."

Jess burst into tears and shot out of the cubicle. Barbara went after her. She caught up with her after a couple paces. "Come on," she said, putting her arm around Jess's shoulders. "You've both had a shock. Matt's taking it out on you, that's all." She led her daughter over to a line of empty seats. The homeless man had finished his tea and sandwich and had fallen asleep. He was snoring loudly while emitting a strong smell of stale urine.

"He might be taking it out on me," Jess said, sitting down, "but he's right. I'm just a gullible idiot. He's been on me all week to take Cleo to the doctor and I refused. I could have killed her."

"I think maybe that's taking it a bit far."

"I was just doing what I thought best. Drugs can have such terrible side effects."

"I know, darling, but doing nothing can have side effects, too."

"So you think that I put my own agenda before my child's health?"

Barbara knew she had to tread carefully. "You made a mistake. But all parents make mistakes. Remind me to make a list of mine. And Matt is just as responsible as you are. He should have forced the issue."

"He didn't have the energy."

"What do you mean?"

"He hasn't had a proper night's sleep in weeks."

"This is about money, isn't it?"

"We're in so much debt. The bank refuses to extend our credit. That's part of the reason Matt's in such a state."

Barbara took Jess in her arms and rocked her. "Shh . . . It's going to be all right. Stop worrying. We'll sort something out."

But she didn't have the foggiest idea what.

Once Cleo had been moved to the children's ward, Matt went home to relieve Jean. The head nurse told Jess it would be fine for her to stay the night and went to find her a camp bed.

It was almost one when Barbara got home. Ben was just leaving. "Good Lord, where on earth are you going at this hour?"

"I'm meeting some friends at a club in Shoreditch. It never gets going before two. And anyway, you should talk. Where have you been? I was really worried. I must have sent you half a dozen texts."

Barbara explained about Cleo. "Sorry. I wasn't checking my phone. I did think about going outside to call you, but I assumed as it's a Saturday night that you'd be out and you wouldn't hear the phone."

"So is Cleo OK?"

"She'll be fine. The doctor said she'll need to use an inhaler from time to time, but the chances are she'll grow out of it."

"I bet you anything Jess was trying to treat her with sugar pills."

"Ben, please don't start. I'm too tired."

"Well, I hope you told her what an idiot she is."

"No, Matt did. They had a fight."

"Jess is such a bloody flake. She needs to sort herself out."

"You're probably right. But please don't say anything to her. You'll only make her feel worse. She knows she made a mistake."

"Whatever."

"Right, I'm off to bed."

She said good night. Ben opened the front door.

It was then that she noticed the leather jacket he was wearing. Tan. Brand-new. Expensive-looking.

"Ben, hang on. . . . Where did . . . ?"

But he was gone. Barbara began climbing the stairs. So what did a leather jacket cost these days? Two hundred quid minimum. A few weeks ago Ben didn't have the money to buy a pair of Converse. Suddenly he owned a leather jacket.

Weary as she was, she decided to call Frank. He would want to know about Cleo. She did a quick calculation. Mexico was eight hours behind. Frank would probably be having a drink or dinner in some noisy restaurant. The call was bound to go straight to voice mail. But it didn't. Frank picked up almost immediately. He was in his hotel room viewing film footage. After she'd reassured him that Cleo was going to be OK and promised to call the next day to let him know how she was doing, she brought up the subject of Ben's new leather jacket.

"Frank, have you been giving him money?"

"Not recently, no."

"So where did it come from?"

"I dunno." Frank sounded pretty unconcerned. "Maybe he borrowed some cash."

"He wouldn't do that. How would he pay it back?"

"So what are you suggesting? That he stole it?"

"I don't know."

"Come on . . . This is Ben we're talking about. If he gets undercharged in a shop, he points it out. I've seen him do it."

"So have I, but that doesn't mean he'd never give in to temptation."

"Bar, you're exhausted. You're not thinking straight. Ben would never shoplift. . . . I bet he borrowed the jacket off a mate."

"Boys don't borrow each other's clothes."

"OK. So somebody might have given it to him."

"Who gives away a brand-new leather jacket?"

"I don't know. You don't suppose it's got something to do with this secret *thing* he's been working on? Maybe we're ignoring the obvious. Perhaps he earned the money."

"Uh-uh. He would have said. You know how he likes to show off when he sells an article for actual money."

"In which case there's only one way of getting to the bottom of this. You'll have to ask him where he got it."

"Don't worry. I intend to."

Chapter 8

Jess called Barbara first thing the next morning to say that Cleo's cough had improved overnight and the doctors had said she could go home. "The hospital is lending us a nebulizer for a few days, and she's been given an inhaler to use when necessary."

"Well, that's a relief. Give her a big hug from me and her granddad and tell her I'll pop over later."

"By the way, I forgot to say thank you for everything you did last night. Cleo said you were brilliant. And she still can't get over seeing the dead woman."

Barbara laughed. "What are grandmas for, if not for letting their grandchildren ogle cadavers? But I promise you she wasn't dead."

"Well, Cleo's full of it. She even asked one of the nurses how long it would be before the woman's body started rotting."

"You know what I love about Cleo? She's such a girlie girl."

"Isn't she?. . . By the way, Matt's barely speaking to me."

"Give him time. Now that Cleo's on the mend, he'll come round."

"I hope so. Plus it's the money thing. He just spends all his time worrying."

"I've had an idea," Barbara said. It had occurred to her last night, as she'd been falling asleep. "Your dad has a life insurance policy. I don't know what it's worth—probably not much. But I could find out. Maybe we could cash it in."

Jess wouldn't hear of it. "We'll go bust if we have to, but there's no way I'm letting you and Dad give us the little money you've got. It's a wonderful, kind thought and I appreciate it, but the answer's no."

"Well, the offer's there if you change your mind."

Jess said she wasn't going to change her mind and moved the conversation on. She said she'd just been on the phone to Martha. "She said I should try Cleo on licorice and bamboo. She doesn't approve of me letting her have an inhaler."

"And where did Martha get her medical degree? The Hermann von Quack Institute, Charlatanville? I suggest you tell her to stick her licorice and bamboo where the sun don't shine."

"I love it when you make me laugh," Jess said. "When we were growing up, none of the other kids' mums were as funny as you."

She reminded Barbara how every week she would collect her and all her friends from their swimming lesson and sing along to "Crazy Horses" at the top of her voice all the way home.

"They all thought you were weird, but in a good way."

"I can live with *weird*," Barbara said. "It's *normal* I can't stand. . . . So what are you going to do about Martha?"

"I shall politely ignore her. Don't get me wrong—she's my best friend and I love her to bits, but Matt's right. I need to take a step back from the Martha mafia." She paused. "I think maybe I'll go back to regular loo paper, too. I don't want to risk any more illness in this family."

Barbara said that, on balance, that might be a good idea.

Jess said she had to go. A nurse was hovering with Cleo's discharge form, which needed to be signed.

No sooner had Barbara put down the phone than Ben appeared.

He was wearing boxers and a tee. His hair looked even more confused than usual. He was also letting out soft moaning sounds.

"I've got such a hangover." Moan. "We were drinking Negronis until five in the morning." He practically fell onto a kitchen chair.

"Really?" Barbara said, filling the kettle for coffee. "And I bet they don't come cheap? Clubs charge a fortune for drinks."

"I had some money," Ben mumbled before moaning again.

"Where from?"

"Why are you interrogating me? I had some money, that's all."

"But you don't earn anything. So maybe you'd also like to tell me where you got the cash to buy a leather jacket?"

"Selling drugs . . . Shit, my head hurts."

Barbara switched on the kettle. "Very droll. But don't think it hasn't occurred to me."

"What? You honestly think I'd start pushing drugs? Or maybe you think I stole the money."

Barbara sat down opposite him. "People do all sorts of things when they're hard up."

"I get that," he said, looking up at her. "But just for the record, I'm not a shoplifting drug dealer."

"Fine. So how did you pay for the jacket?"

"This really is none of your business, but since you're clearly not going to let it rest, I sold my guitar."

"You sold the Gibson? Why on earth would you do that? It was meant to be an investment."

The limited-edition Gibson had been Ben's nineteenth birthday present to himself. During his gap year, he got a job as a runner with a record company. The pay was lousy, but Ben lived at home rent free (the quid pro quo being that he would put money aside to help pay his university fees) and was able to save a great pile of cash. When he left the job almost a year later, he had fifteen grand in the bank. He set ten aside for university, but he wasn't sure what to do with the rest. The choice was either to go traveling with his mates and spend the weeks leading up to his first term at uni getting loaded in the Andes—or buy his dream guitar. In the end he chose the guitar—a 1954 Fender Telecaster, the same model that Keith Richards had played. He was positively heady with excitement at owning a classic guitar. For the first few days he couldn't stop caressing the scuffed grazed wood. He practiced for hours. He invited friends to come and admire it. It was like he'd just given birth. "You have to come over and see the guitar." Even Frank couldn't resist picking it up and giving it a bit of Dire Straits.

Then Ben had gone to university and formed Grandma and the Junkies. The band, which had come into the world riding on this giant—if a bit green—wave of optimism and hope, went down. That was another reason Barbara felt she had to go easy with him. That said, she was still cross with him for selling the guitar.

"I'm skint," Ben was saying now. "I can't keep taking money from you and Dad. I had no choice."

"But in a few years it would have been worth a lot of money."

"I know, but since the band broke up, I've hardly played the thing. If you must know, I couldn't face looking at it."

She asked him how much he got for it.

"Just over six thousand. So I made a bit of profit."

"And now you're just going to fritter the money away on leather jackets."

"No. I only need one."

"You know what I mean. You'll squander it—spend it on rubbish."

"Why would I do that? I'll spend it on living and hope it tides me over until I start earning some proper money."

"Well, I'm not happy."

"I knew you wouldn't be. That's why I didn't tell you. But, actually, you should be happy because for the time being the pressure's off you and Dad. Plus I've gained a bit of self-respect. It's win-win."

When Barbara called Frank to tell him about Ben selling his guitar, he pretty much took Ben's side. "He's right. It will give him a bit of self-respect, and in the meantime we're saving money."

Barbara was frustrated that neither of them cared about the long game—the fact that the guitar might have been worth a great deal of money one day.

"So how are you feeling?" Frank asked Barbara.

"I'm OK."

"No more panic attacks?"

"Uh-uh."

"So you still angry with me?"

"Of course I am. What do you want from me?"

"What I want is for you to look at things from my perspective."

"Frank, how many more times do I need to say this? I've spent a lifetime looking at things from your perspective. That's the problem."

As usual, they ended the conversation before they got into a fight.

Barbara's medication had put a stop to her panic attacks, but it hadn't stopped her stewing and ruminating about the state of her marriage and whether or not she and Frank had a future. On top of that there was a pile of other worries: Ben's future, Jess and Matt's financial problems. Was Troy OK? How would Freddie do in his assessment and how would his parents cope if it were confirmed that he was dyslexic? The only not-quite-so-gloomy prospect—she hesitated to use the word "bright"—concerned her relationship with her mother. She was convinced that she hadn't been imagining things the other day. For a second or two they really had connected. With her defenses down, Rose had demonstrated something verging on affection.

Over poached salmon and pinot grigio at the Conran Shop—Barbara and Jean had gone there to spend the gift voucher that Barbara had been presented with when she left her job—Barbara told Jean about her "moment" with Rose. "It struck me that maybe it is possible to reach her and that the time has come to confront her about the past."

"Absolutely. Go for it. . . . And while you're at it, you can confront Terence Conran about his prices. You do realize you could have got that light for twenty quid in Ikea."

"No, I couldn't," Barbara said, leaning over to pat the bag containing her tripod table lamp. "The stand is solid beech. You saw how beautifully made it is."

Jean sniffed. "I still think he's taking the piss."

"Maybe. But it hasn't cost me anything, so I don't really care. Anyway . . . back to my mum. You really think I should talk to her?"

Jean didn't reply. She was half out of her chair, staring out of the window.

"What?" Barbara said, putting down her knife and fork.

"That's Jenson."

"Where?" Barbara attempted to follow Jean's line of sight. She spotted a tall guy in a black Fedora and emerald-green overcoat. Ben would have taken one look at him and called him a tool. She couldn't see his face. It was being obscured by a blond girl in a beanie hat who was kissing him. They were both carrying Marks & Spencer grocery bags.

Barbara didn't know what to say. The kiss on its own might have suggested that Jenson was on a gigolo assignment. The grocery bags were the giveaway.

The two women sat in silence as they watched the pair walk away arm in arm. Jean's eyes were glassy with tears. She wiped them with the heel of her palm.

"Do you think that was his girlfriend?" she said. "I mean his proper girlfriend, not just a client."

"I don't know. Does he usually go food shopping with clients?"

"Probably not." Jean was gazing out of the window again. "Wow . . . I haven't felt this jealous since I was in high school."

"Jean, look at me."

It took her a moment or two, but eventually Jean turned away from the window. "I know what you're going to say—that I'm just a stupid old woman who got carried away and I have to end it."

"I don't think you're stupid or old, but yes, I do think you have to end it."

Jean drained her wineglass. "You're right, of course. I can't think what I was hoping for. He's got a life. I will never be more than a client to him." She paused. "Or maybe just a dirty secret that he will always keep from the girl he loves."

"Come on," Barbara said, placing her hand on top of Jean's. "After you've finished with all this, we'll look for another way out of this mess."

But for the life of her, Barbara couldn't imagine what that might be. Meanwhile, Jean suggested they order another bottle of pinot grig.

"So, back to your mother."

"You sure you feel up to discussing my problems?"

"It'll take my mind off Jenson."

"So you really think I should confront her?"

"I do." She said she was amazed that Barbara hadn't done it sooner. "I mean, you're not exactly a shrinking violet. What's stopped you?"

"Don't think I haven't thought about it, but the last thing I want to do is rock the boat. If I upset her, she'll think even worse of me."

"So instead you keep on trying to get her to love you."

"I've been trying all my life. You know when I go round there, I still take her little presents—just like I did when I was a kid—but inevitably, I always get the wrong thing."

"Of course you do. She wouldn't have it any other way. That's her problem, not yours. Come on, Bar—you know you're not a bad person."

"I know it in my head, but I don't *feel* it. Frank doesn't help. When he left, it felt like he was punishing me, and what's more, part of me was convinced I deserved it."

"That's ridiculous."

"I know. What can I tell you?"

"It's time. You need to have the conversation with your mum."

"But I'm struggling with my marriage right now. I don't know if this is the right time. Plus Mum's old. She's getting frail. Surely it would be cruel to confront her this late in the day."

Jean said she took the point about Rose's age. "But it depends how you do it. Be gentle. Don't go on the attack. All you're asking her to do is listen."

Barbara said she still wasn't sure. "I think you're being a bit gung ho. The woman's well over eighty."

"She is, but mentally she's anything but feeble. Look, it's up to you, but it occurs to me that getting some kind of closure with your mother might free you up to think about your relationship with Frank."

"Maybe. I don't know. I've got so much going on in my head right now. Heaven knows where I'd be without the meds."

"Tell me . . . What is it you need to hear from your mother?"

"I know she had a miserable time with my dad, but I just want her to tell me that she's sorry she wasn't able to do her best for me and that she loves me."

"That's not a lot to ask."

Barbara still wasn't sure.

Barbara's wedding day. Her dad is pacing in the living room. They're all waiting for the wedding cars to arrive. Barbara will travel to the church with Stan (if he can get himself out of the house. But the Valium does seem to be working). Rose will share a car with Frank's widowed mother, Betty, who is on her way over in a taxi.

Rose is wearing a cream-and-navy silk two-piece with matching clutch, shoes and wide-brimmed hat. She's standing in front of the hall mirror adjusting it and fussing over the angle. Taking care not to trip, Barbara comes down the stairs in her wedding dress—full chiffon skirt, crocheted bodice, long, billowing sleeves with deep crocheted cuffs. Earlier a hairdresser friend of her mother's came to the house to do her hair. Heavily lacquered seventies flick-ups lap at her beaded Juliette cap.

Stan comes into the hallway but barely notices Barbara because his anxiety is so bad that he's on the verge of being sick. Rose stops fussing for a moment and tells Barbara that the car will be here any minute. She should go and retrieve her bouquet from the kitchen sink.

The doorbell rings. In walks Betty—pretty in peach lace. She takes one look at Barbara and gasps. "Oh, sweetheart. You look stunning. I don't think I've ever seen a more beautiful bride. Goodness. I think I'm going to cry." Barbara takes pleasure in Betty's words but doesn't feel deserving of them. At the same time, she feels a sudden and acute sadness. It will take her years to work out why.

Back home, Barbara was unpacking her precious Conran lamp and fretting about Jean when the phone rang.

"Barbara, it's Jack Dolan."

He said he was sorry to disturb her, but he wanted to ask her a small favor. Freddie had his dyslexia assessment in a few days, and since Sally and Jeremy were away again, he would be taking him. "Apparently they send a written report afterwards. Sally has asked me to take a look at it and then give her a call, but I'm worried it might be all double Dutch to me. I was wondering if you would mind going through it with me."

Barbara said she'd be more than happy to take a look at the report.

"You sure it wouldn't be putting you out?"

"Not at all. I've been thinking a lot about Freddie. I'd be interested to hear somebody else's opinion. By the way, how does he feel about being assessed?"

"I had to persuade Sally to be straight with him about it. Eventually she sat him down and explained why we were worried about him, but it didn't go down well. Before he's even been assessed, he's decided he's thick and good for nothing."

Barbara asked if Freddie's behavior had changed towards his mother.

"Afraid not. Sally and Jeremy are still neglecting him and spoiling him. Poor chap's all over the place—doesn't know where he is."

"I'm so sorry he's going through all this. Say hi to him for me and tell him I'm thinking of him."

"Will do."

Jack said he would call her as soon as the report arrived.

By the end of the week Barbara had made up her mind. She was ready to have "the conversation" with her mother. Jean was right: so long as she took it gently and didn't go on the attack, all would be well. She was due to visit Rose on Saturday with a load of shopping. The supermarket delivery had been a disaster—tasteless apples, brown bananas, Edam that was too cheesy and the wrong brand of water biscuits.

The first thing she noticed when she arrived was that Rose's ankle seemed to be much better. Her walking wasn't quite back to normal, but the swelling had gone down and she was able to put much more weight on it. So much so that as Barbara came in, her mother insisted on taking one of the plastic carriers from her. "Terry's wife the nurse says another few days and I should be completely back on my feet."

Barbara unpacked the shopping and handed the items to her mother.

"What's this you've got me?" Rose said. "I asked for 'light' butter, not 'lightest.' It's full of water. Tastes of nothing. And where are my apricot yogurts? Don't say you forgot my yogurts."

Barbara offered to pop to the corner shop, but Rose put on her martyred voice and said she would manage. Barbara consoled herself with the thought that by next week her mother would be doing her own shopping again.

When they'd finished putting away the groceries, Barbara suggested they have a cup of tea.

"Would you mind making it?" Rose said. "I think I need to sit down again and rest my ankle." Rose headed towards the living room. "Oh, and a chocolate digestive would be nice."

"Coming up." Barbara flicked the switch on the kettle and went to the fridge to get milk. As she leaned in, she saw four cartons of apricot yogurt. Rose still hadn't got through the ones from last week.

Barbara placed the tray of tea and biscuits on the coffee table.

"Would you mind closing that window?" Rose said with a shiver. "It's making a draft." Barbara went over to the window and pulled it shut. On the ledge below was a photograph of Stan in army uniform. She picked it up. "I'd forgotten how handsome Dad was when he was young."

"He was such a catch," Rose said, picking up her cup of tea. "I talk to him every day, you know. Tell him bits and pieces about what's been going on."

Barbara put the photograph back and came and sat in the armchair. "So when you were first married, what was it like?"

"Wonderful," Rose said with a faraway look. "We were so happy." Her fingers started playing with the hem of her cardigan. "In the early days, your dad got a bit low from time to time, but I thought that with time it would pass. I remember how we used to cuddle up on the settee and talk about all our plans for the future."

"Was I planned?"

"Of course you were. We were so excited. Your dad went straight out and bought a book of baby names. I started knitting, but I wasn't very good. I finished one bootee. I think I've still got it somewhere."

Her mother had kept one of her bootees. She never knew that.

"So how did you feel when I was born?"

Rose's face became a smile. "You were such a bonny little thing. Over eight pounds. All the nurses made a fuss of you."

"And you loved me?"

"What sort of a question is that? Of course I did."

So her mother hadn't turned away from her as an infant. That was something. Barbara's heart pounded as she prepared to say what she'd come to say. "The thing is, growing up I never felt you loved me."

Rose didn't react. There wasn't a hint of surprise on her face. It was the oddest thing. Barbara got the feeling that her mother had been expecting to hear these words one day. Maybe she'd prepared herself.

"It was terrible for me, living with your father. After he got ill, he couldn't love me." She sat there unable to make eye contact with Barbara, a guilty but nonetheless fragile, vulnerable defendant pleading her case. "What I mean to say is . . ."

"He couldn't make love?"

She nodded. "I lived almost my entire married life without affection, without the touch of a man. How do you think it was for me? I took refuge in buying clothes—making sure I always looked good. I had to keep proving to myself that I was still attractive."

Barbara moved to the sofa and sat down next to her mother. "I can't imagine what that must have been like." Rose started to cry. Barbara put her arm around her mother's shoulder. "You didn't deserve that."

"No, I didn't. These days they call it post-traumatic stress. When it happens to people now, doctors can help them. They get therapy. Your dad got nothing."

"I know, Mum. It was so bloody cruel. If help had been available back then, your life would have been different, too. I get that. I do understand. But I was just a child. I needed to be loved."

"I did my best." Her mother's words were cold, matter-of-fact. She took a tissue from her cardigan pocket. "What's done is done. Why are you raking over the past?"

"Because I need you to understand that even though you didn't mean to hurt me, you did. I'm still hurting. You were so angry and frustrated about what was happening to Dad that you took it out on me."

"Why are you picking on me? What about your dad? Didn't he hurt you? The man couldn't leave the house."

Barbara is nearly eleven. She's in her final year at primary school. Audi-tions are being held for the end-of-year play—Toad of Toad Hall. She's a shy kid, but inside, extrovert Barbara is already straining to get out. Secretly she fantasizes about one day becoming a famous pop singer or actress. She'd give anything to have a part in the school play. The audi-tions for Mr. Toad—an aristocratic, pompous buffoon who causes may-hem wherever he goes—are held one playtime. The usual live wires and show-offs go along. Barbara stays in the playground, dithering. What she knows, that nobody else does, is that she can do a perfect imperson-ation of an English upper-class accent. But does she dare do it in public? Heart racing and feeling sick, she heads off to the staff room and gets in line. Finally her name is called. She goes in. Mrs. Dean, the deputy head, hands her a script and asks her to read Mr. Toad's opening lines. To get into character, she puffs out her nonexistent stomach and arranges her features to look jovial. "Hello, you fellows! This is splendid. Hello, old Badger. Dear old Ratty . . . How are you? . . ."

Mrs. Dean is visibly shocked. "Goodness, Barbara. That was excel-lent. Why on earth have you been hiding your light under a bushel for so long?"

Barbara doesn't know what a bushel is and is too scared to ask. She gets the part.

On the big night, Mrs. Connell, the art teacher who's made most of the scenery, smothers Barbara's face in emerald grease paint. She gets to wear a red frock coat, an oversized bow tie, and a gold top hat. But the best bit is the toad paunch that she wears under her costume. It's made from a cushion. Mrs. Connell has attached long tapes, which Barbara ties around her middle.

At the end of the show there's a huge round of applause just for Barbara. Rose, who's not known for lavish praise, is quick to tell her how

well she's done and marvels at how she managed to learn all those lines.
Stan, who's going through a particularly bad patch with his nerves, isn't
there. Barbara had begged him to come. Toad of Toad Hall *was funny.*
It would make him laugh. Take him out of himself. He was her dad. He
had to be there. She wanted him to take a photograph of her in her cos-
tume. Rose was hopeless with cameras—even their Instamatic. Barba-
ra's sense of achievement is muted by her father's absence. Her
self-confidence improves a bit, but not much. Overall, she still feels pretty
worthless.

"Of course he hurt me. I'm not sure I ever forgave him for not turning up to see me in *Toad of Toad Hall*, but at least I got some affection
from him. He cuddled me. You almost never cuddled me."

"I don't remember," Rose said. "It was a long time ago. But why
are you dwelling on all this? It does you no good. You should be looking forward, not back." She paused. "And anyway, I did show you
affection. I used to make a unicorn horn with your hair when you
were in the bath and I'd joke about how cabbages would grow behind
your ears if you didn't wash them properly."

"You're right. You did, but that was the extent of it. . . . The thing
is, I know I should be looking forward, but first I need you to understand that because of the way you were with me, I always felt like this
naughty little girl. Even now, no matter what I do for you, I can't get
anything right. Why is that?"

Rose shrugged. "Like I say—I did my best. I still do. If that's not
good enough . . ."

She sounded like Frank.

"After everything I did for him, your father refused to go to the
hospital. He chose to die rather than stay with me. How could he do
that to me?" She wiped her nose with the tissue.

"Mum, we've been over this a hundred times. Dad was mentally ill. He couldn't help it."

"Maybe not, but I've had to live with what he did. It's strange— I've often thought about Hitler's henchmen murdering all those poor wretched people in the concentration camps. But it didn't end there. The lives of those who survived were destroyed, too. Then there were the survivors' children who suffered. But what about the lives of the soldiers who went in and rescued them? Your father never recovered from the horror he saw. Hitler killed your father just like he killed those people in the camps. He may have died decades after the camps were liberated, but it was still murder. I had to watch him suffer, and nobody could do anything."

"I understand all that. You both went through hell. But you dragged me along, too."

"You don't know how lucky you are. You've got Frank, your kids, your grandchildren, your friends. You've had a career. What did I have? Tell me that."

Barbara sat next to her mother, a little girl hungry for a scrap of love or affection. But it seemed that no matter what she said, how much she kicked and screamed, her mother was still refusing to provide it.

She laid her head on her mother's shoulder. Now she was crying—for Rose, for herself, for the whole bloody mess. "I'm sorry, Mum. I'm truly sorry for everything you went through." She wiped her eyes with the back of her hand. "But I just wish you'd been able to show me that you loved me, that's all."

"If you'd walked in my shoes, you would understand."

Barbara was getting nowhere. It wasn't hard to work out why. If Rose dared to acknowledge how cruel she'd been to Barbara, the guilt would consume and overwhelm her. At her age, it might even finish her off. She had to keep it at bay at all costs.

Barbara sat up and looked hard at Rose. "You didn't even tell me I looked beautiful on my wedding day." There, she'd actually said it. After all these years of holding back, she'd come out with it.

"Of course I did! That's a terrible thing to say. What sort of a mother doesn't tell her daughter how beautiful she looks on her wedding day?"

Barbara decided to let it go. She'd said enough. Having promised to go easy on her mother, she'd gone too far.

"I'm sorry," Barbara said. "Forget it. Maybe I'm wrong." She took a breath. "Mum, do you love me?"

"Oh, for goodness' sake. Of course I do. All mothers love their children. Now, can we please stop this? It's doing neither of us any good. Enough now."

Rose picked up the TV remote and hit the "on" button. Green baize and a triangle of red snooker balls filled the screen. They were done. The conversation was over. Barbara said she should probably get going.

Half an hour later Barbara was sitting in Jean's kitchen. Ken had gone to see Arsenal play Fulham. Afterwards he was going out for a drink and a curry with the lads, so he wouldn't be back until late. Since it was past five and the sun was officially over the yardarm, Jean opened a bottle of wine and a jumbo pack of Doritos.

"I went too far. I really upset her," Barbara said, sliding her hand into the Doritos pack for the fourth or fifth time. "I should have left well alone. Now I feel like this great big bully. What was I doing, tormenting an eighty-three-year-old woman?"

"Oh, for heaven's sake. I'm sure you didn't bully or torment her.

Your mother may be old, but from the way you describe it, I think she's being pretty manipulative."

"How do you mean?"

"She made this all about her because she couldn't face taking responsibility for hurting you."

Barbara said she'd had the same thought.

"You were a child. An innocent. Even if she didn't mean to, she abused you emotionally. Not only do you have the right to tell her how you feel, you also have the right to an apology."

"I may have had that right years ago, but not now. Mum's old. My emotions are too much for her to cope with. I left it too late. I missed my chance."

"But you weren't ready to do it when she was younger. You were busy running a home, raising two kids. And anyway, knowing your mother, I'm not sure that if you had confronted her earlier, her response would have been any different."

Barbara shrugged. "Maybe you're right. Perhaps it would have been the same." She took a glug of wine. "All I wanted was for her to acknowledge that I had a crap childhood and to say sorry for her part in it. Then we could have moved on knowing that we understood each other. The only comfort she could offer me was that she'd done her best."

"Nothing else?"

"She said I was planned and how much she loved me when I was born. Oh, and that she still has one of my baby bootees."

"Which proves that until your dad got ill and everything went wrong, she had all the right maternal feelings. And even now she treasures those memories. You have to hang on to that. She didn't set out not to love you."

"I asked her if she loved me now."

"And ..."

"She said she did, and I want to believe her, but I'm not sure her heart was in it. She just said the words."

"Oh, hon . . ." Jean reached out across the table and took Barbara's hand.

"I'm too needy. I know I am. I've got to stop this."

Jean let out a breath. "OK, what I'm about to say might sound harsh, but perhaps you do have to stop. You've reached out to your mother, tried get close to her. But she's made it clear that it's too painful for her. You can't change her, so it's you who has to change. I'm sure she does love you in her own way, and I know that doesn't help much. But it's time for you to stop living in hope and accept that your mother can't give you what she doesn't have."

"Then what am I left with?"

"Frank. Your kids. Your grandkids. Me and Ken. The people who love and care about you."

"Funny how you put Frank at the top of that list. You know as well as I do that Frank only cares about Frank. You said yourself, I probably can't change him."

For a few moments Jean didn't say anything. Then: "All I'm saying is that with a bit of communication and compromise, you two aren't beyond saving."

"I try to communicate. He refuses to see my point of view. And as for compromise, I'm always compromising. Frank never even tries."

"OK," Jean said, raising her palms in front of her. "I've said all I'm going to say. It's your marriage. You two need to sort it out. But meanwhile, try pulling back from your mother. That doesn't mean you have to stop seeing her. It means you must start to disengage from her emotionally. I promise you that in the end it will give you some peace."

"What makes you so sure?"

She smiled. "Come on—how many times have I told you about

my wicked stepfather? I was this little girl whose real daddy had died. I was aching to be loved by my new father, but he saved all his affection for the children he had with my mum. Don't you remember me telling you that in my twenties I was so depressed that I started seeing a therapist?"

"I do, but you never went into much detail."

"OK. Well, she helped me disengage, to stop going to my stepfather for love and affection that wasn't there to be had. Make no mistake, though—pulling back is hard. But if you want to stop the ache, you have to try."

"I get that and I will try. I promise. . . . So what about your ache? Have you managed to stop that?"

"I've stopped seeing Jenson, if that's what you mean."

"Well done. I'm really proud of you. I was worried you wouldn't be able to do it. You will get over him, you know."

"I already have. Now I'm seeing Virgil."

"Virgil . . . Bloody hell, Jean. What are you playing at?"

"The agency said I should give it another go. Try somebody else."

"Of course they did! They want their commission. So what happens when you fall in love with Virgil? Will you carry on working your way through the agency's entire list of men?"

"But suppose I don't fall in love with him? Suppose I've got my emotions in check this time? I think with practice I can handle this. At the very least, I need to give it a go."

"You're crazy. Totally and utterly crazy."

"Maybe I am. But please don't judge me until you've walked in my shoes."

"I'm not judging you. I'm just worried about how this is going to end."

"Well, don't. The worst that could happen is that Ken finds out, and I've told you I don't think it would be the end of the world."

Barbara sat shaking her head and helping herself to more Doritos. "God, we're a right pair. There's you with your gigolos. Me with my autistic husband. Here we are in your kitchen, stuffing our faces and dishing out advice to each other. I feel like we're in some weird episode of *The Golden Girls*."

"I guess that would make me Blanche," Jean said, grinning. "I can live with that. So let me tell you about Virgil. . . ."

By eight o'clock, despite demolishing most of a jumbo pack of Doritos, they were starving. Jean called the local Thai and asked them to deliver two red curries. Barbara switched to Diet Coke because she was driving. By midnight they were "talked out" and Barbara was ready to head home. She hugged Jean, told her she loved her. "Please take care. I worry."

"I will. Love you, too. . . . Oh, quick, before you go, I have wedding gossip. . . . Momzilla has decided to wear white, if you please. Emma finally lost it with her, and they're not speaking. Adam is talking about the two of them eloping. Of course, Ken is encouraging it because he's thinking about all the money he can save."

"So everything's still nicely on track, then?"

"You betcha."

Once she was home, Barbara made herself some hot milk. As she stood waiting for the microwave to ping, she wondered whose problems she'd rather have—her own or Jean's. Was it worse to be loved by a man who had no interest in sex, or neglected by a man who did? She couldn't make up her mind.

Barbara took her cup of milk to the sofa and decided to check what was on TV. For some reason—most likely because her mind was buzzing—she wasn't tired. She went hunting for the TV remote and finally found it down the back of the sofa, along with a moldy crescent of rock-hard pizza crust. Ben. She began channel surfing, looking for some late-night comedy to cheer her up. An hour

later—the hot milk having done its work—she was fast asleep with
The Pink Panther playing to itself. She didn't hear Ben come home.
Nor was she aware of him switching off the TV. And she certainly
didn't hear all the giggles and shushing coming from his room,
which went on until dawn.

Chapter 9

Barbara woke up with a thumping head and a bladder fit to burst. Fearing that her postmenopausal pelvic floor wouldn't take the strain much longer, she practically sprang off the sofa.

She was about to open the door to the downstairs loo when it seemed to do so of its own accord. A young girl appeared. Seeing Barbara, the girl jumped. Barbara let out a tiny, simultaneous yelp. She also let out a trickle of pee, which began traveling down the inside of her leg. The girl—who was in her knickers and Ben's *I Still Live with My Parents* T-shirt that Jess had bought him for Christmas—spoke first.

"Oh, hi. You must be Ben's mum." She was pulling her thicket of slept-in blond hair into a scrunchie. "I'm Katie. Sorry to frighten you. I just came down to make some coffee. I'm afraid Ben and I got pretty trashed last night."

Barbara's profound need to empty her bladder aside, she was in no mood to exchange small talk—and particularly not with some strange girl Ben had hooked up with and got pissed with the night before. He knew the house rule. Only steady girlfriends, to whom she and Frank had been introduced, were allowed to sleep over. She was of the firm opinion—and for once Frank agreed—that they should at least know the names of the women who clogged the shower with their hair, left their used contact lenses stuck to the floor, and finished all the no-fat yogurt.

"Help yourself to whatever," Barbara said, trying to sound hospitable at the same time as tensing her pelvic floor. "There's cereal in the cupboard. Milk and juice in the fridge. Now, if you'll excuse me, I really need to use the loo."

"Oh, sure. Of course. Sorry."

Katie moved aside, offered Barbara a timid smile and headed towards the kitchen. Barbara sat down on the loo and peed most gloriously. At the same time she recalled her prechildbirth, premenopause days, when her undercarriage had been as taut as a drumskin. Back in the day, Ginger Baker could have played a solo on her pelvic floor.

Afterwards Barbara went upstairs and ran a bath. As she got undressed, she considered Katie with her pertness and tendrils of blond hair falling around her face. The only tendrils Barbara owned grew out of her face, not around it, and she had a habit of not noticing them until they were two inches long.

She picked up her foot sander, perched herself on the edge of the bath and began grating the hard skin on her heel. If she didn't do it regularly, she got cracks. As she grated, she reminded herself of her favorite maxim—the one about older women bringing more to the party than a perfect figure (naturally she included pertness and tendrils in this). She supposed her maxim was all well and good, so long as you'd been invited to the party in the first place. These days it felt like it was going on without her.

After a soak in the tub, her headache began to ease. As she

finished getting dressed, she could hear Ben and Katie saying good-bye at the front door. There were a few long moments when nothing was said and she tried to stop imagining the tongue kissing that was going on. Then she heard Ben calling out after Katie, promising to call. The door closed.

"You never mentioned you were seeing somebody," Barbara said, coming downstairs.

"I'm not. At least I haven't been. Katie and I met last night at this club. She just sort of wandered over and said hello . . ."

". . . with her vagina."

Ben screwed up his face. "Mum. For God's sake. Boundaries."

"Er . . . I could say the same to you. You know the rule. No girls to be brought home until Dad and I have met them."

"But Katie's really nice. And you met her outside the loo. Surely that makes it all right."

"Actually, no, it doesn't. . . . So what does Katie do?"

"Trainee investment banker."

"So she's in finance," Barbara said to Jean, who'd called to see how Barbara was feeling after yesterday. (Still a bit wobbly.)

"And your problem with that is . . . ?"

"I dunno. I guess I'm just a bit disappointed."

"What—that she's an evil capitalist and not some nice Marxist feminist he met at the food bank?"

"Very funny. I'm just worried that she may not be right for Ben, that's all."

"Good God, you make it sound like he's already proposed to her. And how do you know she doesn't give to charity or volunteer?"

"I don't. . . . OK, perhaps I've got her wrong. But it still bothers me."

"Maybe it does, but at the risk of stating the obvious, this is Ben's life—not yours."

"Jess and Matt won't like her," Barbara said, thinking about the Occupy London posters in Jess and Matt's flat.

"It's not their life either. The lot of you will just have to butt out."

Jean said she had to go because she needed to get ready for work. "By the way, quick FYI about the wedding—as of this morning Felicity's agreed not to wear white and she and Emma are speaking again. But as a quid pro quo, she wants all the men in top hats and tails. As you know, Ken isn't one to lose his temper, but I think he could be on the point of telling Felicity her fortune. I'll keep you posted. . . . Oh, and Ken and I are off to Devon tomorrow for a few days' break, so I've put your birthday pressie in the post."

One by one Barbara's girlfriends are turning eighteen. Coming of age. Their parents are marking the occasion by giving their daughters pieces of jewelry. Nothing fancy. These are blue-collar families. The lockets, charm bracelets and watches have mostly been bought on the high street. But to the girls showing them off in the school cafeteria they are parental love tokens—keepsakes that they will treasure for a lifetime.

"Mum," Barbara says one night after dinner, "I was wondering if maybe I could have a small piece of jewelry for my eighteenth?"

"What sort of jewelry?"

"I don't know. A locket, maybe."

When Barbara's birthday comes around, Rose and Stan hand her a card. Inside are two fifty-pound notes.

"Buy whatever you want," Rose says.

Barbara goes out alone and buys a gold-plated heart-shaped locket. She shows it off in the school cafeteria. Now she's the same as everybody else. Only she isn't.

Barbara had been trying to forget it was her birthday on Sunday. She didn't feel much like celebrating. Given the choice, she would have spent the day on the sofa drinking tea and watching True Movies back-to-back. It didn't help that friends kept reminding her that this birthday was "the one before the big six-oh" (or as old Mrs. Bernstein down the road put it: "the big six-oy"). On top of that, the Zuckerberg boy was still pushing over-fifties health insurance and cheap funeral plans at her. These days whenever she saw his name, her eyes performed what she could describe only as an ocular spoonerism and the Z in his name became an F.

But wallowing and getting cross with Mark Fuckerberg wasn't an option. By half past seven, Cleo and Atticus would be on the phone singing "Happy Birthday." (They would most likely have been up since six, nagging Jess to let them call.) Then there was the family tradition of the birthday tea party to be upheld.

So she'd wallowed the night before instead. As she lay in bed, she was beset by maudlin self-pity and fear. She hadn't reached the autumn of her days, but summer was definitely on the wane. How much time did she have left? How many more long girlie lunches with Jean? How many more Wimbledon finals? How many more orgasms? They were already pretty thin on the ground. Her life, which had always been about counting up, was now about counting down.

Being an atheist, she couldn't even cheer herself up with thoughts of frolicking in the afterlife. Barbara hated how her mind was attracted to proof and scientific evidence rather than faith. While other people found it so easy to make a case for a divine creator, she wore a *Richard Dawkins Is God* T-shirt in bed.

Religion offered so much more than atheism. For a start, there were all the twofers: Believe in God and we'll throw in free salvation—yours to enjoy for all eternity, no hidden extras. . . . Take the Lord into your heart and we guarantee you free entry into heaven. Rapture for all the family.

As an atheist, Barbara prayed she'd got it wrong. She so wanted there to be a heaven. How atheists had ever managed to sell oblivion, she had no idea. She'd often pictured atheist suits knocking on doors. "Good morning, madam. We're here to share the truth and the light. . . . Here's the thing: Life's crap. Then you die. And when you do pop your clogs, there's nothing. Zip. Bubkes. You cease to be."

Hey! Awesome! Put me down for that.

In twenty years she would be almost eighty. Of course, eighty wasn't what it once was. These days, octogenarians ran marathons and caught sexually transmitted diseases. But once a person hit eighty, oblivion could strike at any time.

Best-case scenario: she fell asleep one night—having danced at her hundred and tenth birthday with her new boy toy, who later made passionate love to her—and didn't wake up.

She dreaded a long, drawn-out illness. Her uncle Sid had died of lung cancer. In his final weeks, he had taken to his bed. Bit by bit, the chintzy bedroom he and Aunty Beryl had shared for fifty years was transformed into a hospital room. First came the oxygen tank. Then the hospital bed with a water mattress so that he didn't get bedsores. A large bottle of morphine stood on the dressing table next to Aunty Beryl's eau de cologne. Sid lay there, parchment and bone and hollow chest rattle.

But at least he'd died at home and not some hospice. Who in their right mind wanted to die among the dying? Or surrounded by a load of caring, sharing hospice nurses hell-bent on making sure you'd drawn up a "good death plan." If you were having an OK day, somebody might wheel you into the hospice garden and sit you on a wooden bench donated by relatives of a former dying person. From there you would, no doubt, have an uninterrupted view of the ornamental fountain and fiberglass flamingos.

Then the memories came flooding back—testaments to her

advancing years. She could remember London in the fifties and sixties when it was still moth-eaten with bomb sites. Sometimes there might be one house left standing in the rubble, its sidewalls blown off. Looking at a cross section, you could see the remains of living rooms. Each one had different flowery wallpaper. But most extraordinary—to Barbara's mind at least—was the column of unscathed fireplaces, each one the centerpiece for five families who'd lived stacked one on top of the other.

She could remember coal fires, thick yellow with pea-soup fogs. When the fog came down, nobody was allowed home after school until an adult arrived to collect them. Mums and dads turned up with torches. People wore scarves over their mouths. It went without saying that Barbara was always the last to be collected.

She could see her parents' black-and-white TV being delivered. Everybody on it spoke like the Queen. She remembered hopscotch and jacks, kiss-chase and riding on steam trains, the coalman, the sweep, the knife grinder, French onion sellers, washing lines full of billowing drawers, families decked out in their Sunday best at the seaside. She could remember *The Dick Van Dyke Show*, *The Defenders* and *My Three Sons*. She could still see the black armbands the day after Kennedy was shot.

Barbara couldn't sleep, so she went downstairs to make some hot chocolate. Her mind went back to Jean's sixtieth birthday party and the comment she'd made—albeit when she was drunk—about the importance of leaving a legacy. Jean had a wonderful legacy: the hundreds, if not thousands, of healthy babies she'd delivered.

For her part, Barbara had all the kids she'd helped over the years. But the truth was she hadn't achieved that much. It hadn't been for want of trying. For once she wasn't blaming herself. She was blaming a system that was underfunded and callous. Many of the children she'd taught over the years had needed a damn sight more than a couple of hours a week spent in her cubbyhole. They'd needed three decent meals a day. Some had needed counseling. They'd all needed new homes. A few she could mention had even needed new parents.

A tiny minority, the ones who managed to get an autism diagnosis or were thought to have serious learning difficulties, got transferred to specialist schools. The kids who were merely "a bit slow" or "lagging behind" or who had emotional problems didn't. There was no budget to help them—beyond what teachers like Barbara could offer. Some of them, the ones like Armani, the confident, likable kids who didn't have a problem beyond their noisiness and attention-seeking personalities, would make their way in the world. Others wouldn't.

Back in bed, she found herself looking at the envelopes on her nightstand. Her birthday cards had come in that day's post, but she'd decided not to open them until tomorrow. In addition to the cards, she'd received a magnificent bouquet of white roses from Frank. They'd come from Stems, the chichi, not to mention pricey, florist down the road. (As part of their chichi priciness, they didn't deliver on Sundays.) The card read: *Sorry can't be there. Missing you. Have a great day. Love you, F. xxxx*

When Frank bought her flowers, it was usually a small bunch of her favorite yellow freesias. On her birthday they tended to go out together to choose a present. The bouquet of roses was unusual—a grand gesture. It occurred to her that he was starting to feel guilty about the way he'd treated her.

In the end it was Frank who called first.

"Happy birthday! Sorry to phone so early, but it's two a.m. here and I'm starting to nod off."

"Don't worry. I was already awake." In fact, she's been sound asleep. She pulled herself into a sitting position. "I'm amazed you stayed up." He was definitely feeling guilty. "And thank you for the flowers. They're gorgeous."

"I'm glad you like them. Look, I'm really sorry I'm missing your birthday, but all being well, I should be back by the end of next month. So I thought we could have dinner somewhere a bit posh and have a belated birthday celebration. Maybe we'll splash out and go to La Buvette."

She didn't say anything.

"But if you don't fancy it, we could go somewhere else."

"Frank, you have to stop this."

"Stop what?"

"Pretending everything's fine between us when it isn't."

"Bar, please. You've got to move on from this."

"I can't. It's as simple as that. You left me when I needed you. I begged you not to go, and no amount of flowers and posh dinners are going to change that. . . ."

"Bar, please. How many more times do we have to go through all this? I'm sorry. I truly am. I don't know what else to say. But I'd signed a contract. There was nothing I could do. And anyway, you've coped really well."

"Yeah," she said. "I've been great . . . just like always. Barbara's strong. She can cope with anything."

"You know what? I can't do this right now. I'm too tired. I need to hit the sack."

"Fine. Go."

"But for what it's worth, I do love you. I love you very much."

She hit "end."

Summer 1977. Barbara and her flatmates graduate from teacher-training college and throw a party to celebrate. Frank, this dreamy-looking cool guy with crazy Bob Dylan hair, comes over and starts chatting her up. He's just finished the BBC's graduate trainee directors' course, and now he's on the payroll. Presently he's researching a film about social division in Britain. Poverty and inequality is his thing, he explains. "I really think filmmakers have the power to make a difference." She is so turned-on.

After a while they go out onto the balcony. They smoke weed and snog. At the end of the evening he asks her out and she says yes.

She wears her new halter-neck dress. Then she worries that he might find her sexier in her Workers of the World Unite T-shirt and CND pendant. But there's no time to change. They've arranged to meet in Hackney—equidistant from them both. She imagines they'll go for a curry or maybe to a cheap falafel place. She won't let him pay. As a feminist, she'll insist they split the bill. It upsets her that she isn't able to burn her bra, but her tits are way too big and left to their own devices would wobble and swing.

Hackney hasn't yet started to get trendy and is still pretty rough. As Barbara waits outside the station, she spies a gang of skinheads with swastika tattoos. They're coming in her direction. She's studying their body language, trying to work out if they're going to approach her and make trouble, when Frank appears. He kisses her on the cheek. "Ooh," shout the skinheads. Then they call him a wanker and a bender and swagger on by.

"Fucking morons," Frank says, before telling her how great she looks in the dress. They set off along Mare Street, and he takes her hand.

"So where shall we go?" she says, aware that she likes the feeling of her hand in his. "There are a couple of great curry places along here."

"Actually, I had somewhere else in mind. I hope you won't be annoyed."

"Why would I be annoyed?"

"'Cos it's not very datey."

A few more yards and they stop outside a white stone church, once grand but now decrepit. Its windows are covered in wire mesh.

He's brought her to church? Crap. Could she have gotten him more wrong? "Well, I see what you mean about it not being very datey," she says. "The thing is, I'm not really sure if I believe in God and I definitely don't go to church. I'm really not up for being shown the light."

Frank looks horrified. "What? No. It's nothing like that. We're headed for the church hall. It's used as a soup kitchen. Totally God-free. I promise. I volunteer here once a week. The thing is that when I asked you out, I totally forgot that I'm supposed to be working tonight. So I thought ..."

"... that maybe I'd like to come along and help?"

"Just for a couple of hours, and then we can go on somewhere—I promise. I know I should have called you to explain. But that would have meant canceling and I thought ..."

"... that I'd tell you to take a hike? Because you made a mistake?"

"It did occur to me."

"Don't be daft. I'd never do that."

"So are you happy to help out for a bit?"

"Absolutely. Lead on."

They walk through the churchyard. It's strewn with weeds, beer cans. The elderly, lopsided headstones are stained and weather-beaten and covered in moss. A few have been smashed or kicked over. They stop to read some of the inscriptions and remark on how long people seemed to have lived in the nineteenth century. They decide it's probably a myth that everybody died young. Then Barbara discovers a small section set aside for children. There are a dozen Ethels, Mays, Ediths and Herberts who fell asleep in infancy. Barbara tears up. Frank notices and puts his arm around her. She likes this even more.

Inside the church hall it's hot and full of people eating and queuing. The place smells of bacon and chips. Occasionally there's a waft of stale urine or robust body odor. There are trestle tables covered in plastic cloths and long wooden benches. Not everybody shoveling up food with plastic cutlery is a filthy, matted-haired crazy. Many of the diners look like regular people—a bit tatty round the edges maybe, but pretty normal-looking.

Barbara notices a besieged-looking, concave woman with three small children. Her cheek is a purple bruise. But the four of them are clean and tidy. Presentable. They probably have a home. Barbara assumes that the woman and her kids have come here to get away, for some respite from her husband's violence. Barbara points out the woman to Frank. "Isn't there a refuge round here?"

"She refuses to go. Insists she keeps having accidents."

Barbara can't imagine protecting a man who beat her.

On another table there's a chap in a grubby business suit and brogues with no laces. He's clutching an old briefcase to his chest. "Alcoholic," Frank says. "Used to be an accountant. Wife threw him out. We get a lot of those."

Barbara thinks about how her friends rail about inequality and poverty, but always from the comfort of a warm flat or a bar with a few beers inside them. None of them—her included—actually goes out and does anything (not that she doesn't have plans to rectify that). And here is Frank with a full-time job, giving up his time every week to get his hands dirty.

A nice middle-aged lady called Audrey welcomes Barbara and gently chides her for wearing such a lovely dress, which is only going to get sprayed in fat. She hands her a pair of tongs and directs her to a hot plate, where bacon and eggs are popping and spitting. A few moments later Audrey produces a pink nylon overall, which she says Barbara is welcome to borrow.

The half dozen or so volunteers cook, serve and make everybody feel welcome—apart from a group of students who have come in pleading poverty. Somebody hands each of them a packet of crisps and a Wagon Wheel and tells them to bugger off. They duly bugger.

There are jokes and laughter. People who have finished eating play
cards. One of the volunteers is on a break. She sits down to play chess
with Briefcase Man. Meanwhile, the drunken crazies rant or stare, silent
and glassy-eyed. Barbara can't take her eyes off Frank as he talks down
a filthy, shoeless man who has come in drunk, wielding a traffic cone.

When Barbara finally looks back at the hot plate, the bacon is turn-
ing black and smoking.

Barbara went downstairs, made herself a cup of coffee and took it
back to bed. She lay against the plumped-up pillows, reflecting on
the past as she sipped. She'd rarely worn her eighteenth-birthday
locket—partly because it had no sentimental value, but mainly
because she didn't like lockets. They were too traditional for her
taste. She'd preferred hippie beads and cowbell necklaces—her
CND pendant, which hung from a leather thong. The locket ended
up in Jess's childhood box of jewels. But her daughter hadn't shown
much interest in it because it wasn't glittery and sparkly. Barbara
couldn't remember when she threw it out.

As usual, Rose's card would contain a check. But these days Barbara had no problem excusing her mother for not making the effort
to buy her a gift. Rose was old. She was able to shop for herself, but
Barbara knew that the mere thought of doing it for somebody else
overwhelmed her. She was lucky that, at eighty-three, Rose even
remembered her birthday.

Once again, Barbara found herself replaying the tape of her big
conversation with her mother. She forced herself to listen to the section about her birth and how her parents had been overjoyed when
she was born. After that came the bit about how Rose had kept her
baby bootee, fed and clothed her, kept her out of harm's way. Her
mother's love tokens: the straws, which according to Jean she needed
to grasp. Her best friend was right. It was time to pull back and to

stop looking for what she couldn't have. To make do. It made perfect sense, but it felt like she'd spent her entire life making do.

She knew she was wallowing in self-pity, but she couldn't help it. By now her mind had turned to Frank and the state of their marriage. Jean thought it could be saved. She was probably of the opinion that Barbara should pull back from her husband as well as her mother—that she should stop looking to him for what he couldn't offer. But she couldn't. A good marriage involved both parties caring for each other. If the giving went in only one direction, it caused anger and resentment. Frank had neglected her for decades and she'd rarely complained. It wasn't that back then she hadn't noticed or cared. She had. But she'd always felt unworthy. Now she was almost sixty. She'd lost her job. She'd been ill. She needed him. He should have stepped up. Surely that wasn't asking too much. But even now she questioned her entitlement. How much love did she deserve? It still perplexed her.

It occurred to Barbara that she needed to see a shrink. Dr. Johal had mentioned that counseling might help her get to the root of her panic attacks. But she knew what had caused them. On top of that, it would take months to get an NHS appointment. And then it would only be with some ineffectual, drippy woman in a calf-length skirt and moccasins. Good shrinks cost money. So that was that.

She knew she had to sit Frank down and force him to listen to her—to make him understand exactly how she was feeling. Unless, of course, he did understand, but like Rose, he couldn't face up to how he'd treated her all these years.

If he refused to make some effort to change, what did she do then? Leaving him was unimaginable. They'd been married for nearly forty years. Two-thirds of her life. The marriage hadn't been terrible or wretched. Barbara hadn't lived with a brute who'd beaten her—merely a self-centered workaholic who took her for granted. A million women could tell the same story. She guessed that most of them didn't leave their husbands. Instead they plowed on in their run-of-the-mill discontent. They carried on because they were scared. Lonely oldness. That's what prevented them from leaving. It scared Barbara, too. But she also feared growing old in a lonely marriage.

There was a tap on the bedroom door. Ben appeared. "Happy birthday, dear Mu-um. Happy birthday to yooooou." He leaned over and gave his mother a kiss on the cheek and presented her with his card.

"You OK? You look a bit down."

"I'm fine," she said, patting the bed, inviting him to sit down. "Just a bit thoughtful."

"Come on, cheer up. It could be ages before you have to keep your teeth in a jar."

"Thanks, Ben. I appreciate that."

He sat down next to her. "You missing Dad?"

"I guess," she said, hoping that would be enough to satisfy him.

"Yeah, I used to hate it when he missed my birthday. But he always made up for it with some amazing present. Do you remember I had Pokémon cards before any other kid in the school?"

"Which meant it was at least a year before you had anybody to swap cards with."

"Yeah. There was that."

He handed her a lime-green envelope. "Jess is bringing your present over later. We went in on it together."

She pulled out the card. *Fifty-nine isn't old . . . if you're a tree.*

"Wow, such beautiful words. You have no idea how much better they make me feel."

"I thought they would," he said.

She opened the rest of her cards. There weren't many. These days most of her friends—and relatives like Pam—put birthday messages on Facebook.

Jean's card made her tear up. On the front was a photograph of two laughing women of a certain age, driving a sky-blue vintage sports car. The roof is down. The pair are wearing funky, jewel-encrusted cat's-eye sunglasses and scarlet lipstick. The backseat is covered with upmarket shopping bags. Inside Jean had written: *Here's to the two of us driving through Paris in a sports car with the warm wind in our hair.*

Barbara couldn't remember mentioning her Lucy Jordan fantasy to Jean. But clearly she had.

As promised, Jean had also sent a parcel. Barbara pulled off the brown paper. Inside a decorated box was another much smaller box. This contained a jar of Eve Lom cleanser. She knew it was Barbara's favorite. What she didn't know was that Barbara had run out weeks ago and that after that scary post-Christmas credit card bill, she hadn't dared buy any more.

Jess's card had hot air balloons on the front. She'd written: *Don't give up, Mum. You're never too old to fly.* Once again Barbara's eyes filled up.

Her mother's message was the usual: *Many happy returns . . . Love, Mum. Buy yourself something with the enclosed.* Inside was a check for thirty pounds. She would treat herself to that chunky Bakelite bangle she'd seen in the vintage shop down the road. It was tangerine with black spots. She would show it off to Rose, who would no doubt hate it, but she wouldn't get upset. Instead she would practice pulling back. She would kiss her, say thank you and move the conversation on.

Earlier in the week Barbara had invited Jess, Matt and the children over for tea. Jess had protested that it was Barbara's birthday and she couldn't possibly host her own tea party, but Barbara had insisted.

They hadn't been to her house in ages. And now that the weather wasn't quite so bitter, Atticus and Cleo could kick a ball around in the garden. Jess gave in.

Inviting Rose hadn't been easy. But in the end Barbara managed to put her emotions to one side and picked up the phone. Rose said that she'd been overdoing it and her ankle had puffed up again. If Barbara didn't mind, she would give tea a miss. It occurred to her that Rose was refusing to come because she was angry with Barbara for raising issues that she would have preferred not to confront. "Mum—about the other day. Are you OK? I really didn't mean to upset you. And if I did, I'm sorry."

"Apology accepted," Rose said briskly. "Now, can we please let the subject drop?"

"I just wanted to check you're all right. That's all."

"Apart from my ankle, I'm fine. Now, then, how's Cleo doing? Is she completely recovered now?"

Rose had shut down the conversation for a second time. Barbara had no plans to reopen it.

Jess and the children arrived without Matt. He'd organized somebody to cover for him at the deli, but they'd let him down at the last minute. Cleo, bright-eyed and back to her old self, was carrying a large plate. On it was a wonkily iced cake, festooned with candles. She held the plate out in front of her as if it were a velvet cushion bearing a precious jewel. "Me and Atticus iced it," she said. Barbara took in the neon-pink icing and marveled at how far natural food colorings had come.

"We were going to write 'happy birthday,'" Atticus said, "but then there wouldn't have been room for the candles. There's exactly fifty-nine. We counted them out to make sure. Fifty-nine's very old, isn't it?"

"Not if you're a tree," Barbara said, relieving Cleo of the cake. "Did you know they live for hundreds of years?" She thanked Cleo and Atticus for all their hard work and said that she couldn't wait to taste the cake.

"Do you want to see my inhaler?" Cleo said. "It's for when I start coughing." She asked Jess to get it out of her bag so that she could do show-and-tell. "You put it inside your mouth, press and then you breathe in the spray really hard." She offered it to Barbara to try.

"I'll have a go," Ben said. "So what sort of a hit do you get?"

"Oh, most amusing," Jess said. She relieved her brother of the inhaler and put it back in her bag.

The kids also presented Barbara with homemade cards. Atticus had drawn Spider-Man, who was meant to be rescuing Barbara from a blazing building. Cleo's picture was of a person lying in bed. "It's that old dead lady from the hospital. Do you think she's in heaven now?"

Barbara figured that if the old lady on the trolley hadn't been dead, she was looking none too well.

"I think she might well be," Barbara said. At the same time she thought it odd that Cleo had decided a picture of a dying old lady would make a nice birthday card for her grandma. Kids were odd creatures.

She asked the children if they would mind going into the kitchen to fetch the paper napkins. Ben went with them to find matches for the candles. He was back a few moments later.

"So, Jess," he said, "did you hear about the bloke who forgot to take his homeopathic medicine and died of an overdose?"

"Mum, tell him to give me a break. I've had Matt going at me. I don't need Ben as well."

"Your sister's right. Apologize for teasing her."

"It was a joke."

"I said apologize."

"What am I? Eight?"

"Ben, for the last time. Do as you're told."

"OK . . . Sorry."

"Whatever," Jess said, glaring at her brother. "You smell."

"So do you." Then: "Ouch! What was that? Did you just pinch me? . . . Mum, Jess just pinched me."

"Good."

Cleo and Atticus laid Father Christmas napkins—the only ones they could find—beside each plate.

"Now can we do presents, Grandma?"

There was posh body lotion from the children. Jess, Matt and Ben had bought Barbara a bottle of champagne and a long silk scarf. Splodges of vivid orange, lilac and fuchsia blended and bled into one another like an expressionist painting. Barbara adored it and insisted on wearing it while she served tea.

After they'd all sung "Happy Birthday," the children put on their coats and went outside in search of spiders. They were pining for Cyril, who had expired before he could be rehomed. The grown-ups sat at the table finishing the champagne.

"Thank you again for my fabulous scarf," Barbara said. She got up and kissed her children in turn.

"I just want you to know how much I love you both. Now you're all grown up, I don't say it often enough."

"Mum's had too much to drink," Ben said to his sister. "Now she's older, it goes to her head more easily."

"Stop it. Can't a mother tell her children she loves them without being accused of senile drunkenness?"

Cleo appeared in the doorway, trainers caked in mud, her head tilted to one side.

"Grandma, is there a spell to make yourself into a mermaid?"

Chapter 10

Later that week, Jack Dolan called to say that the family had received the report on Freddie from the dyslexia clinic. To his surprise, it was all pretty straightforward and didn't need any translation. As Barbara had suspected, Freddie was mildly dyslexic.

"Which means," Jack said, "that he won't need any more coaching for a posh senior school."

Barbara asked if he thought that Sally and Jeremy might like her to carry on giving him extra help anyway.

"I'm not sure he's feeling up to it just now."

He explained that although Sally and Jeremy were slowly coming round to the idea that their son was dyslexic, Freddie hadn't taken the news at all well.

"He was upset before the assessment, but now he's in a real state, poor chap. He's decided he's a dunce. Only kids don't use that word these days. He refers to himself as a 'retard.' I keep telling him that they think Einstein and Leonardo da Vinci were dyslexic, but he's not interested. Sally and his dad are really worried about him. I'm on my own with him at the moment. Usually we get along like a house on fire, but he's even lashing out at me because he's so angry."

"I am so sorry. It can't be easy. Is there anything I can do?"

"To be honest, I could do with some advice. I'm not sure I'm handling the situation very well. I have to admit that I've lost my temper with him a couple of times. I was wondering if you and I could meet up for a spot of lunch and a chat."

Barbara said she would be glad to offer what advice she could. She also had a couple of ideas about suitable schools. They arranged to meet the following day at the Baker's Arms in Islington.

"Sorry to ask you to come to me," Jack said. "But I have to pick Freddie up from school at three."

Barbara had intended to leave home around midday. Even in traffic, the journey wouldn't take more than an hour. Instead she left at ten thirty. While she was having her early-morning coffee, she realized that she wanted—or rather needed—to take a detour . . . to Jubilee Primary. She had no desire to go inside, much less speak to any of the staff. Despite mutual promises to stay in touch, she'd barely spoken to any of them since she left. It was her fault. She hadn't made the effort. She supposed that deep down she resented them all for having jobs. She suspected that for their part, having found out from Sandra that she'd had some—albeit not severe—mental-health problems, they weren't sure what to say to her.

All she wanted to do was sit outside in her car for a few minutes. She was losing her connection with the place and she couldn't bear it. The sane part of her knew that her proposed pilgrimage would only make her more miserable, but she was determined to go.

She sat in the silence—the car windows misting up—staring into the playground, hoping nobody would see her. All she needed was people thinking she'd turned into some psycho ex-employee with a grudge.

The rational part of her had been right. Being at the school only reignited her gut-wrenching feelings of loss, her anger at being cast aside. She knew she should drive away. But again, she couldn't. Instead, she got out of the car. Before she knew it, she was crossing the busy main road and walking into the Orchard Farm Estate. She found herself heading for the bench in the playground—the one she'd come upon that day in the rain—the day she got fired. What was she doing to herself? Was this some kind of Magical Misery Tour?

As she sat down, she noticed that the bench was covered in the same graffiti. Stacey was still a slag. Everything about the place was the same. The litter. The dog shit. The wind, which still felt like it was blowing in directly from the Russian Steppes.

As usual, the playground was empty. Barbara wondered why. Save for the wind, it was an OK enough day. Parental lethargy was the all-too-likely answer. But she suspected it was a lethargy born of despondency and depression. She imagined all these babies and toddlers stuck in smoke-filled flats day after day, filling up on junk, the TV blaring.

Her gaze shifted from the playground to the boarded-up community center a few yards away: a gray, stained-concrete lump spray-painted with fuzzy penises. Even in its short-lived heyday the place hadn't been up to much. Inside, if Barbara remembered rightly, there had been a hall—just about big enough for a couple of table tennis tables—and a couple of toilets.

When the community center closed, Barbara remembered Sandra going on about how it failed only because the council refused to move with the times and get some commercial backing. This would, she said, have paid for decent equipment, a full-time manager on a proper salary and competent, enthusiastic staff. In her opinion, the local council should have appointed somebody to go out and woo the banks and big businesses. But it hadn't happened. "They couldn't be bothered to get off their backsides. Nobody cared. Shame on the whole bloody lot of them." It wasn't often that Barbara agreed with her boss, but she had on this occasion.

Sandra—in a rare moment of derring-do—had written a letter to the council begging them to reopen the center. Some low-level functionary had written back pleading poverty: *Sadly no monies are available to ourselves to reopen said building at this present moment in time.*

Barbara stared at a spiky scrotum and wondered if it was worth contacting the council again to see if they would be prepared to renovate the building and reopen the center. Maybe she could set up a committee of local do-gooders and get a petition going. Lord knows she had the time, and after all the years she'd spent doing battle with social services, the idea of taking on the council didn't remotely faze her.

She got up and ambled over to the concrete lump. Only now did she notice that the asphalt roof had pretty much collapsed. One of the boarded-up windows had been bashed in, so she was able to peer inside. It was dark, but she could make out enough to see that floor was a lake of water. The place stank of rot and wet and urban fox spray. She could make out a couple of car tires lying on the floor, along with an overturned supermarket trolley and great chunks of what she took to be collapsed roof.

Barbara was no expert, but it seemed to her that the building was beyond repair. What it needed was bulldozing and replacing. A new community center that was more than just a brutalist concrete hall with a Coke machine would cost, what? A million? Maybe more. Because of cuts in central government funding, the council had even less money now than it had when they shut down the center. The situation was so dire that they were closing nursery schools and drop-in centers for the elderly. There was no point approaching them about the community center. The idea was laughable.

The sky had clouded over. Thinking it might be about to rain, Barbara decided to head back to her car. She'd reacquainted herself with the school and the neighborhood—for what it was worth. Now it was time to go.

She'd walked a dozen paces or so when her phone rang. It was Sandra. She sounded as if she was on the verge of tears.

"Sandra, what on earth's the matter?"

"I just got a call from Maureen at social services. Troy's mum is in hospital. The boyfriend came back in the middle of the night and went for her with a hammer."

"Jesus." Barbara should have been shocked, but she wasn't. Instead all she felt was rage. "That poor girl. I knew he'd come back. I just knew it."

"He was high on drink and drugs apparently. The police found him on her bed, semiconscious, with a needle in his arm. She's in the hospital with serious head injuries. They've put her on a ventilator. They're not sure if she's going to make it."

Barbara's fury and fear over Tiffany turned to panic. "What about the kids? Are they OK?"

"Troy and Lacie are at the hospital being checked out. Apparently Troy tried to get away on his bike, but he fell off and hurt his shoulder. Otherwise he and Lacie appear to be fine—physically at least. I don't know how much Troy saw of what happened. Maureen's with them at the hospital. She wanted me to call you because Troy is really distressed and asking for you."

"Me? But doesn't he have family? Grandparents, aunts, uncles?"

"Apparently there's nobody."

She was right. Barbara remembered Tiffany telling her that her family was either dead or locked up.

The receptionist at the ER remembered Troy and Lacie coming in with a social worker. "Police dropped them off. Both in their pajamas, poor little mites. The boy was covered in mud. He didn't say a word. Apparently, the mother's in the ICU. So what happened?"

"The thing is, I'm in a bit of a hurry," Barbara said. "Do you happen to know where they are?"

She seemed annoyed that Barbara wasn't about to furnish her with all the gory details. Nevertheless, she directed her to X-ray. Troy was having his shoulder checked out. The attack had happened in the small hours. Why was he only now going to X-ray? Surely they hadn't kept him waiting all this time. Then it occurred to her that the police would have needed to take a statement from him. Troy would have been in shock. It had probably taken forever to get anything out of him.

Barbara got there just as Troy was being taken into the X-ray room. The radiographer was telling the woman with him—Maureen, she assumed—that she would have to wait outside. The door closed.

"Maureen? Hi, I'm Barbara Stirling—Troy's teacher. We spoke on the phone."

"Of course." Maureen offered up a weary smile and the two women shook hands.

"So how is he? Where's Lacie?"

Maureen explained that Lacie had been given the all clear by the doctors and was on her way to emergency foster care. Troy would join her later. "He's in a terrible state, poor lad. He's hardly said a word. It was a real struggle for the police to get anything out of him. But all the time, he's kept asking for you. He says you're his favorite teacher."

"I guess I've taken him under my wing lately. . . . So, did he see the attack?"

"Apparently not, thank God. He'd escaped on his bike by then."

Barbara looked at Maureen in her battered boots, her trench coat that wasn't long for this world. Judging by her pallor and puffy eyes, she'd just come off a night shift. Either that or she'd been woken out of her sleep by a call from the police and had dragged herself out of bed, not knowing what horror she was going to find when she reached Tiffany's house. Maureen was underpaid and overworked. Barbara understood all that. But it didn't stop her being angry.

"When we spoke," she said, "you promised me faithfully that you would look after this family."

"We did our best."

"I'd hate to see your worst."

Maureen didn't get angry. Instead she let out a slow breath. "Look . . . Wayne was off the scene. Tiffany was coping. We found a way for her to claim extra benefits to help with her bills, and the children seemed to be doing OK. There was a case conference and it was decided . . ."

". . . to stop visiting."

"Not entirely. But we scaled back visits, yes."

"And this is the result. Wayne came back and beat Tiffany half to death. The woman's on a ventilator. She might die."

"I know. And I don't know what to say other than I'm sorry."

"What bloody use is *sorry*? This is a tragedy that should never have happened. Those kids might be about to lose their mother because the department—which you head up—decided to 'scale back visits.'" Barbara was aware of balls of spit coming out of her mouth.

"Barbara, you need to calm down. Getting angry won't do anybody any good."

"Don't tell me what to do. I won't calm down. This family is just another statistic to the police and social services. You don't care. Not really."

"You know what?" Maureen came back, finally losing it. "You're right, we do get hardened. And if you did my job, so would you. It's how we survive. And given the resources we have, we do our best. I do my best. This time I made a bad call. I got it wrong and I will have to live with my mistake. Like I said, I'm sorry." Maureen was tearing up. Barbara knew she had gone too far. Maureen wasn't as hardened as she made out.

"You'll make sure the children are kept together, right?" Barbara said, the accusation gone from her voice.

"Of course. We'd never let them be separated."

"I guess that's something. . . . Look . . . I'm sorry for losing my temper. I know your job isn't easy. If I'm honest, it's me I'm angry with—for not going to see Troy and checking they were all OK."

"You can't blame yourself," Maureen said. "I was in charge. In my defense, I did try to get her into a women's refuge, but she was so convinced that this Wayne character wasn't coming back."

"I know. I tried too."

"And then what do you know? . . . He came back. I should have assumed he would. They always do."

"Hindsight's a wonderful thing," Barbara said.

She found herself glancing at the hospital clock. It was after twelve. She remembered her lunch date with Jack. She needed to postpone it. She excused herself, went over to the drinks machine and called his number.

"Good God," he said after she'd explained what was going on. "So, is the mother going to make it?"

"They don't know. . . . Anyway, I was wondering if we could take a rain check on lunch."

"Absolutely. No problem. Do what you have to do."

———————

The woman radiographer held Troy's hand as he came out of the X-ray room. He looked so pitiful in his faded Spider-Man pajamas, which were at least two sizes too small for him and covered in dried-up mud from his fall.

Troy didn't run sobbing into Barbara's arms. Instead he trudged towards her. His exhausted, puffy face was streaked with muddy tears.

"Wayne hurt my mum."

"I know, my darling." She sat down on one of the metal chairs and lifted him onto her lap.

"He kicked the door down. I ran away to find the police. It was dark and I was scared and I didn't want to go to the people next door 'cos he would have bashed them up, too, and then I fell off my bike and hurt my shoulder and my bike's all bashed up and doesn't work anymore and then the police brought me and Lacie here. . . ."

Finally it was all tumbling out of him.

Barbara wrapped him in her arms. "You're a good boy. You did the right thing. Are you OK?"

"My shoulder still hurts. I want to see my mum, but the nurses say I can't because she's too sick. So when can I see her?"

"Probably not today. I think we'll need to wait until she's feeling a bit better."

"So I'll be able to see her soon?"

"I'm sure you will." She tried to wipe away the streaks of mud from his face, but they weren't budging.

In the end, Troy's shoulder was only bruised. He would be in "discomfort" for a few days. If it got too much, he could be given Tylenol. He was free to go.

"Where am I going to stay?" Troy said to Barbara, as the three of them headed to the lift. "Can me and Lacie come and stay at your house?"

"I can't think of anything I'd like more," Barbara said. "But I don't think I'd be allowed. You have to be a properly qualified foster carer to look after children, and I'm not qualified."

"But you're nice and kind. And you're a teacher. You're my favorite teacher, and I know Lacie would like you. It would be good fun."

"I'm sure it would, but Maureen has found you a nice family to stay with until your mum's better and I absolutely promise to come and visit. How does that sound?"

"I don't want to sleep in a stranger's house," Troy said. "I want to see my mum."

Maureen reached out and took his hand. She explained that Carole, the lady he and Lacie were going to stay with for the next few days, was a lovely, kind person. "And she has hamsters and guinea pigs. If you ask her nicely, I'm sure she'll let you keep one of the cages in your room."

"But what about my mum? I want to see her before I go to bed."

"You'll see her soon," Maureen said, welling up.

"Good."

He wasn't happy, but he seemed to have accepted that there was no chance of seeing his mum today. He turned back to Barbara. "Miss, why did you stop being our teacher?"

"I didn't want to stop. It's just that the government couldn't afford to keep me on. Then I got sick. So I left a few months before I was meant to. I'm sorry I didn't have a chance to say a proper good-bye."

"I was upset."

"I know you were." Barbara gave him a squeeze.

"Will you come back?"

"I very much doubt it."

"I hate the gov'ment."

"Yeah," Barbara said. "Me, too."

They stepped into the lift.

"The police have caught Wayne, haven't they?"

"They have," Maureen said. "And I promise you that he will go to prison for a long time."

"Good. Is my mum going to die?"

"Oh, sweetheart, we hope not. The doctors are doing everything they can, and these days they can do some pretty amazing stuff."

"Taylor at school—her mum died."

"I remember," Barbara said. "That was very sad."

"They buried her in the ground. So now she's all on her own in the cold and the dark. If my mum dies, will they bury her in the ground?"

Barbara's heart was practically in bits. "Tell you what, let's not think about that now. What we need to do is focus on her getting better."

"I could pray," Troy piped up.

"Good idea."

"Will you pray, too?"

"Of course I will. Tonight. Before I go to sleep."

"And so will I," Maureen said.

"And what about if Wayne escapes and comes to get me?"

Barbara and Maureen exchanged glances.

"Wayne is locked up in a prison cell," Barbara said. "He's being guarded by lots of big, strong men. He isn't going to get away—tonight or ever."

"But on TV people escape from prison," he said.

The lift pinged. They had reached the ground floor.

Chapter 11

Barbara arrived home just as Ben was getting ready to go out. He was sitting at the bottom of the stairs doing up his Converse. "I'm going to put in a few hours at the food bank and then meet Katie from work. I'll probably spend the night at her place."

"Sure," Barbara said, not really engaging. She hung up her coat. "Have a good time. Is there any wine left in the fridge?"

"I dunno. I don't drink wine. Plus it's three in the afternoon. Since when did you start hitting the bottle in the afternoon?"

Barbara kicked off her shoes. "For your information, I never *hit* the bottle. But since you ask, I'm having a crap day and I could do with a drink."

"What happened? You're not ill again, are you?"

"No, nothing like that. I'm fine." She perched herself on the edge of the hall table and told him about Troy and Lacie. "The mother's on life support. They don't know if she's going to make it."

"Shit. Poor kids."

A text landed on Ben's phone. As he read it, he grinned. *Bound to be Katie,* Barbara thought. His fingers hit the keypad. "OK, I'd better get moving. You going to be all right? I can stay if you want."

"I'll be fine," she said. "I might have a lie down."

There was no wine. Or Scotch. She made a cup of tea and took it to bed. She got under the duvet without bothering to get undressed and watched *Deal or No Deal.* She wasn't sure when she drifted off, but when she woke up the seven o'clock news was on. She realized she was starving.

She made scrambled eggs on toast and wondered how Troy was getting on in a strange house surrounded by strangers. Maybe she should call the hospital to see how Tiffany was doing, but Maureen had warned her they probably wouldn't tell her anything as she wasn't family or from social services. Maureen had promised to call as soon as she knew anything. Barbara finished eating, put her plate in the dishwasher and wiped the toast crumbs off the worktop. Then she wandered around the house, picking up newspapers and magazines, plumping up cushions. She didn't know what to do with herself. She needed somebody to talk to. She called Jean, who said she'd literally just walked in. Jean had been teaching her prenatal class for single teenage mums. She'd been doing it free of charge for twenty-five years.

"It wasn't just social services who fell short," Barbara said after she'd finished telling her what had happened. "I did. I should have gone round there to check they were OK. Then there was the school. Why weren't the staff keeping a lookout for signs that he was distressed? Every adult in that child's life has let him down. Not one of us could help him. It's pathetic. No—you know what? It's not pathetic. It's wicked—that's what it is. Absolutely bloody wicked."

"Come on," Jean soothed. "Nobody's been wicked. People just took their eye off the ball. And you have absolutely nothing to feel guilty about. You've been sick. You've had enough on your plate. If anybody was to blame, it was social services and possibly the school."

No sooner had she hung up than Jess called. "Ben just phoned me. He told me what happened to that poor woman and that you seemed pretty upset. Do you want to come over?"

"That's kind of you, but I'm fine. Just tired. It doesn't help that there's been no more news from the hospital. I can't help feeling that I let the poor kid down."

Jess said much the same as Jean. The responsibility lay firmly with social services.

"I know," Barbara said. "But you have no idea how hard-pressed they are. . . ."

"That's their problem. They should campaign, go on strike, lobby the government for more funding."

Barbara was too tired to argue—to make the point that most of them were probably too worn-out to campaign.

She took a shower and went back to bed. Afterwards she said a prayer, not simply because she'd promised Troy that she would, but because she felt a genuine need. "Please, God, don't let Tiffany die. Please." Barbara wondered how many atheists sent up prayers to the god they didn't believe in when they or somebody they cared about was in desperate need.

Maureen called first thing the next morning to say she'd been on to the hospital and there was still no change. Three of Tiffany's girl-friends from the estate were taking it in turns to sit with her.

"Would you mind if I went to see Troy?" Barbara said. "I feel like I'm all he's got right now."

Maureen said she didn't have to ask. "Go whenever you like."

A few minutes later, she texted Barbara the address.

Carole, the emergency foster carer who had offered to take Troy and Lacie for a few days—until a more permanent placement could be found—lived less than half a mile from the Orchard Farm Estate. What a difference a few streets made. The three-story Victorian house was bang in the middle of a row of smart, gentrified houses. There was barely a house without plantation shutters, bay trees in zinc pots and a muted Farrow & Ball front door. Then there was Carole's: seventies aluminum window frames, the walls covered in crazy paving cladding. It stood out like a garden gnome in the Conran Shop.

Carole, fiftyish, baggy tee over equally baggy jeans, opened the door carrying Lacie on her hip. The toddler, all clean and glossy of curl, was chewing on a half-peeled apple.

"Hi. You must be Barbara. Maureen said you'd be popping over. Come on in." The women shook hands, and Barbara chucked Lacie under the chin. "Hi, noodle. How you doing?"

"Not been a moment's trouble—have you, my darling?"

Lacie grinned at Carole and threw the apple on the floor.

Carole laughed. "Actually, I take that back. She seems to get a real kick out of dropping her apple and watching me bend down to pick it up."

Carole stood Lacie on the worn needlecord and retrieved the apple. She went over it with her fingers, pincering off bits of fluff and schmutz. Finally she handed it back to Lacie, who trotted off down the hallway, making a beeline for the living room. Carole quickened her step.

"No, not in there, poppet. Your brother's napping on the sofa." She took Lacie's hand and pulled the door closed. "We had him up half the night," Carole said to Barbara. "He just lay in bed sobbing for his mum. Poor little mite's exhausted."

She led Barbara into the kitchen. "Excuse the chaos," she said as Barbara dodged a spinning top, a bumblebee kiddie walker and a jar of what looked like homemade chutney. "How on earth did that get there?" Carole said, bending down to retrieve the jar. She placed it on the worktop next to a line of similar ones, all hand labeled and with pretty gingham covers. By now Lacie was making little "eh, eh" noises and lifting her arms to be picked up.

"Let me take her off you," Barbara said, but Lacie wasn't having it. The moment Barbara went near her, she howled.

Carole scooped up the child. "Not to worry. She might need changing." She pulled Lacie's diaper away from her back and sniffed. "Nope. You're still good." She blew a raspberry on Lacie's tummy. The child burst out laughing. Carole blew another and another. In the end, Lacie was laughing so much she began to hiccup.

"Right," Carole said to Barbara. "Sit your body down and I'll put the kettle on." But all the kitchen chairs were occupied by bits of domestic detritus: a bag of potatoes, assorted cardboard picture books and a pile of clean laundry.

With her spare hand, Carole slid the laundry—along with a fat ginger tom who'd been fast asleep on top of it—off a kitchen chair and onto the floor. The cat let out the meekest of protests—as if he was used to being evicted from warm, comfy spots. He scratched a war-torn ear and ambled to his cat door.

Carole got busy making tea. Barbara offered to help, but Carole insisted she was used to doing things one-handed. As if to prove her point, while she waited for the kettle to boil she bustled around picking up a bowl of half-eaten, soggy Coco Pops left over from breakfast, mugs of coffee that had been abandoned after one sip because there hadn't been time to drink them.

Barbara sat taking in the display of children's art. Every inch of spare wall space was covered in drawings and paintings. There were odd-shaped heads sprouting arms and legs, handprints galore—each with somebody's name. Then there was the corkboard with its patchwork of overlapping, curling photographs—some badly faded with age. They were all of children: babies, toddlers, older ones, teenagers.

"So how long have you been fostering?" Barbara said.

"Since the eighties, but it feels like forever. Mike and I have never actually sat down and counted how many children we've had through our door, but it must be in the hundreds."

She explained that she and Mike, a fireman, hadn't been able to have children, so they'd decided to foster. Along the way, they'd even adopted two girls who'd been sent to them.

"Of course they're both grown up and married now, with children of their own." For a moment she looked wistful. "But raising them wasn't easy. Both of them came from wretched backgrounds. They couldn't trust adults or believe that anyone could love them. It took us years to gain their trust. When I think back to the tantrums, all the kicking and punching . . ."

"How on earth did you cope?"

"You just have to keep reminding yourself that the hell they're putting you through is nothing like the hell they've come from. Still, I'm guessing that doing the job you do, you know all this."

"Actually, I'm not teaching anymore—at least not at Jubilee. I just got made redundant. Cutbacks."

"What is it with the bloody government? They make a short-term gain by getting rid of special-needs teachers like you. But in the long run, uneducated, unemployable kids become out-of-work adults—some of whom will turn to crime and will cost them a fortune."

Lacie was nodding off on Carole's shoulder. There was a playpen over by the French doors. Carole laid her down on the soft foam floor and covered her with a blanket.

"Like I said, this one hasn't been a moment's trouble, bless her, but I'm really worried about Troy. He's distraught. I've been cuddling and comforting him as much as I can, but the poor mite's inconsolable."

"I'm not surprised, but I'm not sure there's much else you can do—or any of us can do."

The ginger tom reappeared with a clatter of his cat door. He moseyed over to the pile of washing and stepped onto it. Afterwards he performed the customary feline round-and-round-in-circles ritual before settling himself down again.

Just then Carole's mobile rang. "OK, Doreen, don't panic. No . . . please . . . you have to calm down. I'll call them to find out what's happened. The van's probably stuck in traffic. No, of course you won't go hungry. They'll be there. I promise." She ended the call and explained that her elderly neighbor, whom she kept an eye on because the poor soul had no family, was in a panic because Meals on Wheels hadn't turned up. "If you could bear with me for a sec, I need to make a call."

Carole was making quite an impression on Barbara. The woman had been up half the night trying to comfort a severely traumatized little boy—not to mention look after his baby sister—and here she was the following morning, full of beans and taking on even more problems. She'd even found time to make chutney. Barbara was no shirker, but Carole was in a different league. Right now Barbara felt she had more in common with the cat dozing at her side.

Carole was still on the phone to the Meals on Wheels people when Troy appeared, spent with exhaustion. He climbed onto Barbara's lap. She wrapped her arms around him.

"You OK? How's your shoulder?"

"Still hurts a bit, but it's getting better. . . . Last night when I had a bath, Carole put bubbles in the water. We don't have bubbles at our house." He paused. "Have the doctors called from the hospital?"

"No, my darling, they haven't, but I'm sure they will."

"When I'm a big man, I'm going to kill Wayne. I'm going to shoot him and bash him to bits."

"And who could blame you," Barbara muttered under her breath. "So, how do you like Carole? Have you met the hamsters yet?"

"She's nice. She let me have the hamster cage in my room, and Dave the cat slept on my bed. I like it when he purrs."

Barbara asked Troy if he was hungry. He shook his head.

"Have you eaten anything this morning?"

"Toast."

"And he left most of that—didn't you, poppet?" Carole said, off the phone now.

"I just want to see my mum! I wanna see my mum! I wanna . . ." Troy threw himself onto the floor and began kicking and hitting it with his fists.

Carole sat down beside him. She made no effort to restrain him. Instead she stroked his head and gently shushed him. His body shook with sobs. "I want to see her. Let me see her."

"She's still not well enough, my darling. I know you're sad and angry and missing her, but the doctors are doing all they can, and as soon as she's feeling a bit better, they will let you see her."

"When will that be?"

"I don't know. A few days maybe."

"You promise?"

Carole hesitated. "No, sweetie. I can't promise."

This set him off again—kicking and howling. The two women looked at each other, eyes filling up. Barbara felt heartbroken and powerless. One look at Carole told her that she felt the same.

Finally Troy wore himself out and his tears dried up. Carole held him in her arms and rocked him. Suddenly he pulled away.

"Have you got any crisps?"

Carole looked bemused. "I've got some salt and vinegar Hula Hoops," she said.

"Salt and vinegar's my favorite."

She got up and went over to the kitchen cupboard. Troy followed her.

"Tell you what, hon. You eat these, and when you've finished, you can help me feed the hamsters. OK?"

He nodded and wandered back to the living room to watch TV.

"Poor little sausage," Carole said. "Give him an hour and he'll be throwing himself on the floor again. He's been like this all morning."

"It's how he deals with stress," Barbara said. "He often had tantrums in school."

"It breaks my heart to think what he must have been through—even before yesterday."

Barbara glanced over at Lacie, who was still sound asleep. "Listen, I know Maureen should be asking you this, not me, but would you consider having Lacie and Troy for more than just a few days? Even if Tiffany makes it, she's going to be in hospital for weeks. After that she'll need time to convalesce. And you're so amazing with them."

"I'd keep them in a heartbeat, but Mike's the problem. Now that we're older, he thinks we should restrict ourselves to emergency care only." She explained that he was now working only part-time at the fire department in preparation for retirement. "He's determined for us to have more time to ourselves."

"I totally hear you, but couldn't you ask him?" She was aware of the pleading tone in her voice. "It's not going to be forever ... six weeks maybe." She'd pulled the figure out of the air. She hadn't the foggiest notion how long Tiffany would be in hospital.

———

Maureen called as Barbara was getting into her car. "I just spoke to one of Tiffany's doctors. It's not looking good. She's still on the ventilator. And there's a possibility of serious brain damage. They're planning to do a load of tests today."

There was nothing to say. "OK, let me know as soon as you have any more news."

"Will do. How's Troy?"

"Pretty traumatized, but he seems to have taken to Carole. I really like her. She's great with both of them. I don't suppose there's any way you could put some pressure on her to keep Troy and Lacie for a bit longer? I hate the idea of them being moved again—Troy in particular. I think the stress would be too much."

Maureen agreed. "But it's Mike who's going to need convincing." She said she would call and try a bit of gentle emotional blackmail on him.

When Barbara got home she found a voice mail message from Frank from the night before. "Just checking in. Nothing urgent. Still bat-shit busy here, but all looking good. By the way, I Skyped with Jess earlier. Did you know that Ben was seeing somebody? That should cheer him up a bit. Oh, and she told me about the kid from your school and his mum. Terrible thing. I don't know what to say. Hope you're OK."

By now it was lunchtime. Barbara made herself a couple of slices of cheese on toast and, almost as a reflex, switched on the TV. She would spend the afternoon vegging out in front of some made-for-TV courtroom drama and getting more maudlin. She needed to get out of herself—one of Rose's favorite phrases.

Not that watching crappy TV would really take her out of herself. What she craved was inane chatter, some gossip and a giggle.

Camp David. She picked up her phone and spooled through her contacts list. Could he possibly fit her in at such short notice? she asked the receptionist. Funnily enough, they'd just this minute had a cancelation. He could see her in fifteen.

Camp David—he of David and Jonathan in Hackney Fields—welcomed Barbara with double kisses and, when he saw her roots, a theatrical look of disgust. "Mrs. S, please don't tell me you've actually been leaving the house like that. Come on—let's get you sorted out." He called out to one of the assistants, "Tracey, a gown for my lady."

Tracey brought her *Hello!* and *OK!* and cucumber-infused water to "flush out her toxins." While the colorist painted her hair in "something a bit more tonal than usual," Barbara sipped her water and soaked up the showbiz gossip in *OK!* while in the background Cher belted out "The Shoop Shoop Song." Half an hour later her color was cooked and she was at the backwash being shampooed. "Water temperature OK for you?" Tracey inquired. Barbara said it was perfect. As Tracey got busy rinsing off the excess hair dye, she rattled on about her hen night the previous weekend. A group of them had gone to Amsterdam and her friends had made her go around the city carrying a large inflatable willy. "But it was a giggle, and to be honest, I was too stoned to care.

"Would you like a head massage?" Tracey said as she combed conditioner through Barbara's hair.

"That would be lovely," Barbara said.

The massage lasted ten minutes. Barbara relished every stroke and touch. At one point she felt herself drifting off. Barbara was a great believer in the therapeutic power of nonsexual touching. There wasn't enough of it.

Tracey towel dried Barbara's hair and took her over to one of the big leather chairs, where David was waiting. He asked if she'd like something else to drink. "A cappuccino would be great," she said.

"Trace—if you please, a frothy coffee for Lady Barbara."

He ran his fingers through her wet hair, flicked it to one side and then the other, pushed it behind her ears and then brought it forward again. He said he was loving the color and suggested that she save the white roots for Halloween. He swept her fringe back off her face. "You, know I've been thinking about your hair. . . ."

He probably hadn't been thinking about it at all. But she loved the way David always managed to make her feel as if she were the only client in the salon. "So I'm thinking we should keep the basic bob, but maybe cut in some layers and perhaps go for something a bit more choppy—something with a bit more movement. It's not doing very much at the moment, is it?"

Was hair meant to actually *do* anything? But Barbara trusted David and said she was happy to leave the decision to him.

For the next hour, he wheeled around on his stool snipping and slicing, fretting about getting her fringe right. She liked it left long, but not so long that it went in her eyes. He told her all about Tony, the new man in his life. He'd bought David pecs implants for his birthday. The two of them were also planning a trip to the Antarctic to see the penguins. He turned to wave good-bye to a client. "Bye, darling. See you soon." He wheeled his stool close to Barbara. "Eighteen stone that one was. Full-body lipo. I kid you not. Lost half her body weight."

The stylist working next to David had overheard.

"David, you can be such a bitch."

"Hark at you, baldy. I suppose you do realize that in that turtleneck you look like a roll-on deodorant."

Barbara was laughing so hard that David had to stop cutting.

"So anyway," he said as he started up again. "Me and Tony are thinking about getting married."

"Is your mum OK with it?" Barbara knew that David's mum was a strict Catholic.

"She's all for it. Says she sees no reason why gays shouldn't be as unhappy as straight people."

Being around the fun and repartee at the salon always cheered Barbara up, but today it had really taken her out of herself. She felt lighter. Less doom-laden. The hit wouldn't last long, but she intended to hang on to it for as long as she could.

Back home, she was about to call Jack to reschedule lunch when he called her.

"I just wanted to find out if there was any news," he said. "I haven't been able to stop thinking about that poor woman and those children."

She told him how much she appreciated him calling. "Troy's pretty traumatized, But Tiffany, the mother, is in a very bad way. She's on a ventilator. They're talking about brain damage."

"Good God. I'm so sorry." He sounded genuinely upset. "Look . . . say if you're not up to it, but I thought after everything you've been through, you might fancy meeting for a drink?" He said Freddie had gone on a school trip to see *A Midsummer Night's Dream* and wouldn't require picking up until later.

She didn't hesitate. She'd pretty much come down from her trip to the hairdresser and all she wanted to do was talk. "You know what? I would absolutely love a drink."

They arranged to meet at the Queen Victoria, which was pretty much midway between Islington and Hackney.

Since neither of them was driving, they decided to share a bottle of wine. "You've changed your hair," he said as they sat down. "Suits you."

"Oh, I just had my roots done, that's all. According to my hair-dresser, they were frightening the horses."

Despite playing down the compliment, she couldn't help feeling flattered. Was Jack Dolan flirting with her?

"Well, I never noticed. And, anyway, at least you've got hair." He leaned forward to show her how he was thinning on top. She told him to behave and said that for a man of his age he had a great head of hair.

"So how are you doing?" he said, pouring them each a glass of wine.

"I can't stop feeling guilty," she said. "I should have kept an eye on Troy. I should have called in at the flat, just to check everything was OK."

"Suppose you had visited. You might well have come away thinking all was well and the boyfriend could still have turned up later and gone berserk. It was the family's social worker who failed, not you."

"That's what everybody says—even the social worker."

"And has it occurred to you that *everybody* might be right?"

"Possibly," she said, managing a smile.

"It can't be easy going through all this with your husband thousands of miles away."

"It's not easy. But I'm used to coping on my own."

He didn't say anything. It was as if somehow he'd sensed that she was troubled about Frank's absence and was inviting her to open up.

"I won't say it hasn't been hard sometimes," she went on, "particularly when the kids were young and Frank was away for months at a time making some epic about the Palestinian struggle."

"I can imagine."

"But as he keeps reminding me, I knew what I was getting into when I married him. I never complained. I just got on with it. But then . . ." She found herself telling him about the panic attacks. "I'd just lost my job, I wasn't well and Frank was due to start filming in Mexico. I begged him not to go, but he went anyway. I'm so angry. It's pretty much the first time I've ever asked anything of him."

"I think you have every right to be angry."

"Maybe. But sometimes I don't believe that."

"I'm not with you."

"Let's put it this way. I have rather a lot of emotional baggage."

"Like what?"

"It's all very boring. These days I even bore myself. Honestly, you don't want to hear it."

"Try me."

Usually she would have held back. She wasn't in the habit of sharing personal stuff with people she didn't know. But she felt herself drawn to this man. She'd seen how he was with Freddie. There was a warmth and kindness about him—an air of old-fashioned uprightness and integrity. She could be wrong, but she felt she could trust him.

"Well, long story short . . ." She heard herself telling him more about her marriage, her dad, Rose's inability to show her much love or affection.

"You were an innocent child who deserved to be loved. Surely you realize that?"

"Of course I do. Intellectually. But sometimes I still think I don't deserve to be loved."

He nodded. "Yes, I can see how that might be." His face broke into a smile. "Remind me to tell you about Nanny Fredricks sometime. Wonderful woman. She used to hit my sister and me with a butter pat. If we'd been really naughty, she made us have a cold bath."

"How frightfully English," Barbara said.

"Didn't do us any harm, though. In fact, I developed a rather fine stiff upper lip."

She peered at his lip and agreed that it was indeed a fine specimen. "So, Jack, how old are you? If you don't mind me asking."

"Not at all. I'm sixty-three."

"Do you mind being it?"

"My body creaks and aches. Death seems more of a reality—particularly since Faye died. But no, on the whole I don't mind. Nothing seems as urgent as it once did. I've got nothing left to prove. All in all, I'm more at peace with the world."

She hesitated before asking her next question, but went ahead anyway. "Would you be offended if I said that the world has treated you quite well and perhaps that's why you're at peace with it?"

"You mean I have money?"

"Partly that. But also you're happy to be retired. You've achieved all you wanted to achieve. I haven't. I lost my job way before I was ready to go. I know I'm nearly sixty, but I don't feel old. I have so much more to give and nobody will let me."

"Then you have to work out some other way of doing it."

"I know, but right now I'm stumped."

"You've been through a lot recently. Give it time."

He topped up her glass.

"So were you and Faye happy?"

"Extremely. Without wishing to appear smug, we adored each other. We had our ups and downs like most couples, but we got through them."

"You must miss her."

"Every day. But one does one's best to move on. Being in London doesn't help. All our friends are in Gloucestershire. I barely know anybody here. And adore Freddie as I do, there are times when I could do with a bit of adult company."

"I bet. . . . So how's Freddie doing?"

"Not too well I'm afraid. Actually, I was wondering if I could ask a favor." He explained that for once Sally and Jeremy were both in the country. So if she felt up to it, maybe they could all get together to discuss Freddie's future over a family dinner. "I do a tolerable shepherd's pie, and it makes much more sense us all getting together rather than me relaying information back. But if you don't feel up to it, please feel free to say no."

Barbara said she would be more than delighted to come over. They made a date for that Friday.

When she arrived, Jack was in the middle of making a salad to go with the shepherd's pie, which was browning in the oven. "Sally and Jeremy shouldn't be long. They've both texted to say they've left work. Meanwhile, Freddie's up in his room, sulking. I don't know what we're going to do with him. He simply refuses to accept that he's not a dunce."

"How about if I talked to him?"

"Would you? As you're a teacher, he might listen to you." Jack said he'd finish making the salad and call Freddie down.

"The shepherd's pie smells amazing," Barbara said, sitting down at the breakfast bar.

"I hope it's OK. I taught myself to cook—after a fashion—when Faye got ill. Before that she always said that I needed a map to find the kitchen. I may not be any great shakes, but I've come to rather enjoy cooking. I find it incredibly soothing."

Barbara said that her love affair with food preparation had ended when she had children. "I started off cooking from scratch, but they were both picky eaters and of course they always demanded different things. Fool that I was, I gave in to them. Then they'd leave half of it and I'd think why do I bother? In the end I resorted to fish sticks, beans and sausages. They were much happier, and so was I."

"Nothing wrong with a decent banger," Jack said, pouring them both a glass of wine.

"True, but I could only afford the indecent sort."

That made him laugh. Just then Bertie appeared and began sniffing around the stove, making little whimpering sounds. "You'd think this animal never gets fed," Jack said. He went to the fridge and produced a handful of raw ground steak, clearly left over from the shepherd's pie. He dropped it into Bertie's bowl. The dog was straight on it, his tail wagging like an out-of-control metronome.

"So, any more news on Tiffany?" Jack said, rinsing a red pepper under the tap.

"They've been doing tests to check for brain damage. We're still waiting for the results. Troy is so distressed. I visit him most days, and each time I go, he gets hysterical. He just wants to see his mum."

"Why can't he?" Jack suggested that seeing her covered in wires and tubes would be better than what might be going on in his imagination.

"Maureen's been to see her. She thinks that bearing in mind the state he's already in, seeing his mum like that would freak him out. On balance, I think she's probably right."

Jack nodded. "And what about the boyfriend?"

Again she reported what Maureen had told her—that once Wayne had regained consciousness, he'd been charged with attempted murder. Now he was in custody, waiting for a trial date.

"Troy told me that when he grows up he's going to kill him."

"Who could blame him?"

Jack began chopping the pepper.

"My, what excellent knife skills you have. I thought you said you were no great shakes. This is like watching a proper chef."

"It's a man thing," Jack said. "When I first started cooking, I spent a fortune on Japanese knives. Faye had never bothered. Once you have the kit, the pressure is on to learn how to use it."

"I own posh knives, but I can't say they've had that effect on me."

"That's because you're a woman. You don't need to show off. Men have that hairy-chested, alpha-male thing going on. Not that I'd describe myself even remotely as an alpha male. I'm more your delta or omega type."

"What rot. I'd say you were totally up there. You're tall, good-looking, slim." She felt her face redden. Now she was the one doing the flirting. She was blurting out thoughts that a wiser person, one who hadn't just downed an entire goblet of wine, might have decided to keep on the inside.

"You're most kind," he said. He scraped the diced red peppers off the chopping board and onto the bowl of salad. Then he reached for the balsamic vinegar and olive oil. "So, I'm guessing this Wayne character has his own story of childhood neglect and brutality to tell."

"Bound to," Barbara said, putting her hand into the salad bowl and helping herself to a slice of cucumber. "These people always do. No doubt it will all come out in court."

"So how do you break that cycle of violence?"

Barbara delivered her well-worn speech. It was all about lifting people out of poverty, improving education and giving them a stake in society.

She apologized for getting on her soapbox. "I just get so angry—that's all."

"Don't be sorry," he said, topping up her glass. "You have every right to get on your soapbox. Believe me, I feel the same way as you do."

"Really?"

"Don't look so surprised. Us poshies can be liberals, too, you know."

She was coloring up for a second time. "Of course you can. That was stupid of me. I'm really sorry."

He laughed. "Please . . . you have to stop apologizing. In fact, your prejudice is a perfectly fair one. Nine times out of ten you'd be right."

"Maybe, but it was still rude of me." She took a glug of wine. "I guess I'm not at my most diplomatic just now."

"Why do you say that?"

"I'm worried about Tiffany. Plus I'm still feeling guilty. But I am trying to ease up on myself. . . . Look, I'm sorry. I shouldn't be sitting here drinking your wine and boring you like this."

"Barbara, will you stop apologizing? And, anyway, I'm not remotely bored."

"That's very kind of you to say. But I know I go on. I've been driving my kids around the bend. . . . So, enough of me. Why don't we get Freddie down from his room?" She reached into her bag and took out her copy of *The Fabulous Fart Machine*. "I thought he'd like this to remember me by."

"I don't want your book." Freddie was stomping into the room. "And I don't want to remember you." He picked up a packet of crisps that was lying on the breakfast bar and glared at Barbara. "You told my parents I'm a retard. Now they're going to send me to a retard school."

"Freddie! Don't you dare speak to Barbara like that."

"It's true." He ripped the cellophane packet apart and half the contents fell to the floor.

"It is not true. Barbara helped you. Now apologize. Then you can go and get a dustpan and brush and clear up this mess."

"You do it." Freddie turned to go, clutching what remained of his packet of crisps.

"Freddie, don't go," Barbara said. "I know you're upset, but please could we have a talk?" She asked Jack if there was somewhere she could speak to Freddie alone.

"Of course. So long as he agrees to calm down and behave." He turned to Freddie.

"Take Barbara upstairs to the living room. And no more rudeness. Do you understand?"

Freddie stood scowling and didn't move. "I don't want to talk."

"Please?" Barbara said again.

"Go on," Jack said. "Do as you're told."

Freddie wasn't prepared to defy his doting grandfather the way he defied his mother. He led the way to a chintzy pristine drawing room that clearly hardly ever got used. Two sofas faced each other. Opposing factions with a coffee-table no-man's-land between them. Freddie sat down on one sofa. Barbara was about to take the other, but decided it would look far too confrontational. She decided to share Freddie's sofa, but was careful to place herself at the far end so as not to crowd him.

"OK, you're pissed off with me," she said. "I get that, and I really am sorry I upset you."

"Why did you have to say anything? They sent me to see this woman who made me do all these puzzles and stuff. And I couldn't do them. Then she told Mum and Dad that I'm a retard."

"No, she didn't. That's utter nonsense and you know it. I told your parents that I had concerns about you because I wanted you to get the help you needed. Come on, Freddie. You know you were struggling at school. Your teacher knew you were struggling.

Eventually she would have convinced your parents that there was a problem."

"No, she wouldn't. Mum thought she was an idiot. I would have managed."

"Don't kid yourself. You would have carried on thrashing around and ended up very miserable."

"I'm miserable anyway."

"Meaning?"

"Mum and Dad think I'm a retard. They're having all these arguments about me. Sometimes I'm not even sure they love me."

"Come on, Freddie," she said gently. "You know perfectly well they don't think you're a retard. And they adore you."

"No, they don't. Mum and Dad think I'm in the way. And they cover up for it by buying me stuff. They think I don't get it, but I do. I've called ChildLine. Three times."

"You have?"

This child might be dyslexic, but he was more than a tad precocious.

"And what did ChildLine have to say?"

"The lady said that for my age I was very articulate and mature."

"Ah, so not a retard, then. Unless, of course, she was lying just to make you feel better."

"Stop making fun of me. Anyway, she said that I should tell my parents how I feel. But they're never here, and even when they are, they have important work stuff on their minds. . . . By the way, I know what 'articulate' means. I just can't spell it."

Barbara laughed. "And you still think you're thick?"

"How do you know I'm not?"

"I know because I have spent years working with children who have learning difficulties. Yes, your brain is wired a bit differently from other people's and, yes, you have problems processing, but you are not stupid. You've just told me that you know what 'articulate' means but you can't spell it. That pretty much sums up what's going on in your head. You are a bright, highly intelligent young man who happens to have a bit of mental block around spelling and arithmetic. So do millions of people. With the right help, you will learn to compensate and work around it. In the end nobody will be any the wiser."

"You're wrong. My parents are looking at all these special schools for me. I'm going to end up in a school for retards."

"No, you're not. You're way too bright. You need to be in a regular school, where you can get some extra help. Now, tell me something. How would you feel about boarding school?"

"That means I have to sleep there, right?"

"Yes, but only during the week. You'd come home every weekend. I have a school in mind that I think you'd really like."

"I dunno. Maybe," he said, shrugging. "I don't see Mum and Dad during the week anyway. So what's it like?"

Jeremy Fergusson poured himself another glass of wine. "So you're telling us that this place has no school uniform, pupils call teachers by their first names and they keep sheep."

"They also keep pigs, cows and chickens. As well as being a school, Larkswood House is a proper working farm. The kids are expected to help out for a couple of hours each week. They get to see calves being born, milk the cows, shovel chicken shit. They all adore it."

"Great. And where do they have lessons? In the milking shed?"

Sally glared at her husband across the kitchen table. "Jem, do you have to be so rude? Barbara's trying to help us. And Freddie's made it clear that Larkswood House appeals to him and that he'd like to take a look round."

Freddie had gone to bed a while ago, leaving the adults to drink coffee, finish what remained of the wine and discuss his future. Barbara was starting to wish she hadn't told him about Larkswood House before mentioning it to his parents. Educational traditionalists like Jeremy Fergusson tended to sneer and be against it.

"Sorry. I apologize," Jeremy said to Barbara. "It's been a long day. And you have to understand that this thing with Freddie has been terribly stressful."

Barbara looked at Jeremy, his patrician frame cloaked in his rich man's suit, his annual bonus no doubt accruing in some fancy high-yield investment fund. She wanted to tell him that he knew nothing about real stress—the kind of stress people on the Orchard Farm Estate lived with. Of course she said nothing. Jeremy and Sally were entitled to their own stresses and strains. It wasn't for her to judge—even though she already had.

"I know it hasn't been easy," Barbara said. "But Freddie's dyslexia is fairly mild. He won't get into Eton, but he'll be fine in a mainstream school like Larkswood House, which has a dedicated team of teachers who work with dyslexic pupils."

She explained that she had an old friend from teacher-training college who taught there, that she'd visited several times and had always come away impressed. She described a state-of-the-art campus based around an old manor house. The school had a performing arts studio, gym, swimming pools—indoor and outdoor—tennis courts, sports fields. "It's liberal, relaxed and the kids live in houses with house parents. There's a real family atmosphere."

"I don't understand," Jeremy came back. "If this place is so great, why have we never heard of it? Nobody's ever mentioned it to us."

"People tend to disapprove of the noncompetitive ethos. Essentially, the school concentrates on producing happy, confident kids who are able to make their way in the world. That said, all the pupils take the traditional exams, and most of them—even the dyslexic ones—do pretty well. You can check out their results online."

Jeremy wasn't about to be won over. "What's the betting they all do yoga during break?"

"Oh, and I forgot to mention, it's vegetarian."

"Of course it is."

"Well, I think it sounds terrific," Sally said.

Jack said he had to agree. "I think it might be just the ticket for our young Fred."

"I'm not so sure," Jeremy said. "Freddie needs discipline. He's a brat, and he's out of control."

Barbara watched Jack as he battled to stay silent. In the end the words burst out of him. "And whose fault is that?... Yours." He looked at Sally. "And I include you in that."

"But we give him everything," Sally said. "He's just so ungrateful. You know how he treats me."

"You give him everything apart from what he actually needs. It's a classic tale of the spoiled little rich kid. And it's staring you in the face. It beats me why you can't see it. That lad is crying out for love and attention. He acts out because he's trying to get you to notice him. Good God, it's not bloody rocket science."

Barbara had made it clear to Jack that Sally and Jeremy's parenting skills were none of her business and that she wouldn't interfere. But now she had some information that she thought she ought to share. "As you know, I had a chat with Freddie before dinner and he told me that he feels as if he's in the way. Did you know he's been calling ChildLine?"

Sally's eyes widened. "What? Are you serious?"

"He's just attention seeking," Jeremy snapped.

Jack couldn't take any more. "Of course he's attention seeking. Can't you see that the poor kid *deserves* some attention? Why don't you get it?"

Sally looked at her husband. "Dad's right. You know he is. Do you honestly think that our son was born a brat? We've made him the way he is."

Jeremy went on the defensive. "You should have given up your job when he was born, like I told you."

"Why? Because I'm his mother and that's what proper mothers do? You earn less than me. Why didn't you give up your job?"

"Look," Barbara broke in, "blaming each other isn't going to help. The past is done. What you need to do now is plan for the future—Freddie's future."

Jack was looking thoughtful. "I hate to put the cat among the pigeons, but given that Fred already feels that he's in the way and has been calling ChildLine, do we really think it's a good idea to send him away? Won't he feel even more rejected?"

Barbara looked directly at Sally and Jeremy. "OK, am I right in thinking that neither of you is prepared to give up your job, or work fewer hours, to become a full-time parent to Freddie?"

They shuffled, toyed with their empty wineglasses. "Probably not," Sally said.

"Right. Well, in that case, we have to think about the next-best option." Barbara emphasized again the warm family atmosphere at Larkswood House. "The teachers and houseparents get to know the kids really well. He will be really cared for and nurtured."

"By strangers," Sally said. "Great."

"Your choice," Jack came back. "It's either that or you let him go to a specialist day school in London and come home every night to au pairs. Because I'm not going to be staying forever. Believe it or not, I do have a life."

Neither Sally nor Jeremy spoke.

Barbara made the point that Freddie need only be a weekly boarder at Larkswood House. "He'll be home every Friday night. On the weekends you need to put away your BlackBerries and laptops and have some proper family time. If you put in the effort, he will start to feel loved and his behavior will change."

Sally looked at her husband. "You know, Jem, spending more time together as a family would probably do us all good."

Jeremy didn't exactly roll his eyes, but the expression on his face radiated cynicism.

"So what's this place going to cost us?" he said.

Barbara smiled. "Ooh, I'd say an arm and a leg and several bits of offal."

As Barbara didn't have her car with her, Jack insisted on driving her home.

"I just want to say how much I appreciate everything you've done for Fred these past weeks," he said as they pulled away. "You've been brilliant."

"You are most welcome. Deep down, Freddie's a good kid. And like I keep saying—very bright."

"You don't have to tell me," Jack said. "And I will keep on at Sally and Jeremy to spend more time with him."

"It's all he needs."

"Unlike my son-in-law, who deserves a right royal kick up the backside."

Barbara laughed.

"He suffers," Jack went on, "from what I call 'entitlement' disorder. Jeremy thinks that being rich gives him the right to get his own way. He—and Sally, too, for that matter—simply assumed that Fred would waltz into Eton or Westminster. When something goes awry, they panic. Plus they worry about what their friends will think."

"I understand," she said. "You don't have to apologize. . . . So do you think they might go for Larkswood House?"

"If it's everything you say it is, then I'm sure they will. And Fred certainly seems up for boarding."

"Funny, isn't it?" Barbara said, shaking her head. "How one child's educational problems can get sorted pretty much overnight—so long as his parents have money. It's so bloody unfair. Kids like Troy just get left to rot."

"I know. The system stinks. But I'm not sure what we as individuals are supposed to do."

"Get up off our backsides. Make a difference—that's what I set out to do when I went into teaching."

"And you did what you could," Jack said. "You can't save the world."

"I know. Besides, I have a husband who is already doing that."

As they pulled up outside her house, Jack turned to her. "Barbara, don't take this the wrong way, but I was wondering if you'd let me buy you dinner sometime."

"Jack, don't take *this* the wrong way, but are you coming on to me?"

He smiled. "Do you always say precisely what's on your mind?"

"Not always, but mostly." She paused. "But seriously, I'm married. I'm flattered, but I'm . . ."

"A beautiful, intelligent woman who is with a man who doesn't deserve her."

And there he was, moving in, gently cupping her face in his hands and kissing her. She found herself kissing him back with an urgency that startled her.

"I'm sorry," he said afterwards.

"For what? For kissing me?"

"No, for criticizing your marriage. It was wrong of me."

"Don't apologize. You're only echoing what I've already told you."

"So, say you'll have dinner with me."

She felt a wave of panic. Instead of letting it engulf her, she managed to ride it. "All right. Yes. I'd like that."

Chapter 12

Which Font Are You? Barbara was on Facebook doing BuzzFeed quizzes. Pam's old school friend Heather Babcock had got Courier. She'd posted: Huh and here was me thinking I was more of a Times New Roman sort of a gal. Barbara got Requiem, which pretty much reflected her mood.

In the "Which Actress Would Play You in the Movie of Your Life?" quiz, she landed Tina Fey: "bright, bubby, sparkling personality, doesn't take life too seriously." Yep, the BuzzFeed elves certainly had Barbara pegged. To her, life was just one big ol' shindig.

She was trying and failing to take her mind off Tiffany and the children for a few minutes. In other matters, there was also Jack's kiss. It had thrilled her, overwhelmed her—left her feeling giddy and wanting more. When was the last time she'd felt like that with Frank?

If Jack hadn't done the gentlemanly thing and said he needed to get back, she might have ignored her son's whereabouts and invited him to share her bed—or at least the bed in the spare room. It appeared that her hitherto sluggish libido had suddenly been recharged—with a vengeance. So much for antidepressants suppressing one's sex drive.

She knew perfectly well why it had happened. He was the grieving widower. She was the forlorn wife. They were both lonely and found each other attractive. Jack had listened to her, taken an interest in her—flirted with her. She'd found it intoxicating. Nevertheless, she was old enough and wise enough to know that jumping into bed with another man wasn't going to solve the problems she was having with Frank. It could only make things more complicated. Suppose she fell in love with Jack? What then? Her life was strenuous enough right now. She couldn't cope with the added stress of an affair. She needed to break it off now, before it spiraled out of control.

Bored with quizzes but still looking for something to take her mind off things, she spooled through the rest of her newsfeed. Somebody had posted a picture of a puppy dressed as Yoda Dog. Below it Pam had put up one of her inspirational quotes: Joy is what happens to us when we allow ourselves to recognize how good things really are. Fabulous. Barbara could print that out and stick it over Tiffany's hospital bed.

She hadn't posted a Facebook status in ages. But she didn't have anything to say—nothing cheerful, at any rate. If she was honest, she was getting fed up with Facebook. The pictures of puppies and kittens, the affirmations, the show-offy snaps of Pam and Si sipping neon cocktails by their pool had always irritated her. Lately they made her angry. It seemed that the only reason people went on Facebook was to inform everybody how perfect their lives were. If they weren't doing that, they were airing their first-world problems: Noo! Our neighbor has the same Laura Ashley wallpaper as us. The corner shop just ran out of pickled cherries—it's like North Korea here. Crap, I have to reset my password again. My Brie is too hard.

Then there were Sally and Jeremy, who weren't her Facebook

friends but whose world had been rocked because their son couldn't get into the "right" school.

Sally had called this morning to thank Barbara for all her help.

"Honestly, Barbara, I don't know what we'd have done without you. I can't tell you how enormously grateful we are."

"I really didn't do that much."

"You did heaps. Without you, it might have been years before Freddie got his dyslexia diagnosis. And I do hope you can forgive Jem for his behavior last night. He finds it very hard to cope when things don't go his way. We both do. Anyway, we've made an appointment to go and look at Larkswood House. I'll keep you posted."

A couple of hours later, a bunch of calla lilies was delivered to Barbara's door. They arrived in a green and gold Harrods van and came with a handwritten card: *Dearest Barbara, Just to say how simply marvelous you've been. Muchos hugs from all the Fergussons.*

Barbara knew she was being mean and uncharitable—particularly to Sally and Jeremy. She thought back to last night and how she'd judged them. She had to keep reminding herself that they weren't bad people. They'd sent her flowers, for crying out loud. Her Facebook friends weren't bad people either. They were just regular middle-class folk caught up in their middle-class lives. She understood that. She was one of them. God help her, hadn't she been known to curse when the supermarket had no quince jelly to go with her manchego? But—if she could toot her own horn for just a moment—she had the good sense not to moan about it on Facebook. She even had the good sense not to moan about it at home. If she did, Ben and Jess would come down on her. "Mum, will you just listen to yourself? Just go away and check your privilege." She'd Googled the phrase a few years ago, when the kids first started to use it, and discovered that as a white, middle-class Westerner, she had no right to moan about anything. The notion was crazy, but like a lot of crazy notions, it contained a scintilla of sense.

Barbara closed her laptop. She needed to set the table. Jess and the kids were coming for lunch. She'd just opened the cutlery drawer when her cell rang. It was Jean calling to see if there was any news about Tiffany. Barbara told her what Maureen had told her earlier: that she had an appointment with Tiffany's doctor in the morning to discuss her test results.

"But I don't think the prognosis will be great," Barbara said.

"And the children?"

"I'm planning to drop in a bit later. I'm just praying that the foster parents will agree to look after them for a bit longer. I can't stop worrying about them, but Troy in particular, because he's that much older and he understands what's going on."

"Of course you're worried. I'm worried and I'm not even involved. It's crap you're going through this on top of everything else. You need cheering up. How's about I treat us to a boozy dinner next week, somewhere ludicrously expensive?"

"Actually, Jack Dolan has just invited me to have dinner with him. You know, Freddie's grandfather. Widower. Lives in Gloucestershire. I'm sure I mentioned him."

"You did. So when you say he's asked you to have dinner with him . . ."

"I'm saying he's asked me out on a date."

"Blimey."

"And that's not all. He kissed me last night. And the worst part— or maybe it was the best part—was that I kissed him back. You have no idea how much I wanted him. I haven't felt so horny in years."

"Tell me about it." Barbara took this to mean that things were all pretty tickety-boo with Virgil.

"But has it occurred to you," Jean went on, "that what you felt last night might not be real?"

"Oh, it was real, all right."

"No, what I mean is that it probably had more to do with . . ."

". . . me being furious with Frank and wanting to punish him. I know. I get that. But it was still amazing."

"I'm sure it was, but please tell me you're not going to pursue this. You'd be playing with fire. What if Frank found out? I know he's behaved badly—and not for the first time. But even so, he doesn't deserve to have you cheat on him."

"But Ken deserves to have you cheat on him?"

"My situation is different and you know it. I've told you that it wouldn't be the end of the world if Ken found out about my extra-marital activities. If you cheat on Frank, you could lose him."

"I know, and that's why—reluctantly, I might add—I've decided to put a stop to it."

"Thank the Lord for that. You're doing the right thing. I mean, what would it have achieved?"

"Great sex, for a start."

"You don't know that."

"Believe me, I do. He wasn't kissing you."

"If you're going to be missing out on sensational sex, you have my sympathy. Of all people, I know what it feels like to be in that position. But even so, you have to end it."

"I've already said I will. I'll call him. But I can't begin to tell you how much I don't want to."

"Gran'ma, do you want to hear a riddle?"

"I'd love to."

"What's brown and sticky?"

Jess rolled her eyes. "Atticus, please. We're eating. That's disgusting."

Atticus clapped his hands. "Aha. Gotcha. It's not a *pooh*.... It's a stick!" Atticus and Cleo shrieked at the hilarity and wittiness of it all.

"OK ... I've got another one," he said. "How do you sell a deaf person a chicken?"

"I don't know. How do you sell a deaf person a chicken?"

"OY!! MATE!! DO YOU WANT TO BUY A CHICKEN!!!?"

Barbara roared. Jess rolled her eyes. She'd probably heard it a dozen times before. "OK, you two. If you've finished eating, take a piece of fruit and go and watch a DVD for a bit."

They refused to budge. "Grandma's got Skittles in her cupboard," Atticus said.

"Fine," Jess came back. "You can have Skittles."

Barbara looked at her daughter. "Really? You sure?"

Jess nodded. "Go ahead. I need to talk to you in private."

Barbara shared a packet of Skittles between two bowls and handed them to the children.

"Atticus has got more than me."

"Cleo, don't push your luck," Jess said. "I'm sure you've both got exactly the same. Now, scoot."

A few moments later the *Chicken Run* music started up in the living room.

"So, no Ben?" Jess said.

"He texted to say he'd be back around lunchtime. He spent the night at Katie's." Barbara paused. "You know she's training to be an investment banker?"

"Yeah, Ben told me."

"I have to say I'm surprised he's dating somebody who works in the City."

"What you actually mean is that you're disappointed."

"Well, aren't you?"

"No. Not really," Jess said.

"Hang on. Am I'm losing the plot here? I take it that you do remember the 'Occupy London: Banks Own You' poster that is hanging in your loo as we speak."

"Yeah, well, maybe I've eased up a bit. I can't get angry with people anymore just because they choose a career in finance and make a pile of cash. Good luck to them is what I say. Can you imagine for a moment what it must be like never having to worry about money?"

"Money doesn't necessarily make people happy."

"I know, but at least you can be miserable in comfort. Matt and I were struggling day in day out to make ends meet. We were both exhausted. If it hadn't been for Ben, I don't know what we'd have done."

"Ben?"

"Yes. He's invested twenty grand in the business."

"Very funny."

"I'm not being funny. I'm serious."

"Ben . . . Your brother, Ben, has invested twenty thousand pounds in the Green Door? Excuse my French, but your brother doesn't have a pot to piss in."

"He hasn't told you, has he?"

"Told me where he got twenty thousand pounds? Er . . . no, he has most definitely been keeping that to himself."

"OK, this is none of my business. You need to talk to him. . . ."

"I'm talking to you," Barbara came back. "What's going on?"

Jess took a breath. "Ben has been playing the stock market."

"Now I've heard everything. Don't be so ridiculous. What does Ben know about playing the stock market?"

"A hell of a lot, actually. He's been doing it for months."

"Sorry, you're telling me that Ben has been buying and selling stocks and shares . . . from his bed?"

"Yes."

"And that he's made twenty thousand pounds in a few months?"

"Correct. Actually, I think it might be more than that."

"What? Oh, please . . . And if that's true, he must have needed a pretty hefty sum to start him off. I know he got six thousand from selling the Fender, but that wouldn't have been enough, would it?"

"He actually started playing the stock market way before he sold the Fender. He only did that to make some cash to live on while he reinvested his capital. He felt so guilty about living off you and Dad."

"OK, so where did he get the initial investment?"

"You need to ask him. And anyway, Ben's an adult. It's his business where the money came from."

Barbara was beginning to panic. "Just tell me he didn't do anything dishonest."

"Oh, what, like selling drugs? He told me that's what you thought he'd been up to. Why can't you trust him?"

"I was frightened. I overreacted. I said I was sorry. So you promise me he's done nothing illegal?"

"I promise. All I can say is that he acquired some capital and he's been reinvesting and growing it."

"I don't know what to say. For once in my life I'm absolutely speechless."

"Look, Mum, I know you're shocked, but Ben has done something really kind and generous. Matt and I were at the point of going bust. Ben has saved us. Please don't be cross with him."

"I'm not cross," Barbara said. "So this was the mystery *thing*. . . ."

"What?"

"Nothing. He hinted at some secret project, that's all. I assumed he was working on some music story or another. But why on earth was he so determined to keep your father and me in the dark?"

"Like I said, you need to talk to him."

Jess and the kids were getting ready to leave when Ben turned up. He put his rucksack down on the kitchen table.

"Hey, all. God, I'm starving." He grabbed a cold roast potato from one of the kids' plates.

"Hey, Uncle Ben," Cleo said. "Do you want to hear a riddle? What's brown and sticky?"

"Er . . . that would be a stick."

"Aw. You got it." She turned to her brother. "He got it."

Ben ruffled Cleo's hair. "That's because not so long ago, I was a kid, too."

"Come on, you two," Jess said, standing up. "We ought to get going."

"Why the rush?"

"Mum wants to talk to you."

Ben looked at his mother. "OK, what have I done now?"

"Jess told me about all the money you've made on the stock market."

Ben glared at his sister. "Oh great. Cheers. Thanks for that."

"It was an accident. I didn't mean to."

"I thought I told you to wait until I'd spoken to Mum."

"I did. I mean, I thought you had." Jess finished helping Cleo on with her coat. "Look, I think we'd better get going. You two need to sort this out." She paused. "Ben, I really am sorry."

He shrugged. "Don't worry. It's not your fault, I guess. I suppose I should have said something earlier."

Jess waved good-bye and began steering the children to the door. "No, you can't tell Grandma the gorilla joke. It'll have to wait until another time. We have to go now." A moment later they disappeared into the hall and the front door opened and closed.

"Look, Mum," Ben said, sitting down at the table. "Can we not make a big deal out of this?"

"All I want to know is where you got the initial capital."

"You still don't trust me, do you? OK, if you must know, Rich Steve had some spare cash."

Rich Steve, so called because his father owned a Ferrari concession, had played bass guitar in Grandma and the Junkies.

"I made some investments on his behalf," Ben continued, "and took a cut of the profit. That's all. I acted exactly like a stockbroker."

"And what if these investments had gone wrong?"

"Steve knew the risk. I didn't promise him anything. And like I said, the money was just knocking around. He can afford to take a hit. But as it goes, he turned a decent profit and so did I. Once I had a decent amount of money, I started buying and selling on my own account." Ben unwrapped a Pop-Tart and dropped it into the toaster. "Mum, can I tell you something?"

"Go on."

"I'm good at this. I think I have a bit of a talent. Katie thinks so, too."

"Of course she does. You're sleeping with her."

"Why would you say something like that? It's so mean. She happens to know what she's talking about."

"OK, I apologize. I take it back. So what are you telling me? That you've read a few books, had a bit of luck and suddenly you're a stockbroker?"

"No, I'm telling you that I've read loads of books. I've also been taking advice from various contacts I've made in the business. A couple of my friends have got dads who are stockbrokers. But most of all, I'm telling you that I have an instinct. I have no idea where it came from, but it's here, inside of me."

"Ben, how much money have you actually made?"

"I dunno. About thirty-five K over the last six or seven months."

"But why didn't you say anything?"

"First, I knew you wouldn't approve of me taking Steve's money."

"Too bloody right."

"Plus at the start it was just an experiment. I had no idea if I would make anything, so I decided it was best to keep quiet. I was desperate to stop taking money from you and Dad, but I had to keep re-investing."

"Maybe, but you could have put a few quid our way."

"If I had, you would have interrogated me like you did when I bought the leather jacket. The other reason I said nothing was because I knew the whole making-money thing would upset you."

"Maybe it would have, but . . ."

"No, Mum. No buts. You and Dad would have disapproved. Don't try to pretend you wouldn't. When we were at school, the assumption was that Jess and I would go to university, study something liberal and artsy and go into jobs that would be meaningful and worthwhile. You were so bloody hot on the idea that we had to contribute something to the world."

He was right. She didn't have a leg to stand on.

"But Jess went into business," she said, still trying to fight her corner. "Dad and I didn't complain."

"No. Because it was all green and ethical. You could justify that."

"And we didn't complain when you said you wanted to be a music journalist."

"Because in your book that came in the artsy category. But making money almost as an art form is an entirely different matter. Every time I thought about telling you, all I could see was the disappointment on your faces. If I'd said anything, you and Dad would have done all you could to dissuade me. I couldn't let that happen. So I said nothing."

Barbara could barely take in what she was hearing. "I can't believe a child of mine had to keep his career choice a secret."

"Well, I did."

"Are your dad and I so unapproachable?"

"No, of course not. You're the complete opposite. But at the same time, you both have this bee in your bonnet. You know, for all your liberal talk, the pair of you can be pretty narrow-minded."

Barbara sat there, pulling bits off a paper napkin. "Wow, do I feel like a crap parent."

"Come on," Ben said gently. "You're not a crap parent. You're a great mum. And Dad's a great dad. But you have to admit this whole 'you can't work in finance' thing is an issue with you. In some ways you're like a pair of old hippies."

Barbara had no comeback. "What can I say? Maybe we are."

"Jess has always been more like you and Dad." He paused. "But once I offered to put twenty thousand into the Green Door, suddenly the capitalist monster wasn't quite so despicable. I know that sounds unkind, but . . ."

"No, it's OK. She admitted as much just now."

Ben sat munching his Pop-Tart. "So, are you ashamed of me?"

"What? Good God, no. Of course I'm not ashamed."

"OK, disappointed, then?"

She took a moment to consider. "I'd be lying if I said I wasn't. But I'll get over it. The point is that you're doing what you want to do, and in the nicest possible way, you're flipping us the bird. How great is that?"

"And you know who I got my stubbornness from? . . . You."

"Well, I'm glad to have been of service," she said. "I just wish you'd let your dad and me in and we could have supported you more."

"Are you joking? Dad wouldn't have supported me. I still think he's going to raise the roof."

"No, he won't. Believe me, he'll just be glad you're off the parental payroll."

She asked him where he planned to take things from here.

"The stock exchange runs a post-grad trainee stockbroker scheme, and I'm going to apply for next year. And don't panic. I'll be funding it myself."

Barbara got up and wrapped her arms around her son. "Good for you. . . . You know what? It's about time somebody in this family made some money."

"I agree, because it means that when you get old, I'll be able to stick you and Dad in a really nice care facility."

"What more could any parent ask for?"

Before Barbara set off to see Troy, she called Jack. She came straight to the point, said that the kiss had been a mistake and that she owed it to Frank to try to sort out their relationship.

"You're right. Of course you need to focus on your marriage. I crossed a boundary last night. I took advantage of you, and I'm sorry."

"No, you didn't. I kissed you back—remember?"

"Do you think that we could possibly still have dinner . . . as friends?"

"Come on, Jack. Don't kid yourself. After what happened, we both know that's not possible. . . ."

"Of course it is. I promise faithfully to behave. It's just that I really enjoy your company, and I get so damned lonely in London."

"I understand, but it's too risky. I'm sorry, but the answer has to be no."

She could feel his sadness from down the phone. "OK. It's

probably for the best. I shouldn't have put pressure on you. So is this good-bye?"

"Not exactly. You have to promise to e-mail me and let me know how Freddie's doing."

"Of course I will. And, Barbara, I'm really sorry."

"Me, too," she said.

Chapter 13

Tiffany's test results confirmed everybody's worst fears. Her brain injury was catastrophic. There was no hope of her regaining consciousness.

Two days later the ventilator was switched off. Her best friends—Kenzie, Lexi and Leanne, who had been keeping vigil at her bedside—were with her.

When it was over, Maureen called Barbara. Their conversation was brief. There was nothing to say that hadn't been said, no emotions left to express.

"By the way," Maureen said, "I don't know how you'd feel about this, but Carole and I think you should be the one to tell Troy. Of the three of us, you're closest to him. There's nobody else."

Barbara wasn't sure she could face it. How could she find it in her to inflict more pain on that poor child? But Maureen and Carole were right. It had to be her. And deep down—contradictory as it seemed—she wanted it to be her.

Maureen promised that she and Carole would both be there to offer support.

A few hours after Tiffany died, Barbara and Maureen were sitting on Carole's living room floor next to Troy. He was lying on his front, building Legos. Carole sat on the sofa with Lacie on her lap. The woman's eyes were puffy from crying, but right now she was cooing and dangling a fur bird in front of Lacie, not a tear in sight.

"The thing is, my darling," Barbara said to Troy, heart racing because she had no idea if she was about to handle this the right way, "your mum was so badly hurt that her body simply couldn't keep going. She tried and tried to get better because she didn't want to leave you and Lacie, but in the end she was just too tired."

Troy looked hard at Barbara. "Is she dead?"

"I'm afraid she is."

Barbara glanced at Maureen. The two women prepared themselves for the explosion. Instead Troy sat there, apparently gathering his thoughts.

"I knew she was going to die."

"How?"

A shrug. "Where we live lots of people die. So, is she in heaven?"

"Of course she is," Barbara said. "She's out of pain and she's happy. And I promise she's watching over you and Lacie."

Troy nodded. It took a few moments for the agony to show itself. His face contorted. Barbara held her arms open and he launched himself into her. The anguished howls and sobs, his pitiable cries begging for his mum were muffled by her body. Barbara held him and rocked him. She stroked his head. Had he been one of her own she couldn't have felt more gut-wrenching emotion. Her tears fell onto him. What words could she offer? She refused to shush him or tell him it would be all right.

It was Maureen who managed to find something appropriate to

say. "We're all here, my darling." She was kneeling beside him, rubbing his back. "We're all here. You're not on your own."

Carole held Lacie. She put her lips to the child's blond head and wept. Lacie fought the embrace and demanded to be put down. Carole let her go. Oblivious, the child toddled off to find her toys.

Carole joined the others on the floor.

For the time being, Troy was cried out. He clung to Barbara, breathing in fits and gasps.

"Come, sweetheart," Carole said. "Let's wipe that nose." She produced a tissue and pincered the stream of snot.

"What's heaven like?"

"Nobody knows exactly," Carole said. "But it's a place where there's no hitting or crying and nobody ever gets hurt."

"Can me and Lacie go there? Then we could see Mum."

"No, my sweet. Only very sick or old people get to go."

"That's not fair. So, who's going to look after us?"

"Well, I was wondering if maybe you and Lacie would like to stay here for the time being. But only if you want to."

He didn't have to think. "I do want to. And so does Lacie. I like you and I like this house and I like playing football with Mike—especially when he lets me win."

"OK. Then that's a deal." She scooped him up and wrapped him in her arms.

"Shall I be the one to tell Lacie that our mum's died?"

"You could," Carole said. "But she's ever so little. I'm not sure she'll understand."

Troy nodded. "OK . . . But we have to be kind to her and look after her because she hasn't got a mum anymore."

"We do. But Lacie's going to be fine. I don't want you to worry."

"OK . . . So, can I go and play in the garden now?"

"Of course you can," Carole said. "But are you sure that's what you feel like doing?"

"Yes. Can I take Dave?"

"If he'll go."

"He likes sitting with me on the trampoline while I stroke him. I can tell him about Mum."

"Good idea," Carole said. "Now Dave's getting on a bit, he's a really good listener."

Dave was under the table, licking his paws. Troy picked him up. The cat let out a tiny yelp, but that was the extent of his protest. Troy trotted off, his face buried in Dave's fur.

"One minute he's howling like a wounded animal," Maureen said. "The next he wants to go out to play."

"I suspect it'll hit him in waves," Carole said. "This won't be the end of it, by any means."

Maureen said she would arrange some counseling for him. "So, Carole, since you've invited Troy and Lacie to stay for a while, I'm assuming you've cleared it with Mike."

"Not a problem. I called him before you got here to tell him about Tiffany. He suggested it before I did."

When Barbara got home, she found a voice mail message from Frank. "Ben just called me. Good God. The kid wants to be a stock-broker. Can you believe it? So that was the *thing*. And on top of that, he's made all this money. Nobody in my family has ever made money. Who'd have thought one of our apples would fall so far from the tree? To be honest, I'm still trying to get my head around it. I'm sure you feel the same. But the main thing is we're not supporting him anymore. So if he's happy, I'm happy. Oh, and before you say any-thing, yes, I've said sorry for not having more faith in him. We had a long chat, during which I demolished several rather large humble pies. I think he understood that it was all panic on my part. Anyway, I'll be back soon. I'll e-mail with the actual date as soon as I know. Then you and I can sit down and have a long talk."

So she'd been right to tell Ben that his father wouldn't have a problem with him becoming a stockbroker. This came as some relief. If she was honest, it had occurred to her that Frank might throw a fit and give Ben a hard time. The last thing she wanted was a rift between father and son—another reason for her to be at loggerheads with Frank.

It was the end of Frank's message that concerned her. He wanted to have a long talk. About what? Unless his position changed, what was there left to say? She decided not to call back. She didn't feel up to it—not after what had happened today.

Instead she texted him to say she was proud of Ben, too, and completely OK with his decision. She also thanked him for apologizing.

Also Tiffany died today. In the end they switched off her ventilator.

He replied almost immediately.

Bloody tragic. Hope you're OK. Thinking of you. x

She tried calling Jean to give her the news about Tiffany, but her phone was switched off. She was probably at work. Barbara lost track of Jean's hospital shifts.

She was desperate for somebody to talk to, for a shoulder to cry on—quite literally. As if on cue, her phone rang. Jack. He seemed to have a habit of calling when she was feeling wretched. She decided to let the phone ring. Talking to him would be a mistake. Seconds went by. Then, thinking it was about to stop ringing, she snatched the handset.

"Jack. How are you?"

"Look . . . I know I shouldn't be calling, and feel free to tell me to bugger off, but I've missed hearing your voice. . . ."

"Tiffany died today."

"Oh, Barbara. I'm so sorry. How are you bearing up?"

"Not great."

"Tell you what—why not meet me for an early supper? It might help to talk and get a couple of drinks down you."

"I don't think that would be a good idea."

"Barbara, I'm offering you friendship. Nothing else."

"I'm sorry, but I'm really not up to it."

"But what good is moping?"

"I don't know, but it's what I feel like doing."

"It's up to you, but just to let you know—I thought I'd pop into Adriatico for a quick bite around six. I can't stay long because I've got a neighbor looking after Freddie and she needs to get home. But if you change your mind and feel like joining me, I'll be there."

She thanked him and said she'd think about it. Not that she had any intention of going. The idea of knocking back Barolo at Adriatico while Tiffany lay in the morgue was unthinkable.

She made tea and turned on the TV. But she couldn't concentrate. She couldn't read the newspaper either, or even a crappy magazine. She emptied the dishwasher, tidied the countertops, folded laundry. All she could think about was Tiffany and all she wanted to do was talk. Against her better judgment, she picked up the phone.

An hour later Barbara and Jack were sitting opposite each other, downing wine and olives.

"Thank you for inviting me, but it feels so wrong to be here enjoying myself."

"I get that, but you need cheering up."

"It feels way too soon to be cheering up."

"Poppycock. You're entitled to a few hours' break. You can go back to being sad tomorrow."

"You're being very kind."

"You sound surprised. After the time you've had, why on earth wouldn't I be?"

"Well, I appreciate it."

Jack noticed her glass was empty. He drained his own and refilled both glasses from the carafe.

They both ordered the same—minestrone followed by home-made gnocchi. From then on they did their best to keep the conversation light. They avoided any more talk of Tiffany. Their mutual attraction was also kept well off the agenda. Instead Jack steered the conversation to what he might buy Freddie for his birthday and the fact that Sally was making no effort to find a new au pair because he was so good at the job.

During dessert, Barbara's phone rang. She'd meant to turn it to silent. She knew it would be Rose calling to moan at her. She'd promised to phone and take down her shopping order, but what with everything that had been going on, it had completely slipped her mind.

"I'm going to ignore it," Barbara said. "It's my mother. I know what it's about and it'll keep."

"No, please take it. You don't know—it could be important. And I need to pee anyway."

Jack got up and headed towards the gents. Barbara hit "connect."

"Mum, before you say anything, I'm sorry. I know I promised to call, but I've had a rough few days and I simply forgot."

"Where are you now?"

"Out having dinner with a friend."

"Well, I hope you're enjoying yourself. Meanwhile, I'm sitting here waiting for you to call."

"I'm sorry. I'm a horrible, selfish person. I don't know why you bother with me. Look, I'll call you tomorrow. We'll sort it all out then. Bye, Mum."

Barbara put her phone back in her bag, surprised at how calm and unrattled she felt by her mother's implication that she was selfish. Right now, sitting in this restaurant, a plate of profiteroles in front of her, she was in no doubt that she'd spent her life doing her best to be a good person. Of course she hadn't always succeeded, but imperfection was part of being human. She wasn't sure how long this certainty would last, but it felt like the first glimmer of a breakthrough.

Jack reappeared and sat down. "Penny for them."

"It's nothing much. My mother just accused me of being selfish, and for once I just let it roll off me."

"Good for you. Because the last thing you are is selfish. I could have told you that and I've only known you five minutes."

She reached out and took his hand. "Thank you. You have no idea how much I appreciate that."

"Well, it's true."

They started chitchatting again. He said he was off to Gloucestershire for the weekend. He needed to check on the house and pick up his mail.

"Take me with you."

Jack put down his coffee cup. "Excuse me?"

"Take me with you."

"Why?"

"You know why."

"Barbara, we've had this conversation. You need to work on your marriage, not have an affair."

"Then what were you doing calling me and telling me you missed me?"

"I'm a lonely old fool."

"And I'm lonely, too. We're both crying out for some fun. This doesn't have to be anything serious if we don't want it to be. Call it a fling. Call it grabbing at a moment's happiness after all the crap we've been through. I mean, where's the harm? Who's going to find out? I'm almost sixty. Isn't it time I took some pleasure for myself?"

"Barbara, listen to me. You've had one hell of a day—one hell of a few months. You're feeling lousy. You're exhausted. You've had a bit to drink. Your mind is all over the place. . . . Of course you can come with me to Gloucestershire. I can think of nothing I'd like more, but I hate to think of you doing something you're going to regret. Please, I beg you, take some time to think about this. . . . Now I think I should get the bill."

Barbara finally got through to Jean the following day.

"Bar, I'm so sorry. I honestly don't know what to say. Those poor kids. That boyfriend of hers is a monster. I hope he goes down for life."

"He will, but it's not going to give Troy and Lacie their mum back."

"I suppose social services will have to start thinking about finding them adoptive parents."

"I guess so. I hadn't thought about that." She would raise the subject with Maureen.

"So how are you doing?"

"I'm just so sad. What can I tell you? One of the worst things about it all—apart from her kids being orphaned—is that she left no legacy. No mark on the world."

"She left children. They're her legacy."

"I know, but I feel there should be something more. Tiffany shouldn't be forgotten. People need to be reminded of what she went through, how she suffered."

"But she won't be forgotten. Apart from her kids, her friends will remember her. Then there's you and Maureen . . . all the other people who knew her."

"It's not enough."

"So what are you thinking? Some kind of memorial?"

"Possibly. I'm not sure."

As Barbara's thoughts petered out, Jean changed the subject. "So were you on your own last night? Why on earth didn't you come over to me? I was home by six."

"I tried to get you, but in the end I had dinner with Jack."

"Please tell me you're joking."

"I didn't want to go. It felt wrong. But I was desperate for somebody to talk to."

"For heaven's sake, Bar, you said you'd nip this thing in the bud. What's going on with you?"

"OK, I have something to tell you, and I want you to promise not to get cross."

"What now?"

"I've decided to spend the weekend with Jack in Gloucestershire." Silence.

"You're not saying anything."

"What do you want me to say?"

"I want you to tell me that you get it. The thing is, it's been such a lousy few months. I've been ill. Frank's been so bloody mean. I'm lonely and miserable. I've been at the end of my tether. I'm just desperate to feel the sunshine."

"So book a cheap holiday."

"Now you're being mean."

"I'm sorry, but I don't know what to say—other than you're completely mad."

"That's rich, coming from you. How is Virgil, by the way?"

"Bar, I'm trying to help."

"I know. And I'm asking you if having a fling would be so terrible? Does it make me a bad person?"

"Of course it doesn't make you a bad person. But if Frank were to find out, all hell would break loose and I suspect you'd lose him.... Of course, deep down that might be what you want."

Just as Jack had, she pleaded with Barbara to think carefully before she acted on her crazy impulse.

Barbara thought while she trawled through eBay, looking for a bike for Troy. Since his was ruined, she thought a new one might cheer him up. He could ride it when Mike took him to the park. She thought while she waited for her Irish stew to *ping* in the microwave. She thought while she watched *Roseanne* reruns. She lay awake most of the night thinking. Should she put her marriage at risk for a bit of fun? A bit of hanky-panky, as Rose would call it. But her marriage had been at risk long before Jack came along. Jack was caring and attentive. He worried about her. She had never realized that kindness could be so sexy. She didn't want to walk away—at least not yet.

So long as she kept her affair secret, Frank would never find out. No harm—or at least no additional harm—would be done.

Barbara called Jack the following morning.

"I haven't changed my mind. I want to come to Gloucestershire."

"Are you absolutely sure?"

"Yes."

Chapter 14

J ack picked her up early on Friday morning. That way they
would miss the lunchtime exodus of weekenders heading off to
their second homes in the country.

He put her bag in the trunk and turned to her. "You can still back
out, you know."

She kissed him firmly on the mouth and climbed into the car.

"What did you tell Ben?" he said.

"Nothing. He spends weekends at his girlfriend's place."

The plan was to drive straight to the house. Jack would give the
place the once-over and collect his mail. Later on they would check
into a local pub with rooms. Neither of them was comfortable with
the idea of making love in the house that Jack had shared with his
wife.

Two hours later they were driving along narrow Cotswold lanes,
skimming the ivy and ferns that sprouted from the drystone walls.
Behind these the fields were yellow with rapeseed. Honey-colored,
limestone villages nestling beside millstreams and Saxon churches
came and went. The guidebooks described these places as idyllic,

rural retreats, but they gave Barbara the willies. This was prime Tory terrain, where no black face dared to venture. Behind the mullioned windows of the cutesy tea shops, locals downed scrumptious scones the size of cushions and fretted about immigrants.

At one point the trees on either side of the road arched overhead so that the tips of the branches met and formed a dark, leafy tunnel.

"Almost there," Jack said.

She felt her stomach tighten. This was followed by a surge of emotion that she couldn't explain—other than that it wasn't entirely pleasant. She put it down to nervous anticipation.

After a few hundred yards Jack swung the car onto a gravel drive. At the end stood a Georgian limestone house covered in creeper. "Oh my Lord," Barbara said as they pulled up. "This is so grand. I take it the butler has informed the under parlor maid to build a fire in the library."

"Come on. It's not that big."

"You think? OK, so what are we looking at? Eight bedrooms?"

"Ten and a boxroom."

"Practically a slum."

"I can take you home, you know," he said, grinning.

"Not on your life. I want the guided tour."

As soon as they were inside, Jack disappeared into the kitchen to switch on the heating and read the mail. "Feel free to take a wander." She could tell he didn't feel comfortable showing off the house in person.

Leading off the wood-paneled entrance hall were two living rooms, a formal dining room and a library. The original limestone floors had been covered with shabby antique Persian rugs that had no doubt cost a fortune. There were grand stone fireplaces with brass surrounds, lots of dainty Georgian furniture and feather-backed sofas that cried out for dozing Labradors. In the main living room, which looked out onto an acre of pristine lawns and to the gently sloping Wolds beyond, a grand piano was festooned with family photographs—all in ornate silver frames. Barbara picked one up. It was a photograph of Jack and a woman she took to be Faye. They were standing, each with an arm around Sally, who looked to be about sixteen. Judging by Jack's buttonhole and Faye's hat, it had been taken at a wedding. In her powder-blue silk suit and under-stated jewelry, Faye radiated simple, effortless elegance and good breeding. In another picture, taken years earlier, she was on the beach helping Sally build a sandcastle. Faye was wearing a sundress, which, along with her mane of shoulder-length hair, was billowing artfully in the sea breeze. Barbara thought of her own family beach snaps: her looking like she'd just been swimming in a volcano, the kids covered in mosquito bites and—the bit you couldn't see—Frank swearing because there was sand in the camera lens again.

The house was all so feminine: from the eggshell blues and dusky pinks to the chintz and tassels and heavily draped swag tails at the windows. Jack's builders may have restored the structure, but the decor had without a doubt been down to Faye. Everywhere you looked, she was here.

Barbara found Jack in the cream Shaker kitchen, unloading bits and pieces that he'd picked up for lunch from his local deli. She offered to help, but he insisted he could manage. "And I've put the kettle on," he said.

Barbara took in the green Aga, the rows of cookery books, the Cath Kidston oven gloves and tea towels. Like the rest of the house, it radiated warmth and coziness. She gazed at the long pine dining table, which probably seated a dozen people—maybe more—and imagined the boozy, friend- and family-filled Sunday lunches and celebrations that must have taken place in this kitchen.

There was another family photograph sitting on the breakfast bar. Faye was cradling Sally as a newborn. "I love that picture," Jack said. "She's so happy. She was ecstatic when she became a mother. It was all she'd ever wanted. But one was enough. Faye liked tidiness and order. Children got in the way of that."

Barbara asked if he regretted not having more.

"Sometimes, but it meant that she always had time for me. I would be the first to admit that I was very spoiled." He poured boiling water into a red spotted Cath Kidston teapot. "You remind me of her."

"Me?" Barbara laughed. "Yeah, posh, refined and the perfect consort. You've got me pegged."

"I don't mean in that way," he said. "She was strong. After her diagnosis the doctors gave her nine months. She lasted three years. You have that kind of strength."

"And look where it's got me—a husband who takes me for granted."

She noticed Jack's bag of golf clubs leaning against the wall. For a shameful, unforgivable moment, she was wanted to call Frank and tell him that she'd found Jack's bag of golf bats.

"Maybe I should take up golf," Barbara said. "I need something to keep me occupied."

"I have to say it's kept me sane. When the weather's good, I play most days."

"Don't you find it a bit tedious?"

"Not really. A round of golf, a pub lunch with a few of the chaps and . . ."

"And what?"

"I suppose what I'm trying to say is . . . and then the day's almost over."

"You still struggle to get through the days?"

"Some are worse than others," he said.

Barbara felt her stomach lurch.

She poured the tea while Jack found plates and cutlery and laid the food out on the table. They ripped into the baguette and spread it with pâté and smelly French cheese.

"So what are your plans?" Barbara said, helping herself to some sun-dried tomatoes. "I mean, you must feel you're rattling around in this house. Have you thought about selling it?"

He didn't reply.

"I'm sorry. That was tactless."

"I'm not ready to let go of this place. Not yet."

He meant that he wasn't ready to let go of Faye. Something chimed in Barbara's memory. This wasn't the first time he'd mentioned how much he missed Faye. She remembered them discussing her death, their near-perfect marriage and how he struggled without her. So why had he kissed her, agreed to them spending the weekend together?

After they'd eaten, Jack made coffee and they took it into the smaller, more cozy living room. The mantelpiece was decked in ornamental elephants. A couple had to be a foot tall. Some were barely an inch. There were wooden ones, china ones, some made of terra-cotta. A couple were encrusted with glass jewels. Barbara picked up one of the twee, twinkly elephants.

"Cute, aren't they?" Jack said. "Faye had never shown a moment's interest in collecting, and then suddenly, after Sally left home, she got this bee in her bonnet about elephants. Everywhere we went she insisted on coming back with one. Of course, they're ten a penny in India or Africa, but you try finding an elephant in Reykjavík."

"I bet."

"Sally used to tease her about it and told her she was turning into a dotty old woman. But I found it rather appealing. I liked the idea of the two of us growing old and a bit eccentric together."

They sat side by side on the pretty chintz sofa, sipping their coffee.

"We're a funny old pair, you and me," Barbara said.

"In what way?"

"OK, tell me this: Why did you kiss me the other night?"

"That's an odd question. I'd have thought it was pretty obvious. Because I find you immensely attractive and I was overcome with desire. Why did you kiss me back?"

"Same reason."

"So?"

"So don't you find it odd that we're sitting here drinking coffee when we could be in our room at the pub enjoying glorious afternoon sex?"

"But we've just finished lunch. It's nice to have coffee after lunch. We're not exactly teenagers. We're simply taking our time. Aren't we?"

"Maybe."

"Barbara, what exactly are you saying?"

"Well . . . I think we're both putting off having sex. I know I am. I got this odd, slightly queasy feeling earlier, as we pulled onto the drive. I put it down to nerves, but I know perfectly well what it was—guilt. Despite all my bravado, I can't bring myself to cheat on Frank. He's behaved badly, but he doesn't deserve that."

His face didn't register a glimmer of surprise. "Well, it's not like I didn't try to dissuade you from coming. . . . So why am I trying to avoid sex?"

"You're seriously asking that question? You need me to tell you that you're still in love with Faye?"

He didn't say anything.

"And to put it bluntly, I have no intention of being made love to by a man who's still nuts about his wife. So what was the real reason you kissed me?"

"I told you the real reason."

"No, you told me part of it."

Jack reached forward and put his mug down on the coffee table. "OK . . . The truth is I thought that having a relationship with you would help me get over Faye—stop me living in the past."

"So you were using me?"

"No, of course not. It wasn't like that. You're a beautiful, intelligent, sexy woman. I fell for you the moment I met you."

"That doesn't mean that you weren't using me . . . in the nicest possible way. Just like I was using you—to get back at Frank."

"Good Lord. We've got ourselves into a right old pickle. But I want you to know that even if I was using you—in the nicest possible way—I did genuinely fall for you."

She took his hand. "And I fell for you. It was your charm, your immense kindness. Oh, and the fact that you remind me of that actor—you know the one . . . that rather handsome, white-haired chap in *Mad Men*. I can never think of his name."

"Me neither, but I think you'll find he has a lot more hair than me."

"No, he hasn't. But we're getting off the point. The fact is that neither of us is in the right place to start a relationship. I don't know much about coping with bereavement. I didn't really grieve for my father—at least not in the traditional way. But I don't think people are meant to *get over* losing loved ones. You were married to Faye for three decades. From what I've read, the trick is to learn to live alongside your grief."

"What can I say?" He paused and took a long breath. "You're right, of course. Sleeping with you would feel as if I were cheating on her."

Barbara put her arm around his shoulders and kissed him on the cheek. "It's OK," she said. "I'm not offended. I get it."

"I'm so sorry. I thought I could do this. I'd convinced myself that I was ready."

"And the truth is," Barbara said with a weak smile, "that neither of us is ready. It's funny how complicated and emotionally fraught people's lives can be—even at our age. I thought my friend Jean and her husband had the perfect marriage. Turns out her husband's never really been interested in sex. She loves him and doesn't want to end the marriage, so now she keeps a gigolo on the side."

"How frightfully Latin. Good for her."

"I'm inclined to agree." Barbara was suddenly overcome with guilt. "Please don't tell anybody I told you all this. Jean's my best friend. I'd hate her to think I'd been gossiping."

"Of course I won't, and anyway, who am I going to tell?" He paused. "So, will you at least stay for the weekend? I know some great walks, and there's this pub that does a fantastic Sunday roast."

She shook her head. "Thank you, but I'd rather head back to London."

"Then I'll take you."

She said there was no way she was about to ruin his weekend and she was more than happy to take the train. But Jack insisted. He said it was the least he could do.

Half an hour later they were back in the car.

"I've been thinking," Barbara said. "Why don't you go back to work? The challenge might be what you need."

"No. I'm happy with my golf. I'm not like you. I don't want to fight the dying of the light."

"Good Lord. You make it sound like you're ready to pop your clogs right now."

"Not remotely. What I am ready to do is embrace a new phase in my life. I'm done with deals, the cut and thrust. I don't mind showing up to the odd business meeting, but mainly I want to take walks, watch the seasons change, read all the stuff I never got round to."

They spent the next half hour in comfortable silence. While Jack listened to the afternoon play on Radio 4, Barbara closed her eyes. She tried to doze, but her thoughts turned to Tiffany—the moment of her dying. Over the last few days, she'd pictured it again and again: holding her hand; Tiffany lying there, still wearing her eyelash extensions, looking as if at any moment she might wake up; that terrible tattoo on her arm. When the tears came and she could bear the sadness no longer, she tried to think sweeter thoughts. But tropical beaches and her grandchildren's laughter refused to come. Instead she found herself on the Orchard Farm Estate, in front of the community hall. The image roused her and she opened her eyes. The idea felt as if it had come slap bang out of nowhere. But it hadn't. Ideas rarely did. She knew it had been brewing for a while—even before Tiffany died. The seed had been sewn the day she'd peered in through the bashed-in window of the community center and decided the council would never consider rebuilding it. She waited until the afternoon play had finished before saying anything.

"Jack, can I ask you a favor?"

"Anything." He switched off the radio.

"On the way home, could we take a detour via the Orchard Farm Estate?"

"Of course. But why on earth would you want to go there?"

"I've had this insane idea—at least you'll probably think it's insane. And I'd like your advice."

In fact, she wanted rather more than his advice, but that could wait.

"What sort of an insane idea?"

She said she would explain when they got there.

———

The late-afternoon sun shone down on the Orchard Farm Estate, partially lifting it from its gloom. A handful of kids were skateboarding and doing wheelies on their bikes. A gaggle of mothers was gossiping in the playground while they kept half an eye on their toddlers.

"What a bloody godforsaken place this is," Jack said.

"You should see it in the wind and rain."

"So what is it you want to show me?"

She led him to the derelict community center.

"OK," he said, his brogues sidestepping a dog turd. "And you've brought me here because?"

"How much would it cost to demolish this place and put up a new building?"

"What sort of a building?"

"A new community center. But four or five times the size."

"Five times?"

"At least. It's a big plot, and it doesn't have to be a single story. I'm thinking of a place dedicated entirely to women and children. There's so much domestic violence on estates like this. Women need a place where they can feel safe, where there are people who can advise and help them. I was thinking that maybe it could be run in association with the local women's refuge. On top of that, I want it to be somewhere for local women just to hang out and where their kids can play. Oh, and plus it has to provide after-school activities for older kids."

"Of course it does. . . . And you came up with all this in the car?"

"Let's say the idea sort of crystallized in the car. And this would only be phase one."

She could see that Jack was trying not to smile. "And phase two would be?"

"A small special-needs school. I thought about involving Larkswood House. The parents are wealthy. Lots of them have dyslexic children. I thought about asking them and the school governors to help raise money to sponsor it. Maybe in time the two schools could even link up in some way."

"Good Lord, you're not asking much, are you?"

"I know, but I can't sit back and let Tiffany's death be for nothing. I have to do something. And this feels like a good place to start. You think I'm completely bonkers, don't you?"

"Completely."

They did a tour of the plot. There was a good deal of open space plus a car park at the back.

"Well, I suppose if you incorporated the car park, you could fit a decent-sized building here."

Barbara said it would need to include offices, a large area for women and children to hang out, a kitchen and a café.

"Oh, and an outside play space for the kids." She paused. "So I guess what I'm asking you is this: if I could convince the local council to come on board, do you think your company would give me . . . us . . . a deal on the building costs? . . . I never told you that chutzpah is one of my more endearing personal qualities."

"And one I highly approve of," Jack said, laughing. "So, what sort of a deal would you be looking for?"

"I don't know. Off the top of my head? A fifteen percent discount."

"Tell you what. You get the project off the ground and I'll do the whole job for the cost of the materials."

"Are you serious? Why would you do that?"

"Because I want to."

"Hang on. . . . If you're doing this because you feel guilty about our failed weekend, please don't. I'm just as much to blame as you are."

"It's not that—at least not entirely. If you can make this thing happen, it would be my pleasure to back it."

"But it's too much. I can't have you do it for cost."

"Don't be daft. Of course you can."

Her eyes met his. "No. Really. I can't."

"Why? Because you think you don't deserve it?"

"I don't know. . . . Maybe."

"Good Lord, Barbara. For an intelligent woman, you're being terribly dense. This isn't about what you deserve. It's about the people you're trying to help. And for the record, after the rotten time you've had, I think you're entitled to a break."

She reached out and took his hand. "What can I say? . . . Thank you."

"My pleasure. But there's something I need to ask. . . . If we're to become business partners, presumably we're still going to be friends."

"We can manage that, can't we? We're both grown-ups. We've talked. We understand each other. I think we can move on, don't you?"

"I do."

"Good. That's settled."

"Of course, you do realize I've got to get this proposal past my board of directors?"

"Heavens. I hadn't thought of that."

"Don't worry. I'm just teasing. It won't be a problem. I still own fifty-one percent of the shares. It's my vote that counts. But even with my company cutting you a deal, it's going to cost the council a million pounds or so for building materials."

"Blimey. As much as that?"

"Could be more. The problem is they haven't got that kind of money—not these days."

"OK. Then I'll raise it."

"How?"

"I haven't the faintest idea."

Tiffany was to have a state funeral—in the sense that the state would pick up the bill. It was destined to be a cheap municipal affair. She would be dispatched in a basic pine coffin. An indecently short cremation ceremony would be led by a dreary clergyman with about as much charisma as broccoli, who had never set eyes on Tiffany or her children. It would be held in one of those sterile seventies chapels with tacky stained-glass windows and fake wood paneling. Velvet curtains would open on cue, and Tiffany's coffin would disappear, silently on rollers—into the furnace. Only it wouldn't. Crematoria were always understaffed and there was a constant backlog. Tiffany would have to wait her turn, along with all the other cadavers. After the cremation, her ashes would probably be guarded by social services until Troy and Lacie were deemed mature enough to take charge of them. Meanwhile, there would be no grave for them to visit, nowhere for them to lay flowers. There would be no memorial, no marker to let the world know that Tiffany Butler had ever existed.

But the state hadn't reckoned on Kenzie, Lexie and Leanne. Maureen told Barbara how the friends—who had previously taken it in turns to sit at Tiffany's bedside—had shown up at her office one day: three gum-clicking girls in tracksuits and hooped earrings, wanting to know who was "the head one" they should speak to about the funeral. They were less than impressed with what the state had to offer. For a start, there was no way Tiffany could be cremated. "She was, like, well—scared of fire, innit." And she believed in God, so they wanted a proper vicar bloke doing the honors in one of those old-fashioned churches like on *Downton*. And she should be buried in a churchyard with a gravestone and everything. They also wanted proper religious hymns: "Candle in the Wind" and Robbie Williams singing "Angels."

"When I told them there was no money for anything fancy," Maureen said, "they really had a go at me. They said that Tiffany had been through enough and that the least she deserved was a decent send-off. I couldn't argue with them."

"Tell you what," Barbara said. "Why don't I ring round some of the local churches, explain how Tiffany died and that she has no family and see if we can't get some kind of a reduction on a church service and burial?"

Barbara thought it would be easy. There wasn't a priest in the land who wouldn't ask themselves—what would Jesus do? They would all be falling over one another to give their services for free. But the local clergymen were of one voice: charity-wise, all their money was spoken for. She was just about to give up when Maureen called back. She'd been chatting to one of the women who ran a local women's refuge. It turned out her husband was vicar of Saint Catherine's in Dalston and they had a burial fund to help poor parishioners. Tiffany could be given a church funeral and be buried free of charge.

In the end there was quite a turnout. Kenzie, Lexie and Leanne brought their boyfriends—all of whom appeared to have gone out and bought black bomber jackets and matching ties for the occasion. The Indian chap from the corner shop where Tiffany bought her fags and mags came with his wife. Sandra was there with a handful of teachers from school. Maureen came with a wreath of sunflowers, which she laid alongside the others.

The hearse pulled up outside the church entrance. There were teddy-bear wreaths on top of the coffin. There was one made of white chrysanthemums trimmed with pink ribbon that spelled *Mum*. Alongside Tiffany's body, Kenzie and the others had placed

Tiffany's hair straighteners, her liquid eyeliner, mascara and her phone, fully charged, so that people could text her. She was wearing her best tracksuit.

Troy was veal-white. Mike kept a protective arm around him. Meanwhile, Carole held Lacie and fed her Cheerios to keep her quiet. At one point Mike and Troy started playing rock-paper-scissors. When Carole shushed them for making a noise, they started giggling like a couple of conspirators.

"Mike's been doing his best to cheer him up," Carole said to Barbara and Maureen, "but the poor kid's terrified of watching his mother being buried in the ground. I'm still not sure we should have brought him, but his counselor said he needed to say good-bye and that if he didn't come to the funeral, it would always be a mystery to him and he could grow up resenting being kept away."

Mike was crouching down in front of Troy. "You see, the thing is, when they put your mum in the ground, it's only her body—the bit that doesn't work anymore. But your mum's soul is up in heaven."

"What's a soul?"

"Well, it's the real her, the bit you can't see."

"You mean like a ghost? Ghosts are scary. They come and haunt you."

"That's not true. There are no such things as ghosts. And anyway, why would you ever, in a million years, be scared of your mum? She loved you and she still does. She would never, ever want to frighten you."

Troy reached for Mike's hand, still not convinced.

The coffin was carried up the aisle to the accompaniment of Jay Z's "Hard Knock Life." Barbara probably wasn't alone in thinking how much poor white kids identified with black ghetto kids these days. The reverend Nick said that he hadn't had the privilege to know

Tiffany, but he knew something of the hardships she had faced. He spoke of a loving young mother who struggled alone to raise her children and whose young life had been cut short in the most appalling circumstances. He hoped that everybody would take comfort from the fact that she was now out of pain and her struggle was over.

The reverend motioned towards Mike, who in turn looked at Troy. "You sure you're up for this, mate? It's OK if you're not."

But Troy was already on his feet. He and Mike made their way hand in hand down the aisle and stood beside Tiffany's coffin. Reverend Nick explained that Troy had a few words he would like to say.

"I can't believe this," Barbara whispered to Carole. "He barely said a word in class other than to have a tantrum."

Carole said he'd found his voice because he was doing it for his mum.

Troy looked at the coffin and laid his hand on the wood. Reverend Nick handed him a microphone. Troy took a piece of paper from his pocket, unfolded it and began to read.

"My mum was pretty and beautiful and good and kind and she would snuggle up with me and not let me drink too much Coke because it's bad for you." His voice quivered and trembled, but it rang out. "Me and Lacie loved her very much and we will never forget her. Not ever. And we hope she's happy up in heaven and the angels are looking after her." The reverend handed Troy a single white rose. He laid it on the top of his mother's coffin. Mike mouthed, "Well done. You OK?" Troy nodded and Mike gave him a squeeze.

The congregation listened to a CD of Robbie Williams singing "Angels." Mawkish as it was, tears fell like rain.

In the end Troy couldn't manage to be there for the burial. He waited with Mike at the front of the church while people followed the coffin into the churchyard. Kenzie, Lexie and Leanne were on their phones texting.

"Have those girls got no respect?" Maureen hissed to Barbara. "They were meant to be Tiffany's friends."

"I'm guessing it's Tiffany they're texting—to wish her a safe journey to the afterlife."

"Fabulous. All we need now is for her phone to go off in her coffin and a hundred people are going to start fainting and having hysterics."

But it didn't—at least not so that anybody could hear.

When the service was over, Barbara took her turn to shovel earth onto the coffin. As the heavy London clay landed with a thud, fury bubbled up inside her.

Everybody went back to Carole's for tea and bridge rolls. Lacie had dozed off in the car on the way home and was napping in her cot. Troy had the TV on quietly at one end of the living room. "He's a bit overwhelmed," Carole said to Barbara. "I thought it would calm him down."

"How's he doing generally?"

"The sadness still overwhelms him, and apart from Mike, he's pretty wary of men. But he's started counseling with this lovely lady. She doesn't think he's ready to go back to school yet, but we'll get there."

Then she excused herself. The reverend Nick was on his own, looking a bit lost. "I should go over and have a chat—say thank you for everything."

Barbara made her way to the buffet table and helped herself to a bridge roll.

"Barbara." The voice came from behind her. "How are you?"

She turned. "Sandra! . . . I'm so sorry we haven't spoken. I should have called. It's just that there's been so much going on and . . ."

"Stop it. I'm just as bad. I could have called you. But I knew you still weren't well, and I wasn't sure if you'd appreciate me phoning. . . . Anyway, I just want to come over to wish you luck with the community center project. It's a marvelous idea. Carole's just been telling me all about it. I knew you'd find your feet again. I'm so pleased."

Barbara thanked her.

"I also wanted to let you know that I'm resigning."

"But why?"

"Oh, come on, Barbara. There's no need to be disingenuous. We all know that Jubilee and I weren't a match made in heaven. I was completely out of my depth. Everybody knew it. Only they were too polite to say."

"What will you do?"

"I don't know. I'll probably leave teaching though. To be honest, that's about as far as my plans have got."

She looked over at Troy, who was still watching TV on the sofa.

"How's he doing? If you ask me, he should be back at school by now. I think the routine would do him good."

"His counselor doesn't think he's ready. But Carole says he's doing a lot better."

"That's good. . . . Look, I want you to know that the staff and I did everything we could for Troy."

"I know you did," Barbara said. At the same time, she couldn't help wondering if that was the whole truth. Had the staff been instructed to look out for signs that Troy might be in distress?

"When that monster goes on trial and the story hits the local paper, I'm not having some ignorant hack accuse me of failing in my duty of care. I won't stand for it. The school is totally blameless. Nobody could have known that this Wayne character would come back and do what he did."

Barbara noticed Sandra's eyes were filling up. "Of course they didn't. None of us did."

"If you'll excuse me, I should say good-bye to Troy." She produced a handkerchief from her jacket pocket and blew her nose.

"Of course . . . And, Sandra, good luck."

"You, too."

She turned away and headed towards the sofa.

"Isn't that Sandra? Troy's head teacher?" Mike had appeared. He was helping himself to a glass of wine.

Barbara nodded. "There goes another one who blames herself for what happened. Only Sandra's not the sort to admit it."

"Maybe she's got the right idea. At least that way she gets fewer sleepless nights. And the truth is, nobody could have done anything. The whole thing is such a rotten, bloody mess. But you can't keep dwelling on it. We have to think about those kids."

"Speaking of which, you and Troy seem to have become really good mates."

"He's a great lad. With a bit of love and attention, he'll really come into his own. And Lacie's such cutie."

"You could always adopt them."

A smile drifted across Mike's face. "I love the casual way you managed to slip that in. Carole put you up to it, didn't she?"

"No. She hasn't said a word. Promise."

"Ever since Tiffany died, Carole hasn't stopped talking about us adopting them. As far as she's concerned, it's a no-brainer. But I'm not sure that at our age, social services are going to agree with her."

"You sound like you're hoping they won't agree."

"Don't get me wrong. I've fallen in love with them as much as Carole has, but if we adopt them . . ."

"There goes any hope of a quiet life."

"Carole says we'll find ways of building in 'us time,' but I'm buggered if I know how."

"Well, you've always got me—and Maureen, too, if I know her.

We'd be more than happy to help out occasionally. In case you were worried, neither of us has the remotest intention of disappearing from those kids' lives."

"That's kind. And don't think I'm not grateful. But even with a bit of help, it doesn't alter the fact that raising two kids at our time of life isn't going to be easy."

"So will you apply to adopt them?"

"Carole's already got the forms. Meanwhile, I'm trying to convince myself that peace and quiet is vastly overrated."

"Poor old Mike. All that moaning and in the end you're such a pushover."

"That's what I keep telling Carole."

"Well, I'm sure she appreciates it."

Just then Barbara caught sight of Troy wandering around looking lost. "Hey, you . . . finished watching TV?"

"Boring."

"Well, I've got something for you that might cheer you up."

"What is it?"

"It's in the garden. Why don't we go and take a look?"

Barbara and Mike followed as Troy went tearing into the kitchen and out the back door.

Troy's mouth and eyes couldn't have got any wider. "Wow! Is that for me?"

"Of course it's for you."

Leaning against the back wall of the house was a shiny red bike.

"Looks brand-new," Mike whispered.

She said that it was, pretty much. The eBay seller had bought it for his son's birthday, but the kid was a bit of a geek and asked if he could have a more powerful computer instead.

Troy darted over and hugged Barbara around the waist. "This is the best present I've had in my whole life."

He looked at Mike. "I want to ride it. Can we go to the park? Please can we? Please?"

"Of course we can."

Troy frowned. "Mike, I know my mum died and everything . . . and I should be sad . . . and I am sad. I'm really, really sad. But is it OK for me to be just a tiny bit happy as well?"

Mike put his arm around Troy's shoulders. "Of course it is. That's precisely what your mum would want."

"Right. Let's go, then. I'll race you to the park."

Barbara nudged Mike. "Peace and quiet really are overrated."

"Maybe, but make no mistake. I plan to be back in time for the football."

Chapter 15

Frank arrived home with a tan and an inch or two extra around his waist—on account of his epic consumption of enchiladas and refried beans. After he'd unpacked he promised that they would sit down and have "that talk."

"But do you mind if we leave it for a few days? Right now I haven't got the energy. I'm completely done in."

Barbara let him be. If, now that he was home, he was running scared and trying to put off discussing their marriage, she wasn't too bothered. She still doubted that it would achieve much. Plus she also had other things on her mind.

She fretted about Troy. Whereas Lacie had no comprehension of her own tragedy and had settled down very quickly with Carole and Mike, her brother was still prone to tantrums and moments of despair when he screamed for his mum. Carole was pragmatic. They were taking each day as it came. She was also busy working on Mike, trying to persuade him to let her fill out the adoption application forms. She would call Barbara every couple of days. "It's like chopping down a tree. I can hear the creaking. Another week and I know he'll give way."

In quiet moments Barbara found herself wondering if she should push Frank into having the state-of-their-union talk. She had made up her mind that when they got around to it, she wouldn't tell him about Jack. It could serve no purpose. Jack was on her mind, too. She wasn't grieving exactly, but she couldn't help wondering what might have been, had the circumstances been different.

Along with worrying about Troy and reflecting on her marriage and her relationship with Jack, she was wondering how one set about raising a million quid. When she mentioned her plan to Frank, he was taken aback but clearly impressed.

"It's an absolutely amazing idea. So, do you think you can pull it off?"

"I don't know. I was hoping you could help me brainstorm fund-raising ideas."

She was aware that at some stage she would need to tell him about Jack's financial offer. But for now she said nothing.

"Sure. But it'll have to wait until after I've finished this edit."

Frank spent most of his time in his study watching the rushes from Mexico. Occasionally he would call her upstairs to take a look at something particularly poignant—a skeletal psychiatric patient tied to a chair, inmates banging their heads repeatedly against walls. But mostly he plowed through the material on his own, making pages of notes as he went.

Adam and Emma were getting married on Saturday. Two days before, Jean called.

"You'll never guess what."

"What?"

"OK, brace yourself. . . . Pam and Si are going to be at the wedding."

"What? You're kidding. How?"

It turned out that Si was related to Felicity's late husband.

"I'm sorry not to give you more warning, but I've never looked at Felicity's guest list and I literally just found out. Will you be really miserable?"

"Don't be daft. Of course not."

Barbara was telling a white lie. She could just about tolerate Pam and Si, but Frank really struggled—with Si in particular.

From the moment he got up on Saturday, Frank didn't stop moaning. He moaned about having to spend the day with his sister and brother-in-law. He moaned about having to schlep the sixty miles to Berkshire for the wedding. Plus he didn't see the point in weddings anyway. It wasn't marriage he objected to—just lavish wedding receptions. Why did people waste all that money? Weddings were a bloody inconvenience. The truth that dare not speak its name was that nobody liked them. "You have to buy a present. Women always need a new outfit. They're just a damned inconvenience."

"You're just pissed off that Pam and Si are going to be there."

He insisted it wasn't just that. "Wedding receptions are boring and pointless. Remind me again why Jess and Matt bothered with one."

"To annoy you," Barbara said.

Inside, the tiny country church was decked in sweet-scented lilac. Emma wore an off-the-shoulder gown and a tiara that had belonged to her grandmother. ("All I inherited from my grandmother," Jean had said when they last spoke, "was her Second World War gas mask.) Adam, Oliver and their father had finally acceded to Felicity's directive and were looking uncomfortable in their morning coats and top hats. Jean looked elegant in gray silk. She'd also been to see Camp David, who had tamed her flyaway hair and cut it into a geometrical bob that took years off her. Felicity peered out from under a hat with a flying-saucer brim and walked round as if she had a perpetual stink under her nose.

The reception was held at a country-house hotel a few hundred yards from the church.

"We haven't said hello to your sister and Si yet," Barbara said to Frank as they each accepted a mini quiche from a passing waitress. "We ought to go and find them."

"Frank! Bar!" Pam had appeared from nowhere. "We've caught up with Jess and Ben, but we've been looking for you everywhere. Where have you been hiding?"

Frank kissed his sister and told her how well she looked.

"That's Spain for you. We eat a strict Mediterranean diet. Lots of fruit and veg. No saturated fat. And judging from the look of you . . ." She patted her brother's stomach. "You could benefit from taking a leaf out of our book. Barbara, what are you feeding him?"

"Hi, Pam," Barbara said, ignoring her sister-in-law's question-slash-insult. "Good to see you. Where's Si?"

Si appeared on cue, holding with two champagne flutes. He handed one to Pam.

"It's only cheap prosecco," he said.

Barbara told him to keep the information to himself. "If the bride's mother finds out, she'll have a fit."

"Ah, clearly a woman of culture and discernment," Si said. He turned to Frank. "So, Frank, what car are you driving these days?"

"A black one."

Si roared and turned to Barbara. "I always forget what a great sense of humor your husband has."

"Now, Barbara," Pam said. "When are you and my brother going to come and visit us in Spain? We've got loads of room."

"Yep. We've got two spare bedrooms," Si said. "Both en suite of course. Best thing we ever did, moving to Spain. Life's one big holiday. During the day we laze by the pool."

"*Infinity* pool," Pam corrected him.

"Sorry. Infinity pool. And in the evening we barbecue some fish, down a bottle of sangria.... It's the life, I'm telling you."

"And the peaches," Pam said. "You want to see the size of the peaches. They're nothing like we get at home. Twice the size."

"More like three times," said Si.

"And it's the same with the oranges."

"Huge. Like footballs."

"And the flavor. You wouldn't believe the flavor."

"So what do you like about Spain apart from the fruit?" Frank inquired.

"No bloody immigrants," Si bellowed.

"Apart from you and all the other English expats," Barbara said.

"We don't count," Si said. "We pay our way. We're not spongers."

"And the crime is nothing like over here, is it, Si? Of course, years ago the Spanish used to execute people by garroting them. I think that had an effect on the crime rate."

"To be honest," Si continued, "I can't think of a single reason why you'd want to live over here in the cold and the damp."

"Oh, I can think of a few," Frank said.

Barbara asked how long they were staying. "Only the one night. We've got an early flight in the morning."

Si dug Frank in the ribs. "You can't keep us away from the place."

Thank God, Barbara thought. That meant they didn't have to invite them to stay.

Pam and Si were unrelenting. Over dinner Barbara and Frank, along with all the other guests at their table, were treated to a history of the Costa del Sol—average climate, rainfall, a description of

Marbella's Golden Mile, which, would you believe, was actually four miles. The only time they let up was during the speeches.

By eleven Barbara and Frank were making noises about leaving. Si tried to persuade them to stay. "But I haven't had a chance to dance with your lovely wife yet," he said to Frank.

Barbara cited throbbing bunions. After promises to come to Marbella to sample the big peaches, they made their escape.

"I can never get over how different you and your sister are," Barbara said.

She knew the reason. Frank had been the golden boy. His parents had had no ambition for Pam. She'd learned short-hand typing. Frank had gone to university.

"It's actually very sad," Frank said. "Our mother was a bit like yours in that she had no hopes or dreams for Pam. But whereas you stood up to Rose and got to university, Pam just accepted her lot." He paused. "Like I always tell you, you're a strong woman, Barbara. Always have been."

On Sunday the whole family—plus Katie—came for lunch. Katie brought Barbara flowers, offered to lend a hand in the kitchen, and after lunch she took Cleo and Atticus into the garden to hunt for four-leaf clovers.

"And before you ask," Ben said, clearly anticipating a barrage of questions from his sister. "Yes, she votes Labour and, yes, she believes in greater accountability and regulation of the financial markets. Oh, and she makes annual donations to charity. That do you?"

Jess held up her palms. "What? Don't look at me. I never said a word. You know how I feel these days about people making money. As far as I'm concerned, the two of you can go off and make as much as you like. Believe me, Matt and I aren't complaining."

"I'll drink to that," Matt said.

Frank raised his glass. "Me, too. Good luck to the both of you."

Rose had missed this part of the conversation. She was too busy staring out the window, watching Katie playing with the children.

"Take it from me," she said to Ben. "You need to grab that one fast. Girls like her don't stay on the shelf too long."

"Thank you, Nana. I'll bear that in mind."

"Well, make sure you do."

For once Barbara was inclined to agree with her mother.

By five everybody was gone—including Ben. These days, he was pretty much living at Katie's.

Frank said he would help Barbara load the dishwasher. She scraped plates, rinsed them under the tap and handed them to him.

"When I was in Mexico," he said, "I went to a Frida Kahlo exhibition."

"I love her paintings. Did you know she spent much of her life in terrible pain from a back injury?"

"I did. Her self-portraits radiate such amazing strength and resilience." He paused. "She reminds me of you."

"Ah . . . That'll be the mustache and the monobrow."

"Behave. I mean she was a powerful, strong woman, like you."

Barbara placed a dishwasher tablet in the compartment, touched the hot wash symbol and closed the door. "OK, that's enough. I don't want to hear it anymore."

"Hear what?"

"I am fed up to the back teeth with everybody—and you in particular—telling me how strong I am."

"But you are."

"Yes, and all our married life you've used it as an excuse to neglect me."

"This again. Why can't you get it into your head? I had to go to Mexico. I know you weren't well, but I had no choice."

"You know what? There is always a choice. You *chose* to go. It wouldn't have been easy, but you could have rearranged things and gone a couple of months later. You abandoned me when I was at my most vulnerable. I have never asked anything of you, and the only time I did, you refused me."

"But I knew you'd be OK. You had people around. And look at you. You're full of plans to rebuild the community center. Somebody who's suffering doesn't do stuff like that."

She felt as if she were hitting her head against a brick wall. What did she have to say to convince him that she wasn't always strong and that it was cruel to use her strength as a stick to beat her?

"Believe that if you want to, but I'm telling you from the bottom of my heart that I'm still suffering over the way you behaved, and the fact that you can't see that is making it worse."

"I don't know what to do. I don't know how many more times I have to say it: I love you. I love the kids. I do my best. I've always done my best. This is who I am, and I'm sorry if you can't accept that."

Frank and Rose both seemed to think that claiming they'd done their best excused their behavior.

"And what about who I am?" Barbara said. "I have made compromises for you all my life. Have you ever made one for me?"

Instead of waiting for a reply, she asked him to sit down. "There's something you should know."

"What?"

They sat at opposite sides of the table.

Until now Barbara had had no intention of telling him about Jack. But she felt she had no option. He needed to know why she'd almost had an affair.

"While you were away," Barbara said, "I met somebody."

"What's that supposed to mean?"

"I came very close to having an affair. In the end I pulled back—in fact, we both did. Nothing happened, and it's over."

Frank sat staring at her. "You've been seeing another man? I don't believe you."

"Fine. Suit yourself."

"What sort of a man? Where? When?"

"He's the grandfather of this boy I've been tutoring."

"I don't understand. Why would you do something like that?" Even with his tan, she could see the color draining from his face. He looked like he'd been poleaxed.

"He listened to me. He took an interest. He cared."

"I listen to you. I care."

"I have to fight to get you to listen to me and you know it. God, Frank, you even ask me to speak faster."

"I don't mean that. It's a joke."

"Well, I've never found it very funny." She swept some crumbs onto the floor. "I'm lonely. I've been lonely for years. Even when you're here, you're absent."

"But you didn't sleep with him?"

"No. I decided that no matter how angry I was, you didn't deserve that."

"Why should I believe you?"

"I don't care what you believe. And, anyway, whether or not we slept together isn't important. I got close to him. We connected. That's the point."

"I don't know what to say. Have I been such a shitty husband?"

"Not entirely, but yes—a lot of the time you have. But I realize now that I colluded with you. Because I thought I didn't deserve to be looked after, I gave you permission to carry on behaving badly. I take full responsibility for that."

He said he needed a drink.

"You drank loads at lunch."

"I don't care."

He went into the living room and came back with a bottle of Scotch. He opened it and half filled a tumbler.

"Shouldn't you put some water with that?"

"No! Just shut up telling me what to do." He looked like he wanted to hit her. Instead he jerked back some Scotch. "Why are you telling me about you and this guy? Are you doing it to punish me?"

She hadn't thought about it until now. "You know what? I think maybe I am."

"So is this it? Are we over? Do you want me to leave?"

Jean had warned her. If she told him about Jack, she could lose him. "No. I just want you to understand. . . . Frank, you need to see what I did in context."

"Context? What bloody context?"

"I have enough trouble accepting that my mother was and never will be the mother I need her to be. I know that when I need love or comfort, I can never turn to her. I'm learning to deal with that, but what I can't cope with is you never being there for me. When two people love each other, they should want to care for each other. I have always cared for you, and all I've gotten in return is your self-ishness."

"What do you want me to do?"

"It's not what I want. It has to be what you want. If you want to change, then do it."

"I don't know if I can. And particularly not now after what you've done."

"I didn't sleep with him."

"Yes, but you wanted to. And like you said, you connected. You think I don't appreciate the significance of that? Well, I do. It may surprise you, but I'm not quite as autistic as you think I am."

"No . . . you're not," she said.

"How could you have done this to me? To us?"

"I didn't set out to do it, but I was at rock bottom. Then Tiffany died. You weren't here."

He stood up. "I need to get away. I need to think."

"Frank . . . please . . . I didn't sleep with him!"

"Yeah, so you keep saying."

He picked up his keys and wallet and said he was going to spend the night in a hotel.

The door closed. Panic overwhelmed her. What if he didn't come back? Who would she grow old with? But in spite of the panic, a part of her felt relieved. She couldn't continue in a lonely marriage. Right now the ball was just as much in his court as hers.

The following day he called to say he wouldn't be coming home other than to pick up his clothes. He said he was moving in with Martin, the cameraman he'd worked with in Mexico. Martin had just got divorced and was renting a flat with a spare room.

"Presumably you think I've lost him," Barbara said to Jean.

"Look, I'd be lying if I said it wasn't a possibility. But I suspect that when Frank sits down and takes stock of everything that's happened, he'll realize what a selfish sod he's been."

"But can he change? You said that at his age it could be too late."

"I don't know, hon. I really don't know."

Jess and Ben were upset, but not surprised when they found out their mother's relationship with Jack. The only thing that amazed them was that she hadn't slept with him.

"Then again," Ben said, when the news had sunk in, "I suppose at your age, relationships are more about companionship. You just want somebody to watch the telly with."

"Believe that if you want to, but for your information, sexual desire doesn't end the moment people hit fifty."

"Er . . . Too much information. Plus I happen to know for a fact that you and Dad only ever did it twice—to make me and Jess. Please can we leave it at that?"

Jess was less cavalier. At one point she started weeping and said she didn't want to be the child of divorced parents. Again Ben was there with the wisecracks. "We could always ask them to wait until after we're dead."

But for once Ben and Jess were in agreement. Much as they loved their dad, they couldn't defend him. He had brought the situation on himself. That said, they were both on the phone to him every day, worrying about how he was coping living off takeaway in a grotty flat in South London.

"He keeps saying how much he loves you," Jess told Barbara. "And you love him. You know you do."

"Of course I do. I always will. But sometimes love isn't enough."

"That's such an old cliché. Of course love's enough."

"No, it isn't, and one day when you're a bit older you might understand. I'm sorry if that sounds patronizing, but I'm old. So shoot me."

Frank kept his distance. He didn't visit or call. Barbara prayed that he was using the time to reflect.

Meanwhile, she decided, she could either sit and mope or get busy. She chose the latter. That was what strong people were supposed to do, wasn't it?

She started by calling Maureen. "Have you got a minute? I've had this insane idea about rebuilding the Orchard Farm community center. . . ."

Maureen listened. "O . . . K . . . And you think you can raise a million quid?"

"Why not? People do stuff like that all the time."

"OK, so what's your plan?"

"I don't actually have one."

"Ah . . . I'm thinking that's probably the insane part."

"But do you think it's a good idea in principle?"

Maureen said she thought it was a great idea . . . in principle.

"Right, then, who do I speak to at the council? I can't do anything without their backing."

"You need to speak to somebody in the buildings and recreation department." As it happened, Maureen knew somebody. He was married to one of the social workers in her office. "Leave it with me. I'll see what I can do."

Rob Truswell, the chap in the buildings department, agreed to see her and, to give him his due, he didn't laugh. "It's a wonderful idea and one I, personally, would support wholeheartedly if you could raise the funds. But believe me, a few bake sales and fun runs aren't going to get you what you need. And fund-raising aside, have you any idea of the processes this scheme would need to go through at the council? There would be planning meetings, finance meetings, building-regulation meetings—meetings about meetings."

"I get all that, but let's suppose for one daft, crazy moment that I could raise the money—would it be something that the council would consider?"

"I can't tell you. There would need to be a meeting . . ."

"Are you telling me to give up on this before I've even started?"

"No. I'm telling you that you have no idea of the obstacles you'd be facing."

"People might say that's a good thing."

Rob Truswell smiled. "Here's my advice. Go away, see how much money you can raise and then come back and see me."

"And then you'll call a meeting?"

"And then I'll call a meeting."

Sandra had always insisted that the reason the original community center failed was because the council had never got commercial backing. "It's a no-brainer," she'd said. "These days you have to get into bed with big business."

Barbara remembered thinking at the time that this made sense. But she had no idea where to start. Then it occurred to her that Sally and Jeremy worked for banks, which most likely had charity divisions. She called Sally and explained about her plan for the community center.

"Everybody thinks I'm bonkers, and maybe I am, but . . ."

"Of course you're bonkers." Sally laughed. "But I know for a fact that therein lies your strength. Only a bonkers person with absolutely no idea what they're taking on would even contemplate doing what you're trying to do."

"So you think I should give up?"

"Don't be so ridiculous. Of course you shouldn't. Did Wellington give up at Waterloo? Did Scott of the Antarctic give up?"

"Scott froze to death."

"Yes, but he didn't give up. At boarding school we had this Latin motto, which loosely translates as: 'Chin up, chest out and don't let the blighters get you down.'"

Sally and Jeremy both contacted their banks' philanthropy divisions and arranged meetings for Barbara.

The first was at Sally's bank, Premier Star. She was expecting a cozy, informal chat over a cup of tea and a Garibaldi biscuit. Instead she was shown into a glass-and-chrome power-meeting room on the fifteenth floor and was confronted by a dozen suits with legal pads. She joined them at the long boardroom table. They were clearly expecting some slick pitch and a PowerPoint presentation and she had nothing. She wasn't just out of her depth. She was sinking without a trace—and she hadn't even begun.

Barbara introduced herself and thanked them for agreeing to see her. "I'd like to begin with some statistics. On average, one incident of domestic violence is reported to the police every minute. Two women a week are killed by a current or former male partner. . . ."

The woman who appeared to be chairing the meeting removed her specs. "Yes, we pretty much know all that. But time is a bit limited, so if you could take us through your actual plan. Do you have a written proposal?"

"Er, no. I apologize . . . but I can certainly get something to you." Barbara stuttered and stumbled her way through her plan.

"So do you have architects' plans and an EBC?"

"EBC?"

"Estimated breakdown of costs."

"Not as such. But we need to raise just over a million pounds."

"How much over?"

"I'm not quite sure."

She had lost them. It hadn't occurred to her that these days people pitched for charitable donations and support the way they pitched a business plan. She had never felt so old or out of touch.

"Look, you're right I have come unprepared," she said. "And I'm sorry. But here's the thing. A few weeks ago a woman called Tiffany Butler died when her ventilator was switched off. She was the mother of one of the children I used to teach."

Barbara told them Tiffany's story. "Orchard Farm Estate, where she lived, is one of the most notorious and neglected public-housing estates in the country. The community center was shut down through lack of funds, and women and children have nowhere to go—nowhere to get advice, counseling or just hang out with their kids. I want to change that. I've had a fantastic costs-only offer from a major building company, and now I just need a million pounds or so to do it."

She thanked them for listening. They thanked her for coming and said they'd be in touch. She couldn't get out fast enough. She sat in Starbucks and called Jean. "I've never felt so humiliated in my life. How could I have been so stupid not to prepare?" Jean tried to calm her down with talk of learning curves and how she wouldn't make that mistake again.

A few days later she got a letter from Premier Star saying that they thought her cause was commendable but on this occasion they wouldn't be able to offer financial support. They wished her well.

She called Jack.

"I need to put together a brochure to support my pitch—with EBCs. Can you get some figures over to me?"

"No. Not until you've got an architect and a structural engineer on board and you can show me some plans."

"But how do I do that if I haven't got any money to pay them?"

He suggested she try Rob Truswell at the council. "It seems like he's prepared to take you seriously, so ask him if you can use council architects. That way the project stays in house and costs are kept down."

"Of course. That makes perfect sense." She said she would call Rob Truswell straightaway.

"Barbara, before you go, there's something I need to tell you. I'm sorry to announce this over the phone, but everything's happened to fast. I'm going abroad for a while."

"Why? How long for?"

"I don't know. A year or so. Maybe for good. I need a fresh start, and I'm not sure I can do it in this country. I thought I might go to Portugal. The climate's great. The golf's good."

"But what about Freddie? He'll think you're abandoning him."

"He's starting at Larkswood in September. I'll make sure I'm back to see him for the holidays. And I think Sally and Jeremy need some space to start reconnecting with him."

"So your mind's made up."

"It is. I need to get away from that house."

"Then sell it. Surely that would make more sense?"

"I'm not ready. But I'm hoping after a few months away that might change."

She wasn't sure if putting geographical distance between him and the Gloucestershire house would separate him from his grief, but it was clear he wasn't about to be dissuaded.

"By the way," she said, "Frank's back. I told him about us."

"Why would you do that?"

"I think I wanted to hurt him. It felt like the only way I could get his attention."

"How did he take it?"

"He's moved out. He said he needed time to think."

"I wouldn't have thought there was much to think about. Your husband is a selfish idiot."

"I know, but he's my selfish idiot."

"Does that mean you still love him?"

"I don't think I ever stopped—not really. But I need him to change, and I'm not sure he knows how."

Jack said what Jean had said, that discovering she'd almost had an affair might be the jolt he needed. "You need to give him time."

"What other choice do I have?" she said.

Jack said he thought it would be for the best if they kept contact to a minimum from now on. "I've done enough damage, and if Frank comes back, I'd hate him to think we were still in touch. I'm sorry if that sounds harsh."

"It does, but you're right. It makes sense."

He said he'd appointed somebody at his company to take charge of the community center project.

"He'll give you a call to introduce himself."

"Jack—before you go . . . thank you."

"What for?"

"First of all, for your support of my lunatic scheme. But also just for being there. And listening."

"The pleasure was mine," he said.

"So as you can see," Barbara said to Rob Truswell at the council, "I'm in a complete catch-22 situation. I know this is a huge ask, but is there any chance you could get council architects and engineers to draw up some plans for the new community center?"

Rob Truswell agreed that it was a huge ask. It was also out of the question. The council didn't have the cash to spend on schemes that probably wouldn't come to anything.

"OK . . . OK . . . What about students? Suppose I approached the London School of Architecture and perhaps the engineering department at one of the universities? Maybe some final-year students would be prepared to take it on."

Rob Truswell said it was highly unlikely. "They'll all be up to their eyes studying for their finals."

Barbara decided she had nothing to lose. She e-mailed the relevant heads of department at both institutions. A week went by and she heard nothing. Then she started to receive e-mails from individual students, registering interest in the project and wanting to know more.

Barbara e-mailed back to say she'd decided to hold an informal explanatory meeting outside the community center and anybody who was interested in taking part in the project was welcome to come along.

She called Rob Truswell to invite him.

"But you can't use students," he said. "They don't have professional qualifications. The council would never approve plans from unqualified people."

"But they would if your architects and engineers had given them the once-over. They have professional qualifications."

Rob Truswell sighed. "Maybe."

"So will you come?"

"On the grounds that it will look a bit more official if I'm there?" he said.

"Sort of. Please?"

He said he would.

Half a dozen engineering and architecture students showed up. Barbara outlined her plan as best she could and explained what facilities would be needed. "The rest is up to you and your imaginations. But please don't get too carried away. We need to keep the costs to a minimum."

Barbara couldn't believe how enthusiastic these kids were. They were full of ideas and questions and rough sketches. Rob Truswell asked them to submit their initial drawings and plans by the end of the month and that he, Barbara and the architects and engineers at the council would consider them all. "The person or group who wins the tender will be informed within a week or so."

It wasn't a hard decision to make. Most of the plans paid no heed to what Barbara had said about cost. They were full of mezzanine floors and all-weather play areas with fancy retracting roofs. An architect student called Hannah, working with her engineer boy-friend, came up with the winning design. It was nothing fancy. In fact, it wasn't much more than a two-story box, but she'd thought about light and space and how one area connected to the next. She'd kept to the brief. Hannah and her boyfriend, James, couldn't get over winning their first commission. Barbara couldn't get over winning her first battle.

Jack provided her with costings and Barbara was able to write her proposal complete with plans and ECBs. She sent this—ahead of their meeting—to the head of the charity division at Jeremy's bank, Mutual Chartered.

Because she knew what to expect, Barbara was even more ner-vous before this meeting, but even with her declining, postmeno-pausal memory, she managed to learn all the facts, figures and costs by heart. When she came away, she felt she'd done OK.

As usual, they said they would let her know.

Frank returned home one rainy Wednesday night. She was watch-ing a rerun of *The Golden Girls.* The doorbell startled her. She looked at her watch. It was after ten. She assumed it was Ben. He must have lost his key. She opened the door without even bothering to look through the spy hole.

"Frank. What on earth are you doing here?"

"I sort of thought I still lived here," he said, wearing his meek face.

"Of course you do. I didn't mean it like that. I meant why are you here so late? And how come you didn't you let yourself in?"

"I didn't want to frighten you. . . . So can I come in?"

"Don't be daft. Of course you can come in."

He hung up his wet coat and they went into the kitchen. She asked him if he'd eaten.

"Chinese."

"Ask a silly question . . ."

Frank sat down at the kitchen table and began fiddling with the pepper grinder. "So, the kids tell me you've started fund-raising for the new community center."

"Yes. I'm pretty crap at it, though." She told him what had happened when she went to Premier Star. "But I'm hoping I've got my act together since then. I've just had a meeting with Mutual Chartered."

"And?"

"Oh, you know . . . the usual. They'll let me know. I'm not holding my breath." She paused. "By the way, the council have agreed to call it the Tiffany Butler Center. Troy's going to be over the moon."

"I bet he will."

"If it ever happens," Barbara said.

"It will. If anybody can make this thing happen, you can."

She said she wished she had his confidence.

Neither of them spoke. In the end Barbara broke the silence. "So, Frank, have you come her for a particular reason?"

He stopped playing with the pepper grinder and looked at her. "I want to come home. I've missed you."

"What you mean is you've missed me running around after you."

"That's not fair. I've really missed you. And I've been doing rather a lot of soul-searching. On top of that, I've had several lectures from the kids about my behavior over the last few decades."

"The kids? I had no idea they'd spoken to you."

"They're pretty mad at me. Bar, you have no idea how much they adore you. To put it mildly, they think I've got a lot of groveling to do."

"I don't want you to grovel. It's just that now we're getting older and we don't know how much time we've got left together. I want you to start putting some effort into this marriage."

"Maybe it's a generation thing, but it never really occurred to me that marriage requires effort. I sort of thought you got on with life and the relationship took care of itself."

"Well, now you know that's not how it works."

"I do. Look, I know I can be a self-centered prick. But I want you to know how much I love you and that I've always loved you and that you're the only person I can imagine growing old with."

"I love you, too, but it won't work if things don't change."

"OK . . . well . . . first I think we should spend more time together. You were right when you said we needed to reconnect. Now the weather's warmer I thought we could take the odd weekend away. And I've also decided to stop looking for so many foreign stories. There are plenty over here to keep me occupied."

"You are going to stop traveling?" Barbara said. "I don't know what to say."

"Not entirely, but I promise to cut back. I'm never going to be the perfect husband, but I will try harder to make you happy."

"That's all I ask. But are you sure you can do this?"

"I want to try. So can I come back?"

"It's odd. I want to say yes, but I'm really scared."

"What of?"

"That you'll let me down again."

"I won't."

She reached out and took his hand. "OK. You can come back, but only on the understanding that you keep to your word and work at this."

He got up and put his arms around her. "I promise. I love you."

"I love you, too."

He pulled away. "One thing I need to ask. I know you and this guy didn't sleep together, but how serious was it?"

"Like I said, he listened. He was there for me when I needed a shoulder. But there's something else."

"Christ. What now?"

"You need to know who he is."

"Why?"

"Because his company is helping to fund the new community center."

"You're kidding."

She explained.

"I don't get it. What on earth did you have in common with some mega-rich mogul?"

"He wasn't like that. And that's all I'm going to say."

"So if you are going into business with him, that must mean you're still in touch with him?"

"I'm not going to lie to you. I might need to speak to him from time to time, but he's moving to Portugal. My main contact with the company is through his CEO, a chap named Stuart."

"You promise?"

"I promise."

"I guess I have to take you at your word."

"You do. I also want you to know that my relationship with Jack Dolan would never have gone further than it did."

"Why?"

"Well, apart from me realizing that you didn't deserve to have me cheat on you, he was still in love with his dead wife. On top of that, I would have struggled to fall in love with a man who played golf every day and was raring to embrace the life of a professional retiree. I think I would have come to find it deeply unsexy."

"So am I to extrapolate from what you've just told me that I am very sexy?" He was already sidling up to her.

"Frank, don't get carried away. Remember you still have groveling to do. . . . That said, would you like to come to bed?"

"I would. Very much."

"But what about your pill?"

He grinned. "I took it before I left."

A year later...

Dear Barbara—

I know we said we wouldn't exchange e-mails, but I just had to drop you a line to say huge congratulations. Stuart, my CEO, just e-mailed me to say that you'd raised the first half million pounds and that building work is about to start. It's a sensational achievement in such a short time, but I never doubted you could pull it off. If next year goes as well as this, you'll have the center up and running in no time. So proud of you. More to the point, I hope you're proud of you.

I'm loving Portugal. I ended up buying a villa in the Algarve. Great weather. Great golf. What more could a chap want?

My big news is that I've finally sold the Gloucestershire house. It wasn't easy, and I'm not ashamed to admit that I shed more than a few tears. Like you said, the pain of losing Faye hasn't gone away, but I'm learning to walk alongside it.

I might even start dating. Just between you and me, there's a rather attractive widow I have my eye on. She's another expat. We met at a golf club dinner a few weeks back and got along famously. Turns out she has the same handicap as me. I'll keep you posted.

BTW, Sally told me that you and Frank are back together. I'm so glad. I hope all is well. I often think of you and the time we spent together. I will always have fond memories.

All my best and congratulations again.

—Jack

●   ●   ●

Jack! How wonderful to hear from you. So glad you're enjoying Portugal and that you found the courage to sell the house. I know it must have been a wrench, but I'm sure it was for the best. And yes, do let me know what happens with your expat widow! I so hope that something comes of it. After everything you went through with Faye, you deserve some happiness.

Thank you for your kind words about my fund-raising efforts. And you're so right—for the first time in my life, I am proud of me. To say this has been a mad, chaotic year would be putting it mildly. And let me say from the start that none of it could have happened without you. In fact, I was about to send you a thank-you e-mail, but I've been struggling to find the words to express my appreciation and gratitude. I will never forget your kindness and generosity, not to mention the faith you had in my harebrained scheme. I came to you with this crazy idea, and instead of laughing it out of court, you immediately agreed to help. I have no idea why you chose to believe in me, but I will always be in your debt. The only way I can hope to repay it is to keep working to make this project a success.

The fund-raising really kicked off after Mutual Chartered pledged twenty thousand pounds. I won't say that finding sponsors hasn't been a struggle, not to say a steep learning curve for me. First I had to get a website up and running. Then I took a course on how to use social media to raise money. You can follow me on Twitter if you like. I've become a prolific tweeter. Of course, I'm still not sure I really know what I'm doing, and even now I get nervous when I make a pitch to a bank or some huge multinational, but over the months it's got easier. That's not to say that I don't spend nights awake worrying that I'm not up to the task and that I won't be able to raise the next half million. But then I think about Tiffany and my stubbornness kicks in again.

Oh, and FYI, I'm also speaking to the head of Larkswood House about rolling out phase two of the project. I've already found a site about half a mile from Orchard Farm, which would be perfect for a small school for kids with special needs. By the way, Sally tells me Freddie is thriving at Larkswood after a bit of a rocky start. I get the impression that these days she and Jeremy are putting in much more of an effort with him. Long may it continue!

Troy and Lacie are doing well, too. Carole wanted to adopt them pretty much from the get-go, but her husband, Mike, took some convincing. Long story short, the adoption is due to be finalized in the next couple of months. Lacie is gorgeous and chatters away—especially to Dave the cat. She calls Carole and Mike "Mummy" and "Daddy." Of course, she will have no memory of her real mum, which is desperately sad. But at the same time,

Carole and Mike will be able to provide her with a stable home and a real future.

Because they live in the wrong zone, Troy had to change schools. He's missing his friends, but he's glad to be away from Orchard Farm. He says that going back to Jubilee would have brought back too many bad memories. The new school is giving him loads of extra help—as are Carole and Mike—and apparently he's improving no end.

In other news, Ben is loving his stockbroking course. That said, now that he's in a class of other aspiring brokers, he's discovering he's not quite the financial genius he thought he was. He's also moved in with Katie, who yells at him when he doesn't pick up his dirty laundry or help with the housework. I love her.

Jess and Matt sold the Green Door. They're hoping to open a new deli in a busier location, where there's more passing traffic. If that does well, they'll be able to give up the catering side of the business, which will give them more time for each other and the children. All body parts crossed.

Frank moved back in round about when you left for Portugal. He's more attentive than he used to be. We have date nights. We have the odd cheap weekend away. He does his best to listen more. But Frank will always be Frank—obsessed with his work—and I have to accept that.

I won't pretend there aren't times when I'm still lonely in my marriage. But I've stopped struggling. I've stopped fighting for perfection, which isn't there to be had. I've realized in my old age that there's a certain freedom in that.

My friend Jean continues in her own imperfect marriage. She's just changed gigolos—again. They tend to say good-bye when they've saved enough money to pay their university fees or whatever. I think Jett is number six. She insists that this no-strings, extracurricular sex has saved her marriage. I still worry about one of these guys turning violent, or that her husband might find out, but she says she's doing what she needs to do and that she intends to carry on until either her libido or the money runs out.

My mum is still an issue. But these days I don't tell her much about what's going on in my life. It's a shame, but at least I'm not disappointed by her reaction. The more I pull back, the more I disengage, the less she upsets me. It's hard work, but I'm getting there. And the other day she presented me with the single bootee she managed to knit before I was born. It's truly awful— misshapen and full of dropped stitches, but I'll always treasure it.

Despite all the angst and sleepless nights, the Orchard Farm project has been the making of me. What upsets me is that my happiness has been born out of such tragedy. At the beginning I also worried that there would be some hostility from the residents. I was scared that they would see me as this white middle-class do-gooder and hate me. But it hasn't happened. Having worked at the local school, I got to know a lot of the parents, and I think they put in a good word for me with the rest.

Tomorrow is my sixtieth birthday, and to celebrate Frank's taking me to Venice for a few days. The only downside is that I won't get to check how the building work is coming along. I like to take a look every day. I kept telling Stuart that work shouldn't get under way until I've raised the entire million pounds, but he seems to have faith in my fund-raising abilities. I'm guessing you put in a good word for me?

So today we're unveiling the foundation stone of what will be known as the Tiffany Butler Center. Troy is tickled pink that it's being named after his mum. I'm making a speech thanking all our sponsors. Naturally, Dolan's is top of the list. Troy will do the actual unveiling. The mayor and the local press will be there. It's all very exciting. I'll text you some pictures. If anybody had told me a year ago that this was how I'd be spending the day before my sixtieth birthday, I would have laughed.

Once again, thank you for your friendship and all your support. I think of you, too, always with warmth and affection.

Take care. Enjoy the sunshine.

—Barbara

Barbara hit "send," wiped away the tear that was trickling down her cheek and went into the kitchen to make a cup of tea. There were still a few minutes before she and Frank needed to leave for the unveiling ceremony. While the kettle was boiling, she checked her Facebook page. She'd posted her last status a few days ago:

Drumroll please. HALF-MILLLION-POUND target reached!!!!!!!!! Building work on the Tiffany Butler Center just started. I'll be thanking each of you individually for your astonishing fund-raising efforts, but meanwhile, huge thanks to one and all. Of the £500,000 raised, more than £50,000 came from individuals. I couldn't have done it

without all you wonderful people. And a special thank-you
goes to Troy Butler, who raised a hundred pounds by
cycling ten times round his local park. That's five miles!
Love you, Troy.

There were now two hundred "likes," seventy comments and
thirty-nine shares. Jess had commented: Yay! Go Mum! Ben had said:
Oy, Mum, lend us a tenner.

Even Pam—who didn't really approve of the poor—had gotten
involved. She had rounded up her neighbors and was organizing a
sponsored calamari-eating contest. Men only, of course. Us girls are
too busy watching our waistlines!

Barbara was still laughing at this when Frank appeared, asking if
she thought he should wear a tie to the unveiling. She said maybe he
should since the mayor and the local councilors were bound to be in
ties.

"But I hate wearing ties."

"OK, then, don't."

"No, I should. It's a formal occasion and I don't want to let you
down." He lifted his collar and laid the tie across the back of his
neck. "By the way, I just wanted to tell you again how proud I am of
what you've achieved. You are an astonishing woman."

"I don't know about that. And I've still got such a long way to go."

"You'll get there."

"I hope so."

"I know so." Frank finished tying his tie and looked at his watch.
"We should get going."

"Be with you in sec," Barbara said. "I just want to read the rest of
these comments. People have been so generous with their time and
money. I can't believe it."

"Well, you should believe it. You're bloody good at persuading people to part with their cash. You've finally found your calling."

"A bit late in the day, maybe. But yes, I think I probably have."

She spooled through the comments. Meanwhile, on her sidebar, the Zuckerberg boy was trying to sell her a walk-in bath and she didn't even notice.

Sue Margolis was a radio reporter for fifteen years before turning to novel writing. She lives in England with her husband.

Connect Online

suemargolis.com
facebook.com/suemargolis.books